☆♡☆　IT'S A HIT!　☆♡☆
Praise for
BOBBY REX'S GREATEST HIT

"The warmth, fears, cares, loneliness, and adolescent dreams of the author's characters are stunningly created."

Booklist

"VIBRANT AND JOYOUS."

San Francisco Chronicle

"FRESH AND WISE. 'Pally Thompson' is a clear-eyed, country-style heroine who deserves a hit song."

Publishers Weekly

"A GRAND NOSTALGIA TRIP THROUGH THE 1950s AND EARLY 1960s . . . a fine and entertaining new work."

Atlanta Journal-Constitution

"Sad and sassy . . . sweet and rhythmic . . . an impressive debut."

The Kirkus Reviews

Also by Marianne Gingher:

Teen Angel and Other Stories of Young Love

BOBBY REX'S GREATEST HIT

Marianne Gingher

Copyright © 1986 by Marianne Gingher

All rights reserved under International and Pan-American Copyright Conventions. Published in the United States by Ballantine Books, a division of Random House, Inc., and simultaneously in Canada by Random House of Canada Limited, Toronto.

Library of Congress Catalog Card Number: 85-91127

ISBN 0-345-34823-6

This edition published by arrangement with Atheneum Publishers. ESSAYS ON GEORGIA LIFE copyright © 1985 by W. Wilkie Collins. Reprinted by permission of Harper & Row, Publishers, Inc.

This edition is not to be sold outside of the United States of America, its territories & its possessions, & Canada, excluding the Dominion, the Dominion of Canada.

This Edition published by arrangement with Atheneum Publishers, a division of Macmillan, Inc., and Atheneum Publishers, an imprint of Macmillan Publishing Company, Inc.

Printed in the U.S.A.

BALLANTINE BOOKS • NEW YORK

Library of Congress Catalog Card Number: 86-3427

ISBN 0-345-34823-0

The excerpt from "Home-Coming" appears in THE ESSAYS OF E. B. WHITE, copyright © 1955 by E. B. White. It is reprinted by permission of Harper & Row, Publishers, Inc.

Parts of this novel have appeared as short stories in the following magazines: *North American Review*, *Redbook*, and *Seventeen*.

This edition published by arrangement with Atheneum Publishers, a division of The Scribner Book Companies, Inc.

Printed in Canada

First Ballantine Books Edition: December 1987
Second Printing: September 1988

TO BOB
AND TO MY PARENTS, ROD AND BETTY JANE,
WITH LOVE AND GRATITUDF

Familiarity, that's the thing—the sense of belonging. It grants exemption from all evil, all shabbiness.

—E. B. WHITE
"Home-Coming"

CONTENTS

☆♡☆　　☆♡☆　　☆♡☆

Part I: 1961

☆♡☆　　☆♡☆　　☆♡☆

LETTERS

☆♡☆　☆♡☆　☆♡☆

Dear Shilda,

  By now you've heard it, and I want you to call me collect as soon as possible. I don't know what to do. They played it on WCOG for the first time yesterday, and my phone's been ringing off the wall ever since. Johnny Dee, the disc jockey, called me for an interview! "You are Pally Thompson?" he said. "Did you know there's a new single out by Bobby Rex The Man Moseley with your name on the label?" "Pally?" I said. "Not just 'Pally,' " he said. " 'Pally Thompson.' Your whole name. It's the title of the song, like 'Stagger Lee,' " he said. "Just turn on your radio and I'll play it again within a half hour. It's dynamite." So, Shilda, I sat by the radio and smoked a whole pack of cigarettes and bit off all my nails twice, waiting. Finally, he puts on the song and I'm hearing things I don't believe and thinking how many more minutes until they ban this song? I mean, Shilda, he doesn't boldface say that we Did It. But you can sure guess what's going on from the lyrics like you can guess in "Sixty Minute Man." And there can be no doubt it's me he means. Like what other Pally

3

Thompson could he mean? Especially if she lives in Orfax and "goes down" with him to Sawyer's Creek. Goes down—*you see the sort of lyrics I mean? Please call as soon as you get this. Help!*

Love,
Pally

☆♡☆

August 6, 1961

Dear Pally,

Why didn't you ever tell me about you and Bobby Rex Moseley? All those years I was spilling my guts right and left to you, but you never once fessed up. I mean, what are best friends for? I'll call when I can stop crying. Like maybe never!

Shilda

☆♡☆

August 9, 1961

Dear Shilda,

I'm writing this letter in red ink to symbolize a true heart's blood spilled in your direction. You've got to believe me that Bobby Rex made the whole thing up. All I know is that the song's a big lie and my life will probably never be the same again. Two weeks ago I was a little nobody picking out my wedding invitations. Now I can't walk into the Cash and Carry without some jivey fourteen-year-old cornering me for an autograph. Billy has even suggested that we postpone the wedding until all this blows over.

Poor Billy. He just thought he understood a town like Orfax. Picture this: we're sitting on his porch swing after a nice candlelit supper. We're sipping wine out of jelly glasses and the moon's that hard kind of full like honeydew, so heavy-looking in the sky that you wonder *what keeps it from falling. We already feel so married, I just can't tell you. He's put the radio in the window and turned it on real low: somebody like Patsy Cline or Connie Francis, somebody with an aching, lovesick voice is coaxing us along. He's unbuttoned my blouse, and there's something about the way he's touching me that makes my heart feel peaky. My skin sort of lurches toward him, and I just want to go ahead and do it on the porch swing. The air has that sweet, loaded-down scent of honeysuckle, the trees seem ignited by the moonlight, and there's that tambourine sound of tree frogs and cicadas that I love. I feel that at long last I have absolutely everything. A dangerous thought, because the instant you take note of such bliss, it's bound to start disintegrating. Happiness is something that you shouldn't ever notice. Suddenly, then, "Pally Thompson" comes on the radio, and for the first time I smell dog do in the neighbor's front yard. It's as if that song comes rushing out of the radio like some terrible chaperone. I even find myself buttoning up my blouse as fast as I can. Billy says, "Why are we acting like this, Pally?" And I don't answer him because I don't know.*

We sit on the porch swing and go over it and over it, again and again. How I probably only had three or four conversations with Bobby Rex in my life. How he never once held my hand or gazed into my eyes. How he was always the teenage idol type and nobody with any sense ever messes with them.

I can look at Billy and tell I've convinced him, almost. Not that I'd have to be a virgin for him or anything so ridiculous. He's been married before, Shilda, so it's not that he expects me to be a virgin and him the first, last, and only. He just wants me to be truthful. *So I am, Shilda: every boring detail of my life told and retold to him. I've told all there is to tell without* inventing *stuff to make my stories seem more convincing.*

But there's this tiny speck of doubt haunting him,

when all is said and done, that I can't seem to nuzzle off. You can almost see it on his face like shadow, a clouding over of his features, as he turns toward the radio and hears how Pally Thompson lay down on the creek bank among all those other flowers: Sweet Betsey, Black-eyed Susan, wild Violet. Only she didn't just lie there, fairest of them all like in some fairy tale. No, she "opened up" for him. Opened up! Now really, Shilda! Did Bobby Rex The Man Moseley honestly believe people were going to think of flowers blooming when they heard that stupid line? It's 1961, for Pete's sake!

Pally

☆ ♡ ☆

August 13, 1961

Dear Pally,
  So sue the son-of-a-bitch.

Shilda

☆ ♡ ☆

August 16, 1961

Dear Shilda,
  For your information Joe Parker was all for suing the socks off Bobby Rex. He talked to this lawyer he knows over in Greensboro, and Joe said that at first the fella seemed real eager about the prospects.
  I have to tell you something now that I never told you. If I didn't think I could trust you, if I didn't think you were true-blue, Shilda, I wouldn't tell you this. But to prove I have nothing to hide, here goes:
  No lawyer will take my case because at one crazy point in my life I really was alone with The Man at Sawyer's Creek. Don't faint. It just happened, Shilda. Nobody planned it; we just sort of coincided. The reason I never told you was because it happened the night

of Eddie's accident. Lord knows you had enough going on not to hear me blathering about some weirdo chance meeting between Bobby Rex and myself. But there's one more thing, Shilda, which I swear to God I can explain: I was naked.

It's not at all what you're thinking. He probably didn't even realize I was naked. He probably couldn't even see, it was so dark! The whole thing's complicated, but it has an explanation. When you come down for our wedding—when and if it ever gets off the ground—I'll explain everything in 3-D and Technicolor.

Love you,
Pally

☆ ♡ ☆

August 20, 1961

Dear Pally,
Like I told you on the phone, now you're talking my language. It's always been mysteries I hated.

Maybe you ought to come to Newark for a few days until things cool off in Orfax. I could go ahead and take my vacation, and we could take the train into New York and goof off like we always planned. How about me getting some tickets to the Ed Sullivan Show *so we can see Bobby Rex Moseley LIVE—before we kill him? Hardee-har-har-har!*

Sorry I gave you such a hard time, but that's what true friendship, like love, is all about. Let me hear.

Shilly

☆ ♡ ☆

August 20, 1961

Miss Pally Thompson
Rt. 1, Narrow Gauge Road
Piney View Trailer Park
Orfax, N.C.

Dear Miss Thompson:

Congratulations! Billboard *notes that in the three weeks since "Pally Thompson" hit the charts, it's skyrocketed to number one in Germany, Japan, Canada, and some little doodad country called Liechtenstein. It's also number two in Great Britain and France. We at* Rockola Magazine *mean to let you know you're an international star, kid! Of course, here in the States, "Pally Thompson" is standing all over "Stand By Me." And by comparison "A Little Bit of Soap" is a complete washout! "Pally Thompson" is also running circles around "Runaround Sue," and wow! is Dion sore!*

But all our ravings aside, would the real Pally Thompson *please stand up? We'd like to pay $1,000 for an exclusive interview. Thanks to Johnny Dee at WCOG for sending us your way. We're listening.*

Buzz Wheeler for
Rockola Magazine

☆♡☆

August 22, 1961

Dear Mr. Wheeler,
I can't do an interview because there's nothing I can say. I never once went out on a date with anyone remotely like Bobby Rex Moseley much less The Man himself! It was always the short fat boys who called me up, the ones with warts and sweaty palms and nervous tics and goofball conversation. No dreamboats ever cruised down my river—and you can make whatever you want of that!

I told the lady who called me from Teen Scene *and*

the man who called up from Life *the same thing. This is all I know, for free: I barely knew Bobby Rex Moseley. I can't think why he'd use my name in a song, except maybe he liked the roll of it in his mouth. Maybe it rhymed nice. It's just an old nickname my daddy gave me, made up from Valerie, my real name. If you want to know about Bobby Rex Moseley, I suggest you write Phoebe Jenkins MacAdoo, his ex-girl friend. Or get in touch with somebody who really knew him like his brother, Leon, or Doodle Washington down at Narrow Gauge Esso or Hogan Royal. They aren't named "Pally Thompson," but Bobby Rex could've written a whole lot truer song about any one of them. All I want now, Mr. Wheeler, is to get along with my wedding plans. I don't need any new wrinkles. All I want is to marry Billy Pickup and have a family and feel as happy when I mop the linoleum as the ladies in those Spic'n'Span ads.*

Sincerely yours,

Valerie Thompson

☆ ♡ ☆

August 24, 1961

Dear Pally,

The other day when I heard "Pally Thompson" I realized that when the train whistle blows it's at this very meaningful moment, like when you two are supposedly Doing It. I had this senior English teacher up here who was real wild, Miss Blondell, and she was always telling us what things stood for, and they always stood for sex. Miss Blondell told the whole class how trains can symbolize dicks, only she said "phallus" in class, real righteouslike. Anyhow, Bobby Rex or some other wiseass —maybe one of Miss Blondell's ex-students—knew exactly what they were doing when they put those train whistles into the song at strategic moments.

But the real reason I'm writing is to tell you that I

bought your and Billy's wedding gift today and it's 100 copies of the new Bobby Rex album called—can you take it?—''Pally Thompson.'' Wait until you see the cover. Maybe it was an accident, but the girl lying in the grass has just blown her last Oasis cig. There's a crumpled-up pack in the weeds nearby. Pally, you and I both know that nobody in their right mind smokes Oasis cigarettes except you!

Love,
Shilda

P.S.
Just fooling about buying all those albums. But I did get you and Billy joke gifts for you to wear on your honeymoon: two matching T-shirts that say in great big letters: I AM NOT PALLY THOMPSON. Haha! For real!

☆ ♡ ☆

August 25, 1961

Dear Bobby Rex,
  It's me, Pally Thompson . . .

☆ ♡ ☆

August 25, 1961

Dear Bobby Rex,
  I'll come straight to the point . . .

☆ ♡ ☆

August 25, 1961

Dear Bobby Rex,
  If you don't feel like writing the truth, please tell me what you'd like me to think. Enclosed is a self-addressed and stamped postcard for your convenience . . .

☆ ♡ ☆

August 25, 1961

Dear Bobby Rex,

No offense, but your song just seems like awful bad timing . . .

☆ ♡ ☆

August 27, 1961

Dear Pally Thompson,

Maybe this letter won't ever reach you. All I know is that you live in Orfax like the song says, but according to Billboard you really do exist. I'm risking it, aren't I? It could be just a made-up story they're passing off on all us ignoramus fans.

To tell you something about myself, I am twenty-six, married, and the mother of four little girls—future Shirelles! And I will NEVER EVER outgrow rock 'n' roll! ! ! In spite of my motherly duties, I keep my radio on night and day. I was born and bred to the beat of the Top Forty, and just because I'm on the shady side of my twenties doesn't mean I'm starting to sing along with Mitch. What were you doing Christmas Eve, 1954, when Johnny Ace died playing Russian Roulette? I was lying on the bed listening to "Pledging My Love." Pally, I just adore remembering things. Also, according to Billboard, you're a Virgo—like me!

Well, enough about me. I'm mainly writing to congratulate you on your ability to inspire that marvelous song "Pally Thompson." Somehow you really got to your man. When I hear a line like "Touch my skin and the fire begins and we can't stop and there's no end," I get chillbumps and want to fall in love all over the place. Not that I'm not still crazy about Jack, my husband, but more and more we're just too comfortable with each other. That line in "Pally Thompson" reminds me so much of what it's like to be newly together. I'm not very good at describing passion, but I do know that it doesn't have a thing to do with feeling comfortable. *It's full of zoom and heat the way "Pally Thompson" is.*

One piece of advice: if Bobby Rex Moseley seems to ignore you lately (I saw a picture of him in Star Magazine *with somebody like Brenda Lee) don't give up. If a little bit of fame goes a long way, then a lot of fame goes a long way and back again! He needs you more than ever now. He needs you like an anchor. I want to tell you that I speak from experience.*

A couple of years ago, my husband Jack went off on a fishing trip to Canada with a bunch of his buddies and caught this 18 lb. Great Northern pike. When Jack slit the fish to clean it, he found a Zippo lighter inside. Surprise, surprise, the Zippo lit on Jack's very first flick. So Jack wrote a letter to the company because he thought it was all so amazing. So did the Zippo folks. They made up a great big testimonial ad about that fish and used Jack's real name: ZIPPO LIGHTER FOUND INSIDE FISH LIGHTS ON VERY FIRST TRY! You wouldn't believe all the letters people sent us. Other Zippo enthusiasts wrote to tell us their personal success stories with Zippo lighters. There were lots of fishermen who wrote Jack, too, asking about which lake he liked best in Ontario—there are only about a billion lakes up there! —what lures he used, etc. The local paper wrote Jack up. He was on the radio. Zippo ran a full-page ad in Life *magazine, big as could be. There wasn't a picture of Jack in the ad, just a big splashy Great Northern pike, baring his teeth. I have to tell you that Jack was pretty hard to live with until all this blew over. But it does blow over, Pally. Just wanted you to know. The consolation prize of getting to be twenty-six, soon to be twenty-seven, is that you do start to figure things out a bit. Although, to be perfectly honest, you might be able to figure things out faster, but all of a sudden there*

*seems like more to figure out! Oh well. Best of luck to
you.*

Admiringly,
Doris Purdue
Palmyra Drive
New Orleans, La.

☆ ♡ ☆

August 30, 1961

Dearest Billy-Boy,
   *You are a grown boy, almost twenty-nine now, and
far be it from me to tell you how to run your life.
Remember the little present I gave you on your twenty-
first birthday? I cut them off myself and put them in a
box all neatly gift wrapped for you to open:* apron strings.
   But I can't help wondering what you ever did *with
them, Billy. The first time your father and I gave you a
haircut, we were careful to save every darling curl we
snipped. To this day I can lay my hand on the envelope
that holds them. Just give me a moment's notice. What
I'm saying, Billy, is that just because we purposely cut
ourselves off from things, doesn't mean we need lose
them* forever.
   *Remember when I warned you about Donna's health?
I always said she was the frailest little bird of a girl I'd
ever met. She had absolutely no appetite except for
vegetables and fruit. Didn't I tell her over and over that
red meat would put color in her cheeks and pep up her
blood? Especially while she was pregnant. And* you!
*Studying to be a veterinarian, taking it so calmly that
she didn't eat meat.*
   *Then, after the babies were born and she was drag-
ging around on that diet of sunflower nuts and soybean
bread, didn't I warn her that only red meat would help
replenish all the blood she'd lost? You'd think her doctor would have told her* that *much. So when we got your*

telephone call that she'd simply dropped dead, just dropped mysteriously dead where she stood, rinsing out baby bottles at the kitchen sink (she didn't make enough milk to breastfeed, that should have told somebody something!), I was horrified, but I wasn't surprised. Some people's hearts just stop for no good reason, the doctor told you. Pshaw! I said at the time and am still saying. Some people's hearts stop because they don't nourish themselves properly.

I felt uneasy about your marriage the first time I laid eyes on Donna, God rest her thin little soul. The first time you brought her to eat Sunday dinner with us and she refused that slice of pot roast, I said to myself: there's a weakness there. Lack of flexibility is a weakness. I foresaw dim things. I never spoke of all this to you, Billy, mainly because of those apron strings. But I'm not about to make the same mistake twice.

I think it's wonderful that you think you've found somebody you love. It doesn't bother me that she's only eighteen. It doesn't even bother me that she's your former baby-sitter, although what must the neighbors be saying now? I don't even care that she's from the backwoods and has no plans to further her education. In fact there are many things about her that I applaud. I admire her robustness. In the photo you sent, she looks as tall as you. She looks strong. Her teeth look good. Usually girls who tan easily and darkly are relaxed and even-tempered. I'll bet she takes vitamins, and I'm happy to know she's grown up around farms. I'd bet money that she knows the value of red meat. I also think that it's a miracle, this day and age, for a young girl to know how to make a pie crust from scratch. But Billy, I have heard the song "Pally Thompson" and although your sisters assure me that I'm making a mountain out of a molehill, I can't get it out of my head that you are about to marry some rock-and-roll star's concubine! There now. I've said it. The word was burning a hole in my tongue. Oh, Billy-Boy, I only beg that you think of the children. This is the woman they'll grow up calling "Mother!"

It's your life, and Lord knows I've given you enough 2 cents worth of advice to make you a millionaire by now, yet you still aren't. So whatever you decide is all right with Dad and me, of course. But I just had to get my feelings out in the open so that you could never say later that I hadn't warned you. And now—tick-a-lock-tick-a-lock—I'll just lock up my lips and throw the key away.

Devotedly,
Mother

☆ ♡ ☆

September 1, 1961

Miss Pally Thompson
Route 1, Narrow Gauge Road
Piney View Trailer Park
Orfax, N.C.

Dear Miss Thompson:

Rockola is now willing to pay $2,000 for an exclusive! If what you say is true, that you never knew Bobby Rex Moseley well and that the song "Pally Thompson" is not about you, then our editor wishes you to consider for comment this explanation of the song's title. You've read in all the fan mags how shy and private The Man is in real life. A zillion bodyguards. No interviews. Dark glasses night and day, except when he's on stage. Well, how does the notion grab you that the song "Pally Thompson" is The Man's attempt to reach out? Maybe it's a song about the way he wishes it had been between the two of you. Think hard. $2,000! ! We're listening.

Sincerely yours,
Buzz Wheeler
Rockola Magazine

☆♡☆

September 6, 1961

Dear Pally,

I'm writing mainly to "regret" your wedding invitation. I'm so pregnant I'm about to bust, and I'm not to travel, doctor's orders.

I assume I was invited since you addressed the envelope to the Jenkins family. Mother told me last night when we talked long-distance. You know I still consider myself part Jenkins even though I married Butch Mac-Adoo from Wilson and we're settled in with the U.S. Army down at Fort Bragg. Butch is a first lieutenant, but I expect his rank will change any minute because he's very determined and his goal is the Green Berets. Everybody down here calls him The Bull. He's so brave that I go around with goose bumps all the time, although Mom says that's the way all brides their first year of marriage are supposed to feel. Anyway, Butch is a man who never learned how to flinch. For example, last night he broke the drill sergeant's dog's neck. I'd give you all the details but it's too long and involved a story. Anyway, he's some hunk, and I'm happy as can be and twice as proud.

It feels funny writing you a letter. Especially since the last time I saw you, we weren't speaking. I was such a nerd back then. You know, I think part of our problem back in high school was that they put saltpeter in all the food. You know what saltpeter does, don't you? Butch had to tell me, and boy was I shocked. Anyway, I'm apologizing at long last for being such a pent-up, saltpetery nerd. Forgive me?

It feels funny writing you a letter because I never dreamed I'd have any need to. For one thing, I never dreamed I'd leave Orfax. I always assumed I'd marry Bobby Rex and stay within gabbing distance of all my old friends. But let me tell you, Pally: I'm glad things turned out this way because Bobby Rex Moseley was a born-deep snob and Butch, thank the Lord, is not.

I expect you're basking in all the excitement of the "Pally Thompson" album. Well, as we said back in high school, don't let it give you a swelled head. Remember, he wrote a song called "Phoebe" back in 1959 and sang it at the high school prom. I pranced around like I was Grace Kelly! Of course he never recorded "Phoebe," and it's just as well because Butch would have knocked his block off.

Anyway, I've listened to that "Pally Thompson" song a lot, and is it just my imagination or is it supposed to be suggestive? It's okay, now, if y'all ever did anything. It's water over the dam, as far as I'm concerned. But I can't help marveling at how you sneaked it by all of us, Bynum and me especially. How could you have operated so seriously right under our noses and we never suspected a thing? Oh well, just another of life's mysteries. Believe me, Pally, it's okay and I hold no grudges. I've got everything I want right here in this little base duplex with Butch. But probably—I really shouldn't admit this—if Butch hadn't come along and swept me off my feet, I'd be hating your guts right now. High school casts such a shadow, doesn't it?

Hope you have a great wedding and a romantic honeymoon. (Pack plenty of K-Y jelly and don't use the rhythm method like we did!) I highly recommend the Starfish Motor Lodgette down at Myrtle Beach. They throw in free pink champagne!

Best Wishes,
Phoebe Jenkins MacAdoo

P.S.

Maybe we can get together some time and compare notes, if you get what I mean? Maybe you ought to burn this.

September 10, 1961

Dear Bobby Rex,
   I should be really furious at you, but lately I'm not . . .

☆ ♡ ☆

September 10, 1961

Dear Bobby Rex,
   Remember me? I probably won't even mail this, but just in case, here goes. Even if I do mail it, you'll never see it. One of your slinky lackeys will slit the envelope with a long red fingernail and skim these words and bleat out a laugh and maybe you'll look up from whatever you're doing and say, "Huh?" and she'll say, "Oh, never mind, nothing." And I guess it amounts to that . . .

☆ ♡ ☆

September 10, 1961

Dear Bobby Rex,
   Of all my fantasies the one I like best is where I ride the Southern Crescent all the way to New York City and into Penn Station. I get off the train with my chin held so high and my manner so bustling that nobody can guess I'm Southern. I'm not wearing tacky, bumpkin K-Mart clothes either. I look tailored, like Jackie Kennedy. I'm wearing a Chanel-cut suit and high-heel pumps and maybe even a hat. But it's a solemn, inconspicuous hat. Nothing flappy or swagged with gauze and flowers. No price tags showing. You might say that I look dressed for business. I hail a cab and pretend to speak French to cover up my Southern accent. Shilda has told me that if anybody up there suspects you're Southern, you get treated like a cream puff, which translates: you get eaten alive. I say to the cabbie, "Chez Ed Sullivan, s'il vous plaît."
   Of course what I'm planning to do is wreck your

show. I suppose that I'm planning to stand up in my front row seat and wave my arms so that you'll notice me and be so stunned that you forget your lyrics right in the middle of that song. I'm aiming to make an impact, see. But even in fantasy I start softening. I get caught up in the sway of the crowd. All around me young girls are talking about you. There is a jittery thrum that hangs over the audience. The girl beside me bites her fingernails. Several girls hold flowers to throw, gifts, dollar bills with their names and addresses and telephone numbers written across them. There's a whole chorus of girls who are crying they're so nervous and happy to be here. They all wear T-shirts emblazoned with the name of your last album, *BOBBY REX, MOSTLY.*

When Ed Sullivan appears, whoops and screams rise and swell from the audience. His lips try to conceal his teeth but a sly smile wins out. He folds his arms and shuffles about the stage talking about what he's got lined up but really only teasing the audience. I feel sorry for all the acts that must come before the main attraction. First there are some acrobats, some jugglers and plate spinners. There's a bear who lumbers through a polka and plays an accordion. There's a comedian with slick hair and a bow tie that you'll remember longer than you remember his jokes. Then, borrowed from Lawrence Welk, the Little Lennon Sisters, who above all else are good sports. Then a drumroll. And the audience tips forward.

The air trembles, there's so much yelling. There's a general feeling of panic that nobody will be able to hear what they came to hear: Bobby Rex, mostly. Singing, breathing, tapping his foot. So girls start shushing each other, stifling their sobs with their hands. The stage is black with one bright spotlight that glows like the mouth of a lighted cave. Maybe you'll show up, maybe you won't. There's an unbearable pause, a delay that suggests you are really too godly to appear any place that's *real. We don't deserve you. But then, miraculously, you walk on stage, holding your guitar, cradling it, wearing your famous simple jeans, the unironed blue work shirts that everybody loves, the unglamorous boots. Scuffed boots! The style you've made famous, unlike Elvis or Jerry Lee Lewis or Chuck Berry, is what's ordinary, what everybody can have. You are everybody's farm-hand, everybody's country classic. You're the boy who bagged their groceries, changed their oil, washed the blackboards after school. Nothing special, that's your label. You belong to everyone, you're attainable. It's a good, good trick, Bobby Rex. There's a rush of adora-tion from the audience as palpable as weather—a mon-soon of sighs. You stroke the guitar like some moony girl's cheek and you sing, "Pally, oh Pally," in your husky, tender, bedeviling voice that makes every girl in all the world wish she was Pally Thompson. Except me, because I am, and they would be so disappointed if they knew . . .*

☆ ♡ ☆

September 16, 1961

Dear Pally,

You need to remember that Bobby Rex Moseley was always like a shadow on spilled oil. Did you ever know him to be any more reliable than a catfish out of water, jumpy and slick? The Man had stars for eyeballs; but you could wish on them all you wanted and you'd be wasting your desire because they were like stars that had died a hundred years ago—the light was still travel-ing down through space to you and you didn't know any better. A lie ain't nothing to him but, say, a suit of glittery clothes. Something to put on; something to slip out of when the heat's on. Remember the summer after his graduation? That's when he and Phoebe Jenkins were real thick and Bobby Rex got a job pumping gas for Hogan Royal instead of working his daddy's tobacco. Said Hogan paid him more, and said it cool and calculated in front of everybody. Oh, he had a plan all right. His daddy stomped around beet-red mad all summer, planning to whup up on Hogan Royal, rumor had it. But that was just more lies.

Remember, Pally? Everybody thought he was saving up his money to buy Phoebe Jenkins a diamond ring, and he just let everybody think it. Dumb sheep, and him a wolf who could sing as innocent as a canary. Nobody knew that Hogan's brother Merve had brought Bobby Rex a poster about that singing contest in Nashville and that Bobby Rex was saving up his money to strike out on his own. He fooled his own kinfolk, and he fooled Phoebe Jenkins. And think of all the other suckers, sitting around all dreamy-eyed at Woody's Danceland, listening to the jukebox, watching Bobby Rex rock his hipbones against Phoebe's and breathe down her blouse. A regular bride and groom they were, a peep show—even though it never felt right, did it? Him such a hunk and her so homely? They were unlikely. But nobody could have guessed that the more money he laid aside for his escape to Nashville, the more he pretended to love her. When he left her flat like that, we should have all felt terrified, Pally. It was as if somebody with an A-bomb for a heart had been let loose on the world. Maybe we can comfort ourselves with the hope that someday he'll self-destruct. Chin up, girl.

Love,
Shilda

☆ ♡ ☆

September 18, 1961

Dear Bobby Rex:
Maybe I should phone you up. If you could just talk to Billy . . .

☆♡☆

September 18, 1961

Dear Bobby Rex:
   With so many real things that happened to write about, why on earth . . .

September 19, 1961

Dear Bobby Rex,
   We've had a huge amazing argument, Billy and me, because I won't give Rockola Magazine *an interview and make $2,000. But don't get the wrong impression of Billy. It's not the money he's after, it's . . .*

September 19, 1961

Dear Bobby Rex,
   I think back hard to that night at Sawyer's Creek, and I go over the details in my mind and the strongest memory I have is that there was no moon . . .

☆♡☆

September 19, 1961

Dear Bobby Rex,
   Here I sit in my wedding dress (Mama has just evened up the hem for me—the wedding's next Saturday), smoking an Oasis, calm as can be. But I don't know how I can be so calm because the man I dearly love has just walked out the door and slammed it so hard behind him that the hinges are still shrieking. I think that they're shrieking this blasted version of "Pally Thompson" just to be extra cruel.
   We all saw you on "The Ed Sullivan Show" last

night. Mama fixed popcorn and root beer and we all sat around playing "I Remember When" about Bobby Rex Moseley. Mama remembered the day you were born. The men put blue ribbons in their lapels. It was at the start of World War II, and you were the first baby born to a war bride.

Joe Parker remembered you hanging out at Hogan Royal's Esso back in elementary school. You were in awe of Doodle Washington because he knew all those spirituals and could reach some bottom notes you hadn't dreamed of yet. The two of you would hunker down in the grease pit and sing "Go Tell It on the Mountain" until you'd built a ring of echoes sturdily around you as a fence. You did the harmony and Doodle pitched the songs low and round-mouthed and torchy. Joe said the grease pit had the best acoustics in Orfax.

People buying gasoline would hear the songs floating out, and they'd climb from their cars and gather around the grease pit, toe-tapping, swaying, until they didn't care whether they bought their gas or not. Maybe all they really needed to keep them motivating was some good music, huh? (That's the way Joe Parker tells it.) Anyway, another boss might have fired Doodle Washington on the spot and figured you, a white boy, knew better than to tempt a colored boy to slack off. But Hogan Royal carried each of you a frosty cold Cheerwine so that your voices wouldn't parch out.

When it came my turn to remember Bobby Rex Moseley, everybody said I could pass if I wanted to. But I didn't, especially with Billy there. I've got a lot to prove to him, and that's the truth. So I said this: "All I ever remember about Bobby Rex Moseley was wanting him because he was so impossible." You should have seen the way Billy stared, but it was the truth.

Once I remember sitting in Mama's car while she ran into the Variety for something and watching you cross the street. You were a couple of blocks away, very *small, and so I put my hand out and kind of covered you up, kind of snuffed you out for a moment to torture myself. Then I took my hand away and let you amble up the street, out of my range, unimaginable. Again, I put my hand out and held a thumb over you and had you the way that children have the moon. But, unlike the moon, you slipped past. You got bigger. You got away . . .*

Part II: 1957–1959

☆♡☆   ☆♡☆.   ☆♡☆

PALLY

THIS SONG IS DEDICATED
TO BILLY PICKUP,
AND I PROMISE HIM
THAT IT'S NO STICK-UP

☆♡☆　　☆♡☆　　☆♡☆

Bobby Rex Moseley was the kind of boy you only windowshopped, so handsome that to look at him made your heart and lips just ache. He was gentle, even kind to cats, but he knew how to use his fists like all serious, worthwhile boys. He could be tender and he could be hard, and knowing which to be when is an art, but he knew. He had a chipped front tooth from when he fell out of the hayloft. He had a cowlick from where his daddy punched him once. Otherwise he looked perfect, like no boy that's real. Except for the surly cowlick, his black hair swept back from his forehead like one deadly, dangerous wave. I mean that it was hair with an *undertow* to pull your heart right down. Now and then he checked it with a black Ace comb.

He'd never been a tall boy, but you thought so just the same. He wore his jeans so tight you had to look away. Sometimes he pulled a hat down low over his eyes. It was a gray felt hat with a blue-jay feather jutting from the band. He wore ordinary boots, but somehow you always thought of them as maroon leather ones with star-shaped spurs chattering at their heels. Whenever he pitched horseshoes without a shirt, girls weren't allowed to watch—I'm talking about the young married girls. Their husbands promised them Whitman's Samplers and hurried them off on errands. Because Bobby Rex Moseley had muscles lurking all over. His skin made you think of brown lake water full of clever jump-up snakes.

But the thing about him that drove all the girls crazy was that he played guitar and sang. When he sang love songs, you knew you couldn't have him. He shaped his lips like a valentine and held them around the most yearning note in the world. He'd drop to his knees and arch his throat backwards like he was begging for his life.

He'd lived in Orfax all his life, but there wasn't a speck of farm dirt under his fingernails. There wasn't manure on his boots. The only calluses on his hands were the guitar-picking sort; his palms were as soft and pink-looking as my own.

Of course I loved him. I pined like every other girl in town. Meanwhile I went out with Bynum Jenkins.

☆ ♡ ☆

Bynum was all right, I could have done a whole lot worse. He was my first boyfriend; by that I mean he liked me for myself, whoever that was, and was not just after my body. He was tall and gawky and so spattered with freckles that he looked like he'd been painting brown ceilings all his life. His best feature was his bangs. They were standouts. Every boy at Orfax High, including Bobby Rex Moseley, who was above most fads, slicked his hair into wings and pompadours and a real popular style where the barber rolled your bangs like a link sausage. This was called a roach. A few boys had crew cuts and flat-tops, but they were the sons of doctors or bankers and everybody expected them to look more city.

Bynum's hair was firecracker orange. It exploded from

his scalp in little smoke-thin sprouts, and he had to visit the barber every two weeks just to keep it under control. To make up for having to mow it so crinkly short, Bynum grew his bangs extra long and he peroxided them. They hung almost to his eyes. He oiled them with baby oil to keep them from frizzing, but they always looked as wavy and pleated as a fan.

I met Bynum in the cafeteria line at school in September 1957, my sophomore year. I was only fifteen then, close to six feet tall and slump-shouldered.

"Hey girl," this boy said behind me. "You got a bent fork."

It was the first thing Bynum Jenkins ever said to me, and as I wheeled around, I found myself facing a boy who stood a whole head taller than me. Slowly my backbone unfurled and my shoulders uncupped. I felt full of gush and generosity. "Thanks bunches," I chirped. But I felt shocked as soon as the words came out. *Thanks bunches?* Only short, flirtatious cheerleaders like Mopsy Brownlee talked gush and got away with it.

I suppose my voice went haywire on me because Bynum was so much taller. Everybody in their own secret way craves to be stood over. I grabbed a new fork and picked up my tray.

"Hey, wait up!" He loped after me. "You're *welcome* bunches."

I knew right off who he was because you just knew everybody at Orfax High. By reputation if not firsthand. Bynum had the reputation of his peroxided bangs. You had to use your imagination to decide what those bangs stood for—nothing else about him had ever made the news. I figured they had to stand for something real wild, although wild bangs didn't fit in with his zithery voice. He was sixteen then and had his own car.

We started going out together some on Friday nights, sometimes Saturdays, too. Pretty soon it felt like we were going steady. Often he'd invite me over to his house for Sunday dinner, which is how I got to know Phoebe, his sister, and his parents.

Hewson Jenkins farmed tobacco like most people around Orfax. He had a lean, squash-shaped face and a prickly gray flat-top he liked to wet down with Vitalis. He was a rawboned, loose-limbed man, even more awkward than Bynum. He always spilled something at dinner: his glass of buttermilk, soup down his Sunday shirt. But whenever he had an accident, he'd laugh like a real rascal. Mrs. Jenkins did not laugh. She had hair that had turned pure white in her twenties and she livened it up some by keeping a pinkish rinse on it. It was the rosebud pink of her skin which only turned shades darker when Hewson had one of his serious spills. She'd ask him to leave the table *immediately* and change into a fresh shirt. But just let Phoebe slip Buddyroll, their Chihuahua, a piece of fried chicken that disagreed with him so that he gagged all over the carpet, and Mrs. Jenkins' voice would ooze with concern. She'd cuddle Buddyroll against her bosom right there at the dining room table and wipe his little mouth with one of her linen napkins.

Mrs. Jenkins wasn't from Orfax. She was from Hopewell, Virginia, the daughter of a high school principal, and she had airs. At dinner there were always napkin rings and little silver dishes for salt with special doll-sized spoons. She rang a tiny china dinner bell between soup and dinner and between dinner and dessert. There was no maid in the kitchen to serve us when Mrs. Jenkins rang her bell, but she liked the idea of "announcing" courses. She had a voice that rippled and shivered like a harp, and when she used words like *entrée* and *sautéed*, something crumbled in my spine. She was always cooking up unusual recipes like Welsh rarebit and lemon mousse, dishes that had to be *explained* before anyone would touch them. But Mrs. Jenkins loved explanations. I guess it was the high school principal in her blood.

Bynum's parents liked me all right because they'd known my daddy. "Your father was a fine, smart fella," Mrs. Jenkins told me the first time I came to dinner, and every dinner since. "Everybody expected him to leave Orfax one day and go off to college and become somebody." Then she'd look away dramatically. "What a loss," she always said. Sunday after Sunday she gave the same sermon. Her voice shook with lament, but it struck the graver pitch of warning, too. One night I'd had my fill. I felt that sickening feeling in my craw that you get when you've taken one bite too many just to be polite. So when she started in on the sorrow Speedy's youthful death had caused, I piped right up. "Why, I barely remember him," I told her brightly. I probably even *smiled*. "I was real, real little when he got killed."

But she didn't bat an eye! "Your daddy was a kind person, good-natured and sweet, and he should have had a long, happy life." She refolded her napkin, which was bright pink and monogrammed with a rose-colored *J*. "Everybody called him Speedy," she said fondly.

"I *know*."

"He liked the fast life," she said then, shaking her head. "He liked fast cars and fast motorcycles and fast— never mind."

"Mama says he was in a hurry all the time," I offered.

"If you ask me," Mrs. Jenkins said, "he'd be alive today if he hadn't wanted too much too fast."

"Now, Mother," Mr. Jenkins said.

"One good thing," I said, "is that he didn't waste any time getting married. If he'd put off marrying, I might not have gotten born." Everybody was looking hard at me after I said that except for Bynum, who was staring at the tablecloth. "He married Mama when they were both seventeen," I said. You could have heard a pin drop. Even Buddyroll gave me an accusing look. Then I remembered that Bynum's seventeenth birthday was coming right up.

With a pert little flick of her wrist, Mrs. Jenkins rang the dinner bell and we started clearing the table.

There was a floor fan in the middle of Mrs. Jenkins' kitchen. It had a round top like a piano stool. While the sink filled with water, I plopped right down on the floor fan and let the cool breeze whoosh up my skirt. I was flaming after all I'd said. Phoebe, Bynum's sister who was my age, got out some dry dish towels. She couldn't stop laughing and shooting me sly looks. I liked Phoebe pretty well, although there was something pouty and spoiled about her. We started washing the dinner dishes; then, out of the blue, Phoebe Jenkins reared back and gave me this squinty, sizing-up look and said, "Pally, do you think Bynum's ugly?"

I was surprised. I'd never much thought of Bynum as having *any* looks, ugly or otherwise.

"No, I don't think Bynum's ugly," I said, although I could have tried harder.

"Yes you do," she whispered. The tone she used encouraged me to confide.

"I like Bynum for *himself*, not his looks," I said.

"Ha! You only like him because he has a fancy-dan car and buys you ball game tickets and because finally there's somebody who likes you that's taller than you."

"I'm crazy about Bynum," I said in a thin voice.

"*Why?*" She narrowed her eyes at me.

"Lots of reasons."

"Name one."

"His personality."

"You're so funny I forgot to laugh."

"Look," I said. "You either like somebody or you don't. Period. Anyway, it's impossible for you to see Bynum romantically because he's your brother."

She paused a moment, shuddering. "Do I look like Bynum?"

It wasn't until then that I realized the whole conversation had been about her from the beginning.

To be perfectly truthful, Phoebe Jenkins was a lot better-looking a girl than Bynum was a boy, but there was this huge family resemblance, as noticeable as a branding. She had the same spattered-looking skin, except hers was paler, afflicted by her mother's chalky pinkness. Her face was long and narrow like her daddy's, but she had a sweet, plump mouth, almost heart-shaped like a little red piece of candy. The showstopper was her eyes: big, blue sentimental eyes, as velvety as pansies. They were eyes that worked on you.

"There's a family resemblance," I said finally.

She barely seemed to hear me. "If only I was real tall like you," she said mournfully.

"Good lord!" I said. "There's nothing tall ever was but goony."

"Tall is graceful," she said. "Svelte."

I sighed. "Well," I said, hoping to change the subject, "the dishes are all done and I think I'd better go on home."

"Wait a minute, Pally. I got to talk to you," Phoebe Jenkins said, grabbing my arm. "Could somebody be drawn to me for my looks?"

I could not resist giving my voice a knowing lilt when I answered. "People are drawn to people for lots of reasons more strange than we could ever imagine."

"Then I'm scared," she said. "I'm afraid he's seeing something that's not *there*."

"*Who* is? What's not there?"

"I'm not gorgeous. I'm passable, but I'm no Mopsy Brownlee."

"Mopsy Brownlee *acts* a whole lot prettier than she is," I said.

"Well, I think she's beautiful," Phoebe said. "Mopsy Brownlee wouldn't have a moment's doubt about it if he told her *she* looked nice."

"Who told her? Who are you talking about, Phoebe?"

She stared at me dead-on, but she blushed when she said his name. "Bobby Rex Moseley," she said. Just the way she said it, kind of bleakly with disbelief, made you know it was the truth.

"Well, tell all," I urged.

"Sh-h-h," she said, "I don't want Bynum to hear." We went up to her room and locked the door.

I managed to coax the whole story out of her. But she enjoyed being begged for details and it took such a long time to pry the facts loose that I got invited to stay for Sunday night supper.

Friday evening she and Fayette Weems had been messing around together over at Fayette's house. They couldn't go out to the Rhapsody drive-in or Woody's Danceland because they didn't have driver's licenses, much less cars. They'd seen the show at the Sunset Theatre in downtown Orfax a couple of times already: *King Kong Versus Godzilla*. There was no good music on the radio, only baseball games and nothing local. They'd ended up playing Fayette's whole collection of Pat Boone records and baking Toll House cookies. About nine o'clock, after they'd eaten all the cookies, Fayette suggested that they walk up to the Tastee-Freeze on Proximity Street for a milkshake. She was a clunky bruiser of a girl who loved to pack in the food.

As Phoebe talked, I had it pictured. Moths strummed the lazy, smoke-colored air around street lamps. Lightning bugs bloomed in the cavey shadows of bushes and trees. There was the whispery sweep of lawn sprinklers, the damping-down smell of burned out, wiry summer grass. Late summer nights around Orfax, North Carolina, are all the same: vivid, quiet, slightly strange, the sky overhead bristling with the pointy light of new autumn stars.

The change of season is so slight that you still don't need a sweater, but just the same the hair lies differently on your arms, waiting for goose bumps. Sometimes, if you listen real hard, you might hear a single ruddy leaf unhinge itself from a dogwood tree and rattle down the sidewalk. There are hardly any mosquitoes left.

"I remember everything I wore," Phoebe told me.

"I hope so," I said. "It's only been two days."

"My white sleeveless Ship'n'Shore blouse and my turquoise pedal pushers. I also had on a new pair of white English knee socks and my saddle oxfords. I looked pretty good."

Proximity Street runs right down the center of Orfax, parallel to Main. The Proximity Street Tastee-Freeze was about three blocks from the heart of town, the one place that stayed open until midnight and that everybody could walk to. It never attracted a rowdy group because most of the rowdy group had cars to drive them places in the county that served alcohol like Woody's and Gizmo's Bar. Mostly the folks who ended up at the Tastee-Freeze on a Friday night were the old creaky people who couldn't sleep or women in roller bonnets with squawking babies on their hips whose husbands were out running around or pitching horseshoes or young kids who didn't have TV sets and would spend all evening clattering up and down the street on bicycles with playing cards jammed in the spokes. You'd never expect to run into any BMOCs there, so it was a safe place to show up in your grubbiest clothes or if you had some loser of a date. Nobody you hoped to impress would be there.

When Phoebe and Fayette arrived, there were just a couple of old farmers in crusty overalls eating cups of vanilla ice cream in a back booth. And at the counter, on one of the red leatherette stools, sat Mrs. Oxendine, drinking a cup of scalding hot coffee and not batting an eye.

Mrs. Oxendine had insomnia, everybody knew that, and she was proud of her ability to go without sleep. She liked to coax the insomnia along, like some shadowy talent, by drinking cup after cup of coffee late at night. In the summertime, when she wasn't working part-time as our school nurse, she opened shop as a round-the-clock spiritual adviser. Most evenings you could find her swilling coffee at the Tastee-Freeze, gearing up for any late night advising she might be summoned to do. My only run-in with her had been the day I had to go to the infirmary when I ran the sewing machine over my thumb in home ec. Lucky for me, she said, it was a basting stitch. Most everybody was afraid of Mrs. Oxendine, which is why she made such a champion school nurse. Nobody goldbricked her because Mrs. Oxendine was an expert on torture. She had a reputation for challenging the sick and testing their pain tolerance.

Mrs. Oxendine lived with her son, Howdy, in a log house way at the back of the trailer park where I lived. The trailer park was called Piney View and she owned it and leased out trailer plots to about a dozen families. Everybody that lived there had to be nice to Howdy, who was a strange, brown monkey of a boy and wore homemade snakeskin belts.

Everybody knew that Mrs. Oxendine was a first-class weirdo, so Fayette and Phoebe took a booth as far away from her as they could get and ordered two chocolate milkshakes. By then the Godzilla movie at the Sunset had let out and a few more people drifted in, but nobody they palled around with much. Then, just as Fayette was beginning to make these gargling sounds, draining the last of her milkshake, the door swung open and in walked Bobby Rex Moseley and his little brother, Leon.

Phoebe didn't even have time to blot her mouth with a napkin and put on fresh lipstick before Bobby Rex noticed them and strolled over.

"Hi there," he said. "What's two nice girls like you doing in a place like this?"

Phoebe shivered with the delight of repeating his words. She hugged herself.

"So what did you say back?" I asked.

She frowned. "It was that dumb old Fayette Weems who answered," she said miserably. Then she tried to make her voice sound real horsey, the way Fayette usually talked: " 'Why, hello, Bobby Rex! We've just finished listening to all my Pat Boone records and eating a whole batch of Toll House cookies and now we've come to the Tastee-Freeze for some refreshments.' *That's* what she said!" Phoebe groaned. "Anybody with half a brain knows that you don't tell a boy like Bobby Rex Moseley the absolute word-for-word truth."

"Not *that* sort of truth," I said.

"You've got to be *mysterious*," said Phoebe. "*I* know that."

"What did Bobby Rex say then?"

"He's a gentleman and he's cool," she said. "He said, 'Phoebe, do you like Pat Boone?' And I said, 'I like Pat Boone all right, but you sing a whole lot smoother.' " She looked up at me, glowing. "Was that too forward?"

"I don't know," I said. "How should I know?"

"I think it was probably too forward," she said. "I turned red as a tomato. Fayette said so. She pointed it out right then and there. She's a fool. I don't know why I mess with her."

"What did Bobby Rex do then?"

"I don't think it was my imagination," she said, gazing dreamily past me. "But I think he turned red, too. Just a little."

"Then what?"

"His little brother, Leon, came up with two strawberry ice-cream cones and told him they were melting. Bobby Rex laughed and introduced us. Leon's real sweet, but he's no Bobby Rex. He's got ears the size of dinner plates and sort of slicked-down, mule-colored hair. He's a little bitty bumpkin of a thing. Anyhow, I said that maybe the two of them ought to share our booth since it's getting crowded in the Tastee-Freeze, only Fayette pipes up that she's finished her milkshake and they can go ahead and take the *whole* booth since it was time we headed back to her house. I could have smacked her, Pally, until I thought what she was already thinking. It was bound to happen: Bobby Rex and me on one side of the booth and her and Leon on the other. So I said: 'Why don't you let me treat you to a cakeroll with hot fudge sauce.' It was a brainstorm, Pally. I think being desperate can make you a split-second genius. As soon as I reached in my change purse, she jumped right up to go order. 'Sit down,' I said then to Bobby Rex. And guess what, Pally?"

"What?"

She sucked in a deep, disappointed breath, then laughed. "Now that Fayette was gone, they both sat down on the same side! Mostly, after that, I talked to Leon," Phoebe said. Her face was radiant, her eyes glistening. She looked pretty. "Boys like Bobby Rex like you to take an interest in their brothers," she said.

"So when did Bobby Rex tell you that you looked good?"

"Just hold your horses, I'm getting there," she said.

I looked out her bedroom window. The sky was dark now and nubby with late summer stars. Suddenly I was ready for school to start. I even wished I had homework. Something to go home and *do*. I craved the smell of new Eagle #2 pencils. It would give me great pleasure to label the dividers in my notebook. I'd print neatly in blue washable ink: GEOGRAPHY, ENGLISH, FRENCH, ALGEBRA, BIOLOGY. Maybe this year I'd keep a neat notebook. Maybe this year I would make all A's. A late summer sky full of stars made you feel robust with new promises to yourself. I felt so restless sitting there in Phoebe's bedroom, her chenille bedspread making little pocks all over the backs of my legs. I felt filled up with myself, with no room for her, and certainly no room for Bynum.

Phoebe Jenkins droned on and on about Leon Moseley and I listened a little, but mostly I thought about Leon. What was it like to be kin to the handsomest boy in Orfax, maybe the whole world? What was it like to have such a popular brother and to be ten years old and have thin, slicked-down mule-colored hair and Dumbo ears? Did Leon know Bobby Rex was handsome? Or did he just stop seeing the handsomeness after a while, come to take it for granted because it was always around? Did Leon even *like* Bobby Rex? Maybe they were friendly only in public; maybe Leon was raging with jealousy inside. Did they ever fight? Did Bobby Rex think Leon was a brat? Did Bobby Rex confide in Leon? Did Leon think Phoebe Jenkins looked pretty in her white Ship'n' Shore blouse and her turquoise pedal pushers, or did he see her as flirty and stuck on herself? Or did Leon eat his ice cream *period* and not think anything much about anything?

"Are you listening, Pally?" Phoebe asked fretfully.

"Of course I'm listening. It's fascinating."

"Okay, then what was the very last thing I said? Just now?"

"You were talking about Leon."

"What did I say *exactly* about Leon?"

I shrugged.

"Pay attention, Pally," she said, "or you'll miss the most important part. I'm counting on you to help me make sense out of it all."

"Why?" I said, more to myself than to her. Why did I suddenly feel so sad? I felt I was doing everything in my life absolutely wrong.

"Because it's all so *mysterious*," Phoebe said. "So out of the blue. I didn't even know that Bobby Rex knew my name."

"Don't try to figure it out," I said wearily. "Just accept it and be happy." I sounded a lot like Betty, my mother, who always made good sense if you stood back from her and forgot she was your mother.

"You just don't understand!" Phoebe cried. "He sat right there, licking his strawberry ice cream and told me I was a real *knockout*. What do you think, Pally? Am I a real knockout? You won't lie."

I felt my eyes looming at her. "Those were his *exact* words? A real 'knockout'?"

Phoebe smacked her pillow with a balled-up fist. "Darn it, Pally. You made me spill the best beans first. I was coming to the compliment, but it needed a buildup. Without the buildup, it sounds like some cheap line."

But I knew Bobby Rex Moseley if only by rumor and reputation. Everybody in Orfax knew he didn't have cheap lines, didn't know one from a hole in the ground. He was pure-mouthed as a baby that way. That was the reason every girl I knew sort of hung her hopes on him. He was different. He was impossible because he was so pure.

☆ ♡ ☆

Bynum drove me home about ten o'clock. We didn't speak for several miles, which was normal. More and more we had less and less to say to each other. I leaned back in my seat and rolled down my window and let the wind sort of wipe me away. The night smelled rich and secretive, like the insides of old pockets. I loved the smell of the countryside. It was a smell so familiar that you forgot about it most of the time: the fragrance of damp pasture grass, peeling fence posts, big, slow-witted animals, aging manure. It was a dank smell that seemed stronger in the dark, with a living quality to it as if it were capable of making shadow and sound. I sucked in a lungful. I opened my mouth and ate it; it had a luscious, bitter taste.

"Godamighty!" Bynum said. I jumped. "I used to think them things was *miles*."

I looked over at him. His long face was lime green in the dashboard light. From the side it seemed shaped like a gourd. I usually didn't watch him while he drove, and it was a real shock.

"Boy, I was a dumbbell," he said, shaking his head. "I really thought them things was miles."

He didn't have to talk hick, but he liked to. He liked to chew tobacco, too, and he was saving up for a tattoo, war or no war. His daddy had gotten a tattoo in World War II. It was on Hewson Jenkins' chest, a battleship with a mermaid lazing on top of it. Mrs. Jenkins had almost left him over that tattoo, Bynum said.

"What are you talking about?" I asked. "What things did you think were miles?"

"Them dotted lines," he said, pointing at the road. "Them painted dashes they use to divide the highway."

"*Whole* miles? Each dot?"

"I thought so. When I was a real little dumbbell. I mean *real* little."

"Wouldn't it be fun if they were whole miles," I said, "and we could cover huge distances really quickly."

"But if they were *real* miles," he said, "then it would be about a hundred sixty-nine of them from my house to yours, and that's too far for this boy." He reached over and squeezed my hand.

"You've actually counted them? Between our houses?"

"Once," Bynum said, "when there was nothing good on the radio."

I felt discouragement blow through me like cold, whistling wind. I shivered.

He slowed the car at the intersection of State Road and Highway 21. "You tired?"

I shrugged.

He turned off on 21 then and bore sharply to the right under an arbor of bloomless wisteria. It was the entrance to a bumpy dirt road that led to Sawyer's Creek. Everybody went down there to make out. I kept thinking about Bynum's mile theory and how fun it would be if some glittery town were only so many painted dashes from Orfax. My best friend, Shilda, had a grandmother who lived in Newark, New Jersey, and Shilda was always talking about how some day the two of us were going to ride the Southern Crescent up there to visit. The main reason Shilda wanted to go to Newark, New Jersey, was that you could be wilder with less guilt in a place where nobody knew you.

"What if instead of six hundred miles, it was only six hundred dashes to Newark, New Jersey?" I asked. Bynum had cut the engine.

"Who in their right mind wants to go to Yankeeland?" He swung his peroxided forelock for emphasis.

"Think of all the things to do, the restaurants and shops. I could take a taxi over to some big store like Macy's and buy your birthday present there instead of at Rice's."

"It's an asphalt jungle up there," Bynum said with authority. "If you didn't get killed in a taxicab, you'd get robbed by some wino. Thanks but no thanks." He ran a hand through his forelock and flipped it out of his eyes. "If it was only six hundred dashes to Yankeeland, we'd have to figure something new out."

He turned on the radio. Vic Damone was singing "Affair to Remember." Bynum leaned over and kissed me wetly through the whole song. Then they played a new record by Teresa Brewer. She belted the song out so enthusiastically I could picture her dimples. With the exception of their different hair colors, she and Mopsy Brownlee could pass for sisters, that's what I was thinking. I'd hardly thought about Mopsy Brownlee all summer. But school would be starting in a couple of weeks, the day after Labor Day, and I'd see Mopsy, who'd be suntanned and blond and wearing the latest style she'd bought over in Greensboro at Montaldo's. "How was your summer?" she'd ask everybody. "Mine was gorgeoceanus," meaning, of course, that she'd spent most of it at the beach.

Some of it was getting awfully old: Mopsy Brownlee's charm, Bynum's Palomino show-horse–style bangs, wet cafeteria trays, pencil sharpeners that chewed up new Eagle #2's because they were too full of shavings. It was getting old and I was weeks from my sixteenth birthday and almost two years from graduation. Life seemed treacherously long.

I took off my blouse and Bynum unhooked my bra and draped it over the steering wheel. Then he leaned slightly forward and kissed it, the bra.

"Ever feel guilty?" he asked with a sly smile.

"About what?"

"It's *Sunday*," he said.

I looked down at my chest. My breasts were as small and round as brown eggs. There was nothing to them. They just hung there, boring and predictable.

"Does Phoebe have freckles on her bosoms?" I asked Bynum.

"Good grief, Pally, what a dumb question."

"Well, does she?"

"How should I know? She's my sister. Gross."

"Are her bosoms bigger than mine?"

"I don't know."

"Well, *guess*."

"I don't *know*, Pally. I don't ever look at her . . . *there*."

"Bobby Rex Moseley told her she was a knockout," I said.

"A *knockout*? Phoebe? One look at her and it feels your eyeballs is knocked out, she's so painful to look at. That's all he meant." Then Bynum started laughing at

his own humor. He laughed so hard that you expected
him to damage himself somewhere. His shoulders rolled
around and he tilted his head back. He couldn't stop
laughing.

I started taking off my skirt and my half-slip, and
Bynum didn't say one word because he was still laughing. His cheeks looked wet with tears. When I got down
to my underpants, I took them off, too. I felt loose and
crazy and like laughing myself. This wasn't *me*. I could
throw this girl away.

All summer we'd ridden around in the red Studebaker
with the Cyclops-Eye speedometer. Everybody had
thought we were whooping it up. But it wasn't like they
thought. Bynum had been so tired from helping his daddy
farm tobacco all day that I usually had to honk the car
every few seconds to keep him perky. We'd parked
down at Sawyer's Creek regularly and made out, but
nothing past the waist.

"Bynum," I said. I took his hand and planted it carefully between my legs.

He stopped laughing, as quickly as if somebody had
stoppered his mouth. He swallowed. I pressed his hand
firmly against me so that he'd know it was no accident.

"What," he said, but it wasn't a question at all.

"Feel me."

"Why." He wouldn't look down.

"Because we never have."

"I'll lose complete control, Pally. Honest-to-God."

"No you won't."

"Yes," he said sadly, "I'll rape you or something."

"I won't let you rape me."

"Fat chance," he said. He flexed his jaw and closed
his eyes. He looked miserable.

"Don't you want something to happen?" I asked softly.

He sighed deeply. His nostrils flared. "Heavens to
Betsy," he said. His voice was pitched high and whin-
nying. "I'm not even seventeen years old, Pally."

"My daddy was married when he was seventeen," I said.

"That's what I'm talking about, Pally," he said.

We were silent for a long time. The crickets hissed in the grass like fire. I could hear the rippling calls of whippoorwills and owls that measured the depth of these woods. Slowly the real Pally Thompson came floating over Bynum's Studebaker, gazing down in judgment, and what she found was this: a lanky know-nothing farm boy with fake-o, stud horse hair, and big, rough shy hands that smelled of hard soap but still had dirt under the fingernails, a boy who sat under his clothes with posture as stiff as a sawhorse. And beside him: a know-nothing jerk of a girl, bent on wasting herself.

I hated Bynum for his calmness and reason. I hated him for the very qualities in a boyfriend that all the magazines said you should be grateful for. His hand felt dead and damp. He'd not moved it, out of politeness. Briskly I peeled it away.

"There."

He looked at the hand as if it were an exotic gift. He flexed the fingers. Then, one at a time, he popped each of the knuckles.

I put on my panties, my half-slip, my skirt. Then I reached for my bra that hung over the steering wheel.

"What are you doing?" he asked. "What did we come here for?"

I let him kiss me. I let him hold my breasts and kiss them, too. There was nothing to it. We'd done that a million times before. When he was ready, we got in the backseat of the Studebaker and he lay on top of me and heaved. Afterwards he had to take his shirttail out so that the wet spot on his pants would be covered. Then he offered me a Chiclet and we drove on home, chewing the gum and listening to the radio.

We pulled into Piney View just as "Party Doll" came on the radio, one of my all-time favorite hits right then, so of course I stayed to hear it through. When the last note was over, Bynum flicked the radio off importantly.

"Pally." His voice was low and sober. I'd never heard his twang so well controlled. "I need to ask you a huge favor. Pally." He swallowed hard. "You won't tell nobody, will you?"

"Tell?"

"You know," he said. "What happened down at Sawyer's Creek just now."

"What did happen, Bynum?"

He wiped his Palomino bangs out of his eyes, but they flopped right back. "Pally, you know and I know that I acted like a queer."

"Forget it," I said.

"I'm not a queer."

"I know you're not," I said. "You probably only turned me down because it's Sunday."

"Thanks, Pal." He kissed my cheek. "Promise you won't tell?"

"Cross my heart."

"Gee, Pal." He hugged me in his hard, awkward, angular way. "Gee, thanks. Thanks bunches."

By the fall of my junior year, especially after what Phoebe had told me about Bobby Rex Moseley, I felt fed up and desperate. I needed a *change*. Mama suggested a home permanent, which was exactly what Mrs. Futrell had told me in home economics.

Home ec. was my very worst course that fall. I burned everything I put into the oven, and it was all I could do to keep from running over my thumb with the sewing machine again. But Mrs. Futrell kept encouraging me. She was an optimist, you had to give her that. And she tried to inspire each of her students by setting a singularly appealing example. She had bleached blond hair that she slicked into a bun and bleached blond eyebrows that she plucked into perfect arches. They sort of sat on her forehead like thin little French fries. She wore spike heels to match all her outfits, and she had about one thousand outfits with coordinating scarves, jewelry, sweaters, and belts. Pinks, corals, and grays showed off her coloring best, she always said. She liked wide belts that flattered her tiny, always-sucked-in waist, and she liked bangle bracelets that tinkled at her wrists, giving an illusion that she was musical. She always smelled good.

That term she decided to devote an entire unit of study to feminine fashion and grooming. The project was called "Make Yourself Over." I was all for it.

Every day Mrs. Futrell marched out her list of beauty tips. She demonstrated the proper application of facial masks (some you could whip up in your own kitchen out of eggs and oatmeal). She performed all sorts of amazing tricks with eyelash curlers, tweezers, lipstick brushes, mascara, rouge, garter belts, and Merry Widows. Once she got an underwear salesman to come to our class and give a talk on Lov-a-Lift bras.

The very worst part of the good grooming unit was the beauty clinics where we had to identify and analyze each other's main flaws and make tactful suggestions. We got rated on hair, eyes, shape of face, height (as if you could do anything about *that!*), hands, and proficiency with makeup. About the only thing on our faces we weren't suppose to dicker with were birthmarks.

"Remember," Mrs. Futrell told us, "what you do to improve yourself improves others."

"Others?" Fayette Weems blurted.

Mrs. Futrell glared at the whole class, daring anyone to dispute her. We were not a very showy bunch of girls, and there she was: a real standout, a real flower of an older woman. I admired her fierceness. She really believed all this stuff we were scribbling into notebooks that we'd either lose or throw away some day. She was only trying to help us catch Mr. Right.

Mrs. Futrell's cheeks pinkened. "Think of life as a gallery," she said, "where everyone is beheld and judged like a piece of art."

Fayette Weems groaned, and Mrs. Futrell bugged her eyes at the class angrily. "Very well," she said tartly. "You don't seem to appreciate metaphor, so I am going to tell you a true story." It was a story she'd saved, you could tell. Her tone of voice, usually so crisp and pert, turned suddenly confessional.

She told about the time she'd driven over to Winston-Salem for a doctor's appointment—she'd thought her plantar warts would have to be removed, but, luckily, the doctor prescribed new shoes. Afterwards, she'd stopped off at the Winn-Dixie there to buy a leg of lamb. She'd decided to fix a special dinner that night to celebrate, and leg of lamb was something you couldn't find at the Cash and Carry in Orfax.

It was late May and very hot. She hadn't dressed properly for steambath weather, but then one must sometimes make sacrifices to comfort in order to look one's best, she insisted. Note: she'd worn nylon stockings and her heavy beige linen suit with a brown silk scarf tucked down inside the neckline. She'd worn her brown and white spectator pumps and had carried a brown and white leather clutch that *almost* matched the spectators. Anyway, it was the best she could do. She'd worn pearl earrings and a matching bracelet.

In front of the grocery store stood a woman from the American Legion Auxiliary selling Memorial Day poppies. Mrs. Futrell believed strongly in the armed services because she believed in sacrifice. She paid a whole dollar for the poppy without a moment's hesitation. But she could not bring herself to loop the poppy through a buttonhole of her beige jacket. It was the wrong look. She knew this bone-deep. You always had to consider the *total* look, and a red paper poppy was simply too flashy to pin on a tailored beige suit. So she quickly slipped it into her purse and hurried inside the grocery store.

She'd just finished selecting the leg of lamb she wanted when a tall gentleman she'd never seen before tapped her lightly on the elbow. "Ma*dam*," he said, and for a split second she could have been in Paris, France. She turned slowly to face the most superbly well groomed man she'd ever seen in her life. In a quick glance she saw that his fingernails were manicured and buffed to an elegant pearl. His silvery hair matched his silver-gray suit handsomely. "Pardon me." An accent hung delicately in his voice like an ornament. When he suddenly took her hand, her knees felt as loose as a couple of Slinkies. He gazed into her eyes steadily, boldly. "In all my life," he said, "I never thought I'd see a dressed-up woman in a grocery store." He had wintergreen mint on his breath.

It seemed to her then that he paid her every proper compliment in the world, some, she thought, in other languages. *Romance* languages. She was certain, for example, that he used the word "magnifique."

"Just look at the way most women show up at a grocery store to shop," he said scornfully.

All around them shuffled weary-looking ladies—young and old—with bleached-out faces, haywire hair, roller bonnets. Here they came, slouching along in their shapeless, faded wrappers, brown wren housedresses, baggy pants held together with safety pins, some of them!

Not for the first time, but with a sudden sharp pang in her chest, Mrs. Futrell realized what a mess most women made of their looks and how offensive it was to others if they went public. She felt embarrassed for all of them. Why, there went a woman in a man's T-shirt! Here came another in bobby socks and bedroom scuffs. Why, wearing bedroom scuffs to the grocery store was almost indecent exposure!

Suddenly the man with the silver hair (whose name she never learned) did something amazing. He took one of her own well-manicured hands and pressed into its palm a one-hundred-dollar bill. "Buy some champagne," he told her. "Please, you must celebrate yourself." Then, almost gravely, he added: "I want to thank you, ma*dam*, for heeding the eye of the beholder."

Of course she was shocked and flattered and bewildered all at once. Her first impulse was to fling the money back at him. She wasn't quite sure it was proper

to take money from a stranger no matter how polite he
was; after all, politeness had its excesses, too. But before she could organize herself well enough to do or say
anything, the man turned quickly and glided right out of
the Winn-Dixie like a mannequin on casters. He had
heavenly posture. At the door he paused only to slip on
sleek, dark, lagoon-green glasses before he stepped into
the sun. He strode right past the poppy lady without so
much as a nod.

"I never found out who he was," Mrs. Futrell said
dreamily.

"Maybe he was somebody famous," I said. "A movie
tycoon, a talent scout."

Mrs. Futrell rolled her eyes. "Of course he was somebody famous. And now, girls, I hope you understand
what I meant when I said that improving your own looks
improves others," Mrs. Futrell said. "Why, that man
made me feel as if I'd made his day." She seemed to
look specifically at me now. "Make no mistake," she
said. "People are watching you and judging you every
minute of your life. And at *your* tender ages, how can
you possibly be sure that the person who judges you
today won't turn out to be your own heart's destiny
tomorrow?"

After listening to Mrs. Futrell's story and attending
my "personally tailored" beauty clinic, I felt doomed.
The consensus of my looks turned out to be this:

Shape of face: Oval, too narrow. Correct with light
foundation at jawline and cheekbones.

Complexion: Clear, but too pale. Use rose-beige
makeup with a dot of rouge. Stop using harsh soaps and
clean face with cold cream.

Hair: Limp, lusterless, nondescript brown. Nice widow's peak, though. Recommend conditioner and permanent. Curls soften a thin face.

Hands: Disaster area. Hangnail problem so bad it
looks like you use a pencil sharpener instead of a nail

file. Let nails grow! Use clear polish. Soften cuticle nightly.

Height: 5′ 11¾″. Wear low-heel shoes, flats, and full skirts. Overblouses help. Stop slumping!

Weight: 126 lbs. Gain 10–20 pounds. Wear knee socks to help round out skinny calves. Wear bulky sweaters and padded bras.

Colors: Avoid wishywashy colors that don't make a strong statement. Best bets: turquoise, maroon, cerise, navy, and colors related to those families.

For our unit exam we were given two weeks to overhaul our looks and follow the suggestions of the consensus. On exam day we were supposed to show up in class groomed, I guess, as if we wanted to attract a talent scout at the Winn-Dixie.

☆ ♡ ☆

So, one Saturday morning, for the sake of the "Make Me Over" Project, Mama gave me a home permanent. When she finished, my hair looked like a major tornado touching down. We expected it to roar, to suck me right up and carry me away. To make matters worse, Joe Parker, Mama's fiancé, dropped by just as we'd both burst into tears and were consoling each other. It was five o'clock and the permanent had taken all day.

Mama looked beat. She wore this old pair of farmer's overalls that she liked to slop around in. They had holes in both knees. Joe Parker gave her a big cheerful kiss and offered her a Chesterfield.

"Well, I've ruined her," she admitted to Joe. "You couldn't get a pitchfork through that mess."

"You want to borrow my hay baler?" Joe asked and they laughed. But they covered up their laughs with their hands and looked at me sympathetically.

"It's not so bad," I said fiercely. "It's a *change*." I stomped out the front door then and walked around the trailer to the backyard. I crawled into the tire swing that hung from an old beech tree. I swung until the sky began to darken. One by one the lights inside the trailer came on. I could smell the hamburgers Mama was frying up for supper and hear her and Joe laughing and popping beer tops. It was late September and cicadas were ringing all around me.

Mama called out the front door of the trailer for me, but I didn't answer. I heard her walk back into the trailer and say something to Joe. Then Joe went out and called me. I kept right on swinging. I felt mean and tight in my heart. After a while he walked back inside, and I could hear the kitchen chair legs scraping the linoleum as they sat down to eat. I could hear the tink of forks and the slow, easy sounds of supper talk.

It was inky dark by the time I unpeeled myself from the swing. There was Mama at the kitchen sink doing dishes, and there was Joe Parker kissing her ear and putting his hands on her breasts. It all meant something. The world was full of other people's doings that got done whether you were around or not. Supper got eaten, your mother got loved.

All around me tired old lightning bugs flickered in the heavy leaves of the beech tree. They made scrambled-looking constellations. Way up I spotted the largest of them all, and I wished on him like a star. I wished for just anything, any old thing at all that would make a difference.

I hadn't felt so gloomy about myself since last Christmas when Joe had given Mama a diamond ring and Bynum Jenkins had given me a lint brush. But what had made me gloomiest was how I pretended to Bynum that the lint brush hadn't mattered, it was the thought that counted. The *thought*!

"Come on, Pally, it's a goofball present," Bynum had admitted to me. "You know I'd give you something better except that I'm flat broke." He was saving every penny he earned working odd jobs for his daddy so he could dude up that Studebaker Commander with the Cyclops-Eye speedometer.

"Seriously, Bynum," I'd said reassuringly. "It's a handy present. I don't have one. I can really use it."

"That's good," he'd said, smiling in spite of his doubts, because I did act truly pleased. Maybe he felt puzzled that I could be satisfied with such a practical gift. It must have made me seem flexible and mature. He looked impressed.

"I just couldn't think of anything really special that I was sure you'd like," he'd said. "I mean, something cheap. Mama picked it up for free at One-Hour Cleaners."

"Stop apologizing, Bynum. It's a fine gift, really. You know I'm sort of messy."

"It's not that I was *hinting*, Pally," he'd said.

The next morning, after Joe had given Mama the engagement ring and they'd clung together like it was their last kiss instead of the beginning of about a billion more, Joe asked me what Bynum had given me for Christmas.

"You'd never guess in a million years," I'd said, "so I'll tell you. It was a lint brush."

"Whoa now!" Joe said. "This girl can tell a joke."

"Honey," Mama said to me, "don't be fresh."

"All I can say," Joe said, "is that if it *was* a lint brush he gave her, then the party's over and it's time to clean up."

"Y'all can borrow it and take it on your honeymoon if you like," I'd said tearfully.

Then I went into my bedroom and shut the door and turned on the radio loud. They were playing "Jingle Bell Rock." I kept thinking: what's your problem, Pally Thompson? It's Christmas morning! The whole damn world is merry as can be. You've got a boyfriend who happens to be a whole head taller than you and calls you his dream girl. Isn't that all you've ever wanted? Well, you *deserve* a lint brush. Then I started sobbing, and I just couldn't stop. "Jingle Bell Rock" was simply too jolly. It reminded me of when I was a kid and Speedy made me a rocking horse for Christmas. He painted the horse a bright, feisty red and fastened a feather plume to the crown of its little leather halter. I was only four years old, but young as I was, I knew a true thing when I had it. I knew we lived in a house with yellow shutters and a chimney built with fieldstones. We had a porch swing and a bird bath and a trellis covered in roses. Back then I remember feeling lucky all the time. In the springtime, the grass in our front yard was woven with wild blue violets and Mama, barefooted, would hang the laundry outdoors. The way the wind would smack those clothes around made them sound mad and put upon, but they looked as twirly and carefree as dancers. The Christmas that Speedy gave me the rocking horse was the last one before he got killed on the motorcycle. And the strongest memory I own of my early childhood is the one of me riding that painted pony in front of the fireplace, staring into the flames as if into a dazzling, open jewelry box, feeling that things couldn't get much better, that I couldn't possibly have more. And probably I was right about that.

☆ ♡ ☆

On Monday I wore the biggest scarf I could find to school.

"Why, Pally," Mrs. Futrell said, clapping her hands together with excitement. "Don't be shy, let's see what you've done."

I peeled away the scarf and everybody gasped.

"Why, it's *you*!" Mrs. Futrell said, beaming, touching my hair. "It's *positively* you."

I don't know what was wrong with me after that, what made me go out of my way to sabotage myself. The least

I could have done was to stop biting my nails. But I chewed them down to nubs. I chewed with purpose, and I savored each bite.

I didn't wear any makeup except for a touch of my old Pretty Please lipstick which the consensus had said babyfied my mouth. The class had recommended some wild strutting shade called Cha Cha Cherry.

I couldn't do a thing with my hair except wash it now and then and try to tame it with cream rinse. It looked like I needed a hammer and forge rather than a hairbrush.

In English class we were reading *Sonnets from the Portuguese,* but all I could think about was Elizabeth Barrett Browning's hair. *She'd* done all right without a home permanent. I'd have bet anybody that her hair was one huge mess, too, because back then people didn't wash their hair for fear of catching pneumonia. Even well people didn't wash their hair for fear of becoming sick. I was just certain that E.B.B. had had greasy, stringy, pitiful hair. But *her* heart's destiny couldn't have cared less because, lucky for her, he liked poetry better than hair. That got me to wondering about the trickery of poetry. It seemed every girl on earth had to have a gimmick going.

The night before the home ec. exam, when I was supposed to present myself transformed, Mama baked Rice Krispie squares. She and Joe and I sat around the kitchen table talking and eating up the whole batch.

Joe and Mama were in great spirits, planning their wedding. It was still a long time off because Joe wanted to build a new house for all of us to live in. But the wedding's being shoved into the future didn't seem to bother Mama a bit. She and Joe acted as excited as if it were tomorrow. When "Love Me Tender" came on the radio, they got up and danced, looking straight into each other's eyes.

"What should I *wear*?" Mama asked suddenly. She

bunched her shoulders like a little kid. You could tell that deciding was more of a delight than a bother to her.

"Why, a fancy white wedding dress, of course," Joe said.

"No, no," she said, laughing. "Not *white*. White's for purity. Not even a wedding dress. You only wear that the first time."

"Well, it's my first time," he said.

I sashayed around the kitchen, my shoulders thrown back, my stomach sucked in so tight I felt like I was an hourglass. I jutted my chin and tried to look snooty. "May I suggest, for your complexion, a fabric of the cerise hue."

"What's she talking about?" Joe asked.

"Oh, it's something she learned in home ec. class."

"You'd look simply fetching in a cerise gown," I trilled.

"What the hell's cerise?" Joe said.

"The color of Strother Mottsinger's old Dodge," I said.

"Whoa now, I like that color," Joe said.

Mama and I rolled our eyes at him and shook our heads.

"Why don't you wear the wedding dress you already have?" I asked.

Mama and Joe glanced at each other and then Joe winked and kissed her on the nose. It was a sweet little upturned nose and he adored it. "That's okay by me," he said. "Make it do, wear it out, use it up, do without."

"People would talk," Mama said. "People would think it was tacky and disrespectful."

"I wouldn't," Joe said solemnly.

"I wouldn't either," I said.

Mama looked pleased. "I probably couldn't get it over my hips now." But her tone was a wondering one. "It's been over seventeen years since I wore that dress. It's turned yellow by now."

"Then nobody would recognize it was the same dress if it's turned yellow," Joe Parker said, and we all laughed.

We sat there drinking our iced tea awhile and then Mama said: "I've got a picture of me wearing it, Joe, if you'd like to see."

I was surprised that she took out the big framed picture of herself and *Speedy* marching up the aisle. She had other pictures of herself alone, wearing the wedding dress. But she chose to show the one that included Speedy, my daddy, whom she'd been crazy-blind in love with, and laid it on the table. I peeked at Joe, feeling sorry for him in a way, but Joe was smiling. If the picture made him jealous, I couldn't tell. He touched it gently as if it were very fragile. He moistened his lips. "Let me tell you," he said to Mama, "I could eat that fairy princess right on up with a spoon."

"Do you like the dress, Joe?"

"Oh boy," Joe said. He studied the picture like he was trying to memorize every detail.

I stared at the image of Speedy. He looked like a boy, young and handsome. He looked so brisk and handsome that I felt sad. There he loped, up the aisle, a tall, stringy farm boy with a big, curvy mouth, just smiling and smiling.

Then, I studied the picture of Mama. What a baby! She was only seventeen. The gleaming satin dress billowed all around her legs because she was running to keep pace with Speedy. She carried a bouquet of blurry flowers in one hand. Her other arm was looped through his, and she looked like she was holding on for dear life. She had a mist of little flowers in her veil. To see her glowing face, so full of confidence and pride, you would have thought she was the wisest person in the world. My heart felt all caved in with pity, watching her face. She didn't know she was flinging herself down the aisle straight toward sorrow and loss. That possibility never crossed her mind.

"Hey," said Joe Parker suddenly, "what's on your feet?"

I leaned closer. In the photograph her shoes looked peculiar and floppy. Since the camera had caught her in motion, one shoe was lifted halfway up and you could see its dirty sole.

Mama giggled. "Oh *those*!" she said fondly. "I wore my old scruffy bedroom slippers. It's a good thing they were white. They hardly showed."

"Bedroom slippers?" I cried. "In your *wedding*?"

"I was a nervous wreck," she said. "I forgot to take them off when I got dressed."

"Bedroom slippers," I said, shaking my head and thinking of Mrs. Futrell's story. "That's practically indecent exposure." I couldn't believe I said that.

Mama laughed. "It was a *mistake*. I was only seventeen and love had fried my brain."

I crawled into bed long before Joe Parker went home. It was a comfort to hear his voice sort of rumbling around the trailer and to smell his cigarette smoke and to know that when there was a long drowsy silence, it was a silence filled with two people loving each other.

I lay very still and tried to remember Speedy's voice, but I couldn't. I love you anyway, Speedy, I said to the ceiling. There was a lacy gray moth on the ceiling going around and around whenever I said "Speedy." I said it over and over and watched the moth dance. I knew I'd forgotten everything about Speedy except that I'd loved him once.

I lay there almost ready for a dream. I couldn't help thinking that if you asked Mrs. Futrell what she'd worn on her wedding day, she would have rambled on and on, smitten with every seed pearl on her bodice. She would have remembered the exact yardage of her veil. She would have described her cream-colored shoes with sassy bows. She would have told you that her bouquet was an arrangement of yellow roses, gardenias, and baby's breath.

But I'll bet if you asked Betty, she would have had to get out her wedding pictures to prove to herself as well as you that she'd even been there.

When I finally closed my eyes, I saw my young baby mama. Her name was Betty and she was striding up the aisle with a wildly handsome boy named Speedy Thompson. I saw her face clearly: bright and sweet as a magnolia bloom. I saw that the difference between Betty then and me, Pally, now, was that Betty had truly been ready. She was so ready that she'd worn bedroom shoes to her wedding. She didn't wear them to be a smart aleck, and she didn't wear them because she was tacky. She wore them because it just didn't matter what she wore.

When I thought about my home economics project, I was sorry I'd bitten off my nails on purpose. I was sorry I'd permed my hair, then cried about it. And as I gazed across the room at the namby-pamby pastel lilac dress I'd hung on the door to wear to school tomorrow, I was sorry about that, too. I wished I hadn't *concentrated* on my ruination. I wished I'd not even thought about it. I wished it had just happened, naturally, like a kind of unblushing nakedness, incurably my own.

III

☆♡☆ ☆♡☆ ☆♡☆

I didn't tell anybody about taking off all my clothes at Sawyer's Creek that night with Bynum. I didn't even tell Shilda Hawk, my best girl friend, though Lord knows she would have offered me hope. Wild notions were always seizing her and lighting her fuse. Once, on a dare, she'd gone to church with nothing on under her raincoat. She'd worn high heels and a hat and nobody had suspected a thing.

I'm not sure why I didn't tell Shilda. It wasn't because I felt ashamed or anything so natural. Maybe I just felt failed. I kept asking myself: what if it had been Bobby Rex Moseley on the seat beside you? How would you have acted then? But I knew the answer and it made no sense. I would have sat primly on the edge of the car seat and picked imaginary lint off my skirt. I would have kept my knees locked tight.

At school it seemed that I saw him everywhere. Sometimes he was with Phoebe, and that about broke my heart. He wore blue jeans all the time and blue work shirts or shirts of soft plaid flannel. His eyes were so blue and his hair so dark that he looked painted onto the world.

I tried to lose myself in something frivolous. I tried out for cheerleader and was the first in my group to get cut. Mopsy Brownlee took me aside after my name had been announced along with the other losers. She'd braided her honey-blond hair for the tryouts and had laced the braids with slim pink ribbons. She wore a gingery cologne that made her smell like a sweet bun. "It was your cartwheels that messed you up," she told me confidentially. "Your legs looked too . . ."

"Gangly?" I offered. "You don't have to tell me, Mopsy. I know what they're like. I've lived with them for sixteen years."

"You're just tall, Pally," she said in a conciliatory way. "You'd make a fantabulous model. I especially like your new permanent."

I guess I went out for cheerleading because everybody else did—everybody but Shilda, who was cynical about peppiness. Shilda watched the tryouts from the stadium bleachers. She sat with the LaMarr twins—Orst and Hogarth—and they smoked cigarettes and told dirty jokes and laughed at all our bodily defects like my skinny legs and Mozelle Barkley's midriff bulge and Fayette Weems's bloody nose. Fayette got a bloody nose every time she stood on her head, but she went out for cheerleading every fall anyway.

After I got cut, I climbed the bleachers and joined them. The LaMarr brothers were huge, good-looking, muscular boys with dirty-blond hair. You never saw them wearing anything but white T-shirts with the sleeves rolled and tight, tight jeans. Even in the winter they didn't wear coats or hats. Around their necks swung heavy metal crosses on chains, but the LaMarrs were not religious. They were identical twins, and the only way you could tell them apart was that Orst smoked Camels and Hogarth smoked Lucky Strikes. Whenever they laughed, they smacked their thighs and went, "Haw! Haw!" They drove a famous gray Chevrolet everybody called the Sardine. They'd blowtorched the top off so that the Sardine was a permanent convertible. But the scariest thing about them was that their daddy was a convict at Central Prison down in Raleigh.

They were wild, tough boys and I'd always backed off from them. But Shilda didn't back off from anybody, especially boys. Although they were still seniors at Orfax High, the LaMarr brothers were twenty years old. Hogarth liked to say they'd failed twelfth grade for two straight years on purpose, that they couldn't bear to leave Orfax High where so many wild women were running around loose and needing service. Everybody knew that Orfax High had the wildest women in the county. Haw! Haw! Then Orst pinched Shilda's knee and Shilda pinched Hogarth's knee and Hogarth pinched mine.

I felt strange, sitting high up in the bleachers, looking down on all those girls still twirling cartwheels and doing jumps. They all wore shorts under their full skirts. Some still wore their crinolines. When you are suddenly flirting with danger but can look down from a new height and see where you were just moments before and observe what a tame and innocent thing it is to flip a cartwheel, it makes you nostalgic. You tend to forget you were sad down there; you forget you felt awkward and too tall.

I looked at Shilda, who was snuggled up between the LaMarrs. Her heart-shaped face tilted first to Hogarth, then to Orst, then back to Hogarth. She knew how to tease better than anybody. Orst and Hogarth looked enchanted. But I expected that at any second Shilda would yawn right in their faces and say that she needed to get home or something. She was always looking to divert herself.

"Anybody got a cigarette?" she asked. Orst fished out a Camel and Hogarth, a Lucky Strike. They each raced to light the cigarettes off the ones they were already smoking.

"Here," they both offered.

I laughed.

But Shilda took the Camel and the Lucky Strike side by side and poked them between her lips. She smoked seriously, her large brown eyes just full of concentration. Orst and Hogarth went to hawing and slapping their thighs like crazy. They thought she was divine.

"Come go with us," they whispered on either side of her. "Come take a ride." Their faces were full of heat.

"You got your car here?" She stared straight ahead, still concentrating on smoking two cigarettes at once. "It's late and I need a ride home." Then she tapped my knee. "You come ride with us, Pally," she said. "It's fun riding in the Sardine." Then she leaned across Hogarth and winked at me. "Hotcha!" she said. She had on these white cowgirl boots.

I couldn't believe her sometimes. "No thanks, Shilda," I said. "I'm walking."

"All the way to Piney View? It's too far to walk after a rough day of cheerleading. Come on now, live a little."

I looked at her boots. My heart felt like they were kicking me. Then I looked at the LaMarrs. They were enormous. They breathed heavy. Their foreheads seemed too short. Their shoulders were as big and square as packing crates. I didn't like the constant hairy smell of their cigarettes. They were twenty years old! They were *men*!

"You all go on," I said.

"Suit yourself," said Hogarth.

"Hey, boys," Shilda said, "don't you get it? She wants us to beg her." She stubbed out her Camel and Lucky Strike at the same time.

"What's her name? Who is she anyway?" Orst said like I wasn't even there.

"Miss Cheerleader," Hogarth said.

Orst guffawed. "Naw, I bet her name's . . . Miss . . . Miss *Cherry* Leader." They were tickled to death with that one and keeled over, hawing. "Hey, Miss Cherry Leader," Orst said, "will you lead us to the cherries?"

"Shut up," Shilda told them. "You boys are crude and rude."

The funny thing was that they shut up. Then Hogarth, who was sitting beside me, picked up my hand. I felt myself wince. His hands were huge and rough as pavement.

"Everything's fine now," Hogarth announced. "I've got her and she's going." He turned to his brother. "But if I take *her,* I get to drive the Sardine."

This will sound hypocritical, but on the way to the Sardine, I thought of Bynum Jenkins and I loved him with all my heart. If his narrow, speckled scarecrow's face had popped out from one of the cars in the parking lot, I would have burst into tears of gratitude. I would have married him. I would have settled for lint brushes every Christmas from then until Hell froze over. I longed to hear his familiar raspy honkytonk voice and to feel those pokey hipbones of his as he lay down on top of me. I craved to go riding down a back road with Bynum in his tomato-colored Studebaker with all the windows down and the radio on. Tab Hunter would be singing "Young Love" in his melting way and I'd put my head on Bynum's shoulder.

Suddenly I understood how grown people could get kidnapped. You were so overwhelmed by the shock of somebody claiming you like property that you just went. You went like there was no other choice, not even to scream. You kept thinking: they don't *really* mean it and are bound to have a change of heart. You held to this dangerous faith that, just like you, everyone is reasonable, way down deep.

I walked beside Hogarth LaMarr with one puny, sweating hand gripped in his, which felt more like an animal trap than flesh and bones. I could feel my own pulse throb, bucking against the force of his hold. I looked back at Shilda, but she was laughing coyly, Orst's arm slung around her shoulders.

We stomped down the bleachers like angry people stomping down stairs. That's the way Orst and Hogarth liked to walk everywhere. They just loved noise. Several girls looked up from their cheerleading or stopped entirely to watch us. I lowered my eyes. I told myself that it was just a ride home. Please, God.

"Where did you say you lived?" Hogarth asked. But before I could answer he turned to Shilda. "Where does Cherry live?"

"Not far," she said. "Over at Piney View Trailer Park."

"All right!" whooped Orst. "We've been to some good parties out there. There's some wild women out at Piney View."

"You a wild thing, Cherry?" Hogarth asked and laughed.

"You just got to humor her along," said Orst. "Get her in a party mood first, right, Shilda?"

The Sardine was a real heap. All the doors were rusted shut and you had to climb in through the hole in the roof. The seat covers had mostly worn off and you sat on jiggling rusty springs. The floor of the car was piled high with trash: empty cigarette packs and candy bar wrappers, skin magazines, water guns. There was even a mousetrap. I saw comic books and some spurs and wine bottles and some old moldy boots.

We zoomed right off. Hogarth peeled three wheels before we were out of the parking lot. He shot right out onto Narrow Gauge and drove fast, one hand on the steering wheel, one hand clamped tight on my own. Every second or two he'd grin at me and squeeze my hand so tight I thought I'd pass out. We roared right past the Tastee-Freeze, the Variety, the Feed and Seed,

Dicks, the Texaco. Hogarth hit all four stoplights on yellow and went right on, 50 miles an hour in a 20 zone. I wanted to shout that he was going to *kill* somebody, to slow down *please*. But just then he lifted his one hand off the steering wheel to wave at Davey Cole, the sheriff's deputy, who was standing beside his motorcycle, drinking a Coke, it looked like. Davey Cole waved back.

I knew I was going to die then. I felt that maybe I was dead already, that I'd seen the accident, heard the impact, watched as our bodies spun through the air, limp as empty sacks. I looked down at my arms and legs and imagined their skin unfurling against the concrete as I bounced and skidded hundreds of feet, skin sluffing from bones as easily as peeling from fruit.

How had I gotten there, in the front seat of that car with the blasted-off roof? I'd never even spoken to the LaMarr boys before. How had I ended up practically handcuffed to one of them when, only a few minutes before, I'd been spinning cartwheels across a breezy football field? Why was life never what you were ready for? It always seemed either too fast or too slow. When I thought about it, death seemed like that, too. I was sure, then, that if the truth were known, life and death were secretly best friends. Why did people pretend otherwise?

I watched the speedometer hit 80 before I closed my eyes and went crazy. I started praying to Speedy. I didn't feel the tears on my cheeks until Hogarth LaMarr slowed the car just enough so that I could smell the sweet, hot sun fragrance of cut hay, drying in the fields outside Orfax. I think it was the smell of hay that made me cry, the extraordinary smell of cut hay.

"Oh, Speedy," I said out loud. "Oh, Speedy, thank you."

"Anytime, Cherry," Hogarth said, pulling me close. Then he kissed me with his hard smoky mouth, and we almost went into a ditch.

We weren't anywhere near Piney View. We were bumping down the dirt road that led to Sawyer's Creek and it was five o'clock in the afternoon.

"I wish we had some Ripple wine," Shilda said. "I'm not "

"Are you hot, too?" Hogarth asked me and winked.

He parked the car in a grove of tall, vine-smothered oaks. The shade was so deep and cool that I shivered. A rich, stinking mud smell rose up from the creek and settled over the heavy grape scent of kudzu hanging above. I could hardly believe the car was stopped, its engine quiet. It was a heap. There were holes in the floorboard. I could see a mushroom growing underneath us. The windshield glittered menacingly with cracks from what looked like bullet holes. The rear window was filled in with cardboard.

I had never loved my life so much. The fact that I'd escaped being wasted by Hogarth LaMarr's recklessness overwhelmed me with gratitude. I leaned right over and kissed the dashboard. I meant to kiss it only once. But I kissed it twice, three times. I kissed the broken radio knobs, both of them. I kissed the springy seat. I kissed my own knees and then I kissed the dashboard once again.

"What the hell?" said Hogarth.

"You've got a live one," Orst said and laughed.

"Pally?" Shilda asked, "are you okay? Honey, you look white as mashed potatoes."

"Did you see what she just done?" said Hogarth.

If they had ignored me I wouldn't have gone on. But because they thought I was acting strange, I started acting that way on purpose. Next, I kissed the lopsided rearview mirror. I kissed my elbows, one at a time.

"Act right," Shilda said sharply. "Enough's enough, Pally."

I kissed the tattered armrest on my rusted-shut door. I kissed the steering wheel real fast, twenty times. Then it came to me. I'd hung around him so long that I was acting just like Bynum Jenkins would have acted in a panic.

"I think we should all go swimming," Shilda announced. "Come on, Pally, be a sport." She leaned close and whispered in my ear: "You're going to get yourself in a lot of trouble, girl."

I kissed her on the cheek, loud.

"Hell," said Hogarth. "I didn't want to bring her."

"All them cheerleaders is the same," said Orst. "I could have told you it would turn into one big joke, bringing a cheerleader along with us. Now majorettes is another story."

Hogarth started swinging his big metal cross in front of my eyes. "Is she going to put out, or is she going to get out?"

"Well, boys, it's hot," Shilda said, "and I'm not wasting any more time sitting here." She uprooted herself from Orst's lap and climbed through the roof of the Sardine. "Let's go." There was a new edge in her voice, a shrill strictness. Her voice seemed to rap against the stillness of the woods as if that stillness were something solid.

"Swimming?" Orst sounded disappointed.

"I'm sorry I don't have my suit with me," Shilda said then. "But you won't look, will you, boys?"

"Goddamn! I heard of you, woman!" Orst shouted.

"It's all true," Shilda said. "Come on then. Both of you."

They scrambled out after her as if the car were on fire. When at last they'd all gone, I slumped against the car door, listening to the racket of my heart, listening to the rip and crackle of underbrush as they trooped down to the creek. Jaybirds were shrieking, but throughout the woods swooped Shilda's laugh, cool and overwhelming. She made wildness seem easy and joyful. She made it seem like casual choice.

But I wasn't sorry I'd gone on like I had. I'd only followed my instincts, just as Shilda followed hers. Overhead, through the lattice of oak limbs I saw an early moon, its profile almost ladylike, dainty. A chin-up moon. I climbed out of the Sardine and started following a path I know that leads to State Road. By the time I reached Narrow Gauge, little bats were circling in the lavender haze above the hayfields and the owls had commenced their shivery, spook show music. I ran on down the side of the highway, and that time I was just as glad as Bynum that those white painted dashes weren't miles. Bynum. Good old Bynum, I thought.

It was close to seven when I got home. There was a note on the kitchen table that said Mama had gone bowling with Joe and to call Bynum. P.S.: "Supper's in the oven." It was a pork chop, navy beans, and a golden square of buttered corn bread. There was pecan pie for dessert, and I was eating the last bite when my phone rang.

I suspected it was Bynum and hurried to answer. When I picked up the receiver and said hello, there was this long, breathless silence and then, although she tried to disguise her voice, Phoebe Jenkins said, "Slut," and hung up.

☆ ♡ ☆

Of course the truth was that I'd acted so pure that Shilda wouldn't speak to me for a whole week after I'd left her with the LaMarrs. But there had been about two hundred eyewitnesses trying out for cheerleader that day who'd seen me stomp down the bleachers holding hands with Hogarth, so I had a bad time coming. Phoebe, and I can't blame her, was spreading all sorts of rumors to protect her brother. Once I saw Fayette Weems shoot me the finger from a school bus, but I pretended not to see. And maybe she was the one who put that loony bin,

Howdy Oxendine, up to phoning me for dates. And then *somebody* passed me a note in French class that said: *Mangez-moi, s'il vous plaît.* They didn't even know enough to use the informal.

Only Bynum heard me out. But he didn't believe me, I could read it in his eyes. He didn't come right out and accuse me of anything, but I knew that his mind still dwelled on that night I'd taken off all my clothes and laid his hand on me. I didn't blame him for thinking that night at Sawyer's Creek was the beginning of my downfall. Even I didn't understand why I'd taken such liberty with our innocence.

We didn't break up, but there was this cool suspicion that hovered over him like an awning. I tried to tease him out of his gloominess; I started calling him Mr. Paul Bearer. But he didn't get it, and it loses something with explanation. We stopped going to the Rhapsody. We never went to Woody's Danceland. And I knew we'd hit rock bottom when he started taking me to the Tastee-Freeze. Mostly we drove all the way over to Greensboro and saw up-to-date movies, movies that usually starred Doris Day or Pat Boone, where the characters cared more for singing than kissing.

All the movies Bynum took me to during this particular time seemed to be about sex and love, but in a real dissatisfying way. Every time somebody in one of these musicals would make a pass at somebody else, the other person would dodge the pass and burst into song or do a little dance.

We didn't stop dating, but I could tell that Bynum was starting to look elsewhere. He'd begun taking stock of his situation, and for the first time he saw his advantage. He was a senior, after all. He commanded respect from a whole gaggle of goosey little freshmen girls. He was tall enough for any of them, he had a proud banner of bangs that people still talked about, and he had a snappy little car. Best of all he had a sister who was willing to fix him up with anybody he chose, a sister who, because she'd started dating Bobby Rex Moseley, was more popular than pizza pie.

Of course the commotion about Hogarth LaMarr and me died down in a couple of weeks. People got tired of feasting on old news and eventually more startling things happened to distract them. For example, one night Willard MacIntosh got so drunk out at Woody's that he started spitting watermelon seeds on everybody. And then there was the news that Mopsy Brownlee got a preengagement ring from some boy in her brother's fraternity down at Chapel Hill. Chester Rice wore earrings to his army interview but got drafted anyway. Some crazy person vandalized school property by breaking into the gym and snipping all the crotches out of all the girls' gym shorts. For a while they suspected Howdy Oxendine, but he was helping his mother hold a séance, and she could prove it. Then Cookie Beasley, a senior majorette, started passing a rumor that she was going to kill herself after the last football game in November if we lost. We lost, but Cookie Beasley was laid up in the hospital that very night, having her appendix out. Everybody said she'd planned the whole chickenhearted thing. But I'd like to know how.

IV

☆♡☆   ☆♡☆   ☆♡☆

Take Highway 21 from Greensboro and ride about fifteen miles—until all the good rock stations fade out. Pretty soon the road narrows and gets twisty and potholed, and you'll start passing a bunch of signs shaped like feet. THREE MILES TO WOODY'S ... TWO MILES TO WOODY'S ... TRY OUR CIDER. No way you'll miss Woody's Danceland. It's a plain, squat box of a building, whitepainted cinder blocks, just baking away like a biscuit in an empty field. Inside, there's nothing but an ancient jukebox and sawdust floors and a bandstand and long pine benches that ooze sap in hot weather. The signs are shaped like feet because everybody dances barefooted at Woody's in the summer. Then, from the time you pass Woody's Danceland, you've got time to smoke one cigarette before you hit the township limits of Orfax.

Orfax, North Carolina. Bird Sanctuary. Population 3,127, only I think they must have counted in the cows, too. It's not a bad town, really. Just plain. The smell of meat loaf is always in the air. Lots of black Fords and Chevrolets, four-door, practical. Black rubber buckle-on galoshes and white metal lawn chairs, rusty push mowers, crabgrass, crumbly tobacco barns, clotheslines loaded down with overalls and chenille bedspreads, birdbaths with metallic balls, white-washed tractor tires with petunias planted in the holes.

By the time I was sixteen I looked around at people who'd made their lifelong homes in Orfax, and I was at a loss as to how they'd stuck it out. How, for example, had they settled, day after day, for the dusty, has-been shopping at Rice's Variety Store? The candy was stale, the magazines and newspapers, yellow. Even the parakeets Wilbur Rice sold were rumored to be ten, fifteen, twenty years old. They all had rheumatism so bad that they could barely hold on to their perches. There was one parakeet named Wild Bill who was so old he'd grown a fluffy little beard under his chin. All he could do was sit on the floor of his cage, and twice a day Mr. Rice hand-spooned him baby food.

Across the street from Rice's was the one decent restaurant in town: Dicks Hot Dogs. The best thing about Dicks was the sign that Dick had painted on the plate-glass window of the shop. It featured a huge, red, naughty-looking hot dog with chirpy blue eyes and a toothy grin. Underneath the hot dog was the slogan: "If you love hot dogs, you'll love Dicks." Somebody had scraped off the apostrophe years ago. Probably the LaMarr twins.

If you wanted something to do in Orfax, you'd need to drive over to Greensboro, twenty miles or so, and go see a movie at the Carolina Theatre. They had a big roller rink over in Greensboro, too, you could case out. Or maybe you'd just get out and *drive,* get some highway air in your lungs, the smell of gasoline rather than manure for a change. If you wanted to dance, there was Woody's. Farther up the road, toward Kernersville, there was Gizmo's Bar. You could brown-bag hard liquor at Gizmo's, but you had to look out for knife fights. Especially if this motorcycle gang called the Asphalt Prophets showed up. Especially if their girl friends were along.

Sometimes there was nothing better to do than drive down to Sawyer's Creek and neck and smell the kudzu. Or maybe park by the old train depot and wait for the Southern Crescent to roll past. Mostly you just waited for something to happen. And usually it happened to somebody else.

There was something about living in Orfax that made you feel you ought to bunch your shoulders. Everybody seemed to have bunched shoulders and narrow faces. It's as if people walked around trying to disappear and got caught somehow halfway.

You *wanted* to disappear in Orfax, you wanted to blend in. Otherwise you were notorious. There was no middle ground. Take Shilda, for example. When she cut loose and started going regularly with the LaMarr twins, she was more visible than the town could stand. Poor *breeding*, they called her upbringing; it was the stock she'd come from, making her run hog wild. That's country people for you: always sounding the farm alarm.

☆ ♡ ☆

When Gloria Hawk, Shilda's mother, left Eddie, she left Shilda behind, too. Shilda was only three years old. Gloria didn't even pack a suitcase. The only thing she took with her was Shilda's first pair of baby shoes, which she'd had bronzed. The only note she left was addressed to Shilda. For some reason Eddie secreted it away in an old Tuberose can, and Shilda didn't find it until she was twelve years old and wanted to try dipping snuff one day. She'd memorized the note before folding it away, and sometimes, as she got older, she'd recite the whole letter just before she performed some wild or devilish act.

Dear Shilly, her mother wrote. *I feel like this house is on fire. The flames are all around me and I must jump to save myself. I would save you, too, if you needed it, if*

I could. Never, never forgive me. It would take too much away. My love forever, Gloria D. Hawk, 1945.

The letter was printed in pencil and the *i*'s were dotted with tiny valentines.

I was always curious about the part that asked Shilda not to forgive her because "it would take too much away." I got a lump in my throat whenever Shilda recited that part. That one sentence had the power to make me see poor Eddie Hawk waking up the very morning Gloria slipped away. I imagined the whole scene, even down to the pajamas Eddie would have worn, flannel ones with some earnest little print like bluebirds. The Cardinals baseball cap he wore all the time rested atop one bedpost. Some corny little needlepoint slogan like HOME SWEET HOME hung framed above the bed. Of course I imagined that it hung a little bit crooked. Early morning sunlight crept through the window blinds, a warm, homey, caramel-colored light that could fool you into thinking somebody was in the kitchen taking care of things, fixing pancakes and oatmeal, grinding coffee, maybe wearing a ruffled white apron tied with a sash. Could even fool you into thinking you heard the radio in the kitchen—"Chattanooga Choo-Choo" or something just as jivey. So when Eddie finally stumbled out of bed and found his bedroom shoes, his robe, the baseball cap, he'd have headed straight to the kitchen, and there she'd be, Gloria, his pretty young wife, dancing as she cooked and wearing the slippery satin mules he'd given her for her birthday and the see-through negligee with pink maribou trim. I always pictured Gloria in something see-through; I just couldn't help myself. And I played this crazy game in my mind: that if Eddie could have just gotten out of bed fast enough and hurried before the morning light changed, before it became harsher, more definite, a different mood altogether, *cooler*, maybe Gloria would still be there and not just a ghostly hope in his poor heart. If he'd just gotten up on the opposite side of the bed, maybe, just done *anything* different, maybe he wouldn't have found the kitchen empty when he got there, the faucet dripping bleakly, the supper dishes still in the sink looking downright rusty with last night's food.

I was always rooting for Eddie when I imagined this scene of desertion. But I was rooting for Gloria, too. I kept searching my mind for those proven things you can do that will keep the one you love by your side forever. Are there really such things? There are all those magazine articles that try to tell you what to do. Some nights you are supposed to serve the one you love pot roast wearing nothing yourself but a leopard skin loincloth. You are supposed to flaunt and offer yourself in weirdo places, then go through with it: the apartment stairwell, a gas station bathroom, on top of your washing machine during the spin cycle.

But even if Eddie and Gloria hadn't been particularly adventurous, I couldn't think what had caused Gloria to feel so stripped of love, so unbearably restless that she'd not only leave Eddie but abandon a baby daughter, too.

I kept thinking: back up, Eddie. Send her roses *yesterday*. Didn't he know any tricks? It wasn't *that* tough to keep somebody with you—even somebody who didn't love you all that much. Look at Bynum Jenkins and me, Eddie!

But who knows what got on Gloria's nerves? Maybe it was Eddie's baseball cap.

I felt certain that Gloria had run off ashamed of herself, so sick and sorry with guilt that she never wanted forgiveness from the one person she truly loved: Shilda. When she wrote that Shilda shouldn't forgive her because that would "take too much away," wasn't she finally thinking about Eddie, too? Wasn't she asking Shilda to love and be loyal to Eddie in her place? She must have thought of Shilda as a precious good-bye gift to Eddie. Her note was so full of remorse that there

must have been hope for them all. That's what bothered
me most about the whole situation: that there had been a
lot of hope, but nobody had known how to handle it.

Rolled up with Gloria's note in the Tuberose can was
also a picture of her in her majorette's uniform when she
was a junior. She wore skimpy sequined short-shorts
and a halter top and high-heeled boots with tassels. She
was twirling a fire baton and kicking one leg as high as
her head. She had short, dark, feathery hair, naturally
wavy like Shilda's, and a dimple in her chin. Her eyes
were so big and dark they looked sooty. Her broad grin
showed off the small gap between her front teeth which
everybody says is the sign of a wild child. On the back
of the photo, written in pencil, was *GLORIA D. HAWK,
Majorette for the Orfax High Twirlettes, Class of 1942*.

Shilda carried the picture in her wallet, and when she
showed it to strangers, she always said that Gloria D.
was the older sister she'd never known who'd died on
her honeymoon in a tragic auto wreck. Once I'd asked
her what the ''D'' in her mother's name stood for.
She'd hardly thought about it at all before she said,
''Devil woman,'' and laughed.

Counting back the years, I figured Gloria was pregnant with Shilda when that photograph was taken. There
she was, seventeen years old, almost a high school senior but without the barest hope of floating free from
Orfax.

Marna told me the whole story one afternoon while
we sat in the kitchen snapping green beans, real slow.
''Gloria Dillard was as smart as a whip,'' Mama said.
''She studied all the time.''

''A majorette?'' I hooted. ''Smart?''

''She only went out for majorettes because she liked
to dance,'' Mama said, giving me a scolding glance.
''She had wonderful rhythm. Nobody had rhythm like
Gloria. She could have joined the Rockettes in a heartbeat.''

"But she was wild, wasn't she?"

Mama regarded me a moment, trying to size up what I was after. "No, honey," she said finally. "Gloria was just young. She was still closing her eyes when she blew out her birthday candles."

"What's that supposed to mean?"

"You can get burned that way," Mama said significantly. "Being so young and blind."

"But when she ran out on Eddie and Shilda, she wasn't so young then. I mean, she *knew* what she was doing."

"She was barely twenty-one," Mama said. "Why so many questions, Nancy Drew?"

"Just asking," I said. "It's the mystery side of Shilda. She never talks about it. I don't think she knows as much as I do from talking with you, Mama."

"It was awful hard on Eddie," Mama said. "It liked to have killed him. He went away for a while."

"So go on."

"It's a long story."

"So talk about how smart she was."

Mama smiled. "She was smart, all right, but she wasn't very wise. She knew all her multiplication tables and square roots," Mama said. "She knew her Latin and I don't mean pig. I can even remember what she read for extra credit in English class: James Fenimore Cooper—yuck! But she didn't know beans about men.

"Her parents were real strict and she wasn't allowed to date. She had to sneak to be a majorette. When her daddy found out, he locked her out of the house and wouldn't take her back until the youth minister over at Holy Methodist could give her a counseling session. The minister's name was Rudolph Von Wicke. He was just out of seminary school, a young, wiry, good-looking boy with hair that lay flat and bright on his head like a red maple leaf. The startling red hair made him seem more approachable than he knew, almost clownish. There was something about him, as I recall, that just seemed *too* eligible. He was a bachelor, young and attractive, but ministers back in those days were supposedly forbidden fruit to all the young ladies of Orfax. Still, you couldn't help thinking how young and good-looking he was when he took your hand and shook it after church. It made you blush. And when a girl blushed talking with Rudolph Von Wicke, he blushed right back."

"Was he the one?" I asked. "The one who carried her off?"

"Rudolph Von Wicke," Mama said fondly, her eyes sparkling with memory.

"The war in Europe was blasting away," she continued. "Nobody knew what was coming for America. Gloria's daddy had a heart attack the summer of forty-one, before her senior year, and died. That was the same summer she marched in a parade over at War Memorial Stadium in Greensboro and met Eddie Hawk. I don't know a whole lot about their romance," she added. "I was too tied up with Speedy to look around and judge others. Speedy and I were still on our honeymoon then and so drunk with love that half the time we didn't eat right. I'd taken my first job with the phone company as an operator. What a laugh! Why, it was all I could do to remember my own phone number back then. I was a mess." She sighed and tapped out a Chesterfield.

"Eddie was a baseball player, but his daddy had owned a hatchery near Kernersville and he'd grown up here. He'd played on a few farm teams around the state, and people talked like if he stuck with it long enough, he'd make the majors. Anyway, the summer of 1941, Eddie pitched a special Army versus Navy game over in Greensboro. He was Navy. All I remember for sure is that he pitched a no-hitter and was treated like a hero that afternoon. The Navy fans carried him around the ball field on their shoulders and he got tossed and kissed by all the cheerleaders plus this majorette from Orfax High named Gloria Dillard.'' Mama crushed out her cigarette. ''I'm fairly sure it was one of those love-at-first-sight to-do's,'' she said. ''Eddie always bragged that after their first date, Gloria was so snowed she went right home and announced to her mother and to Bess, her old maid aunt who'd moved in after Gloria's father passed away, that she'd met the man she was bound to marry. They got married the first of November, before she started to show.''

''Show?'' I asked.

''Well *really*, Pally, you do know that much!''

I blushed, I think.

''Then, Eddie got orders to go to Hawaii and the Japs bombed Pearl Harbor in December, and for weeks Gloria didn't know whether he was alive or dead. Remember, too, that living with her miserable old black widow of a mother and her aunt was in itself no picnic, and on top of everything, she was expecting a baby. Along comes the news that her Eddie is missing in action. Well, I would have gone and lay down on the railroad tracks, belly up.

''I remember running into her at the Variety. She was always shopping for her mother and Bess, buying sad old lady stuff like laxatives and bunion pads and those spiderwebby hair nets that her mother liked to wear and tooth powder for false teeth and gentian violet for their gum boils. She looked so frail and worn out and lonely that I said to her, 'Hey, Gloria, it's awful good to see you. Let's have a Coke and a cigarette?' Her skin actually seemed to lighten when I spoke, she looked so pleased. She'd had to drop out of school, and it was obvious that she missed the company, the youth of it, the silly chitchat and all. She had this hollowed-out look that people get when they're deprived of silly, ordinary pleasures for a real long time. So we sat right down at the counter in Rice's and ordered two Coke floats. Now!'' Mama said suddenly, ''if that isn't the damnedest thing—

that I can remember it was Coke floats we ordered. How about that? I swear, at that particular time in our lives you could almost get high on Coke floats!" She carried a colander of beans to the sink and washed them. "I expect that's enough beans for now, Pally," she said matter-of-factly. "I don't have room to freeze them."

"Joe Parker could eat this many beans all by himself in two bites," I told her, and she nodded, her eyes twinkling at the mention of his name.

"We'll do a couple more pounds."

She resettled herself with an empty bowl in her lap and placed another bag of beans beside her chair. "All we talked about was dumb stuff," she said. "The sort of dumb stuff you're always craving to hear when you're seventeen—no offense, hon. Oh, I probably asked her *something* about Eddie—they hadn't found him yet—and I expect her eyes teared for a second, but that was all. What could she do about any of it, really? She was in a terrible jam. Lord, the whole world was. After Pearl Harbor got bombed, folks stumbled around in a daze. Nobody could believe it. But instead of sad, you felt this blistering anger, this *indignation*. Probably the only choice Gloria had was to keep her chin up. Maybe in her heart she was treating Pearl Harbor like the sorrow that takes place in some popular song. You know it's real; you know it can happen; but you don't have to let it touch you if you don't give in. She had to think positive or she knew she'd end up spending her days in a rocker across from her old widowed mother, rocking miserably in the dark and watching dust grow under the furniture.

"People talked about her like crazy. It galled them to see her out with a friend, say, drinking a Coke float. It seemed downright unpatriotic. People expected her to sit night and day by the telephone and keep her grief private. They expected her to give up fun altogether, as if fun for somebody in her boat was a vice. They forgot

how truly young she was, and that she'd given up everything to become Eddie's wife and a mother to his baby.
That girl was so starved for the company of people her
own age that she'd taken on a stooped and bony look.
By December she was over four months pregnant, but
her stomach looked as flat as mine. Omega Oxendine
passed the word along that in some cases it was possible
to *wish* a pregnancy away. Folks paid great attention to
Omega Oxendine in those days, Pally. Since her childhood she'd been predicting things: the Lindbergh baby's
death, Will Rogers', Jean Harlow's. She'd also predicted
the war. After high school, she went off to California,
became a nurse, and married a Cherokee Indian named
Sky who was a Hollywood stunt man. That detail alone
was enough to give her clout around Orfax, let me tell
you. People treated her like a celebrity there for a while.''

"What happened to Sky?"

"He got killed doing some stunt. Anyway," she continued, "on the afternoon of the Coke floats, Gloria and
I ended up talking mostly about Bea Satterfield's new
boyfriend. We decided he was too short for Bea and too
much of a bumpkin."

"Who was he? Whatever happened to him?"

Mama laughed. "His name was Tommy Lee Brownlee
and she married him and they had Mopsy."

I laughed too. "So you all just gossiped?"

"We just gossiped. It was wonderful. Gloria needed it
like a dose of vitamins. Gossip brought the roses back
into her cheeks. We discussed Bo Moseley's young wife,
Willa, and decided she was too plain for him but we
liked her. We talked about who I'd seen necking down
at Sawyer's Creek lately. Who'd broken up with who,
who was planning to elope. And it seems to me that she
wanted to hear whatever I knew about the Twirlettes—
the majorette team. We talked on and on. In spite of the
war, things still happened. She asked me lots about
Speedy, if being married to him was as fun as it looked.

She thought Speedy looked like nonstop fun, so rambunctious and full of jokes.''

"Was Speedy wild, Mama?"

Her face pinkened. "Oh, I expect I brought it out in him," she said. "I egged him on. I double-dee-dared him all the time."

We laughed together. The beans were all done.

"Why did you and Speedy stay in Orfax?" I asked. "Didn't you ever want to leave?"

"I suppose I did from time to time, the way you yearn for a vacation. But it was always just a passing thought, nothing very permanent. Nothing that messed up your *heart*," she said. "Even after we got married, Speedy and I went down to Sawyer's Creek and the train depot. The train depot was our favorite. We'd park Speedy's motorcycle and lie on a big patchwork quilt in a grove of weeping willow trees, and we'd neck like crazy. It's the summers with Speedy that I remember best—the drenching smell of honeysuckle, the sputter of crickets in the tall grass, that lacy feel of a granddaddy-long-legs stalking across your foot or your arm as you lay there. The stars back then seemed as big and bright as whole moons. You could see the countryside all around you for miles, gleaming in the moonlight as if waxed. On both sides of the railroad tracks there were blankets filled with lovers. It wasn't a private spot, you see, but it was nice. The company was nice. We didn't mind the other people, and somehow we could still forget ourselves, which is why we went there, I suppose. We could forget ourselves because we felt so comfortable. Everything that surrounded us was safe and familiar. We knew that the scream from the woods was just the old barred owl hunting down his dinner. We knew that when some other girl lying on a nearby blanket squealed and jumped up suddenly and said, 'Why, I could just *kill* you for saying that to me!' that she only meant play, that her voice was too soft and cozy for the boy she was with to have intended anything but flattery. Most times we could even tell *whose* voice it was. And by listening carefully we understood whether they were still happy or whether they were about to lose each other. There was real comfort in knowing that sort of thing—especially being newly married and newly alone even if we were together all the time. You find out when you get married or have a baby that there are all sorts of alonenesses you'd never reckoned on.

"Anyway—" She took a deep breath. "You could hear the train coming for miles: the Southern Crescent. First a low-down rumbling in the earth. The willow trees seemed to stop swishing. The crickets hushed up. The approach of that train was a serious event. The air was black and serious and still. It had a weight to it, then the faintest sort of tremble. When it began to smell sparky, we held our breaths in order to hear the train better. And always Speedy would whisper in my ear: 'Hey, girl, let's hop it.'

"Sometimes I knew he wasn't joking. And the insistence in his voice gave me gooseflesh. 'We'd have a big time.' And he'd hug me so tight I'd feel winded.

" 'Where does the train go?' I recall asking him once.

" 'Oh, D.C., Baltimore, New York City, Boston—take your pick.'

" 'What will we do when we get where we're going, Speedy?' I'd ask him, making a game.

"He'd sweep a hand through his dark hair as if the gesture stirred up better thoughts. 'Oh,' he'd say, 'we'll find us a first-class hotel and have them send us supper on a tray with lots and lots of pink champagne. Then, after we eat, if you're not too tired, we'll go dancing."

" 'But if we hop a train tonight, this very minute,' I said, 'I won't have my red high heels, the ones I like best for dancing. You know the shoes I mean.'

"Then, he'd consider everything we'd said, for a moment, and say, 'Well, then we'll just have to find us some place that's got sawdust floors like Woody's Danceland. You don't need shoes to dance in sawdust. You don't even *want* shoes. And there's bound to be a place like Woody's in a great big town like New York or Boston. A place where everybody dances barefoot.'

" 'Well,' I'd say, 'if we're going to ride the Southern Crescent all that distance just to scare up a place exactly like Woody's, why bother? Why not stay right here?'

"And Speedy, who was nearly always agreeable, would hug me half to death and say, 'Okay, we'll stay this time. But *next* time we come to the depot, be sure to wear your red high heels.'

"Then the train would roar past like a solid wall of thunder and, in a way, I'd feel we'd barely escaped going. I'd say, 'Whew!' and cling to Speedy, because there was something almost too thrilling about the Crescent plowing through all that sleepy farmland, something so full of risk that I felt lucky to have been spared.

"I'll tell you, Pally, it was so easy to know and be with Speedy right here in Orfax where we'd both grown up. We knew the background of everything. We didn't constantly have to *explain* ourselves. There comes a real freedom when the both of you know basic rules such as you don't need to wear a sweater out at night around Orfax until the middle of October. Or that the Hershey bars at Rice's Variety are deadly stale, so go use the vending machine at the Texaco and settle for a Butterfinger. Just think about heading to some place new and leaving all that information behind in a cloud of dust! You'd be starting from scratch. How in the world would you ever have the time to love each other? When I look back, it seems that the happiest and safest I ever felt in my life was when I lay in Speedy's arms beside the railroad track and went absolutely nowhere while the Southern Crescent clattered by. I felt lucky that I didn't need to go chasing after something as hazy and uncertain as a dream.' "

After a minute or so I asked her: "But when Speedy died, didn't you feel like leaving then? The memories must have nearly killed you, Mama."

She smiled a thin, wistful smile and wiped her hands on a dish towel. "Once you've felt as lucky as I felt with Speedy the first time around, you're spoiled rotten. You've had it all and lost it all, and what new place could show you more than that? And in a way, Speedy never really left me. I had you, Pally, and now I have Joe Parker. I'm talking about l-o-v-e, honey, and that's the only reason to stay any place on earth."

"Then why did Gloria Hawk leave Orfax?" I asked. "She had love, too. She had Eddie Hawk, a good man, and she had Shilda. What happened?"

Mama said, "You want something to drink? My throat's all dried out." She stirred up a quick pitcher of Kool-Aid and poured two full glasses over ice.

"I couldn't tell you what happened exactly. Nobody knows the true ins and outs of another person's love life. There's always more than one story. But a big problem was Eddie's taking so long to come back from the war. Maybe she got so lonesome with a baby that she was about to die for a man, any man—it can happen, don't smirk. You haven't been lonesome until you've been lonesome with a baby around you day and night but no husband. You'd think it would be just the opposite, wouldn't you? You'd think a baby would make loneliness easy. But the baby just reminds you of all the adult life you're cut off from. Loving a tiny baby can drain up all the joy and cheer you've got. If nobody's around who can help put some back for you, your heart can start shriveling. You usually count on the man in your life to stoke up your cheer. Well, Gloria was out of luck. Remember, Pally, she had *three* people sucking at her: the baby, her mother, and Bess. If it had been just her and the baby living together someplace else, she might have managed the lonesomeness. But there she was: walled up in that dreary house night and day with people to do for.

"I went by to see her after she had the baby. I'd just found out I was pregnant myself and I felt like a kindred spirit. That was in April, one of those cold, dingy Aprils that always happen when you count on an early spring. Even the weather seemed at war with us in those days. Late frost had nipped all the forsythia buds and stunted the dogwood blossoms. We didn't get a single peach off our trees that summer.

"I remember taking two presents along: a little bonnet for the baby and a canister of bath oil beads for Gloria. She acted real pleased about the bonnet, but when she unwrapped the bath oil beads, she burst into tears. She covered up her eyes with her hands and sobbed and sobbed. I remember how sorry her hands looked, too. Like old lady claws they were so overworked, skin so raw it seemed grated. 'It's just that . . .' she said, but couldn't finish. 'Never mind,' I told her, 'you're worn out, that's all.' Then, still sobbing, she managed to say, 'Oh, *thank you*,' her tone laden with such relief that it just about broke my heart. She seemed delivered from something terrible just because I'd noticed the strain she was under.

"It wasn't hard to notice. Her situation was purely awful. The bath oil beads were practically an insult. Why, she barely had time to comb her hair, much less pamper herself with a leisurely bathtub soak. You don't know these things get so difficult to manage until after you've had a baby.

"But the worst part for her, I think, was having to share her bedroom with the baby and Aunt Bess. It didn't look like a baby's room at all. For a long time, until after Eddie was found and had sent money to buy a proper crib, the baby slept in a big cardboard box that Gloria toted home from the Cash and Carry. It said Rinso-Blue on the outside. The room itself was painted the drab color of shirt cardboard. It was supposed to be 'battleship gray.' Her father, a Coast Guard veteran, had painted it himself the summer he had his heart attack. There were plain paper shades at the windows. The only light in the room came from one of those metal gooseneck lamps that always makes me think, to this day, of depressing things like having too much homework and not enough time to complete it, so that you are bound to fail the test. The whole room had that look: like Gloria was bound to fail her test whatever it was. Aunt Bess, a retired science teacher, had moved in with every memento of her past life in tow. She'd stored most of her lab equipment in the attic, but a few of her more personal treasures she displayed on the vanity in Gloria's bedroom: hideous little jars with delicate specimens floating in formaldehyde. Eventually she put the calf's brain in the attic, but not the jars that held her kidney stones and tonsils and adenoids.'' Mama shuddered.

"Why didn't Gloria move out?" I was practically shouting. "*Anyplace* would have been better."

"No money," Mama said. "The little bit Eddie sent her every month went for doctor bills and food and heat and the staples of life—her mother's and Bess's as well as her own. Gloria's daddy had left a mountain of debts, and Gloria possessed one of these overwrought consciences that people sometimes get stricken by when they lose a particularly unlovable parent. I'm not sure why, but they keep thinking that if they can only *do* enough, they'll come to love the dead person the way they might have when the dead person was alive. But, Pally, there's no simple answer to anything where love's concerned. Never mind that if Mr. Dillard had lived to see Gloria pregnant and married before high school graduation, he'd have disowned her flat out. He would have booted her right out of the house and thrown her boot tassels after her."

"Poor Gloria."

"Yes, that's exactly how it was."

"So when did Eddie come home?"

"I'll tell you when," Mama said. "Too late." She lit another Chesterfield and picked a shred of tobacco from her tongue. "Blame the war, blame Gloria's impatience, blame Aunt Bess. It all contributed to Gloria's general downheartedness. Maybe Rudolph Von Wicke was a lot more innocent than everybody thought at the time."

"How did it all start?" I asked. "Did anybody guess or were they able to keep it a secret?"

"*I* guessed," Mama said, and there was a proud color to her voice. "I guessed because I knew how lonesome she was. Other folks just thought of her as a busy new mother. Motherhood is a very preoccupying thing, Pally. People don't expect new mothers to have time to monkey around. And somehow it sort of goes against the grain of nature."

"Did you ever see them together?"

"Once," Mama said. "At a Holy Methodist picnic. It was the first time they'd ever really socialized. But I knew what was happening between them sure enough."

I laughed at her. "You sound like Mrs. Oxendine."

"I *knew*."

"How?"

"Okay," Mama said, settling in. She rested her elbows on the kitchen table.

"Tell *all*."

"First I want to tell you how subtle but particular the stirrings of new love can be. The slightest gesture can give you away. I'm saying, Pally, that just the way somebody opens your front door can be a sign.

"It was summer 1942 now. Lots of fellas were off at war or getting ready to go. Speedy was eighteen, but he wasn't eligible for service. He'd had an awful motorcycle wreck a few years back and broken his hip. It hadn't knitted itself together right, so the army had given him a 4-F and that was that. It about killed him. Sometimes he called me his consolation prize. But he always said it real sweet and laughing so I never did get mad. Anyway, Speedy and I weren't so caught up in the war as some folks. We had a baby on the way to think about, too.

"We'd gone to the church picnic over at Holy Methodist only because it was something to do on a fever-hot Sunday afternoon. There were lots of young people our age about, mostly girls. But there were a few young men who hadn't been shipped out yet or who'd come home on leave and were happy to go anyplace, even church, where they could show off their uniforms. Bo Moseley was there with Willa, I recall. He was as handsome as a prince back then."

"Big old burly Bo Moseley? Phoo!" I laughed.

"More handsome than Bobby Rex."

"Hah!"

"I'd bet my life on it," Mama said almost huffily. "It was a covered dish supper and people had brought picnic blankets to sit on under the oak trees. There were also card tables which the church social committee had set up and decorated. In the center of each table stood a little milk glass vase filled with fresh flowers. I remember, too, that after supper some fellow brought out his harmonica and another, his guitar, and the Reverend Von Wicke proposed that we should all dance, 'if the Spirit so moved us.' Ha ha, his little joke.

"Speedy and I ended up sitting at a card table with the Reverend and Gloria and little Shilda, who was asleep in a picnic basket. Of course Gloria and the Reverend already knew one another from the time Mr. Dillard had made Gloria seek counseling. But conversation went awful stiff. It's always made me nervous to sit beside a minister at the dinner table, Pally. After hearing the food blessed so sincerely, you feel extra-obligated to clean out your plate.

"Conversation tended to hover over the weather. Give Speedy credit for thinking up *that* topic. You should have heard him talk: Boy! were these the worst dog days we'd ever had, Speedy said, and nobody could disagree. When in the world was it ever going to rain again? And nobody could answer that one. Why, the corn was starting to pop right in the fields, and everybody chuckled. You can imagine how much trouble we were having getting up a good, solid discussion. Gloria just sat there, twisting her napkin into a little paper spike and, every second or two, checking the baby's heat rash.

"Reverend Von Wicke looked very prim and miserable in a black wool suit with vest and tie. His face was blistered with sweat, and there were great wet patches under the arms of his coat. On the tip of his long, pointed nose he wore a sweat bead like some sort of ornament. The black suit was so sincere-looking that he looked as if he were planning to bury somebody right after the picnic. I imagined he'd worn such a getup to try to maintain his image of being a serious steward of the Lord. That, of course, meant some degree of sacrifice, or folks would have run him out of town. If he'd dressed casually, it would have struck a lot of us as sacrilegious, I think. We weren't suppose to think of him as having flesh and bones. And, except when he blushed, the skin of his face and hands (which is all I ever saw) was as white and spongy-looking as those little cubes of day-old communion bread.

"The fellows with the music struck up some hoedown type number, and couples started swinging into action. Bo Moseley called for everybody to square off for the Texas Star, a real favorite, and Speedy jumped up and grabbed my hand. Then, the Reverend, all of a sudden, rose and waved his arms in the air. People hushed right up. It looked like an important announcement was at hand. I thought he was going to say a prayer and bless our dancing. He seemed so tall and thin, towering above our table like a dark steeple. His face was so red, it hurt me to look at him. It was such a bashful-looking face, slick with sweat. 'I'd like to put in a request,' was what he said. Then he looked down at his hard black shoes. 'Can you fellas play . . . a waltz?' It was what those boys had probably been waiting for, some sort of holy permission, and they shouted, 'Ho, yes!' and struck up "I'll be Seeing You" in less than a drumbeat. The sweetest music you ever heard poured like syrup all over that churchy twilight. It was settling down kind of music; why, it even seemed to make things cooler. All around us lightning bugs bloomed in the pink air like moony little flowers. You could smell the scorch of the sunburned fields as evening wetted them down with an early dew. Couples paired off and sank into one another. Some of the girls sang along with the music, their eyes closed. All around us, like some new kind of weather, unexpected and magical, we felt the dreamy, slowdown reprieve of that sweetheart music. You could hear nothing but the music and the swish-swishing of skirts and the rasp of crickets in the weedy grass. I'll never forget it. And there was something about the music, Pally, that made everything seem forgiven. Whether it had happened or was just in the making, if it had one thing to do with love, forbidden or not, the music made it feel forgiven.

   "Anyway, Speedy said, 'Hey, let's dance, good-lookin',' close up in my ear. It still thrilled me to pieces to have Speedy whisper stuff in my ear. So there we went, dancing under the oak trees, glued to each other, when it hit me that we'd gone off and left poor Gloria all alone at the table with Mr. Stiff. I knew good and well, too, that there was nothing like waltz music to make you pine for your man. I was just about to say something to Speedy about how he ought to go over and ask Gloria to dance, just out of friendship and comfort, when I saw her locked into a gaze with the Reverend. She was twisting that little worn-out napkin and her feet seemed to be jumping around under the table like trout out of water. Only her gaze was steady. At first I thought she was simply tapping her feet to the beat of the waltz.

Then, the closer I looked, I decided it was her nerves. Reverend Von Wicke was asking her something and she was answering and all the while her feet were shuffling around under the table. Then I saw what she was really doing: hunting for her shoes which she'd slipped off after supper. Reverend Von Wicke had asked her to dance. But the whole time her feet were searching out those shoes, she never took her eyes off the Reverend and what he was saying. Finally she got up from the table and he took her in his arms for the tail end of the waltz. Nobody took much notice of them but me. I expect some folks thought he was merely doing his ministerly duty, dancing with a lonely bride and mother to boot. Marriage kept her safe from him, and he was the preacher, so that was that. I was the only one there who noticed her feet, I think. She was *hobbling,* Pally.''

I gave her a blank look. ''So?''

''Gloria Dillard Hawk was a first-class dancer, a star majorette before she got married and had the baby. But there she was falling all over the Reverend as he spun her once or twice. When I saw what was causing her to act so awkward, I almost burst out laughing. What I saw, Pally, was what convinced me that Gloria had fallen in love with him.''

''Don't light a cigarette *now*,'' I pleaded. She obliged, pushing the Chesterfield back into its pack.

''Well,'' she said, ''when the music stopped and we sat back down at our table, I finally caught a close-up glimpse of her feet. And what I saw was this: she'd gotten her shoes—a pair of white straw high heel pumps—on *backwards*. I mean, of course, on the wrong feet.'' Mama paused importantly.

I laughed. ''But what does that prove?'' I asked her. ''Why would something like that give her away?''

"Think about it, Pally. Here she was so taken with Rudolph Von Wicke that maybe she didn't even *notice* that her shoes were on wrong. And if she *did* notice, well, she didn't make a move to change them."

"So?"

Mama gave an exasperated sigh. "Well, suppose she *knew* she'd gotten them on wrong. Anybody with a clear head who liked to dance would have told their partner to wait up, that they needed to change their shoes around. Big deal, right? But somebody madly in love and hankering after a bit of romance couldn't possibly break the mood of being asked to dance by their dream lover, now could they? There are some codes, you know. What was left to her if she broke the spell by saying: 'Excuse me, Reverend, but my shoes are on backwards'? How would that make a person look but comic?"

"Well, dancing with shoes on the wrong feet was a pretty big risk," I said. "She could have fallen. Or somebody could have noticed it and called it to her attention. That would have been embarrassing."

"But nobody *did* notice," Mama said. "That's how woolheaded people can be. And Rudolph was so gone on her already that he'd forgotten her reputation as a good dancer. I expect other folks thought she was out of practice, if they thought anything at all. They probably figured that motherhood left her no time to practice her dancing."

Mama and I were quiet for a long time.

"Sometimes," Mama said, "if I didn't know otherwise, I'd swear that the Devil invented love and that God didn't have one thing in the world to do with it. Maybe the joke's on us for ever thinking any different."

☆♡☆   ☆♡☆   ☆♡☆

I hadn't seen a whole lot of Shilda lately. She'd taken a
fancy to the LaMarrs on account of their robust looks
and daredeviltry. Mostly she spent her free time riding
around with them in the Sardine. She looked bad. She
had circles under her eyes and hickeys all over her neck.
It hurt me to see her changing from her old carefree
brand of wildness to a new hardhearted sort. We talked
some at school because we shared a locker, but she
always acted bored and impatient, like I was some brat
kid sister and she didn't have time to play nursemaid. I
asked her to spend the night a couple of times, but she'd
always find an excuse. No, she'd say, flicking her tattery
black hair out of her eyes, no, she was going with Orst
and Hogarth that night. Then she'd arch her sooty-
looking eyebrows at me and narrow her eyes like a cat
and say, "But you can come along, too, if you'd like,
Pally. There's plenty of room. Think Bynum would object?" Then she'd laugh in a burst—"Haw-haw!"—close
up in my face. She was always razzing me about Bynum,
as if she had something better going.

One evening Eddie Hawk came by our trailer. He
drove a truck for a mattress company and made runs

every day to Norfolk. But he was usually home to cook a late supper for Shilda and himself. He liked to cook. He liked to keep a tomato garden and put up tomatoes, then make this red-hot spaghetti sauce all winter long he called Cardinal Sauce. Anything red he called cardinal red, after the St. Louis Cardinals. He just loved the St. Louis Cardinals, and red was his favorite color.

I liked Eddie Hawk. He was short and stocky and bald under the Cardinals' baseball cap he wore all the time. When he and Gloria married, they'd had their wedding ceremony over at War Memorial Stadium in Greensboro, where they'd first met, and walked under an arch of baseball players' bats.

Eddie was the only grown man I knew who chewed bubble gum all the time and read the fortunes. He said he didn't believe them, but just try to get him to throw one away. Chewing bubble gum seemed to give him a young face. When Shilda and I were little, he'd taught us card tricks and how to make it look like you were pulling your thumbs off. He taught us how to bird whistle with our hands folded a certain way and how to talk like Donald Duck. Mama always said that when Speedy died, it was Eddie who'd been her greatest comfort.

The Eddie Hawk who came to our trailer that Monday night in December looked worn out. Mama said, "You left your truck running, Eddie." And he had, headlights on, too. But Eddie just shook his head and sat down and said, "Let her run." He slumped back against the divan and Mama poured him a cup of coffee.

"I was hoping to find Shilly here," he said. "I didn't think I would, but I hoped so."

It was late for a school night, eleven o'clock. I was already in my nightgown and had rolled my hair. You had to be constantly upgrading a permanent.

"I'm worried, Betty," Eddie said. He drank the scalding coffee down in one swallow, not even blinking.

"Want a cigarette?" Mama asked.

"Thanks, girl," he said. "Got any whiskey?"

Mama touched his shoulder, gently.

"Well," he said in a defensive way, "I don't keep it in the house no more, not with Shilly gone so wild, and I miss it."

Mama went to the cupboard and poured him half a jelly glass of bourbon. The glass had Archie and Jughead and Veronica and Betty prancing around the sides.

"I just don't know what to do," Eddie said. "It's the damnedest thing." He sipped the bourbon slowly and gritted his teeth over the taste. He swallowed hard like the bourbon burned much worse than the coffee. He turned the jelly glass around and around in his hands as if he was reading the cartoons, but he wasn't. "If only I knew something about girls," he said. "I wish to hell I knew."

"Has she run away?" Mama asked. "Did you have a fight?"

"We don't talk enough to fight," Eddie said. "She just didn't come home last night. I had to leave for Norfolk at five this morning and I saw that her bed hadn't been slept in. There wasn't a note or nothing." He took off his Cardinals' cap and put it on one knee and sort of spun it around a few times. Then he put it back on. What killed me was that he looked so ashamed, like he was the runaway.

"She's okay, Eddie," I said. "I saw her at school today, so don't worry she's been kidnapped or something."

Eddie bluffed a laugh. "That's real good to hear," he said sarcastically. "I'm real glad to get word she ain't been kidnapped."

Mama sighed and poured out another slosh of bourbon. "Some girls get to be her age and just go on a tear," she said. "It's not your fault. It's nobody's fault. It just happens."

"I don't believe it," Eddie said. "If things were regular. If Gloria had stayed. If we were a *family*."

"If, if, if," Mama said. "You're talking like a fairy tale."

"I think she's staying over at the LaMarrs'," Eddie said. "It's posted land, though. I'd have to get the sheriff to take me in there, and what a humiliation. They don't got a phone and those people won't mind using buckshot, I know that. The daddy's down at Central Prison and the mama's done time herself. There's nothing right with any of them, you know that, don't you?"

"It's awful," Mama said. "Maybe you ought to go to the sheriff." Mama lay a hand on Eddie's arm and patted it. "She'll grow out of it, Eddie. I did," she said.

He sighed. "You never went with trash like the LaMarrs, Betty. You had the good sense to team up with Speedy."

"The luck."

"The luck, then. Nobody could fault you for luck."

"But I was wild, Eddie. I went on some tears that like to have done my folks in. Some girls are just crazier than others to be let loose."

"She's ruined her reputation," he said.

"I ruined mine," Mama said. "But look at me now. I got all this." She gestured around the living room. She was gesturing at things that weren't so obvious as the braided rug on the floor. Maybe part of what she pointed to was the lingering smell of the supper we'd eaten together a few hours ago. There'd been dessert, because she always made dessert for the two of us, not just for company. And surely the gesture included the picture on the wall of our long-ago family: herself with a summery tan in a dotted-swiss dress and Speedy, his arm around her waist, and me, no more than three, perched on his shoulder, my hair looking scribbled above my head like loops of yellow crayon. Finally I suppose that her gesture included Joe Parker, who wasn't there but had accidentally left his red windbreaker on the back of our rocking chair like a promise.

"I'm living proof that nobody gets just one chance in this old life," Mama said. And she finished the last of Eddie's bourbon herself and kissed him on the cheek.

"You're swell," Eddie said.

She walked out into the yard with him and they stood beside the humming truck, talking for what seemed a long, long time.

When Mama came back inside she was shivering. I thought she was just cold until I saw the tears weaving down her cheeks. "Poor Eddie," she said, and her teeth chattered. "I wish to God somebody loved him." She sat down in the rocker and cried and cried, and when I put Joe Parker's red windbreaker around her shoulders, she cried even harder.

☆ ♡ ☆

One thing I could have thought to tell Eddie Hawk to cheer him up was that Shilda got bored with her own wildness quicker than anybody I'd ever known. I knew in my very bones that sooner or later she'd drop the LaMarr boys. I got proof of it when we were walking home after school on the Friday that began our Christmas vacation. I was working up my nerve to ask her one more time to spend the night. Lately she'd seemed a little softer, but I wasn't sure she'd accept. I was more or less expecting her to yawn right up in my face and roll her eyes with boredom at the suggestion. We shuffled along side by side in a gray mush of wet and beaten leaves down Narrow Gauge Road. At the intersection with Proximity Street, Shilda would turn left and I'd keep on walking straight a mile up the road to Piney View. Hogan Royal's Esso station was at the corner and sometimes we stopped there for a Coke.

"Want a Coke?" I asked hopefully.

"Nah," she said, but she didn't seem to be in such a hurry.

"Want to come spend the night?" I said. "We could play Monopoly or something." I only said something that stupid because I was nervous.

"I've got to go to this party with Orst and Hogarth," she said, but she said it like it was an errand to the grocery store.

"We wouldn't *really* play Monopoly."

"I know."

The air was bitter cold and a light spitting drizzle annoyed our faces. The whole dreary day was the fuzzy humming gray of a television tube with a bent antenna. Friday. The beginning of Christmas holidays, 1958. Twelve more days until we'd begin the last year of the decade. I could think thoughts like that and get a chill.

Weeks ago the Christmas Jubilee Committee had decorated all the Main Street and Narrow Gauge lampposts with snappy tinsel candy canes, red and silver. You were supposed to think of peppermint and good cheer. But for some reason, those candy canes already looked forlorn, as if they sensed their brand of cheer was disposable, that the very first day after Christmas people would feel sad and restless gazing up at them. They'd been strung up so carefully by the Jubilee Committee. Their bows had been looped with the sort of snazzy perfection the Jubilees were famous for. Those Jubilee ladies really cared. They had a big time hanging the decorations. They brought thermoses of hot Russian tea and homemade sugar cookies and had a party right there on the streets. But the day after Christmas, those same pampered candy canes would be ripped down, roughly, by hired workmen.

" 'Hit Parade' comes on tonight. And 'Sergeant Bilko,' " I said.

She gave me a dubious look. "You don't even have a TV."

"Joe gave Mama one."

"Oh," she said. "But what about Bynum Bigshot?"

"He's working on the Studebaker tonight, installing some new seat covers. That damn car." I said it like that was the only problem between Bynum and me.

She sighed deeply, thoughtfully, and we walked along slowly, listening to the leaves slush under our loafers. We were less than a block from the Esso station when we saw it. Shilda stopped so fast and still it was as if her toes had sprouted roots.

"Is it foreign?"

"Who in hell drives a foreign car?" Shilda said. Her tone sounded almost fearful as if we were getting invaded.

Right beside the ordinary Esso Regular pump was parked a green outer-space style car. Its body was kind of stubby and sleek at the same time, so I imagined that it was changing shape even while we looked. It had this gleaming, conceited grin on its grille.

"Hi, Doo," we both said as we walked up to the car.

Doodle Washington, the colored man who worked for Hogan, was crouched in front of the car, spitting on the chrome bumper and rubbing it hard with a fleecy rag.

"Let's get a Coke," Shilda said as we toured the car. It was a convertible. The top was buttoned up but you could see inside the car and there were two tan seats covered with little sheepskin rugs. There were millions of gadgets and gauges on the dash and a tiny wooden steering wheel on the right side of the car.

"It *is* foreign," I whispered. And then I gasped, because I suddenly spied the very best thing of all: draped neatly over the steering wheel, almost like they were shaking hands with each other, was a pair of chocolate-colored leather gloves. "*Racing* gloves!" I cried.

"Whose car is this, Doo?" Shilda asked.

Doodle only shrugged his shoulders.

"Hi there, girls."

We wheeled around and saw Hogan Royal ambling

out of the station house with this blond-headed boy. It was Hogan who'd called to us and we waved.

"Yeah," Hogan was saying to the stranger, "I was over there in England once, during the war, but I never had the opportunity to tinker on no sporty car like yours. I worked on Jeeps. Nothing but Jeeps."

The blond stranger smiled and nodded. He wore a London Fog raincoat. I knew it was a London Fog because all the Brownlees wore London Fogs. The lapels on the stranger's London Fog were decorated with little triangles of chocolate brown velvet that matched his racing gloves. He had on gray pants and dark brown wingtip shoes, very polished. He was wearing a dark tie. But the thing about him that stood out most was the way he walked. He didn't swish, exactly. He didn't tiptoe. But he walked lightly, seeming to choose his steps carefully, like a tightrope walker. He didn't have a stride as much as he had a routine. He was so tall and lean you might have suspected he wore stilts, and you certainly might have wondered whether he could really fold his length up well enough to fit back inside that tiny car.

I liked him at once. Maybe his lankiness reminded me enough of Bynum's so that I wasn't as self-conscious around him as I might have been. He seemed approachable. But as far as other similarities to Bynum, there were none. He seemed to be from another century at least. He could have been the poet Percy Bysshe Shelley gliding right out of Hogan's Esso, only what a crazy place to visit if you were the ghost of Percy Bysshe Shelley coming to poke around in the twentieth century.

I thought how the stranger would get himself stomped to a pulp if he showed up in our high school where in English class just the *name* Percy Bysshe Shelley sent everybody howling, it was so queer. People always pronounced it like it was full of juice.

"Hi," I said to the stranger, and I knew that Shilda

was shocked. Real tall people have always made me feel chummy right off. "What kind of car's this?"

He smiled slightly with his small, serious lips. "It's an Austin Healey," he said. "It's British."

"Sounds ritzy," I said. "I love the color."

"Really," he said, but it was not a question. "It's called British racing green."

"Do you race?" Shilda said then, jutting one hip against the car. Her skirt hiked over her knees.

The stranger studied her for a moment. He looked amused. "My word, no," he said.

"Well, I was just asking," Shilda said.

"What are the gloves for then?" I asked.

"They're just gloves." He opened the door on the driver's side.

"You from around here?" Shilda asked. "I've never seen you before."

"I'm passing through," the stranger said. "I'm a student down at Chapel Hill." It sounded cool and faraway and lakey, Chapel Hill.

"Well, lucky for you you're not from Orfax," Shilda went on. She had a LaMarr brothers' horseyness in her voice that made me embarrassed for her. "Those fancy wire hubcaps would get gone in two seconds flat." She snapped her fingers, twice, close up in his face.

He sort of laughed at her. She wasn't in any of his college textbooks, that was sure. "Guess I'd better hurry then," he said. I liked the way he wasn't rude back. Watching him fold himself up to get back inside the car reminded me of a butterfly deciding that its cocoon was a better place to be after all.

"What's your name?" Shilda said, still leaning her hip against the car. She had on those troublemaking white cowgirl boots. "Want to take me for a ride?"

He cranked the car up and it sounded nice and puttery.

"Hey, buddy, what's your *name*?" She stuck her

hand through his open window. "Mine's Shilda. Come on and ride me down the road."

He took her hand in a gentlemanly way, shaking only the fingertips. "I'm glad to meet you," he said, so polite you could imagine his sleeves trimmed with lace. "My name's Oscar Wilde." Then he zoomed off.

If we hadn't done Oscar Wilde in October, I might have been fooled, too. Miss Joyner, my English teacher, had read us selected quotes. I'd memorized my favorite: "A worse thing than being talked about, is never being talked about at all."

"Oscar Wilde?" said Shilda. She shot him the finger. "What sort of name is that?"

"He made it up," I said.

"Of course he made it up, the son-of-a-bitch. Isn't Oscar Wilde that baseball player Eddie's so crazy about? As if *that* jerk could play ball!"

"Don't worry about it, he was a snob."

"Mr. Lah-dee-dah," said Shilda twirling around jeerfully.

The rain was beginning to fall harder now and the wind gusted cold around our skirts. The sky looked dismal and set. It seemed bolted over the sun like sheet metal.

"I bet we get some snow tonight," Hogan Royal called from the station house. "Radio says there's a storm moving down from Asheville."

"It's snow, all right," Doodle called from the garage. "I can smell it."

"That damn Sardine," Shilda said. "It makes me sick. It's a hillbilly car, and I'm not the type. You *know* I'm not the type. Tell me the truth, Pally. Don't I look like a scag riding around in that rusty tin can?"

Of course I didn't say one word.

"Class," she said, savoring the word. "*Class*. I need some class for this fine ass." She giggled at her little rhyme. It was a tinkly, mischievous giggle, not the faintest trace of the LaMarr brothers' hawing that she'd fallen into. Hearing her laugh that old, familiar way was like tuning into your favorite song on the radio.

"Let's *do* spend the night at your house," she said excitedly, walking faster, almost trotting. "I'll tell the boys something. It's time that you and me drew up a plan."

"A plan?"

She slapped me on the back. "For getting out of this hellhole, Pally, for living it up like Oscar Wilde. God, Pally, don't you just want everything?" she said.

VI

☆♡☆   ☆♡☆   ☆♡☆

It was sleeting hard by nightfall. We cooked popcorn and made hot chocolate with marshmallows and watched television. It was wonderful to have Shilda back. I felt downright motherly toward her, sneaking cautious glances at her as if I half expected her to disappear any second. I loved watching her whoop and holler over the shenanigans on TV. So what if every now and then she whacked her thighs when she laughed?

"You ought to come over Sunday night, too, Shilly," I said, a nervous wreck to please her. "Ricky Nelson is going to sing on 'Ed Sullivan.' "

"No kidding?"

"No kidding."

She chewed the popcorn slowly, relishing the saltiness. I could tell that she hadn't tasted home-cooked popcorn in a long time.

I felt powerful to have lured her away from Orst and Hogarth. I felt practically villainous myself.

Even though it was Friday night, Joe Parker brought Mama home early because the roads were icing up. Little jewels of ice flickered in their hair and on the shoulders of their coats as they came in from the weather.

They made a great show of how treacherous it was outside, wiping their feet, swatting at their coats, rubbing their fingers in front of the oil heater. They'd driven downtown to the Sunset Theatre to see *Seven Brides for Seven Brothers* and Joe started raving about the dancing acts as being the first he'd ever seen where the men acted like men. He stomped around the living room and jumped over an ottoman to demonstrate. He picked Mama up and slung her over his shoulder and spun around. Then he put her down and grabbed Shilda and danced her right onto the sofa while Mama and I laughed and clapped and hummed some corn-pone tune. But I stopped laughing so hard when I saw how gorgeous Shilda looked in her white flannel nightgown with her long black hair all flung out behind her, tattery-looking as she danced, wild, loose hair that men and boys loved. Her face was pink and perfect as a valentine, her eyes hot and shiny with delight and pouring all over Joe Parker. I could have believed anything, seeing her that way. I could have believed that she was the one who would marry Joe Parker, not Mama.

Maybe Mama noticed, too. She said, "Joe, Joe, easy now, the sofa." As if she'd only just realized they were dancing on the furniture. Then Shilda linked her arms around Joe's neck and kissed him fully, quickly, on the mouth.

"Whoa, now!" Joe said. "I'm out of breath, an old man, now." He hopped off the sofa away from her and fell down on the floor, panting and grinning and holding his sides.

Everybody seemed embarrassed then, the way you always feel when a real good time crashes down because of one fool.

"Look," I said, pointing out the window, "was that a snowflake?" It wasn't and I knew it. I just felt like changing the subject.

Mama parted the curtains a bit further and looked out.

"Is it snowing?" Joe Parker asked her, but he seemed to be asking her something else, too.

"Not yet," Mama said.

We all walked to the window then except for Shilda, who lay on the sofa. The light above the front stoop scratched feebly against the black and brittle night. Sleet popped against the window. I thought the trees looked miserable in their glassy skins, like they couldn't breathe. You could hear the pine trees, top-heavy with ice, whining overhead. The pine trees had shallow roots and were easily toppled by ice storms. The hardwood trees, the oaks and maples and elms and beeches, just gave themselves up to the ice. They were beaten, but they endured because maybe they weren't quite convinced by the ice. The ice just tended to bring out the patience in them; they kept still under their burdens and waited for a thaw. But the pine trees fought like fools. They argued back. They tossed themselves indignantly, complained and labored under their portions of ice until they uprooted themselves.

"Well," Joe Parker said, "this old boy had better get on down the road."

"Don't go," I said. I don't know what I'd seen, but it was something forever and heartless out there in the gloom. I even touched Joe on the elbow. "Just listen to those pine trees," I said. "They're *groaning*."

"If I wait much longer I'll have to put on my chains," Joe said. "But thanks for wanting me to hang around your slumber party," he said to me and kissed me on the forehead. "Good night, Shilda. That was some fine dancing. You wore me out, kid."

Mama and I looked down at our shoes. Joe was just so kind. And for a second real anger throbbed in my heart because I knew Joe Parker would have stayed the whole night if Shilda hadn't been there. He would have stretched out on the sofa like he always did, and Mama would have covered him with the afghan called a Joseph's Coat-of-Many-Colors afghan. It was a play they always put on for me, and I loved it: Mama bending over him, tucking the afghan around his shoulders as if he were another child. "Good night, sweet repose, stick out your head, and cover up your toes."

Of course, some time in the night—and perhaps I only imagined it because of craving such adventures for myself—Joe got up quietly and tiptoed into Mama's bedroom. I'd never once heard the bedsprings creak though. I'd listen hard for them, too, my heart pounding. Somehow in my poor, pure romantic mind I imagined that Joe never actually got into bed with Mama but stood over her, watching her sleep, loving her in a part of his heart too selfless for touch. He was always dressed when I woke up. The sofa cushions always looked roughed up by his tossing. It never occurred to me until much later, after I was married, that the footsteps I thought I heard in the hallway late at night were *Mama's* as she groped her way stealthily toward Joe, who lay waiting on the sofa.

Shilda would sleep on Joe's sofa tonight. Joe would go off into the slick darkness of the ice storm, the glazed roller-coaster ride of Narrow Gauge Road. Nothing but frail, doomed pine trees lined Narrow Gauge Road. There were so many ways to lose him.

Joe buttoned his jacket to the throat and dug some big leather gloves out of one pocket.

"Didn't you wear a hat, hon?" Mama asked him.

"Hat's in the car," he said hastily. Suddenly he'd switched his manner to that of a man sick and tired of being fussed over. He could take just so much caring all at once. Too much concern, and it was an insult. He'd begun to feel insulted when he thought we thought he couldn't drive a car on ice.

Joe put on his gloves briskly. They smelled and looked like huge wet oak leaves.

"Joe," I said, "I saw an Austin Healey car today. It

was up at Hogan's Esso and this snooty guy from Chapel Hill was driving it. He said his name was Oscar Wilde.''

"Who's Oscar Wilde, Joe?" It was Shilda who spoke, but her words, floating up from the sofa where she lay, were like the ghost of her true voice, pale and breathy.

We all rushed over to her because her face was as white as a bowl of milk and she was pouring sweat. I guessed she had cramps, but I wasn't going to say that in front of Joe. I almost felt she deserved them.

"I'm okay," she said. "I think it's just cramps."

Mama took her hand. "Want a heating pad, hon? Some Midol?"

"Put your head down in your lap," I said. "Breathe deep and slow."

She did that while Mama fetched her two aspirins and a glass of water. She sighed and wiped her lush, tangled hair back from her face. How could she look so beautiful even when she felt bad? Even when she seemed so frail there was this rare energy about her, a light that we warmed to, waiting for her to cause some new thing to happen in our lives for better or worse. Slowly her face began to pinken again and she smiled as if to say the rescue was complete, her show would go on.

When Joe left, Mama went straight to bed. She blew us a kiss, closed her bedroom door, and her light snapped off at once. I made more popcorn and halfheartedly brought out the Ouija board. Shilda didn't feel much like playing, but finally we summoned this spirit called O.W. who refused to spell out his whole name. I guessed it was Oscar Wilde and that Shilda had forced the pointer to spell those initials just because Oscar Wilde was on her mind. She hated Ouija more than Monopoly, and ordinarily we wouldn't have touched it. But the TV had already played the national anthem and our only deck of cards was in Mama's room. I didn't feel like talking anymore either, mainly because I was still sulking about her flirting with Joe Parker. She knew it, too.

She yawned loudly.

"Look," I said, "we should go to bed if you don't feel like playing."

"I'm not sleepy," she said, lighting one of Mama's Chesterfields.

"Then play the game *right*, Shilda."

She glared at me.

"You forced the damn thing to spell out O.W. Admit it. That stranger's still on your mind."

"I didn't force a goddamn thing."

"You moved it, I *know* you moved it."

"Well, how else is the damn thing going to get around?"

"What do you mean 'how else is the damn thing going to get around?' *Spirits*, Shilda! Forces we don't know about, forces from . . . Look," I said more calmly. "You have to relax and let the spirits move *through* you. If you're receptive and believe hard enough, it's like you're inviting them to use you as an instrument of communication. A spirit has got to feel welcome before it will take possession of your fingertips. *That's* what pushes the Ouija pointer if you play right."

She exhaled a slow, blue lungful of smoke just over my head. "You and Mrs. Oxendine," she said. "Spirits!" she said. "Haw!"

I slammed the Ouija board shut. "You've got to ruin everything sooner or later," I cried. "And why did you have to go and kiss him on the lips, for God's sake, Shilda?"

"Haven't you ever wanted to kiss him on the lips yourself?" she said. "Look," she said, "I could tell you some things if you weren't so dumb."

"Oh, brother!" I said.

"Oh, brother!" she said mockingly, letting go a fierce volley of smoke rings. They barely wavered from their tight little circles. They looked almost hard, solid. A different night, in jolly moods, we might have tried to scoop them onto our wrists like bracelets.

"Why did you throw yourself at him like that? Why did you act like such a whore?" My voice trembled the way voices forced into cruelty usually do.

But Shilda laughed. "Pally," she said wearily, "grow up."

"You know," I said, "I really really hate you sometimes." My teeth felt all sparky when I said it, poisonous snaky biting teeth. It was the mystery of her that I hated.

"Hate me all you like," she said, tossing her head. "And then what's left? I'm your goddamn best friend."

I felt tears on my cheeks. "But why did you do it? Why Joe? And in front of Mama?"

"Come off it, Pally," she said. "That's not what this fight's about. That's nothing but a little old moment, a little old burned-out match of a moment."

"To you maybe," I said.

"It was nothing."

"It's everything."

She ground the cigarette out in a seashell ashtray. "It was just something to do."

"Something to do!"

"Sometimes," she said softly, "you get one chance at something you know deep down is your last. I mean, it's your last chance forever. The moment and your mood will never coincide again. Joe Parker, that was just *playing*," she said.

She seemed suddenly too old, too hard-as-stones truthful to bear. Her face looked too naked, and her paleness reminded me of some tender white flower that had bloomed crazily, unexpectedly, into the wrong season. "I'm going to bed," I said, jumping away from her. As I marched past the living room window, I didn't even notice that the first ice storm of the winter had turned, quietly, into the first snowfall.

It was not quite dawn when I awoke, but snow brings a false early gleam to the sky. I imagined that it was late. I felt a burst of joy that it really and truly had snowed, was *still* snowing. But the joy had a dragged-down quality to it when I remembered last night's argument with Shilda. I kept thinking maybe we'd just been tired, but that wasn't it.

I lay for a while under my cactus flower quilt and watched the flakes tumble past my window. I turned the radio on and, believe it or not, they were playing "White Christmas." Too much. I turned the radio off and tried to think of something other than having snow for Christmas Day, which was still four days away. You could wish it away by wanting it as bad as some people around Orfax wanted it. I suppose the farmers who had field animals hated the snow well enough. It was no fun to have cows in a snowstorm, that's what Bynum Jenkins always said. Cows were dumb and got disoriented and bawled like babies. Ice on the tree limbs and wires could knock out electricity all over the county, which meant the dairy cows would have to be milked by hand—mostly by emergency volunteers.

But in spite of the cows, I couldn't think of a single person who wouldn't have a smile on their face—at first—when they awoke to find an early winter snow. I thought about everybody I knew and how they'd react when they glanced out a window.

Joe Parker would come over to dig us out and drive us into town, which is where everybody went when it snowed. The Cash and Carry and the Piggly Wiggly would be packed, people stocking up on groceries enough to see them through a blizzard. Of course there'd never been a real blizzard in Orfax, but people always hoped for one. Once or twice a year we got a dinky little snow of around two or three inches that caused bunches of wrecks and school to be called off. Still, as soon as the first snowflake hit the ground, people hoarded up groceries and hoped for a blizzard and talked about how long it had taken them to put chains on their tires or how many hours to dig out some snowbound calf who'd fallen in the creek or how they'd skidded halfway down Narrow Gauge Road before their brakes finally took hold. People would talk about nothing but snow all day. People who hadn't spoken to each other in months, who'd held ironclad grudges, would wave to each other and gesture at the sky. The whole world was suddenly the color of truce. I suspected that if I ran into Howdy Oxendine on a snowy day, I'd probably say, "Howdy, Howdy," like we were pals. And if I ran into Bobby Rex Moseley, I wouldn't be shy, I'd say, "What do you think of all this snow?"

It was bound to happen. I started thinking about Bobby Rex waking up to see the snowstorm. I gave him light blue flannel pajamas that matched his eyes. I made his hair all pokey with dark, sleep-smashed curls and his face pink on one side from hard sleep. I made him smell like I remember Speedy's Old Spice smelling. Just a couple of buttons on his pajama tops were undone so that you still had to guess at his brown, muscular chest. I put him on the bed beside me; we were on our honeymoon in some Alpine lodge. His eyes were closed, but he was still smiling. I loved him just then not because he was so handsome that my heart ached, but because I knew he could feel it snowing in his sleep and was glad. I also knew that Bynum Jenkins would wake up miserable this morning because his daddy kept a dairy herd.

The phone was ringing in Mama's bedroom, and I guessed it was Joe Parker. I wriggled out of bed, put on a robe and some bedroom shoes. I was brushing my hair when Mama burst into the room.

"Where's Shilda?" she cried. "Did she sleep on the sofa?"

"Yes," I said, stunned, "I think so."

"She didn't plan to sneak out or anything, did she?" Mama's eyes looked black and spooky as caves.

"What's going on, Mama?"

"You tell me," she said fiercely. "For God's sakes, Pally, where is she?"

"Well, we did have sort of a fight," I admitted. "Maybe she waked up early and went home."

"Well, if she went home she hasn't gotten there yet because that was Eddie calling from their house. There's been an awful wreck." Then Mama started shaking and crying so hard that I guided her to the edge of my bed and sat us both down. I held her tight, and she felt so much smaller than me that I could have cried. She had bony little bird-wing shoulder blades.

"Is it Joe?" I cried suddenly, and I lost my breath in the middle of asking.

"It's the LaMarr twins," she said.

I felt socked in the stomach. "Dead?" I was surprised I had any voice left at all.

"Eddie doesn't know yet. Nobody saw the wreck. They just found the car a while ago off Highway 21 near the creek. It hit a pine tree and rolled. Eddie said it was still upside down, waiting for the tow truck."

"It doesn't have a roof," I said. "In the winter I think they tack feed sacks over the hole in the roof."

"Oh, honey." Mama hugged me.

"The doors are rusted shut," I said dreamily. "The only way out of the car is through the roof."

Then Mama took both my hands and squeezed them. "Honey, Eddie said there's a girl in the backseat. Somebody last night saw a girl with them at Gizmo's."

I looked at her hard.

"That's why somebody called Eddie straight away. Pally, if you know something, if you know *anything*, tell me."

"I wish I did." I pitched off my bathrobe and slipped on some blue jeans and a sweater.

"It just can't be Shilda," Mama said. "In my heart I know it can't be her."

"Hah!" I wanted to say. "Hah! If you only knew half what I know." But I knew that she probably did.

I left Mama to phone Joe and went out into the storm to hunt for tracks. There wasn't a single footprint in the front yard, and my chest tightened with the fear that she'd been gone so long that the falling snow had wiped away all traces of her direction. Slowly I walked around the trailer and there at the back stoop I saw the faintest imprints of her boots. They seemed to go around and around in circles like she hadn't been able to make up her mind what she wanted to do. It looked like she'd gone outside to take a breath of fresh air but had got to walking around and thinking.

Her tracks were almost filled in with snow. The prints led away from the trailer into the pine tree grove, nothing but pale and secretive pocks of shadow. If you weren't trying to make them into boot marks, you might have missed them altogether. I wondered why she'd taken that direction. There was nothing but more trailers in the grove, and when you came to the very end of the lane—about a mile—there was nothing but Mrs. Oxendine's log house and the barbed-wire fence that separated Piney View Trailer Park from pastures. Through the pine grove was the longest way Shilda could have walked home, if that's where her mind had set her walking. It was also the longest and most roundabout way to reach the LaMarrs' place. Although they could have picked her up once she cut through all the woods and pastures and came out on Highway 21, I just couldn't let myself think that way.

It was early, maybe seven in the morning, but the day pulsed with the fuzzy brightness of snow. I tried to relax a little and enjoy it as it wheeled down in huge, ragged flakes. I caught them with my red gloves and studied them. They weren't anything like the perfect snowflakes you see stenciled on shop windows. They looked almost violent and confused, ripped off something larger maybe, lost bits of nothing, dying in the heat of your hand. They seemed both so beautiful and forgotten all at the same time that it made you ache for God's bother.

I couldn't believe the LaMarr boys were dead. I couldn't believe that Shilda had run off into the snowstorm because of our argument. How did my mind keep from going insane with two such awful thoughts jammed into it at once? I tried to remember what my mind had felt like when Speedy died. Why didn't I go insane then? I was only four years old, that's why. I had a happy, careless little mind back then and didn't see the separate struggling snowflakes. It was a mind that observed the wonder of snow from the big picture window of our yellow cottage among the pussywillow trees. If one snowflake got forsaken by the others and melted down the window glass, I was simply delighted and laughed. Because what was the loss of one snowflake when there would come another and another and its mother and her brother? There just isn't any such thing as *waste* when you are four years old.

I trudged straight down the middle of the pine grove, following Shilda's tracks. There were lights on in most of the trailers, people up and eating breakfast, enjoying the winter wonderland view. The trailers looked particularly cheery under hoods of snow. The bomb-shaped silver ones looked as snug as tin can birdhouses. The boxy ones looked less boxy. The Tilleys' big long yellow banana trailer looked as cheery as a Christmas parade float. For a change the trailers didn't look cheap and makeshift. They looked like tree ornaments nestled in the snow. I turned around and walked with my back against the wind to admire my own little trailer, turquoise, bright as a patch of fallen good-weather sky. It looked brave and hardy.

When I turned back into the slamming snowfall, I'd almost forgotten what I was doing in the middle of a pine tree grove besides admiring the view. The moaning of the pine trees overhead sobered me. They looked cold and cranky. I shook some of the stout little fir trees as I passed. They seemed to leap out from under their cloaks of snow, bristling with gratitude. I started humming some rock 'n' roll tune as I marched along. I could smell wood smoke. Then, squinting against the snow, I thought I saw Shilda. Whoever it was lay huddled near a tree way ahead. Just beyond the tree was the Oxendines' log house. In the snow and from such a distance it looked like a toy, tiny coils of smoke springing from the chimney.

It was Shilda! I recognized her car coat. I started running toward her, but the snow sucked dreamily at my boots and it was impossible to move quickly.

"Shilda!" I cried, waving and panting. "It's me, Shilda! Wait up!"

But it was clear she had no intention of going anyplace. I was certain she recognized me, but she gave no sign. Shilda could hold grudges longer than anybody I knew. But the snow had worked its magic on me and I was determined to make amends and act remorseful and win her back in no time.

She sat hunkered over and still in her navy blue car coat, no hat, no hood, waiting until I reached her before she sank backwards in the snow. Her face was white enough to practically stop my heart. She'd been crying. Her hair looked frozen.

"Shilly!" I dropped to my knees beside her.

"I'm not goofing around this time, Pal," she said, grunting. "I think I'm having a baby."

"Cramps again?" I said. "God, Shilly, maybe it's your appendix." I pried one of her clenched hands away from a soggy pocket of the car coat. She wasn't wearing gloves. I rubbed the hand briskly between my own.

"Worst cramps in history," she said in a husky whisper.

"I'll help you back to the trailer, you're frozen solid."

"No, Pal, I can't make it."

"Of course you can make it."

"No, Pal. *Please*." Her eyes sparkled with a kind of fever. "Listen," she said, and she spoke so weakly that I had to lean my ear to her lips. "Listen now and don't argue," she said. "Get Mrs. Oxendine to come."

"*Mrs. Oxendine?*"

"Quick." She shut her eyes, tears rolling down her cheeks. Snowflakes melted bleakly on her wincing, up-turned face.

"Mrs. Oxendine," I repeated. "Are you sure, Shilly?"

"Well, isn't she a goddamned nurse?" Shilda screamed.

VII

☆♡☆   ☆♡☆   ☆♡☆

When I saw the blood that we lifted her out of, my knees felt filled with a whirlpool motion. I had to sit down right away. Later, Mrs. Oxendine told me that it wasn't as much blood as it looked like. White snow just lent a sharp contrast. Between Mrs. Oxendine and Howdy and me, we carried her to the house and into the bathroom. Then Mrs. Oxendine told Howdy to make some tea and she'd holler if she needed us. Of course I told Mrs. Oxendine I thought we ought to call an ambulance, but she just went, "Hah!" and looked insulted. Then she disappeared into the bathroom with a little black medical kit.

The first thing I did was phone Mama. There was so much static on the line that we could barely talk. I told her Shilda was safe, as safe as anybody could be with Mrs. Oxendine hovering over them (of course I didn't say that with Howdy right there at my elbow). I didn't tell her about the blood and I didn't think to ask about the LaMarrs, I was so upset. Mama said a lot of phone lines were down and Eddie hadn't called back and Joe was having trouble getting to Piney View. Even Hogan Royal's tow truck had gone into a ditch. I told her that

Shilda had really bad cramps but that we'd be home just as soon as we warmed up, don't worry.

When I hung up, I saw Howdy leaning one of his spudlike ears against the bathroom door and grinning. He cut his eyes at me. "You didn't tell your mama about the blood," he said.

"Maybe I didn't feel like it," I said.

"It was lots and lots," he said. "Think she's going to die?"

He shuffled into the kitchen and poured out two cups of liver-colored tea that had been steeping in a big china pot. In all my life I would have never guessed that Howdy Oxendine and I would drink tea together at his kitchen table, just the two of us. There was a new, strange intimacy between us now because of Shilda's blood. I was surprised at how easy I felt in front of him after what we'd both seen. I kept waiting to feel embarrassed, but I felt more and more comfortable.

The tea was hot and bitter, but I didn't ask for sugar. I drank it straight down and my eyes watered. I felt strong and wise in a sort of pioneer woman way.

"It's good tea," I admitted. "It tastes real nourishing."

"She makes it herself," he said. "She grows the herbs and dries them under the house." Then he lowered his voice confidentially. "We got big old hairy spiders down there. We got this deadly cobra snake in an old bird cage."

I ignored him. "Want to play Chinese checkers?" Howdy asked me. I shook my head no. The tea had made me drowsy and I only felt like waiting and thinking.

"I've got dominoes, too."

"No thanks," I said, "I just don't have any spirit for a game."

He jumped up then and switched on the television. We watched Mighty Mouse cartoons for a while, lolling back in pink leatherette and chrome chairs that surrounded the pink Formica kitchen table. Then slowly it began to bother me what was happening. I'd never even been inside the Oxendines' house before, yet there I sat acting downright sisterly toward that moron Howdy and taking it for granted that Mrs. Oxendine's tea wasn't poisoned. No telling what was happening to Shilda! Fayette Weems had an aunt who swore Mrs. Oxendine had cured her arthritis by having her soak in a tub of mud and live earthworms whipped up in the very bathroom where Shilda lay sick.

Just then the toilet flushed and Mrs. Oxendine lumbered out of the bathroom, closing the door behind her.

"Howdy!" she barked. "Run down to the basement and bring up some dried mint. And, Howdy, turn off that damn TV and poke up the fire."

He leaped right up, so quick and obedient you would have thought he was normal.

"Is she okay?" I asked. "Can I do anything?"

"I reckon you could call her husband if she's got one," said Mrs. Oxendine sullenly. "I reckon he'd like to know."

"Husband?"

Mrs. Oxendine stared at me with eyes the cold hard color of granite.

"She's only sixteen years old," I said. "She doesn't have a husband."

"Git!" Mrs. Oxendine snapped at Howdy, and he scrabbled out the door without even putting on a coat. "Now," she said to me, "who are you?" She squinted in the dusky light, sizing me up. Her face looked like it had been built from dried up pottery clay.

"Pally Thompson," I said in a thin voice. "I live in the blue trailer closest to Narrow Gauge. My mother's Betty—"

Mrs. Oxendine put her hand up. "I mean," she said slowly, "who are you to *her*?" She gestured toward the bathroom.

"Shilda's my best friend," I said. "She's like my sister. *Closer* than a sister, really."

Mrs. Oxendine scoured me with her eyes. "Ha!" she said. Her eyes seemed to scrape my very heart. "Ha!"

"What's wrong?" I cried.

Mrs. Oxendine sighed heavily and heaved herself into a pink leatherette chair.

"I think it was a boy child," she said at last. "It's difficult to tell the sex this early, but that's what I think. I have real good eyes."

Mrs. Oxendine must have noticed the look of bewilderment on my face.

"Your sister friend had a miscarriage," she said. "She was pregnant, about three months."

"*Shilda?*" My voice sounded reedy and far away.

"Is that her name?"

"Shilda Hawk," I said, about to cry. "Are you sure?"

Mrs. Oxendine gave me a fed-up look. "I'm going to make up some medicine tea," she said. "It helps stop the bleeding and will numb the pain. She's over the worst. She's got pluck, I'll say that for her."

I looked out the kitchen window at the snow falling endlessly. It was more snow than I'd ever seen in my life. It was enough snow to build igloos, a whole village of igloos, an army of snowmen.

It was enough for horse-drawn sleighs. It was the dream snow of my whole long childhood, falling, unstoppable, at the wrong time. It was enough snow to lie down in and be covered up with in no time, maybe die in. I wondered how we would ever get home. And I wondered if anybody would recognize us when we got there.

The bathroom door squeaked open and Shilda padded out wearing an enormous pink chenille bathrobe that belonged to Mrs. Oxendine. She looked as white as anybody taking their last gasp.

"Lie down on the couch," Mrs. Oxendine said to her sharply. "As soon as that old boy brings up the mint, I'll fix you some medicine tea." She stopped fiddling with the teakettle and stomped over to the parlor stove. "It's cold in here," she said. Then she opened the stove door and poked the logs with the toe of one shoe, a pink patent leather loafer. Amazingly the shoe did not catch fire and the logs sputtered cheerily to life.

"Did Mrs. Oxendine tell you?" Shilda asked me. She was all doubled up and I helped her stretch out on the couch.

"Yes," I said softly. "You look so sick, don't talk yet."

"Okay." She closed her eyes. "I'm scared," she said.

I took Shilda's hand. I looked over at Mrs. Oxendine for help, but she'd seated herself in a bulky recliner, had lit a pipe and picked up a copy of *Life*.

"You're going to be fine, now, Shilda. You're just in a state of shock still. Right, Mrs. Oxendine?"

"I can't believe this!" Mrs. Oxendine exclaimed from the recliner. She cackled and slapped her thigh. "This really beats all! Grace Kelly went out and bought twenty-seven pairs of shoes for her wedding trousseau." She glanced over the top of the magazine at me. "Did you say something?" she said.

Just then the front door blasted open and Howdy stumbled in with an armload of firewood.

"Did you get the mint?" his mother asked.

"Yessir," he said. "My pockets." He let the logs tumble out of his arms beside the stove.

Nobody talked much after Howdy returned. Mrs. Oxendine rattled around in the kitchen, making her medicine tea. All around me the air felt stingy with the smell. Shilda lay on the sofa with her eyes closed, and I stared out the window at the falling, unnecessary snow. It seemed to me that so much time had passed that it was probably already tomorrow. And if it was tomorrow, then our families had given up on us or didn't care where we were or what was happening. I began to think that if nobody worried about when or if you'd come home, then you could just wander and it wouldn't matter. You could live in a manhole, a trash can—just any old place with a lid to keep you dry. The more I thought along these lines, the more lonely and hopeless I felt. Then I began to feel that maybe I'd always lived right there with the Oxendines in their pinky dark log house. Maybe it's where I belonged, staring out into the permanent disrespectful weather. You could probably get amnesia if you thought that way for long.

"Hey you, Sister. Give her this," Mrs. Oxendine said to me.

I took the mug of tea she offered and sat down beside Shilda on the sofa's edge. The tea smelled meaty. It looked as thick as stew with clots of leafy things floating around in it. Its steam made my eyes water. Shilda sat up as if in a trance and drank it right down. She kept her eyes closed the whole time. When the mug was empty, she lowered herself to the sofa cushions again and slept.

A long time passed or no time, it was all the same. I read a bunch of *Life* magazines. I read an article in *Reader's Digest* about a man falling out of an airplane into a snowbank and surviving.

Mrs. Oxendine stayed in the kitchen mixing herbs for a while. Then she unloaded the dryer and started folding clothes. Howdy lay on the floor quietly and played dominoes all by himself. I could hear him breathing through his nose; the air seemed to whistle in his nostrils like tiny flutes playing off key. Shilda slept through everything.

When the phone rang, the sound seemed to splinter my whole body from its heart outward. My skin leaped away from its bones and turned spiky with goose bumps. I could even feel the phone ringing in the hairs on my arms.

But Mrs. Oxendine didn't even flinch. She finished folding what looked like a big beach towel before she answered, and by then the phone had rung four times.

"Speaking," Mrs. Oxendine said. She listened intently

for a while. Every now and then she'd say, "Mmm." A few times she'd grunt, but her face never revealed a flicker of interest in what she was hearing. "I'll tell them," Mrs. Oxendine said, then she hung right up without saying good-bye and started folding the laundry again.

"Tell them what?" I asked. "Was that my mother?"

"Oh," Mrs. Oxendine said matter-of-factly, "I thought you were dozing. That was your mother. She said to tell you that she'd gone to town to buy groceries. She went with Joe Parker in his truck. She left the back door open."

"Is that all?" I said. It sounded like part of such a normal day. I glanced at Shilda, who was still sleeping, who'd slept right through those skin-peeling telephone rings. "Did Mama mention the wreck?" I said cautiously.

"What wreck?" Howdy popped his head up from the dominoes. "What wreck?"

"Shush up," his mother told him and he said, "Yessir."

"Do you know anything?" I asked her.

"It's a serious business, that's all I know. Her daddy's coming to take her home." She gestured at Shilda. "He can't drive way back here, so we'd better take her to your place." She took a big gulp of meaty tea and swished it around in her mouth. She swallowed thoughtfully. "Howdy," she said, "where's your sled?"

"Runners broke off," he said.

She grunted and rolled her eyes.

"We can make a litter!" Howdy said excitedly. "I'll get a blanket and tie it between two poles and drag her there."

Mrs. Oxendine grunted again. "It's a mile walk back to Narrow Gauge. There's a foot and a half of snow, two-foot drifts in places. There's all kinds of tree stumps and potholes and dropoff places. She can't be dragged."

"You and I could carry her," I suggested. "We could make a seat with our arms."

Mrs. Oxendine raked me with her eyes. "It could come to that," she said, "if I was desperate." Then she laughed bitterly. "Ha!" she said. "You're too skinny and he's too short." She looked out at the snow, considering. "Go ahead and get your things together and let's dress her."

Shilda was groggy, but she didn't seem in any great pain. Mrs. Oxendine had washed her clothes and put them in the dryer and they smelled warm and linty. Even her coat was warm and dry.

"Is it *still* snowing?" Shilda asked me.

"Just between you and me, I don't think it's ever going to stop," I said.

"Then we're finally going to have a white Christmas this year," she said and smiled.

"Everybody ready?" said Mrs. Oxendine. She loomed suddenly before us wearing a bright yellow slicker as huge as any tent. She had on pink gloves and a red scarf with pink roses all over it. On top of the scarf she wore a band of furry earmuffs to give her ears extra protection. She had on rubber fishing boots that went almost to her hips. I almost jumped when I saw her. She reminded me of some bear you find in a circus all dressed up in rowdy-looking human clothes. I almost expected her to pick me up and dance me across the room.

"You, boy! Open the door," she said to Howdy. Then she brushed me aside and plucked Shilda from the sofa as if she were no more weight than a bundle of kindling "You let that fire die out while I'm gone," she told Howdy, stomping down the cabin steps, "and I'll skin you alive."

"Yessir," Howdy said, saluting her. And as I hurried past him, in Mrs. Oxendine's frosty wake, he reached out and pinched me, hard, on the ass.

☆ ♡ ☆

Once we got home, home seemed too easy. The air

had a perfumey lightheartedness that seemed false. I felt clumsy inside the trailer. I kept bumping into things. I felt blinded from the snow and my skin smarted. The trailer felt too hot.

I looked over all the things we'd left behind us. I picked them up and examined them as if they were changed: bottles of nail polish, emery boards, a ruffly roller bonnet, the scattered Ouija board letters.

Mrs. Oxendine stayed just long enough to tuck Shilda back in bed and heat up another cup of medicine tea which she'd brought in a quart-size mason jar. She didn't even bother to take off her pink gloves or earmuffs while she heated the tea.

"She'll want to rest. If she starts bleeding again real hard, you'll have no choice. You'll have to call a doctor. Otherwise nobody's got to know a damn thing."

"Thanks, Mrs. Oxendine," I said. "You've been . . . swell."

"Thanks," Shilda said. She was wide awake now and propped herself up on one elbow to drink the tea.

Mrs. Oxendine regarded us coolly. "I know my way, then," she said. She stomped out of my bedroom, down the short hallway to the back door. She left a track of wet grids from the soles of her fishing boots. When the back door finally slammed shut, the whole trailer felt light and airy with her leaving. I felt as if I'd been holding my breath the whole time she'd been there.

"Now what do we do?" Shilda asked me.

"I don't know."

"Do you think Eddie will guess?"

"Only if you get sick again. Then you'll have to get help."

"It was a real shock, Pally," she said, gazing out the bedroom window at the snow.

"You didn't know?"

"I was worried, but I didn't know for sure. Pally, find me a cigarette."

"You should have told me, Shilda."

"What could you have done about it?"

"Nothing," I said.

"You're damn right, nothing."

"Well," I said, "I could have *listened*."

She gave me a blank look, then stared out the window again. "You like to listen, don't you? You like to let me make it real for you."

I didn't know what to say.

She sighed and ran a pale hand through her raggedy black hair. "It's just that you seem to want explanations all the time, Pally. I don't mean that you *ask* for explanations all the time, but you give off this air of wanting them. And you don't just want things explained to you, you want them *justified*. It's really not what you do or say, Pally, it's just how you are. How we're different."

"I don't mean it, however I am."

"Of course you mean it," she said, "it's just your way."

"I'm sorry."

"I know. You're just some weird kind of policeman."

"I'll try not to be."

"Well, I'm *not* ashamed," she said, wiping her cheeks. "Don't expect me to go around now with a long face, feeling ashamed. I did exactly what I wanted to do. I had a goddamn good time, so let's just shut up about it."

"Okay, Shilda."

"Good." She sniffed. "I got off damn lucky, that's all I'll say. I'm a damn lucky duck, I really am."

"You are," I said.

"Not that I don't want a baby some day. I'd like a baby, I really would. But not now. Hell, I'm not even seventeen. I don't want a baby until I've done everything. I don't want a baby until I'm thirty years old. When do your female parts start to dry up, Pal?"

"Mama and Joe want to have a baby," I said. "Mama's thirty-four, so I guess they dry up sometime after then."

"I'll wait until I'm thirty-four then," Shilda said. "I'll play it real close, down to the wire, just watch me."

"Do you feel better?" I asked.

"I can fake Eddie out. I'll tell him it's real bad cramps. The worst. That's how it feels, Pally."

"You look much better now," I said, "but when I first saw you lying in the snow, I was scared to death."

"Let's don't talk about it any more," she said. "Let's forget it. We can pretend it never happened if you'd like to. We can fake it."

"Of course we can," I said.

"It never happened," Shilda said. "It was a dream."

"Of course it never happened."

"Now get me one of your mama's cigarettes before I have a nicotine fit," Shilda said.

I broke open a fresh pack of Mama's Chesterfields and fished out a booklet of matches that read: THE INSIDE OF THIS MATCH COVER COULD CHANGE YOUR LIFE. There was an ad about becoming a cosmetic salesman inside.

Shilda lit the cigarette and smoked it luxuriously. She seemed to suck the cigarette smoke down with her whole body. It seemed to drench her in pleasure, inhaling the smoke, so that she made smoking look nourishing, as irresistible as chocolate.

"Look at us," Shilda said suddenly, dreamily. She inhaled another deep lungful of smoke and blew it out gustily as if it had made her strong. "This might be a happy little slumber party, pure and simple. But," she said, "it ain't."

VIII

☆♡☆ ☆♡☆ ☆♡☆

It was Eddie Hawk who lifted the dead girl out of the wrecked Sardine. Joe and Mama were there too, by that time, bystanders along with the rest of Orfax, huddled along the Narrow Gauge Road bridge. It was a skinny little bridge with spindly wooden railings and a drop of about twenty feet to Sawyer's Creek. It made a clattering sound like a toy train trestle when you drove over it.

Davey Cole, the sheriff's deputy, judged that the car had made the turn onto Narrow Gauge from Highway 21 too fast, skidded on the bridge, and gone out of control while crossing. It hadn't landed in the creek. Instead it plowed down the embankment, flipped at least once, and crashed upside down in a cluster of scrub pines. The whole top of the car was mashed flat down to the window ledges.

"I can't get shut of it," Eddie Hawk said.

"You just knew they were all dead," Mama said. "By the quietness if nothing else. Even the car looked like a body."

"A coffin," Joe said.

They were home, drinking hot chocolate, sitting around our kitchen table and smoking cigarettes.

"Sleazebag car," Shilda muttered.

"I begged Joe not to stop. Just ride on by, I told him. I didn't want to be just another gaper. But," Mama said, "you know how men are."

It was Joe, finally, who convinced everybody that they could lift the car upright. No need for the tow truck or blowtorches or Jim Creed's mules. It took only a half-dozen men, easy as pie, once they shoveled the fenders loose from their snare of ice. A split second after the car was righted, Eddie Hawk went scrambling up on its hood to have a peer inside.

"You tell the rest, Eddie," Mama said.

"Naw," Eddie said, "you go on, Betty, you're doing good."

"You have to tell it," Mama said. "I couldn't look."

"It's funny," Eddie said then, fiddling with his baseball cap. "I can hardly remember a thing. It's like I wasn't there."

"You were there," Mama said.

"I felt insane," he said. Tears pooled in his eyes. "Thank God it wasn't like I first thought." He reached out a hand and patted Shilda's arm.

The dead girl's neck was broken. Other than that there wasn't a scratch on her. There weren't any clothes on her either. Mama and Joe and Eddie didn't mention that detail, but we heard it later at school from everybody who'd been there. Orst and Hogarth were naked, too, except for their boots and the heavy metal crosses they wore around their necks. Nobody found any clothes in the car, only piles of Roma Rocket wine bottles. Another detail Mama and Joe and Eddie didn't mention over their hot chocolate.

Orst and Hogarth had bloody noses. Orst's head was bashed in and Hogarth's back was broken. There was a bone from his rib cage, too, poking through his skin. But wouldn't you know it—they were both alive!

"One of them opened his eyes for a second," Joe told

us. "Whoever it is that smokes Lucky Strikes. There was the butt of one clenched between his teeth when they pried his jaw loose from under the steering wheel."

"Hogarth," Shilda said, swiping at a tear, the first since she'd heard about the accident. She must have sensed that we were all looking at her, not knowing what to say, not knowing how to comfort. She rubbed her eyes briskly and sat up in her chair real straight and said, "They weren't nothing to me but trouble."

"It's not like they're dead, Shilda," I said. "Maybe they'll make it."

"Who in this whole room cares?" said Shilda in this brittle, breaking voice. "Who cares if they die? They did it to themselves. They did it to *her*."

Then she started crying so hard that I was afraid she'd get hysterical and begin spilling her own beans about the miscarriage. I put my arms around her and whispered in her ear, "You'll make yourself sick again, Shil."

"The awful thing is that nobody even knows who she is!" Shilda cried, slamming her fist on the table. "Just this dead wild weed of a girl that nobody's ever seen." She glared at me without seeming to see. "Do you think she's really me? Isn't it possible that I went riding with them and got killed and that what's happening right here and now is only in your imagination? You wish me to be alive and so I am."

"Stop it," I said, hysterical myself.

"Shilda!" Eddie said sharply.

"It should have been me," she cried. "It should've been."

That year was the gloomiest Christmas I ever hope to have. For one thing, the snow made getting out to Christmas shop next to impossible. A hard freeze came along just when the streets had turned slushy so that every place you tried to walk was covered in rumply hard ice. The weather seemed to provide for a natural kind of recklessness.

I ended up doing most of my shopping at the Cash and
Carry grocery store because it was close to Piney View.
It was depressing, shopping in a grocery store for Christmas presents, let me tell you. I was stuck giving Mama
and Joe a lot of *cold* gifts, like port wine cheese in little
mugs you could use afterwards. I managed to find some
suede gloves for Joe on the Housewares aisle and a
lipstick and powder I thought Mama would enjoy on
Beauty Aids. I was tempted to get Bynum a lint brush—
they sold them—but instead I bought him a bunch of
Mad magazines. I bought Shilda a romance novel in
paperback called *Scarlet Permission*. That was the heroine's name. On the cover there was a flamboyant-looking
woman who looked like she was getting raped on horse-
back and loving every minute. The man riding behind
her looked like "Oscar Wilde" sporting a mustache.

Only one good thing happened between the time of
the LaMarrs' wreck and Christmas Eve: I ran into Bobby
Rex Moseley in the Cash and Carry.

I think he was Christmas shopping, too. He came up
beside me as I was twirling the magazine rack and stood
there watching my rejects.

"Where are the funny books?" he asked me.

"I think they sold out of comics," I said. "All this
snow. Everybody's been so bored lately."

"Except for the wreck," he said.

"Except for the wreck," I said and shuddered.

It's funny how we acted familiar even though we'd
never been introduced. It would have felt awkward now
to exchange names in any sort of formal way. He knew
I went steady with Bynum and I knew he went steady
with Phoebe, and since they were brother and sister,
well, it made us almost kin in some peculiar way.

He smelled good. I was that close to him for the first
time in my life. He smelled limey, and there was this
rich wool and leather smell rising off his clothes. I could
have buried my face in his sweater and known he was

handsome even if I were blindfolded; just breathing his
air was enough. I kept my head down and leafed through
a few more books. I couldn't look at him directly. God,
I hate shyness. It can make you downright feeble-minded.
I was burning up with wanting to look at him straight on,
but inside I was daring myself, and once a thing becomes a dare that you are doing to yourself it becomes
the riskiest and most forbidden thing on earth. There
was truly a weight to my eyes and I couldn't lift them.
If my life had depended on it, I couldn't have.

"Any good books here?" he asked.

"I don't know," I said. "I have a good friend who
likes romance books." God, it came out *all* wrong. It
was as if the word "romance" were some great big
neon hint.

"A girl or a guy?" he asked.

"Huh? Oh, a girl."

"When it comes to reading," he said, "people know
what they like and what they don't like. Same as music," he said. "My daddy only reads detective books.
My mom, recipes. My brother's the one who goes for
comics. He's only ten." He laughed fondly. "What do
you like to read?"

"Me?" I couldn't think straight. All I could think of
were the books we read at school. "I like love poetry,"
I said. "I like *Sonnets from the Portuguese* by Elizabeth
Barrett Browning." Even as I was saying it, I winced.
Was it possible that your mind could go suddenly out of
control and make you start flirting without your even
trying? Lord, I couldn't say anything cool. *Love* poetry.
Hint hint hint.

"I like *Romeo and Juliet*," Bobby Rex said, and I
practically choked.

"They banned it this year," I said. "Too racy."

"That's too bad," he said. "It's great. It makes you
feel lucky no matter what's wrong with your life. Nobody has it as bad as they had it."

"I guess not," I said. "I haven't read it."

"You ought to," he said. "If you like love poetry, you'd like it. See you," he said. "Maybe we can double-date some time."

"Good-bye, Bobby Rex," I said. I can't describe how sweet it felt to say his name out loud. It felt like I held a rose in my mouth and was dancing. After he'd left, I wasn't sure our meeting had happened. I have this powerful imagination.

I thought of our conversation the whole Christmas holiday. I read meanings into it that you'd never believe. It got me through.

Shilda was so down in the dumps that Eddie called up his mother in Newark and she insisted that they come visit. She even sent them extra money for a Pullman. On Christmas Eve afternoon at the Kernersville depot, Mama and Joe Parker and I saw them off. Before the train left, Shilda took me aside. She'd written her grandmother's phone number on a slip of paper and told me I was to call if one of the LaMarrs should die. She expected me to call the hospital every day and check on them.

"Okay," I promised her. What else could I do?

"Well, how would you be feeling if this had happened to Bynum?"

"Nobody deserves to die young," I told her.

Tears filled her eyes. "My poor little dead baby," she said. "It never even had a chance."

"Maybe it was just smarter than everybody else," I said. "Maybe it knew better."

She stared at me, her face all caved in with hurt. "That doesn't sound like you, Pally."

"Well, I don't feel much like me anymore," I said. It was true. I didn't. "Maybe I'll never be me again. Maybe that's *good*. Maybe if you don't keep adjusting to all the changes around you by changing yourself, you go crazy. I sure don't want to go crazy."

As I watched her train pull out, I wished I was on it. I

wished I was on it surrounded by strangers. I thought
how easy it would be to change yourself around people
who'd never known you. To be wilder, harder, risk
anything and everything if you wanted. And it occurred
to me that people like Gloria Hawk finally picked up and
went because nobody would let them change. Maybe
leaving what was close and familiar always had less to
do with questing after love and adventure than seeking
breathing space. You mess up other people's worlds if
you change. Whether you like it or not, you are always
other people's security. But how many of them really
care about what you do to yourself when you change?
It's how what you do will affect *them* that matters most.

Mama said: "Well, now, I'm depressed. Shilda acts
like a lost cause."

"Whoa now," Joe Parker said. "Nobody's a lost
cause."

"I wish the three of us could just ride down to Florida
and lie in the sun," Mama said.

"And miss Christmas?" Joe cried. "Not a chance!"

"Eat a bunch of fish, hunt sand dollars, turn up the
radio, and go to sleep on the beach," Mama said wistfully.

"Tell you what," Joe said, linking arms with both of
us. "Let's hurry on home and make us a big bowl of
snow ice cream."

"Yuck!" Mama and I said at the same time.

"You girls are testing me," he said, "but okay." His
brow wrinkled thoughtfully under his coonskin cap. Only
Joe Parker could wear a coonskin cap and get away with
it. "Let's get along now and cook up a giant pot of
popcorn, then spike us some eggnog with the Jack Daniel's you've got wrapped up and hid for me, Betty—"

"What's that?" she said, pretending.

"I'm a wise old fox," he said. "You can't pull no
wool."

And sometimes you knew, plain as day without any
words or thinking, that you could never give it up, your

ordinary and samey little life. Somebody like Joe Parker
would always be popping up to make you snap to.

☆ ♡ ☆

I think what got to me most that Christmas was
thinking about the dead girl. Who was she? How had
she come to pal around on a dangerously snowy night
with the LaMarr boys? Where did she live, and was
anybody trying to find her?

The day after the wreck, the Kernersville newspaper
reported the accident as headline news. There were enormous pictures of all the victims splashed across the front
page. Davey Cole had found the girl's pocketbook and,
according to the newspaper, recovered only "a comb, a
pair of sunglasses, a yo-yo, some bubble gum wrappers,
and a billfold." Inside the billfold was a picture of the
dead girl and a picture of a baby. There was also about
forty dollars. The paper said that the girl's body had
been sent down to Chapel Hill to the State Medical
Examiner's office for autopsy. I shivered when I read
that part.

She looked so ordinary, the dead girl. There was
nothing glamorous or wild-looking about her at all. She
had a plain, sweet, country kind of face, a pug nose and
freckles. She had a wide-eyed honest look about her.
She wore her hair pulled back with barrettes, little-girl
fashion. Underneath the photo was written: DO YOU REC-
OGNIZE THIS GIRL? SEND INFORMATION AND INQUIRIES TO
SHERIFF'S DEPARTMENT, GUILFORD COUNTY. Papers all over
the state ran the same picture and notice, but nobody
could find out who she was. I heard that the FBI got
into it. The only information the LaMarr boys ever gave
before slipping into comas was that they'd picked her up
at the Greensboro bus depot and she'd told them her
name was Susie. Davey Cole told somebody that over at

the morgue in Greensboro, they'd referred to her as "Wake up, little Susie" after the Everly Brothers' hit.

Over and over in my mind I went through the contents of her purse. I've always thought women would be easier to trace than men because of their purses. "Nothing gives away a woman's character like the contents of her pocketbook," Mrs. Futrell was fond of saying. "Her whole personality, her *morals,* are spelled right out by what's inside that little flap of fabric suspended by a handle." Yet it didn't seem to me, thinking about a comb and a couple of photographs and some sunglasses, that Susie had left many clues about herself. Still, I wondered how closely policemen looked at things. I wondered if they knew how to read between the lines. For example it occurred to me that although a yo-yo seemed unremarkable in itself, something quite ordinary for a young girl to carry in her purse, it might have indicated that Susie was much younger than at first believed. A thirteen-year-old might be more prone to fancy a yo-yo than, say, an eighteen-year-old. Then there was the matter of the bubble gum wrappers. What if Davey Cole had only glanced at them, had considered them purely trash, when they weren't wrappers at all but the fortunes that come inside the wrappers. Lots of people saved bubble gum fortunes, Eddie Hawk for one. Those wrappers could have been special fortunes that the girl was saving like souvenirs. Nancy Drew could have figured out what the girl's hobbies were, her likes, dislikes, superstitions, maybe even her hometown, just by reading a collection of saved bubble gum fortunes. It's always the little things that give folks away, but most men are too busy thinking big to notice. Look at Bobby Rex Moseley. There I'd been, carrying on a perfectly normal conversation with him at the Cash and Carry book rack. But the entire time I'd never met his gaze. Couldn't he tell something *extra* was going on? All along he was thinking that we were just talking. All

along he'd noted the surface and let it pull him along as
if he were a buoy on the crest of a wave. If he'd looked
below the surface just once, he'd have seen me gasping.
He'd have seen that I was drowning a whole lot more
than I was talking.

On Christmas Eve we made popcorn, like Joe had
suggested, and we spiked the eggnog with Jack Daniel's. We trimmed the tree and sang a few carols and
Mama and Joe turned up the radio and danced to Christmas songs. But none of us could really put the world's
misery out of our hearts.

"What's Shilda's grandmother like?" I asked.

"She's real nice," Mama said. "She's Eddie's mama,
isn't she?"

"Shilda says she's a lady wrestler," I said.

"Oh, I don't think she wrestles herself," Mama said.
"I think she owns a gym where lady wrestlers work
out."

"It all seems so strange," I said.

"What does?"

"Everything. Just the way life happens. Shilda and I
used to talk about going up north to visit her grandmother on a lark. Now she's gone for different reasons
than we ever dreamed. And here I am, same as usual.
Why is it I always stay so safe?"

"As I recall, you got yourself a dangerous new hairdo
recently," Joe said.

For a long time that night I just lay in my bed, no
radio or light, and thought hard about the dead girl. It
was sort of like having a memorial service for her in my
head. I kept thinking: this time last week she was alive.
Maybe she'd gone Christmas shopping. Maybe she'd
been wrapping presents. This time last week maybe she
was lying on her own bed in her own home, someplace
safe, listening to the radio and snapping her fingers. It
wasn't such a weird thing, what Shilda had said about
maybe being a zombie, thinking she was the dead girl

coming back to haunt us. In a way, lying there in the sort of darkness that feels sad and shapeless and ongoing, I felt I might be the dead girl, too. Her death made me feel contaminated and doomed. I'd ridden with the LaMarrs once. I'd known all along what was coming.

My door cracked open letting in a warm slice of living room light. The air of my tomb smelled suddenly, gaily, of popcorn.

"Honey?" Mama said. "Are you awake?"

"Sort of."

"Want to talk?"

"No, I'm all right," I said. "Merry Christmas."

"Merry Christmas," Mama said. She hesitated, then closed the door.

I heard the television flick on and I lay there and listened to them watching *Miracle on 34th Street*. I could cry just listening to it. Finally I heard them say good night, sort of loud, just in case I was awake so I'd think they were sleeping apart. Then Mama went into her room and Joe made this elaborate rustling sound with his sofa covers. I gave him about ten minutes and, sure enough, I heard him creeping down the hall to Mama's bed. I heard Mama's muffled throaty laughter and him saying shush, and I envied their being together, warm and close and thinking it was such a big secret.

I couldn't go to sleep. I kept thinking of Shilda and the dead baby. I kept thinking of Mrs. Oxendine's death-in-life face. I thought of Gloria's love for Eddie dying. I thought of Speedy and what it must have been like for Mama to lose him. I tried not to think of the dead girl, but her face frowned at me from the shadows. "Okay," the face said. "So I took a chance and lost. It was still a chance. I had a ball." I couldn't believe I could think this way. It seemed blasphemous, thinking of a mouth that was dead, jabbering so glibly. "How are *you* going to die?" the dead glib mouth said. "Are you just going to be sitting in your porch swing some day and fall out and land wrong? Or are you going to wait until you're ninety-nine years old, in a nursing home, and choke to death on your own birthday cake?''

I rolled over and put my pillow over my head. "*Angel*food cake,'' the voice said.

Why did the dead girl's voice sound so much like Shilda's? Any second I expected it to start sounding like my own. I jumped up and dressed, crazy with excitement. Quietly I slipped out the back door of the trailer and into the glittering night. The moon hung above the pine trees, full and bone-colored. But the snow is what lit up the night. It was as bright as beach sand, so luminous that you couldn't see the stars. The air was so sharp with cold that it felt like I was breathing needles. I tied my scarf over my nose and mouth like a bandit; I could breathe without hurting then.

I walked down to Narrow Gauge and started heading up the road in the opposite direction of town. I walked as fast as I could in the crusted-over snow, not thinking about where I was headed. I imagined myself as a knife of some kind. On either side of the path I cut, the darkness fell crackling. I didn't think about anything, only walking, only moving forward through the night. The only sounds I heard were the rapid crunching of my boots and the steely wind gusting across snow-covered fields—a sound like brushed cymbals. I passed the bridge where the wreck had happened, but that wasn't where I wanted to be or why I'd walked so far. I didn't stop. I didn't think two seconds about that wreck. What's done is done, the dead girl's voice seemed to whisper from the black tangle of trees along Sawyer's Creek. What's done is done, what's gone is gone. My heart kept pace with the beat of my boots.

I climbed the hill above the creek and kept going, past the turnoff to Bynum's farm, past the road to Woody's and the junction of Narrow Gauge and Highway 21. Way ahead I could just make out the lights of the last farm before you cross the county line and enter Forsyth County from Guilford. The last farm. I wasn't even out of breath. My legs just pumped away, my forehead perspired. But it seemed like the farther I went, the more energy I had. I could have walked all the way to the moon that night and back if there had been a highway.

I turned into the driveway marked by whitewashed wagon wheels. There was the mailbox, and for no particular reason I pulled the flag up as I passed. I didn't try to act secretive. Anybody might have seen me, except that it was two o'clock in the morning of Christmas Day.

The dogs heard me and they started barking, hollowy howling barks like wolves. The air had been so quiet all around me that when the dogs set to barking it seemed to peel back. I almost expected daylight, the air felt so startled by sound. But it was the barking that made me stop, finally, and realize where I was, realize that I'd walked three miles in the dark on a snowy Christmas Eve all the way to Bobby Rex Moseley's farm just to see the lights shining out the windows where he lived and ate and sang. Just to see if it would thrill me to be so close to him yet hidden by the darkness, and it did.

I stood beside a toolshed, slinky as a thief. "Bobby Rex Moseley," I whispered. "Bobby Rex Moseley, Merry Christmas." Then I stooped down and wrote it out in the snow. One light was on inside the house, a back room light. It was honey-colored, pouring into the darkness, onto the snow. I couldn't stop myself. I ran and stood in a patch of it, and when I did, I glanced up and saw him. He was sitting in front of the window, staring. It was as if he were waiting for me, but he didn't make a sign of recognition. His guitar was in his hands but he wasn't singing. The instant I saw him, I ducked into the shadows and started running. I ran until my heart felt as if it were burning a hole through my chest.

He couldn't have known you, I told myself, over and

over. He couldn't have guessed who you were in the dark with a hat on and a scarf tied over your face to keep warm. And if he did guess, how could he prove it? How could he bring himself to ask you such a crazy thing? But if he asked and you told, I wondered, what would it matter? You begin to think like that after a death-defying act.

IX

☆♡☆　　☆♡☆　　☆♡☆

The big news going around school when we went back after New Year's was that Bobby Rex Moseley and Phoebe Jenkins were preengaged. Phoebe had his class ring. Just as soon as he saved up the money, he was planning to buy her a diamond. Everywhere you went you'd see her with her hand stretched out and a gaggle of little girls hovering around the ring like Girl Scouts warming themselves at a bonfire.

"It just goes to show you that Bobby Rex Moseley is as human as the next guy," Shilda told me. She'd come back from New Jersey looking healed and full of zip. "People treat that boy like he's a statue."

We were in the girls' bathroom skipping gym class and blowing a weed between us. "He's just an old regular boy, that's all," Shilda said. "He's got warts and moles same as everybody else if you look real close. And he's got horns."

"Do you think they've done it?" I asked.

"Why else would he mess with her?"

"But Phoebe acts like such a prude," I said.

"Phoo!" said Shilda. "It's a disguise. I dreamed I was

horny in my Maidenform bra. Sweet little breathy-talking
things are always the truest hellions."

"*You're* the truest hellion," I said, "so what's your
disguise?"

"I couldn't disguise it if I tried," she said.

She tossed the cigarette butt in the john and we put on
fresh lipstick and slunk back into the gym just in time
for our showers.

The other big news was, of course, about the LaMarrs.
It looked like they were going to live. For a while
doctors thought they both had severe and permanent
brain damage, but one by one they popped out of their
comas. Eddie drove Shilda over to visit them on Sundays and she'd come back telling how Orst was already
spouting off dirty jokes. Sometimes he'd get halfway
through a joke and forget the punch line though. The
bad news was that Orst was still paralyzed from the
waist down and that Hogarth couldn't feel a thing below
his chin.

I hadn't really thought of the LaMarr brothers as
human until I heard they were paralyzed. I guess I
thought only difficulty could bring out a person's hu-
manness and they'd never seemed to have any. Suddenly they were slowed—and not just slowed but *halted*.
It had been their speed, their gruff assumption that everybody wanted to go with them when they wanted and as
fast as they wanted that had made them dangerous. Now
like most everybody else in Orfax they seemed gathered
in. Nothing very prickly about them anymore, and in a
funny way that seemed just as scary.

The snow finally melted, but a couple more long hard
freezes dragged it out. It was a close-in winter for sure.
But somehow I was ready for it; for a change I was
willing to try and learn practical stuff. For instance
Mama taught me how to make a pie crust from scratch;
it's one of the most satisfying things I ever learned. The
drab, frigid weather made a perfect climate for reading.

During that winter of 1959 I must have read *Romeo and Juliet* about a million times before the first jonquils appeared in March.

Beyond that, nothing much was happening. Maybe nothing was happening because it seemed that everything that could *had*. Joe and Mama had finally set a wedding date for late June. Joe hoped the house he was building us would be finished by then and the calving mostly over. He could afford to take a honeymoon then, although whenever he and Mama spoke of going off they called it a "vacation" and included me.

"Oh, I don't want to go," I assured them.

"You don't want to see Niagara Falls?" Joe asked, incredulous. "Ride in one of those Maid-in-the-Mist boats right under the waterfall?"

"I'm too young to die," I said.

"It'll be great fun, punkin," Mama said. "We'll have a ball."

"Thanks, but I'd feel funny."

"Don't be ridiculous," Mama said.

"How would you all feel if Bynum and I got married and asked you to come with us on our honeymoon like some sort of double date?"

Mama and Joe looked at each other and smiled. They were on this close-knit lovers' wavelength that they thought I'd never pick up on. But I could tell what they were after: leaving me behind without feeling guilty. I was trying to make it as easy for them as I could, being so difficult.

"I didn't know you and Bynum were still a thing," Joe said then.

"We're a thing, I guess, whatever that is," I said.

"So, what did old Romeo give you for Christmas this year?" Joe teased.

"Son of lint brush," I said, but Joe didn't get my meaning, so I said, "Nail scissors. Actually, a whole manicure set. I really lucked out, eh?"

Every now and then we still went out, out of habit. I
didn't even object when he tooled the Studebaker down
to Sawyer's Creek for a little making out. I expect it's
one of the reasons he hung on to me. He never changed
the routine, though. First a little kissing, his tongue like
a shovel in my mouth. Then he'd unsnap my bra and
start squeezing my breasts. He squeezed with a kind of
farm boy's detachment in milking a cow. First one breast,
then the other in a listless rhythm like it was *work*.
Finally, when he was ready, we'd roll into the backseat
and he'd climb on top of me, grinding himself against my
hipbones until he was relieved. He'd taken to chewing a
plug of tobacco when he was finished.

I don't have an excuse. I suppose I went with him
because you never knew when it might suddenly get
better. Maybe I went because once in a while I could
transform him with my imagination into someone else.
But I got no pleasure. Making out with Bynum felt like it
feels, say, to rub an elbow for a long, long time. You
start out feeling very little and end up feeling a whole lot
less. Every now and then, a mean streak would make
me take his hand and guide it toward my panties. He'd
moan and wrench away like I was a real temptress but,
God willing, he would withstand me. Then one night he
confessed that he'd almost lost control.

"How do you mean?" I said. Pat Boone was on the
radio and Bynum was finished. I was smoking an Oasis
and he'd just bitten off a plug of Red Man.

"I almost unzipped it," Bynum said.

"*It?*"

He looked at me as if I were the cruelest person in the
world. "You know what I mean, Pally."

"What would you have done with it if you'd unzipped
it?" I said mockingly.

"God, Pally," Bynum said, "you can make really
holy things start to sound dirty. You and Shilda Hawk."

"Is it a holey thing?" I laughed. "Maybe you ought to see a doctor if it's holey."

He glared at me. "You've really changed, Pally," he said sadly.

I patted his knee. "Mind if I switch the station?"

"I like Pat Boone," he said.

"I read where Pat Boone eats desserts first," I told him. "He was eating lunch at the Twenty-One Club in New York City, and he told the interviewer that he always ate desserts first. He ordered a banana split with his dinner and he ate it while his dinner cooled. Know why?"

"Why?" Bynum sighed.

"He said he wanted to eat the banana split while he was still hungry. Hell, why did he even bother to order a dinner then?"

Bynum regarded me carefully. "Well, I think it's darn cool."

"I thought you'd like that story," I said.

"Pat Boone is a musical genius," Bynum said, "and in person he's also a really nice guy."

"How do you know he's a really nice guy? You a personal friend?"

"You can just tell to look at him."

"He's a puritan," I sneered. "His teeth are just so neat and round."

"So?"

"He's missing out, that's what. Somebody needs to bust him in the mouth just once," I said.

Bynum looked at me sadly. "Pally, you're about the strangest-acting girl I've ever known." His voice sounded full of pity.

"Just how many other girls have you ever really known?" I said. "Huh? How many, Bynum?" But I hated it when my voice became shriller and more whiny than his.

"Look," he said calmly. "I've got a sister. I know girls."

"Phoebe?" I cried. "What's so damn special about Phoebe?"

"What's it to you?" Bynum said.

I took a deep breath and tried to take charge of myself. "I'm a maniac tonight," I told him. "I just can't figure myself out. Forget it, Bynum. I'm sorry."

"Phoebe likes you," he said softly.

"She thinks I'm a slut. She tried to break us up, Bynum, admit it."

"She just never understood why you went off with the LaMarrs. But she does like you. She wants us to double-date with her and Bobby Rex sometime."

"She does?" My heart was racing. "With her and Bobby Rex?"

"Sure."

"When?"

"I don't know when," he said. "Maybe we should all go to the prom together."

"The prom?" It was months away. It seemed whole countries away, maybe even solar systems. Saturn, Jupiter, Pluto, Prom. It sounded like another planet.

"I thought you wanted to break up, sort of," I told him.

"Heck, no, Pally, unless you want to," he said. "I know I haven't been at my best with you lately. I'll try a whole bunch harder." He put one lanky arm around my shoulder, allowing his hand to flop familiarly on my breast. I swear he didn't fondle the breast, he *chucked* it. "We're good together, Pally, don't you think?"

It sounded like a slick line off some buttery smooth Pat Boone record. But I forgave him on the spot. Wasn't he providing me with a legitimate means to get to know Bobby Rex Moseley better? I didn't have to throw myself at anybody, just go along. Why hadn't I cultivated the possibility sooner? Why hadn't I learned by sixteen to be devious?

"Do you know what Pat Boone says in his book, *Twixt Twelve and Twenty*?" Bynum said.

" 'A banana split a day keeps the doctor away'? No, what *does* he say?"

He looked crestfallen.

"Okay, what did old Pat say?" I lit another Oasis and tried to look agreeable.

" 'It's a wise guy and gal who are willing to let there be some spaces in their togetherness.' " He smiled knowingly at me. And with all my might I smiled back.

☆ ♡ ☆

So, just when it seemed that everything was back to Dullsville with *maybe* a planet, if not a star, rising above the flatlands, Eddie Hawk started acting strange. This was in early, early April.

"I think he's having a nervous breakdown," Shilda confided to me one morning at school. "It's all over some whore who works at the Zanzibar fair."

I gawked at her. "What? Eddie? Come on, Shilda!"

"I swear," she said. "Eddie G. as in goody-goody Hawk. Maybe I've finally rubbed off on him."

"I'm sure she isn't a whore," I said. "It was just your imagination."

"Guess what her name is? It's Kandy Kane."

I cracked a smile then and she said, "It ain't one bit funny, Pally Thompson."

"It's a funny name," I said.

"Yeah, and you'd be splitting your sides if your mama was tangled up with some stud horse Ferris wheel operator named Dick Delicious or something."

"Okay," I said, stifling my laugh, "it's not funny. Sorry."

"Would you skip class with me, Pal?" Shilda said. "I don't feel so hot. I've really got to talk to you."

I had an algebra test first period but I said okay.

"Got any weeds?"

I offered her my last Oasis.

"I can't smoke this shit," she said, but she lit it anyway, and I followed her into the girls' bathroom. The tardy bell had already rung and we were alone. A faucet dripped steadily. There was something spooky about those old school bathrooms: the smell of rusty johnny water and green goo soap and soggy brown paper towels that littered the cracked tile floors. And always there was the nervous, darting smell of a secretive cigarette.

"So what should I do?" Shilda asked me.

"Why are you asking me?"

Shilda French-inhaled her cigarette. "She does this dancing act." Then she rolled her eyes, I guess because my face looked so blank. "She's one of those hoochie-koochie girls at the Zanzibar fair."

Bit by bit she told me the whole story, what she knew of it. Eddie had been acting weird for a couple of weeks, maybe longer. Jumpy. In the evenings he fixed dinner but he wouldn't eat a bite. Every car that drove by stirred him out of his chair and to the window. When the telephone rang, he stumbled all over himself to answer it before Shilda did. He stopped shaving for days at a time. On the way home from his truck deliveries, he'd peel off at Gizmo's to have a couple of drinks. He'd all but quit drinking for years, didn't keep a drop of liquor in the house, but lately Shilda could smell it on his breath when he came home. His eyes had a roaming look, Shilda claimed, detached and restless. It was as if he'd found out he had an incurable disease and was trying to live normally except that the secret itself was poisonous and seeping out of him. That was it: he had this poisoned look. Then, she said, out of the blue he wants to take her to the Zanzibar fair. It's a school night, too. Cold for April and pounding down rain. But she went along. She liked fairs, even dirty little fairs like the one in Zanzibar.. It was a true country fair with sawdust up to your ankles and grimy tents just bursting with freak shows and cheats and pickpockets, geeks, and whores. Everybody said that the fair people paid off the sheriff's people and that's why the gambling wasn't ever raided and the striptease shows so wild.

When Shilda and Eddie arrived at the fair, none of the rides were running. It was raining solid sheets of water, thundering and lightning, too. They parked the mattress truck in a big empty field beside the fair grounds and sat there awhile, listening to the radio. Patti Page was singing "The Tennessee Waltz" and Eddie moved his lips silently along with the words.

"I think the fair's closed tonight," Shilda said finally.

"Looks like it," Eddie said. "Let me go get us some hot dogs though. You sit here."

She didn't want to sit there in the mattress truck by herself while he went to get hot dogs. He'd been acting so quirky lately that she was even afraid he might forget he'd brought her along. She could picture him wandering around the fair grounds in the rain, eating soggy hot dogs, or not eating them, maybe just carrying them.

"Let's go home, Eddie," she said, "I've got a ton of homework."

"You sit," he said. "I'll be right back. I've come to see somebody." It was a snapping voice he used, quick and whiplike. It almost made her jump back.

He was gone a long, long time. Every now and then lightning would blaze over the fairgrounds and she'd try to pick him out from among the dark huddle of tents and trailers. She worried he'd been conked over the head and robbed. It was such a crazy place to be on a stormy Wednesday night.

Finally he came back, just kind of materialized out of thin air, opened the truck door and slid behind the wheel. He didn't have any hot dogs. He wasn't even wearing his raincoat. He looked drowned, and he was shivering.

"Where's your coat?" Shilda asked.

He looked at her, then down at himself. He smiled a creepy little smile. "Did I bring a coat?"

"You had your slicker," Shilda told him.

"Well, I reckon I lost it," Eddie said and snickered. Then he started the truck. His teeth were chattering.

"What's going on, Eddie?" Shilda said. "What's happening?"

"Nothing," he said casually. "Just some private business that doesn't concern your pretty head one bit. Now, let's go get us some supper. I'm starved." He almost seemed bucked up.

"Turn on the heater, Eddie," Shilda said. "You're freezing to death."

"I'm okay." He grinned at her. He fumbled with the radio dials until he found "Thunder Road" and he turned it up full blast.

"Well," Shilda said to me. "I felt about as safe as I used to feel squealing around the backroads in the Sardine. I swear, the speedometer hit eighty and that old mattress truck was just a-rocking and a-reeling. Finally he screeched into Gizmo's parking lot. He was in and out in a flash and brought us each a cheeseburger and a beer."

"Eddie brought *you* a beer?"

"Hell," she said, "it's the least strange thing he's done in weeks. But you ain't heard nothing yet."

They'd gone back to their house on Proximity Street, and Shilda got ready for bed while Eddie turned on the TV and watched "Name That Tune." Shilda wrote the paper she had due on *Lord of the Flies*, which was hard to write because the book jacket didn't tell you that much about the book. By the time she finished, Douglas Edwards was doing the eleven o'clock news report.

"Good night," she called to Eddie, who was half-asleep, sprawled on the sofa and still wearing his wet clothes. He'd rummaged in her purse and found a fresh pack of cigarettes, half of which he'd already smoked. He looked *collapsed,* was how she put it. He'd tried so hard all these years. She'd felt this saddening mix of love and pity for him until it made her insides feel weepy and she had to turn away. She wanted to tell him something sweet and kind and hopeful. She felt it but she couldn't say it. Mush. It was one thing she'd never learned, never been good at. Maybe you needed a mother to teach you the recipe. She stood in front of the sofa agonizing over what she might say that could brighten him. His face looked as vacant as a winter field. A broad sadness dimmed him; it seemed a sadness of wanting without needing. If he wanted her to be there, he didn't really need her. She was so much trouble. And so finally she said: "Maybe, Eddie, maybe it would have worked better if I'd been a boy."

He raised his eyes slowly to look at her.

"Maybe not *better,*" she'd added, "but easier."

He sat up and fished his baseball cap out from under him. He'd squashed it flat. "Oh, I don't know, honey," he'd said, "we're all right."

"Sometimes," she'd said. "And sometimes not."

"People always say that trying's the hard part and giving up's easy," Eddie said then, groaning as he lifted himself off the cushions. "I don't believe it," he said flatly. "Trying's easy because it's all we know." He put the soggy baseball cap on his head. "I got to do the dishes before I go."

"There aren't any dishes, Eddie," Shilda reminded him. "We ate out. We got cheeseburgers at Gizmo's, remember?"

"Good," he said. "No dishes, then. I'll get a move-on, it's past eleven and I'm going to be late."

"Late for what?" Shilda asked him, truly spooked then.

"I've got an appointment."

"An appointment? What *kind* of an appointment?"

"It's real personal, honey, let it lay."

"But you're going out so late!"

"Hey there." He'd patted her on the head. "Since when did you worry about late?"

He came home around three in the morning. He got out of his truck whistling quietly, tiptoed into the house, and undressed in the dark so as not to wake her. He was up at six and fixed bacon and pancakes for both of them. He'd shaved for the first time in days. He was wearing a clean blue work shirt and his eyes almost sparkled.

"Well then," I told Shilda. "All the signs point to the fact that he's having an affair. She loves him, she loves him not, that sort of thing. First he's up, then he's down. It's just like Liz treated Eddie Fisher. First he was with Debbie, then he wasn't, then he was with Liz, then back with poor sad Debbie. It probably made him into a nervous wreck."

"Of course it's another woman," Shilda said. "You act like I'm a blockhead, Pally. The big question, of course, is *who*? Is it the whore named Kandy Kane? Or"—and she raised her eyebrows dramatically—"could it be Omega Oxendine?"

"What in the hell are you talking about?"

"Well, you don't think Shilda Hawk would lie around sleeping while her daddy was out getting into big trouble, do you? Hell, I *followed* him, Pally. That's where he went that night for his appointment. He went to Omega Oxendine's cabin, parked the truck at the edge of those fields near the highway and walked to her place through the woods like he didn't want to be seen."

"How did you ever find him?"

"Oh, I rode with him in the mattress truck, only he didn't see me. I hid under a Serta."

"Good Lord," I said, "how on earth could he be attracted to Omega Oxendine?"

Shilda cringed herself. "Maybe he's just using her," she said.

"Yeah," I said, "maybe love has nothing to do with it."

"Whoever said it did?" said Shilda. "You've got to put romance out of your thoughts completely or you'll never wise up."

The bell rang and the clatter of classes changing sounded all around us. Here came Mopsy Brownlee sashaying into the bathroom to comb her hair. She wore a poppy red cardigan sweater clipped at her shoulders with two little silver poodles on a sweater chain. She wore red fingernail polish that matched her sweater exactly. She had on new brown-and-white saddle oxfords that looked as perky as two freshly shelled black-eyed peas. God, she was neat and clean and hopeful. Her gingerbread cologne hung in the air around us until I could hardly breathe. As she brushed her blond, naturally curly gush of a ponytail, I watched that pert little chip of a diamond flicker on her right hand. That diamond seemed as distinct and remote from me and what I knew about love and life as some distant satellite beaming back messages. A college boy had given it to her, a fraternity pal of her older brother's. She was always going off on college weekends down to the university in Chapel Hill.

Mrs. Brownlee, Mopsy's mother, was all for this engagement; the boyfriend had some sort of scholarship and his father was a professor. I supposed some day Mopsy Brownlee would leave Orfax. She'd marry the prince from Chapel Hill and he'd probably enroll in medical school and she'd get her teacher's certificate and teach something jolly like kindergarten to support them until he finished his degree.

In my mind I played out this scene where Mopsy had

been married for five or six years and lived in California
or someplace too far away for her mother to keep tabs
on her. She had a bunch of kids close together and
couldn't get rid of her pregnancy weight. Then on top of
that, for amusement and because of the kids, she started
cooking all those wonderful recipes Mrs. Futrell had
taught us: Monkey Business Banana Pudding, Hundred-
Dollar Chocolate Cake, Fudgie-Pudgie Brownies. Finally
Mopsy got so fat that she had to wear muumuus all the
time. She stopped wearing shoes altogether because they
cramped her feet, so she slid around all day in bedroom
slippers. She cut her hair real short because it was the
quickest way she could think of to take off a pound. The
little diamond ring on her finger got absolutely lost in
flesh. But even as I imagined all this, watching her in the
bathroom mirror, I couldn't see Mopsy Brownlee as
anything but privileged and happy for the rest of her life.
In my heart I knew this, that fat or not, her kids would
still love her. So would her husband. Her mother might
disapprove, but that would only cheer her sense of re-
bellion, and she was bound to have one. Wasn't it possible that she might turn out to be *happier* fat? I watched
her briskly washing her hands, and I admired her not so
much for her beauty and luck, but for her focus. Success
would never be an achievement for her, just a good
habit.

I looked at myself in the mirror and then at Shilda.
There was such an *unevenness* about us. Why didn't we
try harder? Maybe if we'd try harder we'd be happier. I
glanced at Mopsy again as she slipped a peppermint
under her tongue. How did she manage to give the
appearance of hardly trying at all? It was an art.

Fayette Weems burst into the bathroom and slammed
her books down on a radiator. God, she was a horse. I
felt better about myself when I saw her. Her loafers
were always scuffed and run over and her dirty blond

hair, always greasy. "Hey, Pally," she said, "can I borry somebody's brush?"

I gave her my comb, what else could I do?

"I hear you and Bynum were down at Sawyer's Creek last weekend," she said, grinning. "You two still a thing?" Her teeth were kind of yellow and pointy like candy corn.

"I guess you could call it that," I said casually. "A *thing*."

Shilda snickered.

"He's a real sugarpie, Bynum is," Fayette said. "You're lucky."

"I am lucky," I said, trying to keep a straight face in front of Shilda.

"Guess you'll be going to the prom."

"He's invited me," I said, "so we'll be there."

Fayette handed me back the comb. It had merely furrowed her dank thin hair. "Phoebe told me she wishes that Bynum would wise up and ask me out. I'm more his type."

"Even Bynum's got better taste than that," Shilda mumbled.

Mopsy Brownlee clicked her tongue at Shilda as she be-bopped out of the bathroom. Even taking sides she did with a breezy cuteness.

"Bynum would ask me," Fayette whispered loudly in my ear, "I know it for a fact, except *I* don't put out."

"I wouldn't brag about it," Shilda said.

"You shut up!" Fayette shouted at Shilda. "You're nothing but a big black hairy hole, everybody knows that!"

Then Shilda jumped her. She seemed as dark and ruthless as a panther. Fayette fell backwards over a waste can and flat on her back, yowling and biting and jerking Shilda's hair by the roots. I tried to get between them, but Shilda backhanded me across the chest. Fayette's nose was spewing blood and she was crying

PR6068 .A94 D3 1990 — Reymond Patrick
Daniel d'Esther

PS3566 .R54 B55 1992 Price, Reynolds
Blue Calhoun

30-3011

PE1704   91-45575 CIP

Grote, David. **British English for American readers: a dictionary of the language, customs, and places of British life and literature.** Greenwood, 1992. 709p bibl afp ISBN 0-313-27851-2, $85.00

This work deserves its full title; it is much more than a dictionary of British English. Grote, an American and author of *Common Knowledge: A Reader's Guide to Literary Allusions* (CH, Apr'88), has collected and explained an impressive array of terms for Americans who read British literature or view British television and film. His goal is to help us grasp what is essentially a foreign culture, despite years of BBC programs and the US's kinship with the UK. A mix of gazetteer, historical guidebook, almanac, and socio/political/cultural dictionary, the work includes places, events, foods, flora and fauna, social and legal practices, organizations, and everyday words. The result is a handy, one-stop dictionary of definitions and connotations of terms that can puzzle: Bank holidays, haha, Giro, tripos, bubble and squeak, pantomime, parish, ITV, OBE, cookers, the Booker, the gentleman, Wormwood Scrubs, Fleet Street, etc. A work that will serve students of British literature, television, and film well and delight Anglophiles in general. Strongly recommended for circulating and reference collection in all academic and public libraries.—*M. H. Loe, SUNY College at Oswego*

©1993 American Library Association

and Shilda was crying, but Shilda kept hitting her hard like a boy hits. You could hear bones popping.

"Big black hole!" Fayette kept screaming. "Big black hole!" And Shilda kept hitting. Her hands were red and furious. She had Fayette's arms pinned and she'd sock her everytime she hollered, no mercy. I couldn't stand it; I just knew Shilda was bound to kill her. Fayette had a fight coming, but something terrible was happening. I leaped out the bathroom door and grabbed this boy and said, "Help! It's a fight."

"Where?" It was Bobby Rex Moseley.

"In there!" I pointed to the bathroom door. "It's Shilda Hawk and Fayette Weems and somebody's going to get killed. I can't stop them!" I said it real fast, all in a breath. I was tugging at his arm. He pulled away from me and started running down the hall. "Where are you going?" I screamed. "Come back!"

"I'm going to get a teacher," he yelled.

It all probably happened in less than a minute, the fight and everything, but it seemed like decades. When Mr. Beavers, the shop teacher, plunged into the girls' room, trailing curious students, Fayette was sitting on Shilda's back and had Shilda's head in the john. Fayette was a two-ton truck of a girl.

This happened on a Thursday, and of course Mr. Curry, our principal, expelled us all for a day. That was the rule if you were caught fighting on school property. Shilda assured him that I'd only been an innocent by-stander, but in a separate interview, Fayette assured him otherwise. I couldn't blame him for giving me the boot, although it meant that I couldn't make up the algebra test I'd missed and would have to take an F.

It wasn't until I'd explained it all to Mama and we'd finished supper and, contritely, I'd helped with the dishes, then puffed the sofa pillows up real nice for her to snuggle against and watch Loretta Young and brought her a dish of ice cream with Hershey's syrup dribbled nice all over the top, t! .t I had time to think deeply about what had happened. I flopped across my bed and thought about it listening to the radio. Maybe it was just the rash of slow, melancholy songs they were playing, but I started feeling sorry for all of us. Even Fayette Weems. I kept thinking about her bloody little candy corn teeth until I was almost in tears.

It remained a shabby little scene in my mind, that fight. All of us such losers while Mopsy Brownlee slipped righteously past us before all hell broke loose and Bobby Rex Moseley acted about as cool as President Eisenhower in a crisis. There I'd been, a raving lunatic, snatching at him for help, breathless with panic. And did he lose *his* head? Did *he* make a single mistake? Lose a second of valuable time? No. In less than a heartbeat, he'd not only gotten help, but the right sort, according to school rules. In a panic situation, you could count on Bobby Rex to make the wisest move. It made me swoon in his direction all the more.

What I hadn't counted on was that a fight between Fayette and Shilda could cause Bynum to break up with me. But it stood to reason that Fayette would tuck her tail between her scabby old legs with their run-down loafers and lumber straight to Phoebe. Who could guess what she said about me. All I know is that in the middle of "The Loretta Young Show," the phone rang and it was Bynum. You could practically hear Phoebe breathing down his neck.

"Pally, this is Bynum."

"Come off it," I said, "you know good and well you're Bobby Rex Moseley, stop clowning around." I don't know why I said that, but I did. About the only kick I got out of Bynum was throwing him off guard. "Look, Bobby Rex," I said. "If you don't quit pestering me, I'll have to break down and tell Phoebe. I'm very fond of Phoebe, you know, and I'd never want to do anything to hurt her—"

"Pally!"

"What?"

"I can't stand this anymore."

"What can't you stand, Bynum? Are you losing control? Are you going to whip it out right now?" I glanced at Mama to see if she'd heard, but she was crying over some love scene and blowing her nose.

"Listen," Bynum said with true fury in his voice. I could tell he was speaking through clenched teeth. It almost made his voice sound sexy. "Listen, you," he snarled. "Pat Boone is right."

"Oh my God."

"I'm not fooling, Pally. I'm talking about the wise gal and guy needing spaces in their togetherness. All this time I've been waiting for you, giving you space."

"Waiting for me?"

"Yes," he said. "I've been waiting for you to wise up, Pally, waiting for you to change back to that girl I first fell in love with in the cafeteria line. You were so sweet back then, a little baby angel." I heard him swallow hard. "I want to marry a virgin, Pally. At the rate we're going—"

"I *am* a virgin!" I cried. This time Mama looked up.

"Who on earth are you talking to? Is it an obscene phone call?"

"Yes!" I cried, and I slammed the phone down.

"What did they say? I thought it was somebody you knew. Honey, *always* hang up right away when you get one of those calls."

The phone rang again.

"Don't answer," Mama said.

"Don't worry," I said.

☆ ♡ ☆

The next morning, since I'd been expelled from school, I slept late. Mama had already gone to the telephone

company when I woke up. The trailer smelled of perco-
lated coffee and cinnamon toast and Lustre-Creme sham-
poo. It felt luxurious to stretch out in bed on a sunny
Friday morning and listen to the radio. It wasn't a holiday and I wasn't sick, which made the time feel all the
more expendable.

When the phone rang I almost didn't answer for fear it
would be Bynum hounding me for his varsity jacket
back. But I couldn't be bothered sorting through the
rubble of our fakey little romance just now. There were
better things to do with my free day. I answered the
phone, intending to slam it right down if he was calling.
There was a phone booth in the lobby at school, and it
would have been just like him to put on a show for
Phoebe and friends. But it was Shilda calling.

"Hey," she said, "don't be sore."

"I'm not," I said. "I needed a vacation."

"You're not mad?"

"I'm mad about having to take an F in algebra. But
there's six more weeks of school. I'll rally."

"That's the spirit," Shilda said. "I'm glad you're not
mad."

"Bynum and I are splitsville," I said. "It's final."

"You sorry?"

"We were going to the prom."

"So?"

"It's no big deal," I said. I could never have convinced her that my hunger to be near Bobby Rex Moseley
was greater and more deserving than any other girl's at
Orfax High. I'd never told her I loved him; it was the
one pure secret that I owned. Keeping it to myself
seemed important. It was proof that I could suffer alone
and endure.

"So what are you going to do today?" Shilda asked. I
could hear her puffing an early morning cigarette. "I've
got an idea and it's really wild, Pally. Let's go to the
Zanzibar fair. We could thumb."

"Thumb?"

"It's easy as pie. If you're a girl you get picked up quick. I need you for moral support, Pal. I want us to go to Zanzibar so that I can talk to Miss Kandy Kane."

"*What?* Now listen, Shilda—"

"Something strange is happening under our very noses and there's an explanation for all of it if we're clever enough to uncover it. You've got to help me, Pally. I'm counting on you."

Shilda was always able to make arm twisting dramatic and exciting. She had a way of pleading that made you feel important, even superior. She reeled you right in on the fishing line your very own ego was feeding you. It was outright manipulation but managed so beseechingly on her part that you felt privileged to have been called on. You felt selected rather than coerced.

Eddie had gone out again the night before and stayed out until dawn. She hadn't followed him, she'd been too sick from the fight. They hadn't argued about her fighting, she and Eddie, but then she hadn't given him many details. He'd almost cried when he saw her: the bruises on her face and knuckles, the swollen lip. He'd treated her as tenderly as a baby, drawn a hot bath for her and sprinkled in Ivory Flakes to make bubbles. He cooked scrambled eggs for supper and made hot tea and brought her a tray of food into the bathroom while she was still soaking. "Listen," he'd said, "would you like me to wash your hair or something, honey?"

She shook her head, eyeing him suspiciously. There was an awkward attentiveness about him that made her uneasy. It was the sort of mannered attentiveness usually offered before some terrible brutality. It had made her think of criminals being treated to steak suppers before their heads were shaved for execution. Orst and Hogarth had an uncle whose head had been shaved for execution. He'd killed a woman in a bar and spent three years on Death Row. The woman had asked for it, according to the LaMarrs. The uncle had gotten a stay of execution because finally the woman's girl friend had stepped forward and said the dead woman had jumped the uncle first. Some girl friend. Anyway, it seemed to Shilda that Eddie was preparing her for a terrible shock. His manner was so laden with, well, there was really no other way to describe it but *motherliness*.

"Are you sure you won't let me, honey?"

"I can wash my own hair, Eddie."

"It's just that I thought . . . it's just that it feels so nice for somebody to do it for you," he'd said. "Real luxury. Especially when you're feeling dragged out."

"I feel all right," Shilda said.

"It's something your mama might have offered to do," he'd said, and that made her jump, gave her a chill, as if some body they'd kept buried under the house for years had suddenly unearthed itself and gathered its ghastly, eaten-up shape before them. Then he'd said, "I remember once, right after we were married—we lived in a hotel until I went back to sea—we planned to go to a movie one night. But when I got home your mama wasn't dressed. She wore her bathrobe and she said, 'Come here,' and led me down the hall to the bath. She'd filled the tub with bubble bath and set out glasses of beer and candles on the tub ledge. It was the prettiest bathroom you ever saw, all pink and gold with candlelight. She had the radio on soft, playing the sweetest fiddle music you ever heard, plunky music, the kind that always makes me think of apples falling off trees up Appalachy way in October. That's where we went on our honeymoon, Shilda, the mountains. Anyways, she set me in this tub that looked like it was filled with cake frosting and she bathed me every inch and when she got to my hair, her fingers were so full of magic that I fell right to sleep."

Shilda stopped her story and waited for me to say something, but I couldn't.

"Is it my imagination, Pally, or is something awful wrong with Eddie?"

"What else happened?"

"Well, after he told me about the bath Gloria Devil Woman Hawk gave him, he seemed contented. Almost like it was a confession of some kind. He cleared away my supper and left me alone. When I got out of the tub, he'd gone. He didn't say goodbye and he didn't leave a note."

"Maybe he went back to Mrs. Oxendine's."

"Maybe," she said. "I don't think he went to the fair."

"Why not?"

"Because of something that came in the mail today. A letter from Kandy Kane herself."

"God, Shilda! Did you open it?"

"Of course I opened it," she said defiantly. "I wouldn't have if I hadn't seen the return address and known who it was from."

"Well, spill the beans."

"I'll read it to you, hot off the press: 'Dear Sir, Here are some free tickets to the eight o'clock show on Friday night. Sorry I can never talk when you call or come by. Mr. LaRue pitches a fit. I can meet you after the show for five minutes only or LaRue will beat my butt. But I really don't have a thing more to tell you. Honest to God.' Then, it's signed, 'Sincerely, K.K.' "

"That's a strange kind of *love* letter," I told Shilda.

Shilda agreed. "It sounds like Eddie's *pestering* her." She shivered. "I swear, ever since that dead girl in the Sardine turned out not to be me, I've felt queer. It spooked Eddie bad, lifting her out, I have to tell you. Maybe that was the beginning of all this. Maybe we're just a couple of spooks together, Eddie and me."

"That's silly," I said.

"Then maybe I'm making all this up. Maybe I just want something different to happen. I feel out of practice since the LaMarrs have been laid up. Do you ever think you can work on something so hard with your mind that you cause it to come true?"

"Look," I told her, "you're making me nervous. Let's get the show on the road."

"You mean you'll go to the fair with me? Help me talk to Kandy Kane?"

"I'll think about it," I said. "Bring the tickets along just in case."

"Tickets?"

"The strip show tickets that she sent Eddie. As long as we're going, we might as well do something really wild like see a strip show."

"I've seen them," she said. "They're gross."

"You've seen just about everything," I said.

"Yeah," she said, "and it's a real problem. What am I going to do with the rest of my life?"

"You'll think of something."

"Pally," she said then, her voice suddenly quavering and serious. "Do you suppose there's any chance that Kandy Kane could be . . . her?"

"Her *who*?" I said, but I knew because the thought had come to me, too, that Kandy Kane might be Gloria Hawk; and that would explain everything, almost.

☆♡☆   ☆♡☆   ☆♡☆

X

We met at Hogan Royal's Esso station at about one o'clock. We bought some candy bars and a couple of Dr Peppers.

Hogan was in the middle of washing Mrs. Bea Brownlee's new burgundy Buick that she'd gotten for Christmas. It had black leather seats with burgundy trim that matched a black cashmere coat with burgundy trim that she'd also gotten for Christmas. Everybody was swooning about it, but I don't know. All that flashiness and matching up depressed me about as much as the burley tobacco queen riding her parade float in the Christmas parade downtown. There are some kinds of glamour that are depressing, although I know that sounds like sour grapes. Miss Burley Tobacco Queen always comes out of some pothole place in the county, some other little crossroads place called Silo or Ether or Poke's Corner. She dresses like a tobacco leaf, in a crinkly, brown *cured*-looking dress, and she rides in a gold Cadillac that's had glue spread all over it and loose tobacco and cigarettes sprinkled over the glue so that the effect makes you think of *rusty* glitter. People around Orfax swoon over that, too, but it's too much, isn't it?

"You gals playing hooky today?" Hogan asked us. He turned the hose on and directed it at the little burgundy and white license plate Mr. Brownlee had had made for the front of the car. It said: "Queen Bea."

"Nobody told *me* it was a holiday," Hogan said.

"Let's just say we had a doctor's appointment," Shilda said, holding up her Dr Pepper and laughing.

"I can see you needed one," Hogan said.

She did look pretty banged up. The bruises made her cheekbones look more hollow than they actually were. Her lip was still puffy and she had a lump on her forehead from where Fayette had creamed her head against the toilet seat.

"Did you lay Mr. Curry flat again, Shilda?" Hogan teased.

"Naw, I'm saving him for the last day of school," Shilda said. "This was my warm-up."

"What are *you* doing laying out then, Pally?"

"Oh," I said, "I reckon I'm her bodyguard."

"Hoho!" said Shilda.

Hogan was the sort of man you liked to have ask you stuff. He knew how to be friendly with everybody; he teased right. He was especially popular with the high school boys who brought their rods around. He'd let them borrow his tools on Saturday and monkey around the garage as much as they liked. He didn't mind listening to their radios turned up loud either.

It was older folks who didn't care much for Hogan. He'd gone off to some fancy art college in Georgia before the war and I'd heard people like Hewson Jenkins say that after art college he'd turned queer in his head. He'd come back to Orfax to work for his daddy's sign painting company, but in his spare time he filled up his parents' backyard with these little contraptions he'd taken a hankering to building. He used scrap metal, old pieces of junk cars, metal hair curlers the beauty shops threw out, barbecue grills, radio parts, old toasters, *crazy* odds and ends as long as they were metal. He'd use a blow-torch and solder globs of things together, fashioning little contraptions that you could even ride sometimes.

When Speedy and Mama got married he'd given them this thing to sit on that looked like a motorcycle and a fish combined. It had dainty little pedals made out of eggbeaters. The handlebars were parts of an old tuba he'd uncovered at the Greensboro dump. He'd told them that the suggestion of a motorcycle was for Speedy because Speedy loved motorcycles, and when Mama said, "What does the fish stand for?" he said, "Why, Betty, don't you like fish?" And Mama said, "Well, to be truthful, Hogan, I'm not real crazy about them," and he'd looked at her and laughed and said, "Why, I just love them, myself." Mama was fond of telling that story about Hogan and somewhere in one of the closets of our trailer, that fish motorcycle sat collecting dust.

When Hogan's old man died and left him all his money, Hogan spent most of it buying up junk cars for his sculpture projects. But before he could really get going on his art, the war started. He signed right up and left Orfax and wasn't seen again until the war was over. After that, he stopped making sculptures. He said he'd seen too much devastation and lost heart. Some people said he'd opened a garage because he'd bought so many junk cars as art material and had a ready store of spare parts.

He turned the hose off and wiped his hands on a grimy towel. Then he rummaged in his chest pocket for a cigarette. He smoked Kools, which, I guess, is another thing folks who didn't like him added to their stockpile of reasons why. I'd heard Hewson Jenkins say that maybe the Kools were a reason Hogan couldn't seem to keep a woman. Everybody said that smoking menthol cigarettes could make men sterile.

"Pretty day, ain't it, girls?" Hogan said. "I was fixing to build myself an ark if it rained one more day," he said. He inhaled his cigarette with great pleasure. "Look at that sunshine! I wish *I* could get expelled."

"What's that you say?" It was Doodle Washington who called out from the garage where he was stacking tires. "You want to get *expelled*? Well, you just flap your sassy mouth at me one more time, boy, and you be out on your butt."

Hogan laughed that loud wheezing laugh of his that made me think of a choked engine.

They were always joking around, Hogan and Doodle. They were real buddies, and a lot of people couldn't see that either.

"So where are you girls headed now?" Hogan asked.

"Oh," said Shilda, trying to look real nonchalant, "I expect we'll shuffle up to the Variety and buy us a deck of playing cards and play crazy eights or something fun."

"Sounds nice," said Hogan. "Not my favorite indoor sport, but it'll do." He knew she was lying. He played along. He was a sport, Hogan was.

"You going to get off your lazy butt and wax that Buick?" Doodle hollered at him. "Or am I going to have to expel you?"

"You all need a lift anywhere is what I'm asking," Hogan said. He was always doing favors for you, too.

I glanced at Shilda but her face had closed over our secret, tight and expressionless. I nudged her discreetly, but she ignored me.

"Guess not," I told Hogan. "Thanks, but I believe we'll just hang around Dullsville all day."

"Only reason I'm asking," he said, stamping his cigarette out, "is some convict broke loose from a chain gang over in Kernersville this morning, so it's not the best day to take yourself a picnic down to Sawyer's Creek."

"Some joke, Hogan," I said.

"It's no joke."

"Cross his heart, hope to die, stick a needle in his eye," said Doodle.

"Don't be such a worry wart, Hogan," Shilda said. I could tell she still thought he was kidding.

"What sort of convict?" I asked. "For real, Hogan?"

"Armed and dangerous. For real," Hogan said. "I hate to be a party pooper, girls, and you know it."

"A mean old nasty colored boy convict," Doodle said in a scary voice. "And he's got him a pickax."

"A pickax," Shilda said with disgust. "This is the stupidest talk." She flurried through her change purse looking for a bottle deposit. "Let's get gone," she said to me.

"Of course they might've caught him by now," Hogan said. "It's about twelve miles over to Kernersville anyway, so we aren't in any immediate danger. He's wounded, too, shot in the arm. Still, I'd stick close to home if I was you."

"Niggers gets mean when they's shot," said Doodle.

"Bye y'all," said Shilda. "Let's hit it, Pally."

"Look here," I told her when we reached the road, "it's one thing for us to go bumming a ride to Zanzibar in broad open daylight with a convict on the loose. But what about coming home when it's dark?"

"Shit," said Shilda, rolling her eyes heavenward. "I don't know why I mess with such a chickenshit."

"But Hogan offered us a ride, Shilda. We could have told him where we were going. Big deal."

"Well, I don't want to ride with Hogan," Shilda said, her eyes filling suddenly with tears.

"Why not? You're not making any sense to me. You're the one who's acting like a basket case. I may be chickenshit, but you're crazy."

"I don't want Eddie to find out about this. I don't want to ever embarrass him."

"He won't find out. Hogan's cool."

"I wish we hadn't taken the tickets," she said. "I'm starting to think the whole thing was a big mistake."

"If you threw away her letter like you said, then how will Eddie ever know about the tickets? Tonight's the last night of the fair. After tomorrow she'll be gone for good. You said so yourself, Shilda."

"I know I *said* so." She gave me this deeply unhappy look. "But somehow I think Eddie's mixed up in something that will go on and on. Maybe he's joined the Mafia. How should I know? I just don't want other people involved." She glanced over her shoulder at Hogan's station; he stood in the doorway waving. "Why is everybody in this goddamn town such a *nose?*" she said. She reached in her purse for a Kleenex but couldn't find one. She wiped her face with the sleeve of her jacket. "You know what I wish?" she said forlornly as we walked up the road away from town. "I wish that mean old pickax nigger would come barreling out of the woods and carry me off. That's exactly what I wish. In fact, I double-dee-dare him to. Come on out, pickax nigger!" she called. "I double-dee-dare you!"

In spite of myself I laughed at her. She was outrageous.

"Are you still coming?" She hurried past me. "We'll catch a ride at the junction of Narrow Gauge and 21, I just know it. And if the pickax nigger comes, it will be to carry us off with him to *live*, not die. Don't worry, he'll *need* us. I've got it figured, Pally. He'll need us to fix him food and clean the dogshit off his boots. He'll need us to wash his hair." She laughed heartily and the laugh slithered into the woods all around us that weren't quite green yet. "Men are like that. Trust me."

It seemed unlikely that we were in any danger. I forgot Hogan Royal's warning. The sunlight sparkled in the trees like fallen money. The shadows of the trees were fuzzy with tender spring leaves. Dogwoods, whose blooms had finally unclinched, clouded the woods. Along the banks of Narrow Gauge Road wild forsythia gushed and the flame azaleas seemed to crackle with showiness. Springtime conspired all around us to make us feel better than we probably had any right to feel. Pretty soon we were walking along briskly and making up lyrics to a song about the pickax nigger. We highstepped and shouted across the blossoming countryside.

> Here he comes, swinging his ax,
> But we don't worry, we just relax;
> He looks like he's from the monster pit,
> But compared to us, he's chickenshit.

It seemed like we waited a long time at the crossroads for a car to come along. We smoked a few of Shilda's cigarettes and she gave me another French-inhaling lesson. A stiff breeze had sprung up and the clouds looked rough. The sun darted in and out. I hadn't brought a jacket and realized it was the sort of day that was warm only when the wind didn't blow. You could never count on April around Orfax.

"There's a car," Shilda said, pointing down the hill. The Esso station looked like a tiny white Chiclet. "Get ready." She crushed her cigarette with the toe of one white boot and stuck her thumb in the air.

"Who do you think it is? I don't recognize that car," I said.

"It's probably somebody passing through town then," she said, impatience ruffling her tone.

"Do you think we should ride with a stranger?"

She glared at me.

"But what if it's the convict in a stolen car?"

It was a turquoise Chevrolet with two ladies wearing hats, and they zoomed right past us.

"This is going to take all day," said Shilda glumly. "Nobody comes through Orfax."

Another car was headed up the hill. School must have let out already because it was Strother Mottsinger's flamingo pink Dodge. God, he was a hick. He made Bynum Jenkins seem debonair.

"Put your thumb up," I said to Shilda.

"Forget it," she said, stepping back from the road. "I wouldn't be caught dead in that fairy mobile."

Strother slowed down as he passed and waved. I waved back while Shilda lit another cigarette.

She was so anxious she was doing a little tippy-toe dance, but she didn't realize it and I let it go.

We waited for what seemed like ages for another ride to approach. When it did, I hoisted my thumb. It was a truck, which slowed as it neared us, then pulled over. Doodle Washington stuck his head out the window and waved. "Hey, Shilda! Who's winning?" he called.

She gave him a blank look.

"Crazy eights!" he called. "Remember?" He cackled. "Come along, sweet peas."

His wife, Lady, was in the driver's seat. "Move over some, Doodle, so we can all fit in the cab," she told him.

"Lucky for you sweet peas that Hogan got to thinking what a fine afternoon it would be for fishing. Dog if he didn't close down the station early and expel the both of us."

"Expel?" Lady asked, raising an eyebrow.

"It's also lucky," Doodle said, winking at me, "that I live so close to Zanzibar." He dug something out of his back pocket. "Step on it, Lady."

"Zanzibar?" asked Shilda, her face blanching.

"You dropped these when you was paying for your Milky Ways." Doodle handed her the tickets she'd stolen from Eddie. But Doodle didn't bat an eye. He passed the tickets to her like they were some dull postcards and he was the tiredest postman in the world, too tired and too bored to read what was right in front of our noses: KANDY KANE AND THE TITILLATOR. Those tickets were as flashy as marquees. Say what you want, Doodle Washington was as cool as they come.

It just went to prove that nobody even had to snoop to find out your business in Orfax. We just scattered all the private little facts about ourselves all over. A telephone number of some secret lover scribbled on a Juicy Fruit gum wrapper, wadded up and dropped in an ashtray. You could bet your life somebody would find it and make headlines out of it the next day. Some toddler, fishing out a cigarette butt to chew, would hand that Juicy Fruit wrapper to his mother.

But we did it to ourselves. The whole landscape of Orfax was littered with evidence against every one of us. Everybody always talks about the good old days of small-town living when you could leave your back door unlocked and not fear criminals. Well, you can get so used to that back door being open that you forget you ever had a private life at all.

Doodle directed Lady to drive us all the way to the fair grounds, even though it was a couple of miles beyond their house. We passed their house, a neat square log cabin on about an acre of grass beside a freshly plowed field. There was a scarecrow hanging in the field dressed up in an old Esso uniform. Doodle waved at him and laughed.

"Have you been to the fair yet?" I asked Doodle as we pulled up to the main gate. He and Lady exchanged looks.

"Tomorrow's *our* day," Lady said. "The fair's open until noon." She was a pretty brown-skinned girl about my age. She wore a flowered kerchief and lipstick the powdery pink of cotton candy. You could tell she'd put the lipstick on fresh, right before she picked up Doodle at work. She served soup in the cafeteria at Orfax High.

"Saturday is always colored folks' day," Doodle said.

"Oh," I said. I'd forgotten about that and I felt embarrassed. But Doodle was looking at me and laughing and shaking his head.

"I was just thinking how easy it would be for everybody to spot that convict if he should try to lose himself at the fair."

"They still haven't caught him?" I asked.

"They've got dogs out hunting him. He don't stand a chance," Doodle said. "Y'all enjoy yourselves now. Be seeing you."

☆ ♡ ☆

It cost a buck each just to walk through the gate. We only had five dollars between us plus some change after we'd paid admission. It was a trashy little fair.

First off I saw the ponies—six brown, ratty-looking Shetlands with heavy black western saddles bowing their backs. They were roped together in a circle and there was this line of squirmy, squealing baby rednecks just having a fit to ride them, to spur their little ribs with the heels of scuffed-up school shoes and make them trot.

Then I saw a dilapidated merry-go-round and an Octopus screeching over us and the Whip and a creaking Ferris wheel I wouldn't have ridden for a million dollars.

We rode the Whip because Shilda just adored that ride. For a while I forgot why we'd come. I let the Whip swirl us up and down, and I gave in to its pull and laughed and shrieked and felt like I was twelve years old. I wished I were twelve years old and didn't know anything. I wished I still kept a diary and could jot down all those silly innocent observations I'd written in the little pink diary I'd kept back in 1954. It had had its own little lock and key; the pages had been lined like notebook paper. *Dear Diary: Today I painted my fingernails Rock-'n'-Roll red. Dear Diary: Today Shilda and I learned how to use Tampax. We rigged up these mirrors on the toilet seat so we could see what we were doing. It hurt like hell and we only used the small size. It took me an hour to make mine fit. Dear Diary: Last night Shilda and I tried eating apples in the dark to see who could*

*make theirs sound the most delicious. Dear Diary: I
have the wildest crush on this older boy named Bobby
Rex Moseley. The other day I called him up just to hear
his voice, then I hung up. The next day I called and
said, 'Hello, Blue-eyes.' 'Who is this?' he said. Then I
hung up. I think I'm going crazy. And guess what? I
don't care. Dear Diary: I have this thing about Adam's
apples. They seem real manly to me. What is an Adam's
apple anyway? Bobby Rex's looks sweet enough to bite.
Dear Diary: Want to hear a cruelty joke? How did
Cinderella die? Well, at the stroke of midnight her Tampax
turned into a pumpkin!*

"What are you thinking about?" Shilda asked me.
The ride was over and I was just sitting there all crumpled up in the Whip seat with some dumb, daydreamy
expression on my face.

"A cruelty joke we used to know." I scrambled out of
the seat and followed her down the rickety ramp.

"Sometimes," she said, "I think I've got the biggest
cruelty joke going: my life."

"You haven't got it so bad," I told her. "Things
could be a whole lot worse than they are."

"You mean that I could be married to Orst and Hogarth LaMarr, cruising around town with a baby on my
hip. That's what you mean, isn't it, Pally?"

We ate foot-long hot dogs at the Shriners' Club tent.
Then we bought Krispee-Kreme doughnuts and cups of
coffee and strolled along the midway. Freak show tents
surrounded us. The Amazing Dynamo who would allow
a million volts of electricity to pass through his body!
Alligator Woman, Queen of the Reptiles, sheds her skin
twice a year, and to prove it, see furniture upholstered
in her moltings, plus lampshades made! The Human
Spike, who can hammer nails into his forehead, up his
nose! Midget Siamese twins, joined for life at the head!
Living Cyclops—born not only with one eye but one
ear, one nostril! Torture Chamber: see beautiful women

whipped, buried alive, made to eat live snakes! The Miracle of Life: see the Whole Story, from Conception to Birth.

Before I could protest, Shilda ducked inside the tent and shelled out thirty-five cents. It was a gloomy, dust-colored tent. On a long banquet table sat an arrangement of bottles, the smallest about the size of pickle jars. The stuff inside them looked harmless enough, something like egg yolks and meringue. I suppose that stood for conception. But as we strolled along and the jars grew larger, their contents began to take on the texture and substance of flesh. We'd both seen baby animals born before their time, and the fetuses in the jars could have been those of lambs and kittens, maybe. But suddenly we came upon an ear that could only have been human, lips, fingers glowing bluish in the milky formaldehyde.

"Oh God," Shilda said, pointing. In the last enormous bottle floated an entire human child. It looked much larger than a newborn. Its eyes were open and you could see the tiny bubbles that had formed along its brow and eyelashes. Its skin was yellow and plastic-looking. It might have been a doll, but it wasn't; no doll ever smiled like that. It smiled as if it found our horror amusing.

"Oh God," Shilda said and ran from the tent. Outside, the air smelled suddenly sharp and cool. Shilda thought she was going to faint, so we dropped right down in the sawdust together and she bowed her head and breathed deeply.

"Where did they get those things, do you think?" she said.

"Just don't think about it."

"It should be against the law."

"Look," I said, "it's funny I should be telling *you* this, Shilda, but anybody can do anything."

Two hoods were giving us the eyeball since we'd called attention to ourselves by plopping down outside the Miracle of Life tent.

"I think it would be a good idea if we got a move on," I whispered to Shilda. "Al K. Trash and his buddy, Son Quentin, are about to motivate over our way."

We hustled away, and for a while we sat on a bench near the merry-go-round and watched little children having some good, clean fun. Slowly the sky darkened and the midway turned on its spectacle of lights. We didn't talk about it, but our nerve was weakening. I kept thinking that if they checked our IDs at the door, we'd be dead ducks.

Shilda said, "Well, I expect it's time to turn in our tickets."

"You still want to?"

She gave me a scornful look. I made her so tired. She rose huffily from the bench and without so much as a glance backwards, she strode briskly down the midway. She headed straight toward the All-Girl Revue, whose gaudy, winking lights conspired on the horizon like some brash zodiac with all the answers.

XI

☆♡☆　　☆♡☆　　☆♡☆

Nobody bothered to check our IDs. Nobody looked at us twice. Quickly and quietly the tent filled up with men. The sour smell of beer hung all around us. Once we'd taken our seats and I'd glanced around at the audience, I realized that the sort of folks who came to shows like this weren't the sort to be pointing fingers.

The stage was covered with red velvet curtains stippled with little pinned-up tinfoil stars. The set looked handmade in a hasty, make-do way. You could imagine the whole group of dancers—Kandy Kane, Lolly Popp, Cherry Smash, Honey Buns—as some kind of warped Girl Scout troop, seedy in thought, word, and deed, toiling away on their costumes, rigging their own props. It wouldn't have surprised me if, at the head of them, loomed some Mrs. Futrell type, only she'd be nuts about see-through outfits instead of shirtwaist dresses.

The Titillator looked like a cardboard box that maybe a washing machine came packed inside. It was painted silver and wired with Christmas tree lights. I almost laughed. Two little portholes were cut in the side that faced the audience. The portholes were draped with little fringed curtains.

A tall, whiskery man in longjohns and a cowboy hat sat down next to me. He settled right in and didn't mind staring at both Shilda and me. He didn't lean against me, but he did try to strike up a conversation by asking if I had a cigarette. I pretended that I didn't hear him, but Shilda leaned across me and offered him one. I glimpsed a tattoo on his forearm of a skull and crossbones with the slogan DIE YOUNG emblazoned above it. Every now and then he'd cough this bubbling cough and spit into the sawdust. He reminded me of a LaMarr boy in retirement.

I can describe what I saw at the All-Girl Dance Revue only this way: it was like getting my eyeballs raped. The emcee sauntered out, a monkeyish-looking man in a dusty tuxedo and grayed white gloves. I swear I could smell his hair tonic. He wore rouge and lipstick. He shuffled a little soft-shoe number to "I'm Forever Blowing Bubbles," which was played on this grunting organ off to the right of the stage by an old, blocky woman wearing a car coat. Nobody clapped when he'd finished his dance. He bowed, then introduced himself as Mr. LaRue, owner of the Sweet Shoppe, and the organ blasted out a rendition of "Good Ship Lollipop" while the strippers filed out. They were dressed in gauzy peignoirs and spike heels. You could see their bras and panties through the peignoirs but nothing else. Each of them wore a sugary color: pink, baby blue, lavender, and a color I just know Mrs. Futrell would have called marmalade. Their Mrs. Futrell probably called it yaller.

"That's got to be Kandy Kane in the pink," Shilda whispered. There was a candy cane appliquéd on her bodice. "She has red hair! I wouldn't have guessed that."

I have to say that Kandy Kane was the prettiest, although she tended toward the plump. She had a round bowl-of-pudding type face with dimples in both cheeks and another in her chin like a thumbprint in dough. Her

upper arms were soft and round and jiggly and she had
dimples in her elbows like a baby. Her thighs seemed to
ripple even when she stood perfectly still. She had au-
burn hair that hung halfway down her back in a ropy
braid. A flashy rhinestone cross dangled from a chain
around her neck and blazed in the stage lights.

I think that the most embarrassing part of the show,
even counting when Kandy Kane got into the Titillator,
even counting Cherry Smash's stunt with the Coke bottle and Ping-Pong balls, even counting what Lolly Popp
did with that sailor's eyeglasses, the worst part was the
music. Somehow it was the music that made everything
slimy. I kept gaping at that old whiskery woman hunched
over the organ keyboard in her car coat and romping
through tunes like "Hokey Pokey," and my toes curled
inside my loafers. It was as if she didn't know what she
was there for, that maybe she was so blind and old and
feeble she thought she was playing at some grandchild's
birthday party. The music tried to sugar things up. It
had texture, like a sticky, dripping web you were stuck
in. I wondered how the girls could dance to it, why they
didn't just throw up their hands in dismay and go on
strike. But out from the red velvet curtain pranced Cherry
Smash, just grinding her hips to "Farmer in the Dell."
And Lolly Popp practically strutted right into the audience, she got so keyed up swiveling herself to "Mary
Had a Little Lamb." I tried to figure out if the tunes
selected had any particular dirty meanings, and I suppose you could make a case for them all if you were of a
mind. The LaMarr boys would have whooped and hollered when Kandy Kane strapped herself into the Titillator
to the tune of "Knick-Knack-Paddy-Whack-Give-a-Dog-
a-Bone." It just made me feel shy all over and shiver at
its awfulness.

As for the Titillator, what a joke! Kandy Kane climbed
inside and poked her breasts through the two little portholes. She was wearing sparkling pink pasties with silver

tassels. As "Knick-Knack-Paddy-Whack" thumped along on the organ, she began to rotate herself. The Titillator trembled and its Christmas tree lights flashed on and off. But there was no machine that powered Kandy Kane's spinning tassels. Just her own sense of rhythm. The speed at which the tassels traveled was miraculous. The whole time she spun herself—which must have taken incredible stamina—the face that bobbed above the box was the picture of boredom. Once or twice she gave a vague, distracted smile. She yawned. She lifted her hands out of the box at one point and began to file her nails with an emery board. Shilda laughed like crazy.

She must have twirled herself like that, putting on a show of nonchalance, for about five minutes before the organ began to lose its chirpy sound and wind down. All the men started groaning and hooting and begging her for an encore. But like a real pro she stopped, climbed out of the box, and offered them the consolation prize of the pasties themselves. She peeled them off as carelessly as if they were Band-Aids. And there she stood in nothing but a G-string. All the men around us went wild, jumping out of their seats with outstretched hands.

She looked very pleased, and she kind of hugged herself happily and smiled as the audience applauded and yelled. It was obvious that she'd long ago stopped thinking of her breasts as sex objects. If others thought of them as beautiful and desirable, she probably only thought of them as skilled. She stood on stage in that casual, heaving manner of a tired athlete, cradling her breasts like a couple of sports trophies.

The audience whistled and catcalled as Kandy Kane twirled her wrist in preparation for throwing one pastie. All around us, men hooted and jumped up and down. I felt embarrassed for them.

She finally let it sail, and a tall, gawky farm boy who could have been Bynum Jenkins caught it. I was glad he caught it. Maybe it would teach him something. Maybe, after all the backslapping had subsided and he'd slipped it into his pocket and left his buddies to go home, maybe in the quiet of his room, with the radio on, he'd take it out and inspect it the way you do seashells. People always examine seashells in a way that makes them seem to be looking for something more—a fortune, maybe—to drop right out. I imagined the farm boy, sitting on his bed, feeling puzzled. I imagined him holding the pastie in his big rough hands, his hands brown and calloused, the pastie pink and glittering as a seashell. And I imagined how it wouldn't seem very much of a joke when he found himself alone with it. It wouldn't seem much of a treasure. It would begin to strike him, perhaps, as *silly*, and he would feel amazed to have kept it beyond the moment of catching it. The pastie would become just one more thing to pack in the bottom of his underwear drawer away from his mother.

A burly sailor caught the second pastie she threw and slipped it into his wallet.

The stage lights dimmed immediately, and the organist started pumping out "Harvest Moon" as all four strippers jauntily backed on stage for the grand finale. They were all wearing G-strings. The way they danced then, you could tell that nobody gave a damn about nakedness. It was nothing but *skin*, and skin was only what tied your bones together and kept your organs from dripping out. It was like gift wrapping, so there!

"That was something, Shilda," I said when the house lights came on.

But Shilda looked dazed. "Pally," she said eerily, "I think I just saw Mrs. Oxendine leaving the tent."

"Poo!" I said, laughing. "What would *she* be doing here?"

"What are *we* doing here?" Shilda said, shivering.

I draped an arm around her. "Hey," I said, "we're investigators."

"Well, I think I saw Mrs. Oxendine just now anyway.
I'll bet she followed us."

"Why would she follow us?"

"I don't know," Shilda said. She looked really spooked.
"Except in some weird way Mrs. Oxendine's my fairy
godmother."

"Relax," I said softly.

"She was on the back row, Pally. I felt her."

"That's your guilt talking," I said. "You're still worried Eddie will know we stole the tickets."

"Maybe."

"Besides, even if it was Mrs. Oxendine you saw,
maybe she just likes skin shows. Maybe, deep down,
she's a man."

Shilda rolled her eyes at me.

"Mrs. Ox is okay," I said. "She got you through a
real bad time and kept it secret. I'll bet it's one of the
few secrets that's ever been kept in Orfax. Maybe we
should write 'Ripley's Believe It or Not' and tell them."

But Shilda didn't crack a smile. She lowered her eyes.
"It was never a secret for very long, Pally," she said
then.

"I never breathed a word," I said.

"I know that," she said. "*I* told."

I couldn't believe it. I grabbed her by both shoulders.
"Who did you tell? What a fool! You didn't tell the
LaMarrs, did you?"

She shook her head remorsefully. "No," she said, "I
told Eddie."

I let it sink in. Telling Eddie didn't seem that terrible.
He certainly wouldn't gossip about it. And if she'd had
complications he would have needed to know anyway.
Maybe she'd told him as a safety precaution.

She took out her cigarette pack, but it was empty. She
balled up the pack and threw it. "I told Eddie for one
reason only," she said in this cold, lonesome voice. "I
wanted to hurt him as bad as I could."

"Why, Shilda?"

"I wanted to let him know who I really was."

"He knows who you really are."

"He knows how he wishes I was. He'd failed at having, and I guess I wanted him to fail at wishing, too. It's the meanest thing I ever did. I know it. I'm an asshole."

I followed her up the aisle. I wanted to touch her and bring her back. But to what? Maybe her innocence had never existed.

Outside the tent, the air smelled metallic with cold, spiced with the salty aroma of popcorn and old canvas and the motory, sparking smell of amusement park rides. It was air that plainly bore the familiar odors of pastures and close-lying ferny woods, too, a raw clay-and-pine-tree smell that dulled our sense of trespass. Clearly Shilda had a mission; I practically had to run to keep up. She headed straight for the All-Star Revue dressing rooms, housed in a deluxe French Provincial-style mobile home. All the windows and doors were outlined in titillator lights, flashing on and off.

As we climbed the steps to the door marked with a candy cane, we saw her through a window. She was peeling off her eyelashes and dipping a free hand into the box of vanilla wafers that sat on her vanity. A television flickered in one corner of the room and I could see that "Gunsmoke" was on. I expected a character like Kitty would just have to appeal to the Sweet Shoppe girls. Two of the others were sprawled in front of the set wearing terry cloth robes and sharing a bowl of popcorn. They were taking turns pincurling one another's hair. It could have been Shilda and me.

When Shilda knocked, I jumped. I'd expected her to knock, but then I hadn't. It was a kind of explosion, her knock. The sound of it filled me with shock and fear—as if I'd *heard* the impact of some disaster without knowing what it was all about.

Kandy Kane opened the door right up and stared. The twinkly smell of her perfume engulfed us. "Well, *babies*?" she said. "You chickabiddies lost or have you come for an interview? Ain't you a little *young*?"

Then Shilda said in a calm, level voice: "Please don't scream or anything. I'm Eddie Hawk's daughter, Shilda, and I've just got to talk with you."

There was a trembly pause, then she gasped as if suddenly everything made preposterous sense. "Oh, dear," said Kandy Kane. "Oh, dear." We'd scrambled up the trailer's steps and through the door by the time she knew what had happened. "How did you find me?" she said. She looked more dumbfounded than frightened. "All I can say is that the Lord sure moves in mysterious ways, don't he?" She pointed into the sky and tilted her face and clamped her eyes shut. "Is *this* a sign, Lord?" she asked. She touched the little rhinestone cross necklace as if it were a talisman.

"What's going on?" one of the other dancers asked, flicking off "Gunsmoke."

"Nothing," Kandy Kane said. "But what I want to know is why so much nothing can make me so sick and tired? And me, such an innocent! Why, I'm so innocent I still eat baby food!"

"You want us to call Mr. LaRue, sweet thing?"

"Hell no!" Kandy Kane said indignantly. "Just you two make like a new pair of nylon stockings and run," she said. They disappeared so quickly that it was as if they'd evaporated.

"Hey listen up." She turned to Shilda. For a second her voice softened. She touched Shilda's shoulder. "Why don't you just run along home and talk to your daddy," she said.

Shilda grasped the hand on her shoulder and squeezed it with both of her own. There were tears in her eyes. "You aren't Gloria, are you? You aren't my mama?" Her voice was as thin as a child's.

Kandy Kane looked spooked. She drew back as if bitten. "Why would you ask such a thing as *that*?" Her voice sounded like a flat-handed slap. "I ain't nobody's mama," she said huffily. "No time, no place, no how."

Shilda wiped her eyes briskly. "I don't know why I asked such a dumb thing," she said.

"Looky here," Kandy Kane said, jabbing a finger at Shilda. She acted mean now, fed up. "I don't want no more to do with this, period. I've been plenty of places and seen plenty of things, but I don't ever recollect coming up against two loonies from the same family. You and your daddy, you keep clear, you hear me? And that lawdog your daddy sent over here giving me the third degree! Ever since I've come to Zanzibar I've felt punished. It's my own fault, too. I wisht I didn't have such a generous heart. I wisht it didn't have to bleed for everybody and his brother. I don't know what's wrong with me except I've got this disease called being nice. So listen, kiddoes, I don't have time to fart around. I've done three shows today and I've got a fourth to go. My feet are killing me and my butt'll get kicked if I'm not ready. Shoot! Now I'm out of fucking cigarettes." She slammed her empty pack on the floor and jabbed it with a pink high heel. She sighed, then cut her eyes at Shilda. "Hey, I had a mother once, too," she said. "She was the Grand Champion Asshole of America. Forget looking for your mother. Count your blessings that she ran off sooner rather than later."

Shilda was crying now, her shoulders heaving. "I can't help it," she said to nobody in particular. "I don't know why I'd hoped."

I put an arm around her, but I felt nothing except distance in the rigidness of her posture, the coolness of her cheek.

Shilda looked straight at Kandy Kane. "I'd hoped you were her. More than anything else in the world."

"Aw shit," said Kandy Kane. "I'm not believing

this." But the tenderness came creeping back into her voice. "It's my damned old Achilles heart again." She sat down on a red velveteen chaise longue. "I'll tell you what. First, stop crying."

Shilda swiped at her eyes with both hands, but the tears kept leaking.

"Now hold on, I'm such a sucker," said Kandy Kane. "I'm going to get out of here before I join the boohoo chorus myself, okay? You find some corks for them eyes of yours while I run over to Lolly Popp's room and bum some cigs. We'll clear this up right now, angel baby, you just wait here," she said to Shilda. "I'll be right back and I'll tell you all I know."

Of course I didn't think we'd see her again. We waited a long time. But at last she returned, dressed for the eleven o'clock show in a G-string, pasties, and the gauzy peignoir. She had a whole pack of Pall Malls and we all lit up. "Okay," she said, "here goes nothin'."

XII

☆♡☆   ☆♡☆   ☆♡☆

The whole business with Eddie Hawk had started for Kandy Kane one dismal night in late February. It all came out of a sadsack mood she was feeling. She was living on a little farm where Wundaland Amusements wintered its ragtag troupe. The farm, owned by Mr. LaRue, who also owned the whole fair, was located outside Atlanta. The closest town was three miles down the road, a wide spot in the road about the size of Orfax called Gaiety.

"Wundafarm," as Mr. LaRue called it, was a pretty decrepit place. What had once been a grove of magnolias and oaks was now a ring of stumps out of which reared a drafty, two-story farmhouse with one bathroom and no heat except for coal-burning fireplaces. Just beyond the house was a barn with a sagging roof. Much of the barn's siding had been stripped away and burned as firewood. Beyond the barn were several muddy fields and weedchoked pastures. All the fences were warped and peeling. The blackberry thickets were so out of control that, from the highway, the farm looked sealed off by clumps of barbed wire.

Most of the fair employees continued to live out of

their trailers right on the property, or they pitched color-
ful tents and camped out like gypsies. The Sweet Shoppe
girls and Mr. LaRue moved into the farmhouse. Despite
the tipping floors and flaking ceilings and leaking pipes,
the farmhouse had a large and sunny kitchen. Planted
right in the middle of the flowery linoleum like a musical
instrument—a grand piano—was a real hulk of an iron
cook stove. It had scrolly little feet and six cooking
surfaces. All the Sweet Shoppe girls were basically
homebodies and every one of them loved to cook.

You could get fat, living the way those girls lived all
winter. The employees of Wundaland Amusements didn't
do a lick of showmanship from mid-December until April,
when they packed up for the first show of the season in
Zanzibar, North Carolina. Mr. LaRue had a policy of
letting the Sweet Shoppe girls indulge themselves until
February. Every Valentine's Day, because he loved them,
he said, he put them on strict diets and conducted dance
practices three times a day.

It was sleeting the night Kandy Kane recalled for us.
Late February 1959. She'd worked out after dinner to a
Johnny Mathis record which she'd danced to double-
time, and she was really puffing. She'd sunk herself into
a healing tub of hot water filled with Calgon Bouquet.
She was sipping this peppy health drink that Mr. LaRue
had invented for his dieters: a glass of hot water sprinkled with fruit and vegetable peelings.

She couldn't get rid of her blues. She wasn't sure
why, but recently—maybe it had been the weather—she'd
begun to feel all *pasty* inside, like her organs were running together, like her heart had no sure spot, no focus.
Mostly she lay around reading confession magazines.
The fashion magazines made her feel old and frumpy;
the movie mags made her feel like a lusterless nobody.
But the confession magazines seemed to be about low-
down kinds of trouble that could convince some wormy

reader that her life was tiptop by comparison. For example, when you read about some woman discovering she had leprosy on her honeymoon, you couldn't help but appreciate the rosy glow of your own health and feel privileged.

Still, she'd begun to sense a creeping emptiness about her life. She'd been on the road, performing in girlie shows, for ten years. When she'd joined the Sweet Shoppe, Mr. LaRue had made her an overnight star. She had nice clothes, if a bit filmy. She had the use, anytime she pleased, of Mr. LaRue's snow-white Eldorado. She made damn good money and had even funneled a goodly portion into blue chip stocks for the day when she retired and bought herself a cottage with a rose trellis. But look! She was thirty years old and beginning to sag despite the ferocious dancing and Mr. LaRue's diets. She had no imagination about her hair—she wore it in the same limp, long unstylish do she'd concocted back in high school. The only thing she had going for her was that she danced better than anybody she'd ever seen. Not only sultry but *fast*. Everybody said it was the toughest trick in the book. But look where she'd gotten: she was still performing for horny men in Pothole, U.S.A. Worst of all, she'd never been in love, never known a man she'd *want* to love for more than an hour in some rented bed. It was quite enough to get you down, she'd said, yes it was.

So she was soaking in the tub, mulling over her troubles and feeling emptiness spiking her chest like the Devil's own pitchfork. She'd begun to cry, thinking she'd just die from sorrow right there in the bathtub, when she heard voices raised in argument downstairs. Quickly she'd grabbed her robe—pink Chinese silk, it was, with a green dragon appliquéd on the back—and stepped into her bedroom shoes—pink satin mules with three-inch stiletto heels. All the girls wore high-heel bedroom shoes because Mr. LaRue said wearing high heels all the time, night and day, helped curve a girl's calf into an irresistible shape.

Halfway down the stairs she realized who was fighting: Honey, one of the showgirls, and the midget who was head-over-heels in love with her, Amos Pint. He was always bullying her for dates. Once or twice she'd given in and gone out with him just for a change of scenery. He reminded her of her six-year-old son who was now in the custody of his daddy. She was a tenderhearted person and she'd continued to befriend Amos Pint, only he didn't want her as a friend.

They were having a fight about a tent revival meeting. He said she'd promised to go with him. She said not on your life. When had she ever made such a rash promise? She paced angrily in front of him, tossing her frosted blond hair in all directions and stamping her feet as if to punctuate her outrage. The whole point of going, he argued, was to turn to God for guidance about their romance. He'd decided that the only way to win her love was through prayer. *What* romance? Honey fumed.

They were both shouting, their faces blistery red. Mr. LaRue was hovering nearby, ready to step in and throw Mr. Pint out the door if necessary. Normally he'd allow a fight to run its course because Mr. LaRue encouraged his girls to fend for themselves. They were all strong girls, full of pluck, and it was always better for a woman who'd gotten herself into a jam with a man to get herself out without the help of *another* man, Mr. LaRue contended.

"Hey, look," Kandy Kane called to Mr. Pint from the landing. "If you want a date to some revival meeting, I don't mind going with you." She wasn't sure why she'd offered herself like that or why her skin suddenly prickled with eagerness. It didn't feel like that sad, unlovable skin she'd wanted to sluff off in the bath. She'd felt downright jumpy with wanting to dress up and go some place. Mr. Pint accepted her on the spot, desperate to make Honey jealous.

It was at the revival that Kandy Kane felt her sorrow, not her skin, sluff away. Her skin seemed burnished with joy. She sang songs she'd forgotten she knew, songs her grandmother had probably sung over her cradle in a low, crackling voice. The songs were sung almost lustily, people made breathless by them, rocking to and fro, eyes closed, shoulders loose, heads slack. Mostly they were brooding, masculine hymns: "Rock of Ages," "O God, Our Help in Ages Past," "A Mighty Fortress Is Our God," and the one that haunted her into her very bones, "Leaning on the Everlasting Lord." When had she ever leaned on *anybody* without regret? The people in her life whom she'd chosen to lean on had collapsed under her weight: her alcoholic stray cat of a mother and a series of men as willing to topple as dominoes, one after the other. It had never occurred to her to lean on God. She lifted her face in song and it seemed to float upwards, radiant: a smiling valentine of a face, special delivery, SWAK to God. She felt such a generous outpouring of herself that she grabbed Amos Pint's hand right out of his lap and clasped it to her heart.

"What the hell do you think you're *doing*?" he'd yelped, wrenching the hand away. "What do you take me for—some kind of whore?"

It was all right. She barely heard him. Her gaze was riveted on the evangelist who was cheering her on about love. He read from Corinthians:

" 'And I will show you a still more excellent way,' " he read, pausing importantly. The sweat glistened on his brow.

" 'If I speak in the tongues of men and of angels, but have not love, I am a noisy gong or a clanging cymbal. And if I have prophetic powers and understand all mysteríes and all knowledge, and if I have all faith, so as to remove mountains, but have not love, I am nothing. If I give away all I have, and if I deliver my body to be burned, but have not love, I am nothing.

" 'Love is patient and kind; love is not jealous or boastful; it is not arrogant or rude. Love does not insist on its own way; It is not irritable or resentful; it does not rejoice at wrong but rejoices in the right. Love bears all things, believes all things, hopes all things, endures all things.' "

He was a handsome man, tall and lean, almost *wasted*-looking. He wore a black suit, shiny at the knees and elbows with wear. He was almost bald, but he had a bristling red beard which lent him a biblical kind of dignity. He had a stern manner at the pulpit, but his voice was shrill, nasal, almost apologetic in some faint way. He looked soft somehow, like a sinner himself, and that's what appealed to her. Even more than the gathered-in feeling she drew from the hymns, it's what brought her back night after night for a week. Mr. Pint, of course, wouldn't go with her again. She went alone.

On the last night of Reverend Von Wicke's mission in Gaiety, Georgia, Kandy Kane waited outside the tent to thank him for her healing. She had a hundred-dollar bill that she'd resisted dropping into AT&T that week, and she'd planned to give it to the minister for his work. She'd never felt less empty in her life, and she wanted him to know. She felt an odd kinship with him, a fellow performer.

More important, deep down, she felt astir with something like passion for Mr. Von Wicke, although she was sure it was more what Mary Magdalene had felt for Jesus. She'd smiled, thinking that in another time, another place, it might have been appropriate for her to have offered to bathe Mr. Von Wicke's feet and dry them with her freshly hennaed hair.

He was tired, she could tell. She could appreciate the bone-deep weariness that comes from putting yourself on display night after night to a nameless crowd. She waited patiently for him to gather up his pamphlets from the lectern. A young local boy, probably hired to help out only while the Reverend was in Gaiety, sorted through the collection plates, astonished by the generosity of a dollar bill found here and there among small change, buttons, even ticket stubs. He'd shout when he found a dollar and wave it in the air as if to assure the Reverend that the evening's expenses would be met.

She waited until the boy was occupied with folding up chairs before she spoke. She cleared her voice twice and called out, "Sir!" He was rolling up the dollar bills after counting out three of them for the boy. "Sir?"

He looked up and as soon as he saw she was a woman ("young and stacked," was the way she put it), he showed right away he was no saint. He couldn't help looking her up and down, but he couldn't help blushing either. The way she thought about all that was this: God had designed her to be looked at. She was like a bonus that God had tossed the Reverend's way. Was there more shame in a man's taking a long, pleasing gander at her body than the body of some naked goddess statue in an art museum? To her way of thinking, it was a whole lot more perverted to hanker after a cold piece of stone. Still, the silence was an awkward one, so she quickly withdrew the money from her purse and thrust it at him. "Hey, Reverend," she said, "thanks for everything."

As he took the money and looked into her face, he recognized her as a front-row sitter. He began to speak of how gratifying his experience in Gaiety had been, how gathered-in this particular flock had felt. But the passion he'd displayed at the pulpit had vanished. He was merely talking a stiff and mannerly bullshit. He thanked her for the money, but he didn't jump up and down about it. She sensed a tiredness in him that was more than physical. Up close there was a bleakness in his eyes like fog, a gray color to his skin that, if she'd believed in the supernatural—which she didn't, except for God—she'd have sworn was the cast-off color of her former misery. Was it possible, she wondered, that in resurrecting the faith of wayward lambs, the Reverend took on their burdens and wore them as visibly as a yoke? Now that the zealotry of those tent meetings was past, she'd begun to think maybe she'd overdosed on salvation. She'd rededicated herself each and every night! Wasn't it possible to soak up too much of a good thing? Soak up too much goodness and it was bound to make your shit detector go a little haywire. It was a fact that she felt better for having listened to the preaching and sung about what was holy and everlasting. It all had helped to stabilize her lurching, restless spirit. But it was silly to think she was now as purified as a cake of Ivory soap. "Here," she said, because she couldn't bear the way that he was. "This is probably for the Lord's sake as much as my own." And she kissed him on the lips, sweet and tender. She was surprised when he tipped right toward her. He didn't seem to care about the boy who was folding chairs. He slipped his tongue into her mouth. He drove her to a motel outside Atlanta, five bucks a night for a double right beside the roaring air strip. They made love all night; he was tireless. Just as soon as she'd roll away and start drifting off to sleep, she'd feel a tapping against her, down low, and he'd start into her again, helpless against what he jokingly called the most wayward member of his congregation.

They stayed in the motel beside the airstrip for a week. She was so delirious with happiness that she forgot to call Mr. LaRue. One night there was a knock on the motel door and there stood Amos Pint, tracking her down. The hired boy who'd folded chairs had heard and seen enough so that Reverend Von Wicke wouldn't be allowed to preach in Gaiety, Georgia, again.

Mr. LaRue was mostly worried about her diet. Was she staying off the sodas? Was she eating salads and laying off the fried chicken and burgers all-the-way?

"Tell him," she said to Mr. Pint, who hung on the threshold as if the motel room were contaminated, "that you don't eat when you're in love."

She wasn't in love, of course, and she knew it. But it was the closest thing to real friendship with a man that she'd ever known. They talked their heads off; they confessed things like girls at slumber parties do. They laughed and stayed up late watching Jack Paar with their toes intertwined. They spent a good portion of the hundred dollars she'd given him on the Magic Fingers bed vibrator and rubbers.

On the last night of their honeymoon, he gave her a little rhinestone cross that had once belonged to a girl he'd loved. He knew he'd loved that girl more than life, because in stealing her away from her husband, he added, he'd thrown his own life away. In the end it had been guilt that had separated them, not lack of love. "When you get to Zanzibar," he told her, "remember that you'll be within calling distance of Orfax. As much for the Lord's sake as mine, as much for *love's* sake as anything, please call Eddie Hawk and tell him that the Reverend Rudolph Von Wicke is more sorry than he'll ever know. Tell him that I lost her, too. Tell him that we're brothers of the heart." He'd looked at her and kissed her good-bye and said, "She was a dancer, too."

Of course, when Kandy Kane finished telling her story, Shilda and I had clamored for more. "Is that *all*? Where is she *now*? What happened to Gloria? Where did she go? Didn't *he* know?"

But she only gave us a vague, sorrowful, misty look. "You know," she said, "somehow I think that if I knew the answer to where she'd gotten to and how she'd done it, I don't believe I'd be sitting here myself." She patted Shilda on the head and fluttered her fingers. "Show starts in five minutes, love. I got to make like the ocean and wave. Bye-bye."

☆ ♡ ☆

They'd caught the pickax nigger sometime after nine o'clock. Davey Cole, the sheriff's deputy, told us all about it on the ride home from Zanzibar, where he'd caught us thumbing. He was on patrol. He hadn't participated in the actual capture, of course, but he'd picked up every shred of information on his police radio. The story went that the convict had robbed some clothes off a scarecrow and stolen a mule to make a faster getaway. They'd picked him up on the east side of Greensboro, lying in a ditch where the mule had thrown him. He was so banged up they had to call an ambulance. The fall broke both his legs. He'd picked a mule that had a mind of its own, had taken the bit in its teeth and started running. They hadn't found his accomplice yet, Davey Cole said, yelping with laughter and slapping his knee— the *mule*!

The story was supposed to be funny—we were expected to laugh—but it didn't seem funny at all. It didn't seem right for someone as deadly dangerous as the pickax nigger to be suddenly exposed as a clown.

"Maybe it wasn't him, the fellow they arrested," Shilda said. I could tell that she was thinking like me, disappointed that the pickax nigger had been captured so easily. Somehow he'd seemed a test of our bravery and endurance. Now that he'd been caught, there was no longer a cliff edge to inch toward and imagine falling from, no overhang of danger rising above the flatlands of Orfax. Not even a compelling reason to glance over

your shoulder anymore. Our hearts could slow down.
"I'll just bet you caught the wrong man," Shilda said.

Davey Cole looked at her like she was crazy.

It had started raining and had turned colder. Davey
had switched on the car heater because I was shivering
so bad, but then he'd rolled the window down when
Shilda lit a Pall Mall. Outside you could smell the plush
wet fragrance of spring. The cold couldn't discourage it,
a smell of punch and tenderness. I sat there breathing it
and breathing it, unable to fill myself up. I closed my
eyes and I could have told you when we passed a tilled-up
field or when we passed those newly sprouted fields that
bristled with rye. The smell of the night had differences
in pitch, like notes of music. I knew when we were
almost home because I could smell the jonquils that
banked the highway and bordered the Moseley farm.
There were thousands of them, planted by Bobby Rex's
mother. Every spring, after they'd finished blooming and
their greenery began to fade, she'd dig them all up and
store the bulbs in a cool dark place through summer. In
late fall she'd replant them, thousands of bulbs. The task
was endless, but she loved it. Everybody said so. I
opened my eyes and, sure enough, the car's headlights
set the banks bobbing with pale yellow flowers, huddled
close like newly hatched chicks. The tin mailbox flashed
in the dark: MOSELEY. Once I'd raised its flag. We whipped
on by. In my head I wrote a letter: *Dear Bobby Rex,
Love Pally Thompson*. What a letter! What if I sent such
a letter? What would he think? I felt myself spiraling
with exuberance, hope. There were so many ways, it
seemed to me then, passing the jostling yellow flowers
in the dark, hurrying toward home and comfort, to lose
yourself and start over. The whole trick was not letting
your mind get in the way. Thought could be like a safety
net: you could feel yourself ready to sail high and free,
you could feel yourself loosening your grip, but always

the net of thinking things through lay beneath you. It seemed to falsify your skill. Falling into thought was the way to put off flying. I decided I would go home and write that letter to Bobby Rex. What did I have to lose? And why did I feel it was everything?

Davey Cole rode me right up to the trailer. The light was on over the stoop. Cream-colored curtains hung at the living room window, drawn. There was no cozier feeling in the world than to see them from the outside on a rainy night with a lamp on behind them. It was an old antique brass lamp that had once held kerosene. It had an amber glass globe rather than a shade, and the light it shed on the curtains was rich and brown like creamed coffee. I felt beckoned.

"Thanks, Mr. Cole," I told him. "What time is it?"

He looked at his watch, shook it, listened. "It stopped at eleven," he said.

"Why don't you come on in and spend the night?" I asked Shilda.

"Naw," she said.

"Come on."

"I need to be alone. I need to think about all this. I need to decide what I ought to do."

"You know that we think better together," I told her.

"I ain't got all night," Davey Cole said.

"Just don't take off on any wild goose chase."

She laughed and yawned. "I'm too sleepy."

"Mr. Cole," I said. "If Eddie's not at home, will you please bring Shilda back to spend the night with me?"

"Look here," he said, "this is no private taxi service and I'm no chauffeur. I've bent the rules enough to-night, okay?" He meant that he wasn't suppose to give us a ride home from Zanzibar, legally speaking. Police cars weren't made for public transport, except in the case of *criminals*, was how he put it.

"I've got an idea," said Shilda. "When I get home, Davey can handcuff me to my bed."

I laughed, but Davey Cole gunned the engine.

☆ ♡ ☆

It was after midnight. I knew as soon as I walked inside and saw "Shock Theatre" on TV and Joe sprawled asleep on the sofa. I'd seen the movie they were showing. It was some Paul Anka lookalike in *Cheerleaders from Mars*.

"No wonder he's asleep," I said to Mama, who was wrapped up in an afghan beside him.

She jumped right up when I spoke. "Where the *hell* have you been?"

Joe's eyes fluttered open. Mama strode to the TV and snapped it off. "Do you realize what time it is? My God, Valerie!"

"I'm sorry," I said. "It's probably way past eleven."

"It's way past twelve," Joe Parker said, rubbing his eyes.

"Where have you *been*?" Her voice trembled, her face was flushed. She was fighting back tears. I don't know when I'd seen her so upset.

"I left you a note," I said. "I told you I'd be with Shilda." It all sounded pretty flabby.

"What's happening to your sense?" Mama said, collapsing in a chair. Her shoulders shook with sobs. She put her head on her knees.

"Whoa, now," Joe said. "She's back now, Betty, she's safe and sound."

"I'm sorry, Mama," I said, kneeling beside her. "I would have explained everything, but I promised Shilda I'd keep our plan a secret."

"I've just been frantic," Mama said. She fished out a piece of wrinkly Kleenex from the pocket of her slacks and blew her nose. "So much has happened lately. First that girl gets killed and then"—she glanced at Joe—"Shilda's miscarriage."

I felt my heart boomerang around in my chest. "How did you know about *that*?"

"Honey," Mama said, looking at me with her red tired eyes, "don't you know that I know just about everything?"

"Eddie told us," Joe Parker said.

"Eddie tells me all his bad news," Mama said. "What are friends for? But I'd guessed already, honey. I miscarried once after you were born, Pally."

"Why didn't you say anything though? Why didn't we talk about it together?"

Mama shrugged. "We should have," she said. "There were just too many breaches of loyalty to think about at the time, I guess. We'll talk about it later if you like." She blew her nose. "First things first, Valerie Thompson. I want to know where you've been all night. I called everybody I know. Joe rode the pickup up and down all night. He checked out every place he could think of, every place that was nailed down. He rode way past the Moseley farm in one direction and the interstate in the other, looking in *ditches*."

"Ditches?"

"There was a convict loose all day," said Joe. "He was serving time for attempted rape and murder."

"They caught him though," I said.

"That's beside the point," Mama said. "When I got home from work at six and found your note, he hadn't been caught yet, and nobody knew when he'd be caught or if."

"Look," I said, "do you want to hear my story or not?"

Mama looked suddenly surprised and relieved. "Shilda doesn't mind? It won't be a betrayal, then?"

"Do you know Mrs. Davey Cole, the deputy's wife?" I asked.

"Martha Cole? Sure. What's Martha got to do with it?"

"She still works at the phone company? She's still an operator?"

Mama gave me a puzzled look, then nodded.

"I'd better talk fast then, because Davey Cole knows everything," I said, "so it will be major headlines by tomorrow."

Then I told them all I knew about Eddie's mysterious behavior, how he'd not only acted edgy but mournful. I talked about his late-night rendezvous with Mrs. Oxendine and how he'd dogged the stripper, Kandy Kane. I thought Joe would laugh when I described the Sweet Shoppe show, but he didn't. Neither he nor Mama flinched when I mentioned the stolen tickets. They were listening so hard that they didn't even move to light cigarettes.

"Shilda had hoped that Kandy Kane was Gloria," I said.

Mama clucked her tongue. "Poor Shilda."

"But the *real* story is the one Kandy Kane told us," I said. "I hope nobody's sleepy."

They sat on the edge of their chairs and didn't interrupt me once. Then, when I'd finished, they hounded me for more just like Shilda and I had hounded Kandy Kane.

"Didn't she tell you anything more?" Mama asked. "Well, I think she's hiding something and doesn't want to get involved. Maybe she identifies with Gloria. Do you think she's trying to protect her?"

"No," I said, "I think she's telling the truth. Eddie even sent Davey Cole to Zanzibar to see if he could dig any more info out of Kandy. Eddie thought she might be intimidated by a lawman and spill a few more beans. But she told Davey the same story she told us."

"That was dumb of Eddie," Mama said. "There's something real dumb and undignified about inviting so many folks to gape into an old wound."

"Shilda says Eddie's obsessed with finding Gloria and that's why he's been acting so weird," I said. "I guess when you're obsessed you violate all sorts of common-sense rules.''

"It's not a matter of rules,'' Mama said, "it's a matter of self-respect. Poor Eddie.'' She shook her head. Then she looked at Joe. "You're a man, what can we do?''

Joe shrugged.

"I've tried to talk sense with him,'' Mama said. "But I don't think I've ever known anybody so dense on the subject of love. Doesn't it stand to reason that if Gloria wanted Eddie back, she'd make contact? Pick up the phone and call, write a letter? Maybe even appear at the front door some lonesome night carrying the little bronzed baby shoes she carried off with her thirteen, fourteen years ago? We're talking years and years, now. Eddie's a fool.''

"You ever tried to talk a fool out of being one?'' Joe asked.

"Did you know all this was going on?'' I asked Mama. She nodded. "Eddie tells me all his bad news.''

"Well answer this one, then. Is he having an affair with Mrs. Oxendine? How does she fit in?''

"Mrs. Oxendine fits in because she's so discreet,'' Mama said. "She may be crazy, but she can sure keep a secret.''

"Shilda thought she saw her at the girlie show, stalking us. Could that be true?'' This time Joe Parker laughed. I guess he was finally picturing it all.

"Maybe. Or maybe she was there to get a bead on Kandy Kane for Eddie,'' Mama said. "Eddie hired her as a sort of spiritual adviser, to investigate his future and foresee its direction. A direction that might lead him to make contact with Gloria, I guess.''

"Do you think there's any possibility that Gloria still loves Eddie?'' I asked.

"I think it's possible that she might love the memory of him,'' Mama said, "but memory is the easiest thing in the world to love.''

"Then you don't think she'll ever come back to him?"

"Phoo, no!" Mama said.

"Maybe she's just too guilty feeling," Joe said. "Maybe she loves him like crazy but she's punishing herself for past sins."

Mama gave Joe a wry look, then kissed him on the nose. "You got a lot to learn about women," she said.

"Okeydoke, so learn me."

XIII

☆♡☆   ☆♡☆   ☆♡☆

By mid-May the trees bore their summer growth and days were long and breezy. The gloomy events and dissatisfactions of winter seemed to belong to another age, as extinct and unthinkable as the memories of dinosaurs. I exaggerate, of course.

Mama went on a strict diet to get in shape for her wedding to Joe Parker. I didn't really need to diet, but it was easier than cooking for myself and seemed sportsmanlike, so I joined her. We chose a diet she'd found in *Reader's Digest*, where for one whole week you could eat all the hard-boiled eggs and tomatoes that you wanted, it didn't matter how many. But eggs and tomatoes were *it*. Then, the second week you were allowed to gorge yourself on bananas and skimmed milk. Of course the way the diet really worked was that you were so ill just thinking about eating another tomato or egg or banana that you stopped eating altogether. We cheated, I guess, because after we stopped eating, we tried to live off chewing gum. The sugar in it gave you energy but you didn't swallow anything that could stretch your stomach out of shape. But finally I called it quits after day eight when, in the middle of my book report on *The Scarlet Letter*, I fainted.

That night I got a phone call from Bynum Jenkins. "Hey, you okay?" he asked. "I heard you fainted."

I hadn't talked to him for weeks, ever since Shilda's bathroom fight. And although I can't say that my heart swelled at the honkytonk sound of his voice, I realized I'd missed him. I suppose I missed him the way you miss a wart when it finally goes away. You get used to anything that attaches itself to you.

"What happened?" Bynum asked.

"I didn't think you cared."

"Of course I care." I could hear his radio on in the background, playing some sappy Pat Boone hit. "I just heard this Ray Charles song that reminded me of us," he said.

"I thought you hated Ray Charles," I said. "You hate colored people and you hate jazz."

"I never said any of that," he said. "You're getting me mixed up with Phoebe. Phoebe's the one who hates jazz."

I reached for one of Mama's Chesterfields and lit it.

"I can tell you just lit a cigarette," Bynum said. "I read where everytime somebody French-inhales it destroys a thousand brain cells. Brain cells don't grow back," he added. "Anyway, that song sure put me in a missing mood, and I'm calling to ask if you'll go to the prom?"

I wasn't thinking straight, I mean, I really wasn't.

"You want me to go out with you again?" I cried. "What's the matter, Bynum? Are you horny again? And so *soon*."

"Okay, just forget it, Pally," he said and hung up.

As soon as the phone went dead, I kept hearing a little phrase Mama used about not looking a gift horse in the mouth. I kept seeing Bynum's big horsey teeth and his beast of burden posture. He was a gift horse all right, offering me the prom yet again. He must have known he risked getting the whip. I didn't think long though. I picked up the phone and dialed his number.

On the first ring he answered. He'd probably been sitting by the phone in a stupor of self-pity. His voice bobbled with delight to hear me, and it occurred to me, even while I spoke, softly, without feeling, that it was awful if he loved me, and he probably did. Maybe he loved me as much as he would ever know how to love anybody—how could you gauge another person's feelings anyway? Maybe the way I'd come to feel about Bynum was the way Gloria Hawk had come to feel about Eddie. A feeling of neither love nor dislike but of toleration. It just wasn't enough to tolerate somebody. It felt dim and unnecessary.

"Whew!" Bynum said. "I'm really happy you'll go. It just wouldn't have been the same if I'd asked Fayette Weems. Would it be okay if we double-dated with Bobby Rex and Phoebe?"

"I guess so," I said casually, but my heart was doing the jitterbug.

"They're having troubles," Bynum announced.

"Troubles? What sort of troubles?"

"All I know is that Phoebe cries all the time," Bynum said, lowering his voice.

"Are they breaking up?" I said, maybe a little too gleefully.

"It don't figure," Bynum said. "Bobby Rex just wrote her a song."

"Sounds like they're pretty intimate to me then," I said.

"That's what I think is wrong with them," Bynum said confidentially. "*Intimate* stuff. S-E-X, Pally. We know all about that snake pit, don't we, hon?"

It was all I could do to keep my trap shut, but I did.

"Hey," Bynum said. "You got any plans for Saturday night? There's this movie on at the Rhapsody, *Maniacs on Vacation.* Ever see it?"

"Sounds great," I said listlessly. "Look, maybe we should wait until the prom to see each other. We might have a fight and break up if"—I felt myself wincing—"we don't allow some spaces in our togetherness."

"Aw, honey," Bynum said, his voice soft and zithery. "I can't wait two whole weeks till the prom to see you. There's space and then there's too much space."

"Okay," I said. "Okay." I didn't want to push my luck, right?

☆ ♡ ☆

At school nobody talked about anything but graduation and the prom. All the seniors had this misty look in their eyes, even the hell-raisers. The last couple of weeks of school were always more relaxing somehow because teachers didn't expect much and students were too preoccupied with summer plans and the changes graduation would bring into their lives to study. Nobody even made you spit out your bubble gum. But in spite of leniency, the end of a school year had a melancholy feel to it, like fall. When you slammed your empty locker shut, you felt the echo in your chest.

It seemed that folks took the attitude that graduation was somehow tragic, a kind of group death. The future loomed before the graduates like an open grave.

Poor Mopsy Brownlee. She'd be entering State College in the fall and majoring in home economics. She was in love, but her parents insisted that she finish her education before she marry. To make matters worse, she'd won a scholarship. Between classes, she went into the girls' room to cry. It was even hard for *me* to imagine what the cheerleading squad would be without her next year.

"I know you hate leaving, Mopsy," I said to her one

day. I felt that I had to say something. There were just the two of us in the bathroom and she kept crying and blowing her nose into brown paper towels. "You've been so involved with this school," I said. "Everybody's going to miss you."

She cried even harder when I said this. Her shoulders shook and her curly blond ponytail wobbled. "That's not it," she sobbed.

She was even prettier when she cried. Her eyes were so round and ocean blue that looking into them made me think of portholes. She had that trembling beauty of Miss Americas when their faces crumble under the weight of new crowns. "What am I going to do, Pally?" She dabbed at her eyes with a fresh towel. "What if I make the wrong choice? Nobody will ever forgive me." The preengagement ring that she wore twinkled almost mischievously.

I guessed she was talking about whether or not she was going to throw away her scholarship to State College and marry the fraternity boy against her parents' wishes.

"If you'd like to talk about it some . . ." I said.

"All I do is *talk* about it," she said. "Talk, talk, talk. Night and day." I pictured her flung across her bed whispering her fears long-distance to the boy in Chapel Hill. I pictured a canopy bed with a dotted-swiss canopy and matching dust ruffle.

She looked into a mirror and patted her cheeks. "I look terrible," she said to herself. "I've never let anything get to me like this."

"It's called being in love," I said shyly, although I felt I was being too intimate.

She looked at me and giggled, her dimples pulsing. "Poor Alex," she said. "He's never seen me this unglued. He told me last night on the phone that if I didn't make a decision today, once and for all, he'd drive over from Chapel Hill and hold me down and tickle me until I did."

I didn't think I cared much for Alex after hearing that. He didn't seem like the responsible Joe College I'd pictured. I wondered how Mrs. Brownlee could have approved of somebody so shallow.

It seemed our little chat had cheered her up, so I said, "Well, good luck with your decision. I'm sure you'll make the right one." That was *another* thing about the end of the school year. You began talking like the nothing-fluff you wrote in people's yearbooks. Stay as sweet as you are, I almost told her, knowing, of course, that she always would, knowing that even if she eloped with Alex, she'd send her mother flowers every day until she was forgiven. And she'd name her first daughter Beatrice. And somehow she'd work it all out to finish her home ec. degree, with or without the scholarship. She was just winsome and clever enough to get everything.

"Thanks, Pally," she said. "But I guess one more opinion won't hurt, and it could make a difference. So let me go ahead and ask you what you think, since I never have: Mardi Gras or Midsummer Night's Dream? I've boiled it down to those two."

I'm sure my jaw dropped.

"It's deadlocked," she said. "Half the prom committee thinks a Mardi Gras theme would be more fun. But the other half likes Midsummer Night's Dream because it's more romantic. Since I'm chairman, I have to break the tie. Bootsie Pringle is decorations chairman this year and . . . you know Bootsie, don't you? Well, she's about to have a conniption fit to get started."

"I see, you *are* in a pickle."

"So, which would you choose?"

I only pretended to consider. "I'd go for romance any time over fun," I said.

I told Shilda about my conversation with Mopsy and she rolled around on the floor of my bedroom, she laughed so hard. I told her that there was a very sad side to all of it, too, if you cared to notice. Which of course she didn't. But it seemed perverse to me that a clever girl like Mopsy obsessed herself with the duties of prom chairman, her very soul orbiting that unreal planet of Prom like a space satellite, a cheerleader from Mars. Shilda said what did I expect of pompon queens anyway? People like Mopsy deserved to be drilled by the boy of their screams.

Shilda wasn't going to the prom. Instead she planned to buy a carton of Camels and a carton of Lucky Strikes and go visit Orst and Hogarth that night. They'd been moved to the County Home, which was depressing in a way: so many old folks, plus it smelled like pee. But there were fewer doctors and nurses hovering about than at the hospital, so you could carry on a bit wilder. Both boys were still paralyzed, but Orst was more talkative as days went by. The doctors expected he'd walk again with proper therapy and will. But nobody knew for sure. Hogarth was still pretty much a vegetable and couldn't move a thing below his chin. "Sometimes," Shilda confided in me, "I think Orst is really Hogarth pretending to be Orst. Hogarth was always a little jealous of Orst, and since Orst can't speak up for who he really is, it gives Hogarth the chance to trade places with him."

"You lost me," I said.

"If they'd only take off all those damn casts and wrappings," Shilda said, "I could determine who's who for sure." She winked at me. "One of them's got a birthmark. Guess where?"

"You need to get involved with other boys," I told her. "You could date anybody you wanted to if you gave them the slightest signal."

"I'm sick of boys," she said. "I want me a man."

"I can't think of any men who'd care to go to the junior-senior," I said.

"Hogan Royal might," she said, her eyes twinkling.

"He's probably forty years old!" I said.

"You know what's sexy about Hogan?" she said. "That Esso shirt he wears, the one with his name stitched in red on the front pocket. The top button's always undone and there's a little tuft of sandy-colored hair that grows in the hollow of his throat like a nest." She hugged herself with delight. "He's a nice man. Wonder why he never got married."

"Maybe nobody appreciated him the way you do," I said.

We walked to Piney View straight from school, had a couple of Cokes, and talked all afternoon. It was Friday. Mama would be home from the telephone company soon. She and Joe and I planned to drive over to Greensboro and eat supper at the S & W Cafeteria, then see a double feature at the Carolina. One of the movies was *Solomon and Sheba* and the other had Liz Taylor in it, but that was all Joe had said. He had the hots for Liz Taylor and he admitted it. Mama didn't think much of Liz, the way she'd wrecked up Debbie Reynolds's homelife, but she let Joe have his fun.

I was thinking of Eddie Fisher and it made me think of Eddie Hawk. "How's Eddie doing?" I asked Shilda.

She rolled her eyes at the ceiling. "He's planning another trip. This one's to Danville, Virginia. Mrs. Oxendine picked up another hot tip in her tea leaves."

Every weekend since Kandy Kane had conveyed Rudolph Von Wicke's apology to him, Eddie had gone searching for Gloria. Now that he knew she was free, he saw no reason for her to stay away, feeling guilty. He was a forgiving man; he'd take her back and love her half to death. No harm in trying, right? He acted cheerful, his spirits buoyed by Mrs. Oxendine's encouragement. He whistled until it grated on your nerves, the tuneless happy whistling of a workman. Why, anybody could make a mistake like Gloria had. She'd only been young. Since when was youth a sin? By now surely she was sick and tired of eating in cafés and sleeping in rooming houses. Like any sensible woman she was bound to pine for a home and family.

Meanwhile, Shilda had noted that sly Mrs. Oxendine had taken to combing her hair and wearing a crooked little line of lipstick. Once she saw her in the grocery store buying a calf's tongue and wearing a pair of wobbly yellow patent leather high heels and a flowery muumuu. If the muumuu hadn't been flowery, Shilda might have mistaken it for a tent it was so huge. But it was probably the first time Mrs. Oxendine had ever appeared in public so dolled up. The produce man's eyes bugged out. The butcher dropped his knife.

"What do you mean by *sly*?" I asked.

"I said it right from the beginning: she's in love with Eddie. She's just biding her time. She hasn't had a good lay since King Tut got buried, so she figures she can wait a while longer. But it's okay. I like her," Shilda said.

"Why is she so hot to help him find Gloria then?" I asked.

"Maybe she's sending him out on wild goose chases," Shilda said. "It's all a trick. She's only pretending to be interested and helpful. Extremely helpful women make a man feel weak and needful. Think how many sick men fall in love with their nurses? My theory is that she's sending him out on false searches, waiting till he gets worn out. Then maybe, during one of their crystal ball sessions, he'll lean too close, catch a whiff of her perfume, and presto! Hell, knowing her she probably mixes ether with her perfume and he'll suck in a good whiff and go out like a light. Then she can rape him to her heart's content."

"Lord, your imagination!" I said, and we laughed.

"At least he seems happy for a change," Shilda said. "At least she's giving him hope."

"In this case maybe hope's better than sex," I said.

"But *only* this case," said Shilda.

The Liz Taylor movie, *Suddenly Last Summer,* caught on fire inside the projector, so we only got to see Gina Lollobrigida in *Solomon and Sheba.* It was terrible except for the makeup and the costumes.

Mama and I came straight home and painted our eyes up like Sheba's. We didn't have enough eye makeup to do a really dazzling job, so we used an old set of water colors Mama dug up from my ancient elementary-school book bag. There was even a metallic gold color. Mama got to acting so silly that she painted her navel red like the ruby Sheba had worn.

Joe thought we were a bunch of nuts. He sat in the armchair and watched a Perry Como special. "I want to get me a sweater like that," he said, pointing to Perry. "It looks neat and comfortable."

Mama and I paraded out of the bathroom, batting our made-up eyes.

"Hey, baby," Mama said to Joe, shimmying her shoulders and batting her eyes.

"Hey," he said, but he didn't look away from the TV.

"Joe's my beau," Mama singsonged, strutting in front of the set.

"Hey, honey, I'm trying to watch," he said.

"Well, what do you think of our *eyes*?" Mama said, and she flopped into his lap, giggling. She pulled her slacks below her waist and pointed to her red navel. He looked at her. Then he looked at me. He didn't smile and his voice, when he spoke, was gruff and preoccupied. "Y'all look like a couple of whores," he said.

"Well thanks a lot," Mama said.

"We look like Gina Lollobrigida," I said to him. "We made our eyes up to look the very same way."

"Ha!" said Joe Parker.

"Well ha! yourself," Mama said, struggling out of his lap. "You don't have to be such a grump."

"Y'all expect everybody to think just like you think,"
Joe Parker said. "Laugh when you say laugh." It didn't
seem a bit like him.

"Hey, Joe," I said, "what burr's got under your
saddle?"

"The burr of truth," said Joe.

"Let's talk about it then," Mama said. I have to
admit that she did look pretty funny sitting on the arm of
Joe's chair, trying to be kind and serious toward Joe
with those whorish Sheba eyes. It looked like she was
wearing a Halloween mask.

"I don't want to talk about it," Joe said. "I want to
watch Perry Como."

"*I* want to talk about it," Mama said.

"So, talk by yourself," Joe said. He picked himself
right out of the armchair and straightened up. "I'm
going on home now," he said.

"Joe?" Mama said.

"It'll be all right," he said in a heartless way. He
didn't look either of us in the eyes. He picked up his
windbreaker and I noticed that the cuffs and collar were
frayed. In two long strides he was out the front door and
the screen door slammed shut behind him.

"Good Lord, Mama."

"It's late and he's tired," Mama said. "We did get
pretty carried away."

"What's *wrong* with him?"

"Just what I said, Pally." Perry Como was singing
"Oh, My Papa," and she flicked him off.

"I've never seen Joe in such a huff," I said. "I've
been with you all night, but I never saw any fight."

"There's lots of ways to fight," Mama said vaguely.
"Anyway, don't you worry about it. Joe has the right to
go off in a huff when he feels like it, same as you or
me."

"I guess I expect too much of him."

"You always expect too much from people that you love," Mama said.

She went into the bathroom and took out a jar of Pond's cold cream and began cleaning her face. "I'm real lucky that you like Joe," she said. "It's just one less problem. It's hard enough to get married again with everybody liking each other."

"What's going on? You aren't having second thoughts, are you?"

"About marrying Joe? Phoo!" she said and laughed. She wiped the cold cream off with a washcloth, and dabbed on a bit more. "*Every*body has second thoughts."

"Not you!"

"Why not?" The cold cream gave her an eerie look; she seemed an impostor of herself. "Why can't I back out now if I want? It's my life," she said, almost pouting. She burnished her face with the damp washcloth, then opened my jar of Noxzema. "Mind if I use some of this?"

I shrugged. She seemed to be teasing, but the fact that she could tease about something as serious as breaking up with Joe was getting me down. How could she act so flip? Was she saying that the love in your life could never be perfect? Was she saying that nothing, no matter how badly it had ever been wanted, lasted forever? She must have guessed at my mood, because she tousled my hair.

"You *are* going to marry Joe, aren't you?"

"Of course I am, honey, if he still wants me."

"What's that suppose to mean?"

"Just what I said. Hey, what is this, 'Perry Mason'? Why are you such a worry wart?" Her face was filled with search and puzzlement. "You don't get that worry-wart business from either Speedy or me. It's all your own thing. From out of the blue somewhere. Oh, I forgot about the milkman."

"Very funny," I said.

"I want some cocoa. Would you like some?" she said, slipping her slacks off. She dabbed at her red navel with the washcloth. Then she put on her bathrobe, which was hanging on a door hook. She cinched the sash tight. "Let's have some cocoa if we're going to talk," she said.

She filled two big mugs with cocoa and sprinkled little marshmallows on top. She rummaged through the kitchen cabinets looking for cookies. "Where in the hell are the Oreos?" she said. "All I can find are vanilla wafers. I hate vanilla wafers. Why do I buy the damn things?"

"Joe likes them," I said.

She paused a moment. "Joe *says* he likes vanilla wafers, which I buy especially for him. Then he eats up all the Oreos that I buy especially for you and me. Oh well," she said.

We took our mugs of cocoa into the living room and sat side by side on the sofa. Somehow Joe's glowering presence lingered in the armchair. We found ourselves looking in the direction of the chair while our cocoa cooled.

"We've moved the wedding date back," Mama said at last.

I felt my heart contract in my chest. "*Back*?"

"Until late August, Pally. August the thirtieth."

"That's just a month longer to wait," I said, realizing I was trying to reassure myself more than her.

"But I should tell you that no date is absolutely definite at this point," she said.

I felt a slow tightening in my throat then. "What does that mean?"

"I'm not sure myself," Mama said, and took a swallow of cocoa. "Ouch! It's still hot."

"But why?" I didn't have enough voice left to make the question sound substantial.

"This and that," she said. "You know."

"This and that? Mama, I don't know beans."

"Mainly the house won't be ready until August. All that rain we had in the spring delayed construction, you know that. But the whole truth, Pally, is that the man has got the jitters. Just be patient, honey. He'll come through it. I'm not worried a bit."

"How in the hell could he have the jitters?" I said. "After all this time? He's almost forty years old! We've known him for years!"

"It's *marriage*," Mama said. "Some men think of marriage as like going on a blind date forever."

"Good grief," I said, "you'd think some people could finally grow up."

"Sometimes I think that nobody ever really grows up permanently until they die," Mama said. "And then it's too late to reap the benefits, if there were ever any to be reaped."

"Are you upset?"

"Oh," she said, "I think it will all work out. I love Joe, Pally. You know I do. But I'm thirty-five, I've had a lot of flings and my fair share of luck, so if Joe decides he can't go through with it, I'll have to be brave and take what I've got coming. Sometimes I think we should keep it like it is anyway. I like the way it is an awful lot. Why rock the boat?"

"What way is that, Mama?"

She gave me a tender smile. "Us. You and me, Pally. It's been just the two of us since your daddy got killed, all those years ago in June. June twentieth. Sounds like the date of a wedding, doesn't it?" She stared into her empty mug. "We've done all right, haven't we, punkin?"

"We've done more than all right," I said, hugging her. "I wish I could remember Speedy better."

"I wish you could, too," Mama said. "He was a champion man. I mean a *champion* man."

"Is Joe Parker a champion man, too?"

"*I* think so," she said softly, "but only time can prove it."

"What makes a person a champion man?"

"It's just the way they *are*," she said. "There's no lessons and there's no rules."

"Tell me some more about Speedy, then," I said, because I think she wanted me to ask. "Tell me about the night he died. *Everything*."

She looked startled. We'd never talked much about that night in any great detail. It wasn't anything she liked to dwell on. But I sensed a need to ask her then because I knew that when we were part of another family, Joe Parker's rather than Speedy's, I might not hear the story of Speedy's dying in quite the same way.

"Well, you know, I think about it every day," Mama said. "Good Lord, I remember everything, Pally, down to the fact that I went barefooted to the hospital, wearing a dress I'd been sewing on that was only *basted* together. I was a wreck."

"Of course you were," I said and shivered.

"Speedy and I had had a big fight just before it happened. We loved fighting," Mama said. "One time we hollered so loud that we stampeded Hewson Jenkins' cows. They were grazing in a pasture next to our little yellow house. Remember that house, Pally? It's not there anymore."

"I know," I said. "Mr. Jenkins bought that land and built a duck pond there."

"We were such show-offs back then, Speedy and me," Mama said. "We were loud fighters and we were loud lovers. Even after we got married we used to neck down by the railroad tracks."

"You told me all that," I said.

"Well, we always made up after our fights," Mama said. "We had a rule: never go to sleep still mad at each other. And we never did. Except for this one fight." She shook her head. "It was the dumbest fight we ever had."

"What was it about?"

"You don't even want to know."

"Sure I do. I want to know everything," I told her.

She threw up her hands. "Oh, all right," she said. "It was the dress I was making. Speedy thought that it was too . . . *provocative*."

"That doesn't sound like my notion of Speedy," I said. "That sounds more like Bynum Jenkins."

Mama laughed. "I need to tell you more about the dress so you'll understand. I'd sent off to a store in Dallas, Texas, for the material. A fancy-dan store called Neiman-Marcus. You could buy a ready-made dress out of the same material, but I couldn't afford one of them back then. The ready-made dresses were called Invasion Prints, and they were thought to be very patriotic in a sassy sort of way. The material was printed with sketches from the invasion of Normandy. There were pictures of soldiers and American flags and even tanks crawling all over the dresses. I saw the dresses in a catalog. I ordered three yards of the material and bought a dress pattern I liked and had the dress all basted together the day that Speedy was killed."

"What was so provocative about a dress printed with tanks and soldiers?"

"It wasn't the print," she said, "although Lord knows the material was enough to make you salute. No, honey, it was the *pattern* I'd selected. The dress was too low-cut in the front to suit Speedy. And I have to admit that it didn't have much of a back. To tell you the truth, it was probably meant to be a very sophisticated cocktail dress. It was a case of choosing something I'd liked at first sight without thinking about the repercussions. Where could I have worn a dress like that around Orfax? Speedy's argument was that it was wrong to try to look sexy and patriotic at the same time. It implied that you didn't take the war and all that loss of life very seriously. Wearing a flashy, provocative dress printed with the invasion of Normandy struck Speedy as being about as ridiculous as dressing the Statue of Liberty in a bikini. It was just bad taste.''

"It *does* sound like a silly fight," I said. "I don't think even Bynum and I could top that one.''

"Marriage doesn't usually upgrade the subjects of what you fight about," Mama said. "But I'm not through telling you everything. There was more to the fight than that.''

"Well?"

"His name was Hogan Royal.''

I sat there a minute, trying to absorb what she was telling me. I'm sure I looked shocked. "*The* Hogan Royal?" I said. "You were fighting about *him*?''

"A little bit," Mama said. "Speedy always thought Hogan had a sweet tooth for me.''

"*Hogan Royal*?" I still couldn't believe it.

"Of course nothing, absolutely *nothing,* was going on between Hogan and me. I'll swear it on the Bible if you like. But I was friendly with Hogan. I made Speedy trade at the Esso instead of the Texaco. People around town gave Hogan the cold shoulder after he came back from the war and put himself in business. Mainly because of his oddball sculptures. But also, back then, he used big words, and folks thought he was a college boy show-off rather than a man who was simply smart. He'd read a lot and seen a lot and wasn't afraid to talk about it the way he saw fit. You know me," Mama said. "I can't stand to see a person snubbed by narrow minds.''

"Did Speedy get along with him?"

"Speedy liked Hogan a lot at first. They'd take the motorcycle on a Saturday afternoon and ride it double over to some hill climb or dirt bike race, and I'd stay home with you, Pally, and cook a nice supper for them. I cooked a lot of fish in those days. It was local catch and cheap. I'll bet *that's* why Hogan made us that silly contraption that looked half fish and half motorcycle. I swear! I've never been able to figure out the fish part until now," she said, her eyes shining. "That alone should tell you how little Hogan cared. When he thought about me, he thought of fried fish! Anyway, we'd sit around in the evenings, the three of us, after you'd gone to bed, and Speedy and Hogan would relive the events of the day, the hill climbs, whatever. Sometimes Speedy would ask Hogan to talk about the war, but not often. Speedy was a cheerful man, but there was a shadow hanging over him since the war: guilt for not serving his country. The rest is obvious, Pally."

"When you bought the Invasion Print material, Speedy thought you were trying to impress Hogan, right?"

"I suppose," she said.

"It's all so silly," I said. "It's all so high school."

"Nobody ever gets over high school," Mama said. "I don't know why exactly. It's the one place where you learn everything there is to know about being petty and silly, and you spend your whole life either trying to get over what you learned *too* well, or practicing it since you mastered it."

She took a swallow of my cocoa which I'd let grow cool. "So you can see now, Pally, that the Invasion Print was one thing, but a swoony swanky little dress made out of it was another."

"I can see that."

"So we argued like fools. It was Friday afternoon and I was trying like crazy to finish the dress and wear it Saturday evening when Hogan came to supper. If I'm honest, Pally, I did want to impress him. Just because you get married, you don't stop wanting to impress other men. Usually your husband kind of likes for you to. But you have to walk a fine line. You can look *desirable* all you want, but you'd better not desire.

"When I tried on the dress for Speedy, he hit the ceiling. You think Joe Parker acted bad about our Queen of Sheba eyes? Ha! That was preacher talk compared to

Speedy. Of course I roared right back at him, and I suppose you know I can roar."

"I know," I said and grinned.

"He lit out on his bike then, me trailing him down the road, shrieking as hard as I could, *wounded*, throwing basting pins at him like little darts. Well, you know all the rest, honey." She looked down at her lap and laced her fingers together. She seemed almost surprised to have come up so suddenly against the brick-wall ending of so innocent-seeming a story. She was still stunned by the outcome, almost seeing it fresh. Her face looked white and taut. "The accident didn't kill him outright," she said as if she couldn't stop. "Everybody thought he'd been speeding when they first heard the news, because, Lord knows, he'd done plenty of that. But no, he'd raced his fury out along some back road. Then he headed into town. Right in the middle of downtown Orfax on the prettiest most hopeful summer day you ever saw, Speedy slows for a stoplight, and the car behind isn't paying a speck of attention and bumps him. Nobody sees motorcycles ever. It's just a little tap, though. Everybody who saw it said so. The car wasn't going more than ten miles an hour. But it was enough to send Speedy onto the pavement, smack on his head. He jumped right up, though. That's the odd part. Jumped right up, brushed himself off, did a weavy little walk to his overturned bike and heaved it right side up. Everybody thought he was okay. He *said* he was okay. There was just a little blue knot on his forehead. His elbows and knees were hardly skinned. Are you *sure*? everybody had asked when he started the bike up. Are you sure you're all right, Speedy? The crowd who'd gathered watched him drive the bike down the street. And at the very next intersection, he cut the engine and dismounted. He parked the bike beside the curb, and then he lay down on the sidewalk with his hands under his cheek to make a pillow. When I saw him at the hospital, there wasn't a drop of blood on him. He looked just like he'd looked when he left the house. Only he wasn't angry anymore. He'd slipped into a coma, and he never knew I was there, standing in that basted-together Invasion Print dress, crying my eyes out for him to wake up and get mad all over again at me.''

I put my arm around Mama even though she wasn't the least bit weepy.

''It's the funniest thing,'' she told me. ''In my heart I kept feeling that I stood a whole lot better chance of God heeding my prayers if I'd promise never to fight with Speedy again. But there at the hospital, standing over Speedy's bed, holding his cool and dying hand in my own, all I could think to say was, 'Come on, Speedy, let's fight. Let's have the biggest fight we've ever had, ever. We haven't had that big one yet, Speedy. All the cows in Orfax are waiting to stampede, Speedy.' Pally, I wanted to fight with him so bad I could feel the words boiling around in my chest. I wanted to shake him and hit him, lying there so apart from me. They had to give me a sedative, so I wasn't even awake when he died.

''I'd never even considered losing him. Even with him dying right in front of me, I didn't believe it was happening. So, more than fear, I think I felt impatience. I wanted to get on with things. I expected him to sit right up and tell me he was only playing a mean joke to get even. I thought that any minute the doctor would tell me that Speedy was out of danger so that I could run along to the Cash and Carry and buy the fish I'd be cooking for Saturday night supper. I just wasn't afraid yet because I was so young and spoiled rotten with love. I only remember that huge surge of impatience when I think of standing over Speedy's bed. He'd taught me all about rushing. It's just the way he liked to live, rushing and doing and packing your life to the bursting point.''

''And now it's Joe Parker who's trying to teach you patience,'' I said.

She paused to think about that. "It's never too late to learn, do you think?"

"I don't know," I said. "I don't know anything. And the more I *do* learn, the more it seems I know nothing."

Just then the telephone rang. We both looked at the clock: it was past twelve.

"You know plenty," my mother said.

"Like what?" The phone rang a second time, a third.

"Like who's calling us on the phone right now."

I didn't think twice. "Joe," I said.

She picked up the receiver. "Hello," she said. Then she smiled broadly at me. "You were absolutely right," she said to both of us.

XIV

☆♡☆　☆♡☆　☆♡☆

I woke up on Saturday morning dreading to go out with
Bynum Jenkins. I was so obsessed with dread that when
Mama suggested that we drive over to Greensboro and
eat lunch together at Meyers's Tea Room, I had to run
into the bathroom and dry heave. Normally I'd rather
eat lunch at Meyers's Tea Room than just about anywhere. They serve this specialty ice cream cake with
real hot fudge sauce. Mama's notion was that we'd shop
for prom dress fabric in Greensboro so that we'd be sure
to come up with something unusual. Rice's Variety had
a big sale going on labeled "Prom Dress Fabric," but it
was bolt after bolt of homespun-looking cotton and out-
of-season taffetas, and all the colors were dim and dusty-
looking. Wilbur had tried to make the fabric seem more
desirable by sticking labels on each bolt that used a
popular song to describe some putrid wishy-washy color,
names like "Honeycomb" beige and "Smoke Gets in
Your Eyes" gray. A *gray* prom dress?

We left for Greensboro right after breakfast. I tried to
relax and enjoy the day. The weather was balmy. The
sun popped flirtatiously in and out of petticoat clouds.
We pulled into Hogan's on the way to gas up.

For the first time I not only noticed the sandy-colored hair on his arms, I thought about it. I liked watching his hands work. There was a vigor about them that I admired, a knowledge I felt drawn to. I thought about Bynum's long skinny fingers with the bitten-down nails and feathery cuticles. I thought about how he liked to pop his knuckles all the time and I felt queasy again. I thought about how he seemed to rake me with his hands, never touch. Hogan's hands looked like they knew how to fix anything, a transmission, a broken heart. I felt myself warmed by the sight of them. You're so dumb, I said in my heart to Bynum. You think that manual labor is the president of Cuba.

"You're mighty quiet," Mama said as we drove along. "Feeling okay?"

"Maybe I'm coming down with the flu," I said. "Maybe I'd better call Bynum and tell him I can't make it tonight."

From several miles outside the city limits, you could see the skyline of Greensboro, dominated by the Jefferson Standard Building. I began to feel better, anticipating the stroll up Elm Street, windowshopping, the smell of the Planter's Peanut Shop, the crackerjack aroma drifting out of Woolworth's. I liked the windiness of downtown—dropped papers scuttling down a gutter, hats cartwheeling off heads, the snapping of flags and the rattle of chains against flagpoles. The wind sort of batted you down the sidewalk, huffing up your skirt, turning your clothes wrong side out. Overhead a narrow strip of blue sky flowed as calmly as a river between the tall buildings.

We put several nickels in a parking meter, then we walked to Ellis-Stone and rode the escalator to the basement. There was a fat shiny bolt of turquoise chintz, but that wasn't what I was looking for. I had my heart set on turquoise, though: something gauzy and frilly, something memorable. We went to Woolworth's and Belk's and Fabric Discount. We even cased out Silver's Five and Dime, but we didn't have any luck. Finally Mama talked me into having lunch at Meyers's Tea Room.

She abandoned her diet completely and we ordered fruit salads with fluffy orange dressing and fresh-baked corn bread and hot fudge cake for dessert. We even sent the waitress back for a second basket of corn bread.

A model walked past our table wearing the latest fashion: it was a powder pink shirtwaist dress with a straw belt. Another model strolled by in a navy linen suit and black patent leather pumps. She wore a black straw hat, a fedora, Mama called it.

Mama ordered coffee and we tasted our hot fudge cake. Neither of us could speak for a while, it was so delicious.

We'd almost finished when somebody said, "Why, hello there Betty Thompson, and Pally!" We turned in our chairs to see Mrs. Jenkins with Phoebe. They'd just taken seats at a nearby table and were unfolding their napkins. Phoebe was reading the menu. "Out shopping, girls?" Mrs. Jenkins said in her trilling voice. She wore a pale green suit with ruffled collar and cuffs and a green pillbox hat with a veil. She looked stout and green and frilly as a brussels sprout.

"We haven't had much luck," Mama told her.

"What are you looking for?" Mrs. Jenkins asked, but she didn't pause for an answer. "We just bought Phoebe the most gorgeous dress you've ever seen in your life. Size *three*. Can you believe that there are people who can really fit into size threes?" She rolled her eyes in Phoebe's direction. "And take it so for granted. What size are you, Pally?"

"Size ten," I said.

"Just for *length* though," Mama added. "We always end up taking in the waist of a size ten dress."

"Let's go," I said to Mama. "It's getting late and I ought to wash my hair for tonight. I want to check out Meyers's basement."

Mama motioned for the waitress to bring our check.

Mrs. Jenkins shoved their parcels under the table. I saw several expensive-looking boxes stuffed into gray-and-white-striped Montaldo's sacks. "I don't know why we've come here for lunch," Mrs. Jenkins said. "Phoebe's on some diet and refuses to eat anything but soda crackers."

"The hot fudge cake is fabulous," I said to Phoebe. "You really should break down."

She smiled at me, but her eyes were slits.

Another model walked past our tables wearing a yellow sundress and sandals and a multicolored beach hat. "We saw that outfit at Montaldo's," Mrs. Jenkins said. "The beach hat alone cost thirty dollars. Can you imagine?"

"Whew!" Mama said. "Nice seeing you." She picked up our check.

"Look, Mom!" Phoebe exclaimed. "Is that my dress?"

Another model entered the Tea Room, tossing her shoulder-length blond hair over bare shoulders. The dress was turquoise blue. You could hear it rustling from way across the roomful of tables. It was strapless, designed to look like a long tutu, so gauzy and ruffled that you expected there to be little wings at the back and the model suddenly to take flight. It was a midsummer night's dream kind of dress, as blue as a morning glory but brighter somehow.

"That's it," said Mrs. Jenkins proudly. "That's Phoebe's prom dress. Isn't it the prettiest dress you ever saw in your life?"

Once we were outside the store I said, "Well, that's it. I'm not going to any damn prom."

"Look," Mama said. "There are other colors and other dresses. Let's forget about making you a dress. Let's shoot the works. Would you like to go to Montaldo's and really splurge?"

"No," I said sullenly. "It would be different if I were

going to the prom with Bobby Rex Moseley. But I'm not. I'm going with Bynum Jenkins. Year after year I'm going with Bynum. For the rest of my life maybe. I just don't know how to stop."

"Do you want to go to Montaldo's or not?"

"No," I said. "Well, sort of."

"Now you're talking," she said, dropping another nickel in the parking meter as we passed it. "What does Bynum have to do with any of this anyway?"

I laughed because she sounded so much like Shilda.

"The fairy godmother sent Cinderella to the ball," Mama said, "but the fairy godmother didn't have a thing to do with what happened once she arrived."

That afternoon at Montaldo's, we bought my wedding dress. We didn't know we'd bought my wedding dress, but we had: snow-white organdy, tier upon tier like a wedding cake. It had a heart-shaped bodice and little puffed sleeves with ribbon bows. There were silk gardenias sewn at the waist. In the dressing room, as the alterations lady pinned up the hem and cinched the size ten waist a bit tighter, Mama and I both cried. I don't know why we cried except for our great rare friendship which had brought us to this first shared moment of looking into the mirror and seeing that I was a woman in spite of myself.

☆ ♡ ☆

I suppose I dreaded my date with Bynum because I didn't want to have to bite my tongue all night. I didn't want to have to try to stay on his good side. I'd come too far and seen too much to have to lie the way he liked me to lie. Surely by now he knew that I lied. But Bynum preferred me as a liar; I was easier to be with. If I told the truth about things, I only stirred up trouble, and we'd waste our time arguing rather than groping and humping in the backseat. Only the chance to spend a

single evening in the company of Bobby Rex Moseley
could inspire me.

Why did I hold out hope for a romantic union with
Bobby Rex? What possible chance did I have of luring
him away from Phoebe? I'd mooned over these questions for weeks. Of course there lurked in my heart the
shyest possibility that maybe Bobby Rex loved me already. The hope that something had already passed between us, who knows how, who cares; you don't think
logically when you are moony. You think only in a fated
kind of way.

I'd begun to think in supernatural terms, too. I imagined that when I passed him in the halls at school, my
heart sent messages in smoke, his initials unraveling
from inside me when I sighed. Hadn't Hester Prynne's
scarlet letter grown hot to the touch in the presence of
her lover? Miss Joyner said that the smoldering letter
symbolized Hester's guilt. We were supposed to pity
her. But I felt nothing but envy. Oh, to feel guilty about
unstoppable passion!

Over and over I recounted the few times I'd stood,
always breathless, near Bobby Rex. I told myself that if
he didn't know how much I yearned for him by now,
then the purity between us was perhaps too much to
overcome. Words were utterly useless. Either a person
got the message that you beamed to them and recipro-
cated, or he didn't.

I geared myself up for the date with Bynum thinking
this way. Thinking of Bobby Rex untensed me. We
pulled into the Rhapsody drive-in, and I was just as calm
and quiet as could be. Bynum noticed. During the intermission of *Maniacs on Vacation,* he looked at me and
said, "Tonight you remind me of that little filly I met in
the cafeteria line at school almost two years ago."

"Who was that?" I said dreamily.

"*You,* Pally. My little angel baby sugarpie."

I looked at him steadily. I tried to keep my smile

going, but it felt heavy. "She was nothing but a big turd ball," I said.

Bynum winced. "You've never been able to take a compliment too good, Pally."

"You didn't compliment me," I said, "you complimented a ghost."

He drew away, and his jaw jutted out sullenly.

"I'm sorry, Bynum." I scooted over and brushed my lips against his Adam's apple.

"You just don't seem to understand," he said sadly. "I really do love you, Pally. It's the God's truth."

"Hey, I love you, too."

"No you don't," he said. "I'm not as dumb as you think."

I let it go. The movie came back on and I held his hand. We watched these maniacs put two unsuspecting victims in a couple of barrels. Next, the maniacs hammered nails into the barrels and rolled them down a steep hill. It was a contest of some sort.

"Why don't we leave," I said.

"You *don't* love me, do you?"

"Stop acting silly," I said. "I just suggested that we leave the movie. Where else is there to go but Sawyer's Creek? What else is there to do at Sawyer's Creek than to prove you love somebody?"

"Okay, then," he said, fumbling with his car keys, jamming them into the ignition. "Okay, then. We'll see."

"We'll see what? You're acting like a maniac yourself," I said. "Calm down, Bynum."

"We'll just see if you love me," he said. "Tonight you can prove it."

He'd never acted so dramatic before. He yanked the speaker out of the window and slammed it into the metal holster. He peeled a wheel on the way out of the drive-in parking lot and that seemed to please him. He wore a snarly sort of smile on his lip, but his fury tapered off a bit after the wheel. I didn't really think it was *fury*, though. It seemed more of a momentary rage to be somebody he wasn't, a longing like my own to have somebody he couldn't. For an instant I almost loved him, seeing myself.

"I don't want to go to Sawyer's Creek tonight," he said. "I put a blanket in the trunk, and it's nice out."

"Where do you want to go then?" I asked. His decisiveness unnerved me.

"How about somewhere along the railroad tracks?"

"Okay," I said. I felt caught up as if netted. I felt kidnapped again, the same way I'd felt when the LaMarr boys had stalked down the bleachers towing me along. It was Bynum's decisiveness that surprised and weakened me. I kept thinking: so this is how it's going to be, over and over, already imagining that it could happen without happening if my heart were really elsewhere. I tried to concentrate on Bobby Rex Moseley. I pretended that Bynum was Bobby Rex, riding beside me all steamed up with desire. I told myself that if I could just imagine Bobby Rex's face above me when it was actually Bynum's, then I'd be all right. It would soon be over anyway, and I would have done it once and for all and could get on with my life.

Bynum swerved off the highway and we bumped along the potholed road that led to the dilapidated Southern Railways depot. There were lots of other cars parked among the grove of willow trees that grew alongside the tracks. It was a moonless night, but the sky was overcast and the clouds picked up the glow from town and you could see pretty much. I thought I saw Eddie Hawk's white mattress truck parked over by the depot. But that was ridiculous, I told myself. If Eddie and Mrs. Oxendine were getting together, it wouldn't be in such a public spot, would it? For sure I recognized Strother Mottsinger's pink Dodge. But I didn't see Strother. All the cars looked abandoned, but there were people inside them. You could hear them, and every once in a while an arm or a leg would sling upwards, then snake back down into the husky dark. One car I didn't recognize had a brassiere tied to its radio antenna.

Bynum maneuvered the Studebaker around several willow tree groves until he found a cluster of trees where no cars had parked. He cut the engine and headlights. "I want you to know," he said, "that whatever happens tonight, I'm going to marry you, Pally. You don't have to worry about a thing."

Then he dove for me. A button popped off my blouse; he got my underpants off in one snap, frail little things they seemed. He shoved what felt like all his fingers into me, digging. I could not have conjured Bobby Rex's face for anything. It would have felt like sacrilege. Involuntarily my legs clamped around his hand, every muscle bent on driving him out. He was all over me, strong and intent. He wriggled on top of me, grazing me with his daggerlike hipbones. One hand was halfway to China while the other fumbled with his zipper. "*Please*," I said, twisting under him, truly panicked, "*stop*!" His mouth seemed to swallow my face, his tongue splashing everywhere. "*Bynum, please!*" I felt him shove his penis loose from his underwear. But at the touch of his own hand, he ejaculated. The semen thudded softly against my stomach before he settled his full weight on me like a stone.

"Let me up, Bynum," I said. I tried to keep my voice low and even, but it was quaking. "Let me up, *please*." Had this been done to me, or had I let it happen?

"I got too excited," he said. "I'm sorry I was too fast for you."

I grabbed his hand which lay limp between my legs, and I jerked it and flung it and shot both of my elbows into his chest. "*Get off!*"

He lurched backwards, yowling. "Well, don't tell me that I didn't *try* to please you. What do you expect when I'm a virgin and out of my mind being so close to you? It says in *Playboy* that foreplay is the best part of sex for a girl anyway. What did you expect? Maybe only somebody like Orst LaMarr can satisfy your twat, Pally.''

I hit him then. I hit him so hard that my hand rang. I hit him again, twice more, before he could react and shield himself. My hand smarted as if frostbitten. I hit it against the seat of the Studebaker as if to get rid of it. If I'd had a knife, I might have cut it off as if it were contaminated. I was crying, but the tears didn't feel like tears. It was a seepage that had nothing to do with the rest of my life, seepage from some cesspool part of me.

"You've gone loco," Bynum said. "You're as crazy as a bedbug."

Somehow I'd gotten out of the car without opening the door. I can't remember opening the door. I just simply *willed* myself outside. My throat felt constricted with rage, but I got the words out all right. "Fuck you, Pat Goon," I said, then I ran.

I couldn't run fast enough; it was like falling, tumbling, head over heels in hate, panting, pouring sweat, not sweat, really, but a kind of liquid violence. My chest felt like a pot boiling over. Maybe I ran around in circles for a while; who knows? When I finally sagged against a tree, hugging it, gulping cool, black air from its dark swishing dipper of leaves, I realized I hadn't traveled very far. I felt as if I'd burst into a zillion pieces and it was really only my hands and arms that held the tree. Slowly I felt the sensation of the rest of my body falling into place.

I'd run the length of the willow groves and past the depot where Eddie's mattress truck was parked. I'd crossed the railroad track and a plowed field and entered the woods on the other side. The freshly turned sod of the field had sucked my shoes off, and only now I realized I was barefooted. I heard a trickle of water and knew I was a stone's throw from Sawyer's Creek, if I cared to walk deeper into the dark woods. I sat down

under the tree, and for the first time noticed the mess I
was in. I was sticky all over with Bynum; it felt like
school paste. I took off my blouse and wiped myself as
best as I could with leaves. One bra strap was broken.
I'd left my panties in the car. Somewhere in the woods a
stick snapped; I heard the screech of a hunted animal,
the frantic battering of wings. From where I sat at the
edge of the trees, I could see the depot and the willow
groves and all the cars, dark and quiet as if in hiber-
nation. It looked like somebody in a white blouse or
shirt was running up and down the track. Probably, I
thought, it was Bynum looking for me. Had he worn a
white shirt? I couldn't remember. Maybe it was really
me down there. Maybe the girl who sat under the tree,
contemplating moving deeper into the woods, was more
who I wanted to be than who I was. I couldn't bear the
sight of that ghostly, fluttering person, whoever it was,
searching along the tracks. I took off my skirt and my
tattered brassiere and hurried toward the sound of the
creek. The sky overhead was luminous, clouds like mus-
lin covering the moon. I reached the creek bank and
without hesitation I dropped my bundle of clothes and
slid into the water, up to my waist. I heard the puttering
sound of frogs as they scattered. The silty creek bottom
had a cool, thick, chocolaty feel; I dug my feet in like
anchors. The water felt as warm as my own skin, so that
I had the sensation of having no skin, only suspension. I
closed my eyes and pretended I was nothing but a soul.
I filled my cupped hands with creek water and washed
my face, my arms, my chest, my stomach. When I
opened my eyes, the rock on the other side of the creek
had turned into Bobby Rex Moseley. He was standing,
looking down at me.

"Don't be scared," was what he said. "It's Bobby
Rex Moseley."

I jumped, but I didn't scream. "I'm Pally," was what

I said. Maybe it never really happened, but if it didn't, then I was crazy.

"I know," he said. "What's happened?"

"I don't know," I said. It seemed the only truthful thing to tell him.

"Why are you here?" he said.

I sank myself lower into the water. "It felt like the right thing," I said.

"Are you with Bynum?"

"I was," I said. "Now I'm just here."

He squatted down as if to see me better. "I'm sorry if I scared you."

"I'm not scared," I said. "I'm just surprised." I wished I could see his face better. I wished the moon would peep out for a minute and let me make sure. It was him, I was positive, I would just about swear on the Bible. He had on the denim jacket Bobby Rex always wore, didn't he? His legs looked as hard as pipes in his jeans.

"Are you all right?" he asked.

"I don't know," I said. "Maybe."

Maybe it was my nakedness, maybe it was the darkness, but I felt a loosening of myself. I felt that I could say anything and what would it matter? This time would never come again. Words into the wind: there would be no proof.

"Is the water cold?"

"It's warm," I said. "Come in, if you'd like." How could I have said it? But I did. I felt something rush all around me when I spoke: an undertow, a snake maybe.

"No," he said, "I'd better not."

"Do you love Phoebe?" I asked softly.

He stood up then; maybe he didn't hear me.

"What did you come down here for?" I asked.

"No," he said. Or maybe he said, "I don't know." Which question had he answered?

He broke off a twig from a tree overhanging the creek.

He shredded the tip and stuck it in his mouth. "I ought to make a song about sassafras," he said. "I want to make a song that tastes this good."

"You'll do it," I said.

"Maybe."

"What's going on?" I said then, feeling a jingle of chills. "This doesn't feel real. Is it real?"

I thought he smiled, but how could I tell? "It's pretty real all right." He dropped the twig in the water. "Maybe it's the most real thing of all."

"I feel funny," I said. "Like I could be dead or something."

"You aren't dead," he said.

"How do you know?" I said, shivering. "You could be dead, too, and just trying to trick me."

He laughed and shook his head. "You're great," he said. "This should be a song."

"None of this could really happen," I said, "but somehow it is."

He said: "That's music."

"But why are you here?" I asked.

He shrugged. "I just am. Maybe something led me."

"Something led me, too," I said, thinking it should have been love, but it wasn't.

Beyond the woods we could hear the rumble of the Southern Crescent making its approach. He turned his head to listen. For the first time, clearly, against the dim, curdled sky, I saw his profile. It was Bobby Rex all right. He looked cut from black paper, crisp. You could fold him up real quick and small and fit him in your pocket, maybe.

"Some day I'm going to ride that train, I swear it," Bobby Rex said.

My heart lurched, and I thought of Speedy and Mama. I wanted to say then, I love you, Bobby Rex, I've always loved you, and it hasn't been easy keeping quiet, waiting for the right moment to tell you. I wanted to say all that as the train whistle blew, the Southern Crescent rattling someplace new and fast and heartless, its ruckus drowning out my confession, allowing me safety and truth all at once. But even as the whistle blew, I kept quiet. Something held me back. Call it pride or fear or wisdom. Call it of no use.

Overhead there was the rushing sound of startled birds. I felt the train's vibrations as I sat in the creek, and the whistle blew and blew, frantically, almost like a woman shrieking. With that splitting-open sound, the dreaminess suddenly vanished; I felt alerted to my nakedness and the coldness of the water and just how alone I really was. How much had I told him? What had I saved of any value for myself? Again the train whistle sounded: a wound of sound upon the still black skin of night. There was the wrong, awful scream of brakes, the sound of cars honking, people shouting.

I jumped from the creek and groped for my clothes, but Bobby Rex Moseley was already running toward where something terrible had happened. And as I ran toward the scene of the accident, I knew it was Bynum Jenkins. I just knew it.

XV

☆♡☆   ☆♡☆   ☆♡☆

In the mattress truck parked beside the depot, they found his neatly folded will. They found a good-bye note to Shilda; it was scribbled on the back of an invoice marked PAID. They found the Tuberose can, but Davey Cole assumed he'd been dipping snuff and didn't look inside. They found a shoebox filled with mementos: golden door tassels, old flaky love letters, Eddie's gold wedding ring, his red baseball cap with *Good Luck, Eddie, Love Gloria* written on the underside of the bill. They found his 1958 income tax refund check, neatly endorsed. "Everything in apple pie order," Davey Cole told Shilda. "Apple pie order."

When Mrs. Oxendine told the sheriff's people that Eddie's suicide had been methodical, she only meant that he'd *chosen* to lie down in front of the train and wait. "I commend him for his orderliness," she said at the inquest. She sat dry-eyed, unruffled, before the small gathering of people, the few of us who'd last seen Eddie alive. The only detail that suggested she might have cared the least little bit for Eddie was the wrinkled wad of pink Kleenex she clutched in her hand. She wore a potato sack kind of dress and men's oxford-style tie shoes. Her hair was crammed under a gigantic frayed beach hat.

She'd not been an eyewitness. She'd been expecting Eddie to call on her, but he hadn't shown and hadn't called. She hadn't been alarmed. She only figured that he'd picked up a new lead on Gloria's whereabouts and had gone sleuthing alone. Lately he'd run ads in the personal columns of several newspapers. At first he'd run an ad that read: TO GLORIA, COME ON HOME, WE'VE ALL GROWN UP. LOVE AND I CAN PROVE IT, TOO. EDDIE H. But as weeks had passed without response, he'd decided to give the ad a police-search flavor: MISSING: GLORIA DILLARD HAWK. MOVIE STAR LOOKS, SLIM, 5' 5", DIMPLES, LOVES TO DANCE. MAY BE RELIGIOUS. CASH REWARD FOR INFORMATION LEADING TO WHEREABOUTS.

Anyway, Mrs. Oxendine hadn't thought twice about Eddie's failure to show; he was a jumpy-acting tomcat of a man. She'd made herself a cup of owl's nest tea and settled down to read that book that everybody was so burned up about, *Lady Chatterley's Lover*.

The person with all the facts was Bynum, the one true eyewitness to Eddie's suicide. He stood before us and told everything, but he didn't drag me into it. He could have, of course, but he didn't. I cried so hard while Bynum talked that finally Joe Parker carried me outside to settle down, and Mama fetched me a cone of water from the sheriff's water cooler.

Bynum talked with the face of a very old man. His mouth looked wrenched by the facts. He talked to us as if from some mountain peak where the air was much too thin to breathe, but he breathed it anyway, his face pale and cramped. He wore a black suit and a stark white shirt and a horrible silk tie that was his daddy's and made me think of a turkey's wattle. The tie looked like it was choking him, but he couldn't feel it. He couldn't feel anything anymore except the awful burden of what he'd seen. It was as if every feeling he'd ever had coming to him had been concentrated into the few seconds when he watched the train bear down on Eddie Hawk and cut him in two.

I think I cried because there was no touching him. There was no touching his new wisdom. It was unexpected and unearned, Bynum's wisdom, but it was truly his. Nobody could even come close to him now. We could sympathize or we could condemn, but we couldn't finally know.

He'd gotten out of his car, he said, to stretch his legs, take a stroll, breathe some fresh air. It was a hot night for May. The tree frogs were chiming and the first lightning bugs of the season glimmered in the thickets and above the pastures beyond the railroad tracks. Something else flickered, too. There was no moon, but it was the kind of night where the sky seems lit from other sources, as if the clouds sponged up light from neighboring towns and farms. He saw a white shirt bobbing ahead of him, and he followed it.

"Why?" asked Davey Cole.

"I thought it was . . ." Bynum said, staring at his shoes, "somebody I knew."

He followed the shirt a good distance down the track, past the depot where the track begins to curve and disappear into the woods. He finally called out to it and heard an adult man say, "Get back now, son, get away."

"Did you recognize the voice of Eddie Hawk?" asked another official.

"No sir. All I recognized was that I'd made a mistake and the person I was following wasn't who I thought she was."

Howdy Oxendine poked me.

"I started back toward the car, and then I heard the train coming. I glanced back and saw him walk out on the track like he was hunting something."

"Did you call out to him?"

"It seemed unnecessary at the time, but yes I did. I

mean, you could *hear* the train as plain as could be. But something didn't feel right. I called to him like you might call out to somebody deaf or to a child.''

"What did he do?''

"He brushed off a spot on the ties, some gravel maybe. Then he took his sleeve and rubbed it along the rails like you do when you polish something. It was hard to see, but that's what it looked like he was doing. I was back a ways.''

"What exactly did you do when you saw that?''

"I thought maybe he was drunk, a drunk old tramp. A hobo getting ready to hop a boxcar. But something made me call out to him. I asked could I help him find anything. I told him to hurry up his looking because the train was due in.''

"Did he answer?''

"He said okay and thanks and leave it to him. Then I thought maybe he was some sort of railway official. I believed he knew his business.''

"What would a railway official be doing scrambling around in the dark on a Saturday night at midnight?'' Davey Cole asked.

"He acted like he had business,'' Bynum said again. "Even when he lay down on the tracks I believed he knew exactly what he was doing. I can't describe it.''

"Did the train blow a warning?'' asked a Southern Railway man.

Bynum nodded. His big, red flaglike hands shot up over both his ears. "It bleated all over the place,'' Bynum said. "I can't stop hearing it.''

"So you're telling us that you watched a man lie down on the tracks in front of a train while you did absolutely *nothing*?'' Davey Cole said, rolling his eyes.

Bynum dropped his chin on his chest. "I know,'' he said. "I should have known what was happening. But I didn't. This awful moment came when I didn't know anything, when the whole world was like some big dark hole. I couldn't tell up from down."

Davey Cole shook his head. "A man could be alive today."

"I'd give a million bucks if I'd realized," Bynum said in a pitiful, pasty voice. He rubbed his eyes with his big bony hands. I felt my heart just caving in for him, not because he'd been misjudged, but because he couldn't explain himself. He could never put those men in his shoes. He was only seventeen. All his life he'd kowtowed to adults, trusted them to know what they were doing. He'd had respect for authority drilled into him so deep, it'd made a crater where his common sense should have been. He would never be able to describe for them the disabling hesitation, the self-doubt which had overpowered him as certainly as the lure of death had overpowered Eddie. You spend so much of your youth learning when and when not to hold back because it seems your single power over foolishness. When I thought of Bynum out near the railroad tracks with poor Eddie Hawk, I saw myself sitting in Sawyer's Creek, failing to tell Bobby Rex that I loved him. It was a clear risk that when you held back to save yourself from foolishness, you squandered.

☆ ♡ ☆

They found a letter taped to the windshield of Eddie's truck, a long detailed letter from a music professor at State College in Raleigh named Augustus Fuchs, only nobody could pronounce his last name worth a damn. I don't remember the letter exactly as it was written, but since Shilda kept it and I saw it several times, I can report that the beginning went something like this:

Dear Mr. Hawk:
    I'm writing in response to the missing person's

ad which appeared in Sunday's News *and Ob-server.* Sunday *happened to be my sixtieth birth-day, and my children placed a birthday greeting in the personals. My family has been coming at me from all sorts of humorous angles, trying to pry me loose from a sadness of operatic magnitude which I now believe we share in common . . .*

I'll always remember the phrase "operatic magnitude" because when Professor Fuchs came to Orfax to meet Shilda, he repeated it. Shilda was staying with us, and Joe Parker was there for moral support, and he was not about to let something like "operatic magnitude" sneak by.

"Parlez-vous English?" Joe Parker said to Dr. Fuchs, and Dr. Fuchs blushed and tucked his chin in a kind of self-mocking embarrassment. By that I mean that he *exaggerated* his embarrassment, which seemed real.

"You know, Joe," he said, "I'm blessed with two talents: singer and windbag. I don't know which is most fun."

Later when Joe asked the professor's opinion of rock'n' roll and other popular music, Dr. Fuchs's voice took on a confessional tone. "As a student and teacher of voice," he said, "I know a singer like Del Monaco is first-rate. I know that maybe the greatest tenor of all wasn't Caruso but a fellow named Giuseppe di Stefano. Still, do you want to know whose voice gives me a thrill? It's a toss-up, Joe, between Perry Como and Julius LaRosa."

He was an elegant-looking elderly man with a monk-ish fringe of snow-white hair. He wore square-shaped, old-fashioned-looking glasses without frames. A pocket watch dangled from a chain draped across his globe of a stomach. He left the last two buttons of his vest undone of necessity. He had a fuming kind of face; as he talked, the skin seemed to pinken like a steadily ripening fruit. He gushed words at us, but windbag or not, I liked him.

As we listened to his story, I had the feeling that he was almost singing it. He gestured dramatically. You could tell, although he never said so, that he had loved Gloria Hawk.

He'd come to Orfax not because Betty had called him, but because he wanted to meet Gloria's daughter and tell her everything he knew. Mama fixed a platter of fried chicken and homemade mashed potatoes. She'd simmered pole beans all day in ham hocks and made pecan pie and hush puppies. There were pickled green tomatoes from Eddie's garden. She'd made iced tea with mint from a special recipe called Congressional Tea that Mamie Eisenhower served all the time at the White House and which Mama had copied out of *Ladies' Home Journal*. After supper, as if sensing that the small talk had run its course and the business of his being there was at hand, Professor Fuchs began his story.

That past January, the music department of State College had held auditions for a production of a Gilbert and Sullivan play. The auditions were open to the public, and among those who tried out for parts appeared a woman who called herself Gloria Dove and claimed to be from the mountains. At first all he knew of her was that she worked as a barmaid at a local college spot called the Player's Retreat. She lived in Greenaway's Rooming House on Hillsborough Street. Greenaway's was very particular about its boarders, the professor told us. Mrs. Greenaway only let rooms to neat, quiet working girls.

"She was a beautiful woman, your mother," he told Shilda. "She had black wavy hair, very shiny, that she wore pulled back and braided into a crown on top of her head. She had large, dark, trusting eyes and the sort of constant, wistful half-smile of a daydreamer. She sang wonderfully; but as well as she sang, she danced even better: so nimble that she looked boneless. Sometimes there was as much frenzy as there was grace in her movements, as if all that leaping and twirling would eventually tear her loose from her shadow. She danced as if she wanted to disconnect herself from everything and soar free. Free of shadow, gravity, memory, even instinct. Does that make sense? Remember that I'm a windbag, so back me up if you need to. I'm often 'greatly intoxicated by the exuberance of my own verbosity.' "

Joe Parker got up on that one and cracked himself a beer.

"I'll give you an example of how grounded she was by her instincts, and one in particular. She was always sinking herself into mischief by way of her *maternal* instinct.

"She worked at the Player's Retreat, which is a beer joint in downtown Raleigh where a good-size college crowd hangs out. It's also a hot spot for beatnik types. They've got glass bead curtains sectioning off the booths and red lights and throw pillows on the floor if you want to stretch out. Sometimes there's a little band of flute and bongo players who wear dark glasses and play accompaniment to a variety of haggard poets reciting haggard poetry. I know, dear Shilda, that this is a lot of detail, but I want you to visualize exactly where Gloria went to work each night excluding Sundays. It's a far cry from the Orfax Tastee-Freeze, which is where I stopped on the way here to ask directions. Those folks at the Tastee-Freeze were as nice as could be, so please don't misunderstand.

"Anyway, Gloria was always making friends with the customers. They liked her twangy country voice. Why, right in the middle of a discussion of, say, Nietzsche, Gloria would plop down a pizza somebody had ordered and write out a ticket and say, real cheerfully, 'Y'all come back.' Although none of them would have admitted it, they liked the fact that she didn't wear black turtlenecks and tights and drippy black shawls. Beatnik women dress like they're in mourning. But Gloria mostly wore pedal pushers and puff-sleeved white blouses with little round collars. Some nights she wore saddle oxfords like a cheerleader might have.

"I went there a lot myself, so I observed her plenty. Local musicians hang out at the Player's and some of my long-suffering music students—the ones destined to play jazz, either misinterpreted or ignored. It's a cozy spot to talk shop, drink a brew, and feel like something is bound to happen any minute. Usually it does: a knife fight between some beatnik and a Marine who's staggered in from the street, a lovers' quarrel, one of the waitresses throwing beer in some leering college boy's face, some artiste raving about the rejection of his work and collapsing among all the throw pillows." The professor took a deep breath. "I think I'd really love a beer now, Joe," he said, "if you'd be so kind."

Joe poured the beer in such a hurry that it was pure foam, and Professor Fuchs sipped it happily. "Now, where was I?"

"The maternal instinct," said Shilda.

"Ah, yes! Every Joe College with a problem wound up sobbing on her shoulder. And she'd get so caught up in somebody's tale of woe that she'd have to ask for the rest of the night off. She'd leave in tears. Then there was the time she ran off to New York City with poor Alice's boyfriend."

"*Who's Alice?*" said Shilda and Mama and Joe and I all together.

"It was the beginning of exam week, and some poor Joe College came hangdogging into the bar. He was in deep trouble. He had an F in physics, an F in engineering graphics, and an F in chemistry. The only thing he'd figured to do was not to show up for his exams, flunk everything, then go to summer school and start over, from scratch. He and his buddy started talking about getting away from all their troubles, and you know how bar talk goes. Well, Gloria was waiting on those two,

and you can bet the talk got to flying. She adored lighting fuses under people; why, those boys were popping
up and down on their bar stools because the seats were
getting so hot. Pretty soon they dream up the notion of
taking a little vacation to New York City, where all the
action is. Then they start saying how much fun it would
be to try to *race* each other to New York. Then they
start laughing and drinking and whooping it up, and
finally the bet is made that this Joe College will race that
Joe College to New York City. The first boy to touch
the Empire State Building will be winner and all-time
champion."

"Of what?" I asked.

"I guess fun," said Professor Fuchs, sipping his beer.
"So the first Joe College, the one with all the F's, said,
like a man on the gallows is apt to say, let him make one
phone call. He needs to tell his little girl friend Alice that
he won't be home for the weekend like he planned, that
he'll be racing a buddy of his to the Empire State Building instead. But you all know how such honesty pays,
and what little Alice said to him, and not very sweetly
either. That's when Gloria stepped in and took up his
torch. She could tell his spirits were sagging and that he
might give up the race he was so downhearted at the
prospect of losing Alice. Besides there were all those
exams to think about and he didn't have a cent on him
and he'd lose precious time and probably sober up if he
went back to the dorm for money now. Well, Gloria had
money. In no time she'd whipped off her apron, collected her tips—almost thirty dollars—and they were
off. She dragged that Joe College right out of the bar and
up the road, the whole bar cheering."

Professor Fuchs looked up from his empty beer glass
then. He looked around the dinner table at all of us. "I
shouldn't be telling you a story like this," he said. "It's
not my intention to make Gloria sound silly and reckless. I'm meaning to have you see what a wonderful,

lively person she was, and with all due respect I'm telling you about this episode."

"Did the boy win his race to the Empire State Building?" Shilda asked.

The professor smiled. "Oh, yes. Gloria stayed with him on the interstate and thumbed down his first ride. She gave him the thirty dollars and wished him well, then she walked back to the Player's Retreat and tied her apron back on. When I saw her later that night, she was fretting over that boy as if he were a son. She even called up Alice and tried to patch the romance. In a couple of days she got a postcard from him with a picture of the Empire State building on the front.

"She was always adopting people, snap! like that, and manufacturing huge attachments to them. She adopted me, which is why I speak so gratefully and with such authority," he said.

"Want another beer?" Joe asked him.

The professor waved him away. "In the middle of January we began auditioning for a musical, a Gilbert and Sullivan thing, lots of ballyhooing and dancing. But my heart just wasn't in the show. My wife of thirty-eight years had died of cancer during the fall, and I was a sorry mess. Half the time I didn't shave. I slept in my clothes. I got Mondays and Fridays mixed up, so you know I was bad off. I'd show up at my advanced piano tutorial and try to teach some budding Van Cliburn 'Chopsticks.' Then I'd shuffle into music appreciation class where those kids were all but throwing paper airplanes, and I'd expound upon some labyrinthine explanation of Bach's fugues. Plus I was spending large amounts of time at the Player's Retreat, quaffing beer and listening to the beatniks ramble and flirt wickedly with one another. I'd all but failed to notice the perky Gloria Dove delivering my pitchers of beer almost before I requested them. Once, she slapped down a hero sandwich and a garlic pickle, and when I looked up, baffled, she said, 'Hey, you looked hungry.'

"I rummaged in my pocket for some money, but she put up a palm in protest, a tray bristling with about twenty beer mugs balanced on one hip. 'Shush up and eat,' she said.

"I probably hadn't eaten in days; the sandwich tasted like a banquet. With food in my stomach, my sense of proportion returned to me. I joined a table of colleagues who were all arguing, and arguing very badly, about the merits of atonal music. They seemed overjoyed and patted my back and ordered me a beer, with much celebration of the fact that I seemed to be getting into circulation again. What a gloomy Gus I'd been until that single hero sandwich. It seems silly perhaps, but it was the first time since my wife's death that somebody had picked me out of a crowd to care for.

"I avoided the offered beer and ordered another hero sandwich. When Gloria brought it to me, I recognized her from the auditions. I couldn't remember her name. We'd almost given her the leading role, which we gave to Opel Ambler, a senior drama major and a real primadonna, instead. Every aspect of Opel's demeanor was pure theater. She didn't wear eyeglasses; she wore a monocle, which she switched from eye to eye. She carried a walking stick. She wore brazen, broad-brimmed hats with feathers and fresh flowers in the lapels of all her suits. To tell you the truth, Opel Ambler was a dead ringer for Oscar Wilde." He chuckled mischievously. Then he put a finger to his lips. "Hush, Augustus! Such a fool for digression. Sorry, folks," he said apologetically.

"Oscar Wilde," Shilda said, remembering.

It seemed to me then that a million years had passed since we'd met Oscar Wilde at Hogan's Esso. It seemed, too, that we'd met him on the last eve of our innocence, Shilda and me.

Mama asked if anybody wanted seconds on pecan pie,

and Joe and the professor held up their plates. Then, after he'd eaten the last rickrack of crust, Professor Fuchs settled back in his creaking chair and finished his story.

"The reason I brought up Opel Ambler was to show you what a determined and ambitious lady your mother was up against for a leading role. And of course Opel Ambler considered your mother a hick and an upstart.

"Gloria was cast in a supporting role as a swashbuckling peasant girl, and the role seemed to please her. She was a bright, quick study. She dropped her cajoling twang, adopting a British dialect that made you yearn for kidney pie. She danced like a spider around the other players; it was as if their movements suffered paralysis by comparison. Even when she stood among the chorus, swishing her skirts and rocking to and fro to that guileless music, you picked her out above all the rest.

"We all adored Gloria—even the dubious Opel. Gloria made the play work despite the disparate talents, the froggy voices of so many music students who'd joined the cast only as part of some college requirement. Not all music students can sing, you know. But Gloria cheered them on, rushing here and there between sets, calming stage fright on opening night, disclosing her secret of eating a chocolate bar prior to singing a solo to the jittery Opel Ambler.

"After opening night, Gloria invited us to the lobby of Greenaway's Rooming House for the cast party. She and Mrs. Greenaway, an elderly woman with theatrical aspirations all her life, were on the best of terms. Mrs. Greenaway had once worked concessions at Radio City Music Hall, where she'd run into practically all the stars. She was so excited about the cast party that she'd insisted on concocting the most dramatic hors d'oeuvres I've ever seen. She'd built an amazing little stage out of blocks of cheese and soda crackers and peopled it with Vienna sausages, using olives for heads. One Vienna sausage character wore a flamboyant little boa made from a curl of peeled carrot that had been meticulously fringed. One wore a radish crown. Some had raisins for shoes and others wore little pimento slippers. The orchestra members included a percussionist who hovered over a collection of marshmallows, a wind section all spiky with pretzels, and a bass fiddler sawing away on half a Bartlett pear.

"The cleverness of the food made it downright intimidating. Nobody would touch a thing. But the edible stage was such a conversation piece that nobody noticed the lack of alcohol. Mrs. Greenaway was serving lime Kool-Aid instead.

"It was the first cast party I'd been to without my wife, and despite the merriment and camaraderie, I felt lonely. When you've lived with another person for thirty-eight years, accommodating yourself to their quirks and habits, often spending your time the way *they* chose to spend it, you get very used to playing the accompaniment. Why, a solo performance scares you half to death. I stood in the lobby of Greenaway's feeling like a bashful schoolboy at his first piano recital. My hands felt overly large and dangling. What did I used to *do* with them? Of course, of course, I used to fetch Bonnie's purse from wherever she'd left it. I'd rummage in my pockets for matches to light her cigarettes. I'd mix her drinks, slip her stole off, slip it back on if she was chilly. I'd spread cheese dip on a cracker, even pop it into her mouth if her hands were full. And I hadn't quite realized, until I stood alone in the middle of a party, how much I'd counted on Bonnie's vivacity. She'd always known how to break the ice, introduce the two of us to a stranger, make a joke that would draw someone into conversation, laugh in a way that made somebody feel appreciated. She'd been the sun of our partnership, and I'd been simply an orbiting moon. It's all right. I'd never once resented her gravitational pull; in fact, I'd come to count on it."

"Didn't Opel Ambler befriend you?" I asked.

"She did. And by way of doing so, she was the first person to mutilate the hors d'oeuvre stage. Mrs. Greenaway had insisted that *somebody* do it; and since Opel Ambler was the leading lady of the play and hadn't been able to forget it offstage, she grandly took charge of the demolition. Before I could protest, she'd whisked the boa-draped character right off the stage and popped it into my mouth. 'You cad!' she said, laughing. 'Now you've gone and *eaten* the leading lady.' She stood there giggling and babbling about this and that until finally she got sidetracked by one rakish-looking party crasher whom I recognized as the manager of a local dinner theater, Vic Chance.

"For a moment or two I enjoyed not having to talk with anyone. I missed Bonnie terribly—in a paralyzing way. Then somebody touched my elbow lightly and said, 'You miss your wife, don't you, Augustus?'

"The directness of the question took me by surprise. 'Yes,' I said, not even stammering. 'Yes, I'm afraid I really do. It's a shock, the loneliness and how it drags on.'

" 'I know all about missing somebody,' Gloria Dove said to me. 'There are people who will tell you that you'll get over her in time, maybe even remarry. Certainly your pain will ease with time, they say. Well, maybe your pain will ease a little, and maybe you'll remarry. But you won't get over her. Not ever.'

" 'Thank you,' I said. 'I'm so glad you said that. I've never believed you got over such a loss; you just learn to coexist with it.'

" 'Nothing morbid about that either,' Gloria said. 'It's just a fact of life.'

"We sat down then on an old horsehair loveseat festooned with antimacassars.

"'Have you lost somebody, too?' I asked, although I knew she had; you could see the loss in her eyes.

"'Two husbands and a daughter,' she said then without blinking. 'It's the daughter that liked to have killed me. All these years I've wondered what she'd be like, how she'd look, what we'd talk about if we could meet. I still have her baby shoes. I got them bronzed,' she said. 'They sit on my nightstand and hold my Bible.'

"Then your mother told me the whole story of her courtship with your father, their hasty marriage, the birth of her only daughter, the gradual failing of her love for your father, and her romance with the minister. She never used names. She never told me which town she was from. She spoke so dreamily about it all that it was almost as if she'd forgotten everything except the guilt and the sorrow. After her elopement with the minister, she'd felt like a felon, wanted dead or alive. And over the years her remorse continued to chafe at those chains of love that bound her to the minister, finally loosening them. Of course the more she learned about the Bible, the more she grew to fear her punishment. She was convinced it would descend on her one day, unexpected. From out of a clear blue sky there would drop a rain of toads, a funnel of locusts. How could so terrible a crime against innocent hearts go unpunished? At last, in the fall of 1958, this past fall, she left the minister and came to Raleigh to begin a new life."

"Why didn't she try to come home?" Shilda asked. "Why didn't she at least give it a try?"

"She almost did," the professor said. "This, my dear, is the saddest part of my story."

We all leaned forward in our chairs.

"For months she contemplated the possibility. But this is what she decided: when she'd chosen to leave home, she'd not looked back a single time. Whatever sorrow that had been suffered by those she'd left had been endured and, if not entirely forgotten, certainly diminished. Remember that she'd been gone fourteen years, and that's a long time. For all she knew, Eddie had remarried. Shilda could be engaged. Maybe they'd left town altogether. Maybe they'd gone to Eddie's mother's in New Jersey. And even if they hadn't, what would they *do* with her? The fairest thing was to leave them to their familiar complications. Of course, these were the excuses she made to *me*, Shilda. But the truth I felt was that she longed to return home more than anything on earth. She couldn't sleep at night for remembering Shilda. If she could only see you once, even at a distance . . . Yet she wouldn't yield herself the chance. Maybe God was a dillydallyer when it came to dishing out just deserts, but she wasn't. She wouldn't return because deep in her miserably guilty heart she didn't believe that she deserved a second chance.

"Then, one evening, she rather lost control. It was almost Christmas, and the thought of being alone without any family at Christmastime was too terrible for her. She slipped out of bed and went downstairs to the telephone in the lobby and dialed her old number. Her heart was beating a mad staccato—can't you just imagine how she must have felt after all those years?—and over and over she prayed that Shilda would answer. She'd planned to say, 'Shilda?' and if Shilda answered, 'Yes,' then Gloria planned to hang up. Just the *thought* of hearing Shilda's voice after fourteen years made her practically faint with joy. Her hand was shaking so badly she feared she'd drop the phone. Her palms were gushing perspiration. The phone rang on and on, perhaps because it was so late. Finally Eddie answered. 'Hello?' he said. 'Who's this?'

" 'It's Gloria,' she said then, not able to stop the words. 'Could I speak to Shilda, please?'

" 'Is this a joke?' he said.

" 'It's not a joke. It's me, Eddie.'

" '*Gloria!*' He started crying then. 'Oh, God! Where *are* you? When are you coming home? Oh, Jesus!'

" 'I'm not coming home, Eddie. It wouldn't be right,' she said calmly.

" 'You *can* come home. I swear it. You'll see. I've never stopped loving you. I need you so bad. *Please,* Gloria.'

" 'Stop, Eddie,' she cautioned.

" 'Let me come get you, tell me where you are. Oh, God!'

" 'How's Shilda? How's my baby, Eddie? That's why I've called.'

"He was silent for a long time. When he finally spoke, his voice sounded husky with grief.

" 'I thought maybe you'd heard,' he said. 'Our daughter, Shilda Dillard Hawk, was killed in a car accident several days ago. We buried her yesterday. *Well, how in God's name was I to let you know?*'

"She hung up on him then, aghast. Maybe she hadn't heard right. Maybe she'd gotten the wrong number after all, and it hadn't been Eddie speaking. Maybe whoever it was held a grudge against her and was playing a hideous joke. It occurred to her that maybe it was God.

"She called back and this time he gave her the details. There were so many and she was so shocked that she got them mixed up. The two boys that Shilda had been riding with were alive but paralyzed. The car had flipped over in the snow. The car had no roof and she'd died of a skull fracture and broken neck. 'Good-bye then, Eddie,' she said when he came to a stopping place, sobbing. 'Good-bye, then.'

"So now she could stop pining for home since nothing she loved was there. But nothing she loved was anywhere anymore, and this, she knew, was God's punishment. It was such a long time in coming to her because God was such a Thinker.''

"But why didn't she call anybody else?" Shilda cried. "Why didn't she double-check?"

"You don't expect a father to lie about those sorts of things," Joe Parker said.

"Maybe he thought some big tragedy like that would bring them together in a way that smooth sailing hadn't," the professor said. "Now that I know the truth, that's all I can figure."

Mama put her face in her hands. "What a terrible lie," she said.

Shilda excused herself and went into the bathroom and cried for a while. When she finally came out, she had a brisk scrubbed look to her face. She'd tied back her long black hair in a ponytail.

I kept thinking about Eddie's lie and Gloria's phone call, then Eddie's attempts to find Gloria to at least tell her the truth about Shilda. That must have figured highly in his plan. And I couldn't help wondering that maybe, if she'd seen one of his frantic advertisements, she might have reconsidered and agreed to meet him. The whole story made me think of *Romeo and Juliet*; maybe all love tragedies had less to do with love than missed connections.

"So," the professor continued, "Gloria had tried out for the Gilbert and Sullivan in January in order to throw herself into the effort of forgetting who she was. She called herself Gloria Dove when I met her, and I never knew her by any other name. She was such a success in the Gilbert and Sullivan that we begged her to join our cast for the spring production of *Oklahoma!*

"On the closing night of *Oklahoma!* she was late. It was the last Saturday in April, a balmy night. Little bats fluttered in the twilight. There was the moist tender smell of late-budding trees, the bitter scent of dandelions. I'd opened the stage door that overlooked the Hillsborough Street parking lot. I stood there smoking a cigar, which is my habit prior to curtain rise. A little ritual of good luck, a pose of calmness. Behind me the dressing room was aflutter with prairie-style fashions: hoop skirts being wriggled into, bonnets, the garnishes of wigs with corkscrew curls, aprons, bloomers being fretted with and giggled over. But Gloria's absence was almost palpable. I can't explain why, exactly. The best I can do is to say that Gloria's presence had lent a *validity* to the drama we'd performed that semester. Somehow she'd embraced the stories we'd acted out on stage so wholeheartedly that the dramas tended to become as believable and respected as real life. Her enthusiasm swept over the entire cast; they were bedazzled.

"Of course you all know the rest, from my letter. That night, the final night of *Oklahoma!*'s performance April nineteenth, Gloria failed to show. She crossed Hillsborough Street, right in front of Greenaway's where she'd roomed for many months. Then, right in front of Mrs. Greenaway, who was waving her on and shouting things like 'Bravissimo!' and 'Break a leg!' she disappeared into an automobile piled to the roof with rowdy fraternity boys. It looked to Mrs. Greenaway that Gloria had thumbed a ride.

"Even as I stood chewing my cigar, I think I knew. *Deus abscondi.* I felt a hole in my world, a lapse of continuity. How does one speak of such things without seeming suspect? Then, I just happened to catch sight of this dogwood tree, pink, so loaded down with blooms that it looked fake. There it stood, splendidly showy, in a little circle of unmowed grass at the back of the parking lot. Maybe I was the only person who had noticed it all spring. But it didn't seem to mind its obscurity. It seemed to celebrate it, lifting its limbs almost wantonly to the breeze. I didn't think twice. I found Gloria's understudy and told her to lace up her jerkin."

We were quiet for a long time. Mama and Joe lit cigarettes, and the professor took out a cigar. The sky was dark outside; it seemed very late.

"What do you think happened to her?" I asked.

"Mrs. Greenaway found a note taped to the baby shoes on Gloria's dresser. All the note said was: *Don't worry; this seems to be what I do best.* Mrs. Greenaway called me right away. She was hysterical."

"What did the note mean?" I asked.

"Mrs. Greenaway thought there was some sort of symbolism to the note's being attached to the bronze baby shoes," the Professor said. "Mrs. Greenaway is a highly imaginative if Christian lady, and she thought that Gloria was perhaps with child and hastening off to seek its misfortune. But where would Gloria have found time for such romance, much less heart?"

"She meant she was good at leaving," Shilda said then. "And good at staying away. Her house was on fire again and she was saving herself."

"But she had friends in Raleigh. She had respect," I said. "She'd already started over."

"Fourteen years ago she had Eddie and she had me," Shilda said.

"Somebody reported seeing her at the bus station. Somebody else at the airport. Just last week a former student of mine, who knew of my interest in locating Gloria, phoned me from California to tell me that he'd seen her waiting tables at the Brown Derby restaurant in L.A. A faculty member thinks he saw her in New York City. She seems to be everywhere, you see."

"If only Eddie had told her you'd been *injured*," I said to Shilda. "Why did he say you'd been killed?"

Tears filled her eyes. "It wasn't anything against *me*, Pally."

"What are we going to do now?" Mama said. "What's left? How can we find her?"

"Get real lucky," Joe Parker said.

Shilda and I stayed up most of the night talking. When we finally cut the lights out, I couldn't get to sleep. Moonlight gushed like eerie daylight through the window, and I kept wishing we'd never found Gloria. Even though Eddie's death made better sense now, what good was sense where death was concerned? With death, solution is just a mirage in the heart.

"Are you going to look for her?" I asked into the darkness.

"I've never stopped," said Shilda. "Not since I was three years old."

XVI

☆♡☆　　☆♡☆　　☆♡☆

Of course I didn't go to the prom that year. But I heard about it plenty. Bobby Rex Moseley sang a song called "Phoebe," and people were just oozing over both of them for yearbook autographs before the night was over.

The theme of the prom, as things turned out, was Midsummer Night's Dream, which made a lot of folks mad because the prom committee had booked this old-fogey band called The Hi-Tones that played too much slow music. Mopsy Brownlee had to take up the microphone during the band's intermission because she'd heard so much grumbling. As she explained it, rock 'n' roll wasn't as *romantic* as a Midsummer Night's Dream theme called for. If the committee had chosen Mardi Gras, there would have been plenty of rock 'n' roll. Remember, too, that the committee had been *elected*. It was the first time in her life that Mopsy Brownlee got booed.

When I heard that Bobby Rex Moseley had sung a song dedicated to Phoebe, something got blown out, poof! Night after night I lay in the dark, trying to figure it out. I wasn't sure what had happened down at Sawyer's Creek the night Eddie had gotten killed; Eddie had pretty much gotten in the way of all that. But I must have known all along that the moments between us, which had seemed so full of honest if dreamlike exchange, were nothing but the result of chance meeting. What had I expected? I felt a cold spot in my heart.

I'm not saying I was hardened against him. But it seemed an unforgivable slip in judgment: he'd written a love song about somebody he didn't love. Then he'd stood up in public, basking in the spotlight, and sung that song with his eyes closed, like during some private kiss, his knees buckling as if he were in pain because love hurt him so. But if you want to know the truth, it wasn't the girl he cared for at all; it was the singing.

I'd been wrong to think of Bobby Rex Moseley as pure. Pure didn't have one thing to do with him; he was detached. What's more he couldn't help it, didn't have a single care about his detachment. Didn't recognize it, wouldn't have wanted to. Would just as soon have flicked purity off himself as lint. Of course the more he didn't care, the more you couldn't touch him.

I thought back to the night at Sawyer's, hearing the awful wounding sound of the train, people yelling. I'd jerked myself out of the water. But he'd vanished before I'd hoisted myself onto the creek bank. I'd run as fast as I could across the field, toward the track, but I never spotted Bobby Rex.

When I could finally see what was going on, that somebody had been hit by the train, I quit hunting for Bobby Rex and raced up and down the track screaming Bynum's name. "He's over there," somebody shouted, and at last I found him, near the caboose, huddled down upon himself and wailing like a baby. I threw my arms around him, feeling the wet heat of tears that seemed to have soaked his entire body. At that moment it seemed to me that we'd been through everything in the world together, maybe even marriage. "Oh God oh shit oh God oh shit oh shit, Pally, don't look!" he'd sobbed into my hair. I'd squatted down, hugging him, until the sheriff and the ambulances arrived.

It was much later, after the crowd began to thin out and Bynum and I were slouching toward the Studebaker, that I saw Bobby Rex. He stood quite alone, some distance from the track. His arms were folded across his chest. I don't know what I expected from him. I'm not sure what might have been an appropriate sign for him to make. His face had a flat, resistant quality to it. He didn't turn as we passed him; there wasn't a flicker of movement in him—he might have been stone. He seemed to be studying something in the distance, and I mean a great distance beyond. In his eyes he was gone forever from that place. But what prickled my arms with gooseflesh was to hear him humming steadily under his breath. As we passed him, sure enough, he rocked steadily on his heels, keeping time. The song he hummed had the steadfast beat of a railroad ballad.

☆ ♡ ☆

Fourth of July weekend, Shilda's grandmother flew down from New Jersey and Joe Parker drove us all over to Friendship Airport to meet her.

"Is that her?" I asked Shilda, pointing to a cheerful-looking, gray-haired lady in a prim, gray, vase-shaped suit.

"Hell no," said Shilda with disdain.

"*There* she is then. *That* one, I'll bet." I pointed to a short, hump-shouldered woman who was roly-poly as a biscuit and wore harlequin glasses with sprays of rhinestones at the corners.

"Get serious," Shilda said.

"I hope this is the right plane," Joe Parker said.

"Mavis!" Shilda cried, jumping up and down and waving.

It was hard to think of Mavis Davis as Eddie Hawk's

mother and almost sixty. She'd remarried after Eddie's father had died, and she'd changed her name. She'd liked the way people's eyebrows raised when she gave her name as Mavis Davis. People were so startled that they never forgot you, she said. You had a built-in conversation piece to help you over any shy spots in your life.

Mavis came prancing off the plane in a pair of tight red jeans and a matching red cowboy hat. Her blue canvas flight bag had Budweiser written on it. She wore a white sleeveless sweater which showed off sinewy, suntanned arms. She wore black high heels and pink socks, rolled around her ankles, plus an ankle chain.

I liked her face. Her skin was the color of butterscotch and seemed to lighten from underneath when she smiled, which she did, broadly, as soon as she spotted Shilda. She swiped off her straw cowboy hat and saluted us with it. Her hair was the bright, clumpy color of scrambled eggs.

"Hello, hello, strangers," she said all around. Then she clamped Shilda to her and tears rolled down both their cheeks. Up close you could see that her earrings were made of real pretzels which had been shellacked. A pack of cigarettes bulged in one pocket, and she gave off a smell of wintergreen Life Savers, tobacco, and the closed-up, hair tonic smell of trips.

"Well," she said finally, holding Shilda at arm's length. "Let's have a gander at my little orphan. You look damn good, honey. Cripes! What you've been through!" She had the tiniest and most delicate tattoo I've ever seen engraved right over her smallpox vaccination scar: a neat little sunburst.

We introduced ourselves, then everybody strolled over to the baggage claim chute. "I travel light," Mavis said, holding up her flight bag and sticking out one foot to halt the U.S. Army knapsack rolling by. "This is it," she said briskly. And she insisted on renting a car, even though Mama offered her the use of ours. No, she said, no, she wanted to do a little sightseeing while she was here, a little traveling down Memory Lane. This was her vacation, after all. Maybe she and Shilda would take off and go to the beach for a few days after they'd sorted out their business. No, thanks anyway, she needed a car of her own.

☆ ♡ ☆

All the next week we sorted through Eddie's things. I'd never thought men were savers; I'd never considered them real big on mementos, but he'd never even tossed out Gloria's wedding bouquet. We found it in one of about a million cardboard boxes in the attic, as crisp and singed-looking as a wad of old newspapers. We found her wedding dress, packed neatly in plastic and mothballs. Under the wedding veil lay what seemed to be a tiny shrunken head. It was a baseball with the signatures of all Eddie's teammates. *Good luck*! they wrote. *Hot time tonight*! For a second Shilda cradled it in her palms, then she slipped it under the bodice of the dress. "Junk it," she said to the dress, so we did. We didn't question a single decision, even if it seemed stern and heartless. We acted matter-of-fact, like sailors following captain's orders, disposing of unnecessary cargo to keep a ship from sinking. And every day we worked, the house felt lighter. Joe hauled off box after box in his pickup. Some he took to Goodwill. Some he took to the county landfill. Shilda donated the crate of worn-out catcher's mitts and baseball gloves to Orfax High. They'd grown stiff over the years, coated with a chalky mildew. But you could still rub a clean spot on any one of those gloves and breathe the candy-sweet odor of leather and sweat. We discovered piles of newspaper clippings: baseball games played and lost, sports articles clipped from magazines. There were scrapbooks so loaded with photos of baseball pals and scoreboard news that they wouldn't shut. Items that fluttered out disintegrated midair into ashy powder.

"Junk it," Shilda said tiredly.

Her face looked greasy in the heat of the attic. She fanned herself with a scrapbook and all the pages flew out.

He'd saved every appliance he'd ever bought, every mechanical gadget he'd ever laid his hands on and for one reason or another stopped using. "Jesus Christ! Eddie's Van de Graaf generator!" Mavis cried and threw up her hands. "He built that thing back in high school. You can pass a million volts of electricity through your body with that thing and not get electrocuted," she said.

"Who'd want to do that?" I asked.

"Eddie did," she said almost proudly. "He really loved science."

We plowed past an old waffle iron, a toaster oven with a frayed cord, a mixer with jammed beaters that was still coated with fossilized mashed potatoes, a net sack of Vidalia onions that had withered to the size of peas, several tuckered-out radios and flashlights, a sack of railroad flares. We paused over that sack of railroad flares, then we hurried along. There was a kiddie record player with a Mickey Mouse lid. "Junk it," Shilda said.

Mama uncovered piles of magazines from the twenties and thirties, and we took time to run through a few. It was the fashions that got to us and the advertisements for things that now were obsolete, like ice boxes that really held chunks of ice.

"There's a broomstick skirt," Mama said. "When you washed them, you wrapped them sopping wet around a broomstick to dry. Wrinkles were the fad, can you believe it?"

"Stockings with seams!" I said, pointing.

"Silk," Shilda said.

"See those mushroom heels?" Mama said. "They're

back in style today. Everything always comes back in style. We'd be smart if we saved everything."

"Some things don't," said Shilda, a wistful, glazed look in her eyes. She stared past us out the attic window and down the road. "Things like long dresses with lace collars, pantaloons."

"They're too much trouble," Mama said, "and we're too modern."

"But seems like it's always the most beautiful things that don't last, that never come back," Shilda said. There was an insistent sadness in her voice. But it was her right to be sad, and nobody felt like shooing it away with false humor. "I'm talking about things with tucks and hand-stitched lace and scalloped hems."

"I know," Mama said.

Just then Joe Parker hollered as if something had bitten him. "Great God in heaven! What's *this*?" When he held it up to the light we all gasped, all except Mavis, who scooted right over to where Joe sat; she whisked the jar right out of his hands.

"Aunt Bess!" she cried almost gleefully. In the blond sunlight that slanted through the window I could clearly see the remains of a preserved cat. He'd dissolved into a kind of grayish stew, all but his claws and his yellow teeth and his jellybean eyes. A moment later Joe had ferreted out the other bottles, which contained Aunt Bess's tonsils and adenoids. The bottle with the calf's brain had broken long ago, and Joe held up the dry, brittle remains which looked like a piece of old sponge. "Who's Aunt Bess?" Shilda asked.

So we called it quits for the day, and Joe made fresh lemonade and Mama and Mavis fixed roast beef sandwiches the New York deli way, according to Mavis, who lathered them with brown mustard and horseradish that materialized from her knapsack along with some very special pickles labeled Polski Wyrob.

Then we sat right down among all the packing crates

and Mama told Shilda everything she knew about Eddie
and Gloria's past together. It was the same story she'd
told me the afternoon we'd snapped beans, even her
digressions about Speedy. As I listened to the way she
told the story, I recalled our earlier conversation about
the old-timey fashions found in magazines, and Shilda's
yearning for the frills of old-fashioned clothes. Now I
knew it wasn't the lace Shilda had yearned for, it was
the caring that put the lace on in the first place. Everything worthwhile came from caring: being cared for,
caring about somebody, taking care to do this or that,
taking care of your health, sending a care package, driving in the snow very carefully. I listened to the reassur-
ing way that Mama told the story, anecdotes of joy and
sadness. The story seemed to envelop Shilda. She wore
a bright and listening expression. In the version Mama
had told me, there had been an airiness in the telling; the
story had seemed more like entertainment. But this time
Mama offered it as a gift. Handmade with the greatest of
care. Her voice sounded sturdy, deliberate, as if creat-
ing something durable, a *mending* kind of voice that
went in and out of something very worn but well worth
saving. A voice as deft as a darning needle.

By the end of the week we'd sorted and hulled out
everything from old toothbrushes to Shilda's potty chair.
We'd uncovered in the basement freezer the top layer of
Eddie and Gloria's wedding cake, glittering under stalac-
tites of ice. We'd junked lampshades with hula skirts of
fringe, cracked baseball bats, boxes of expired season
tickets to ball clubs all over the state, snapped fishing
poles, galoshes as holey as sieves, sacks of old Coke
bottles—what for?—shoeboxes full of pennies, funny
books, dog show trophies—where on earth *from?*—a
Boy Scout pup tent so lightweight that Mavis rolled it up
like a flag and popped it into her knapsack, no further
ado.

But whenever we came upon a nostalgic item now

amidst the rubble, like the wedding cake top or, say, a bright pink teddy bear that he must have won for Gloria at the fair, pitching baseballs at some silly target, maybe, we no longer clammed up and avoided talking about Eddie's past. He'd had a past: cluttered and sad, but happy sometimes, too. He'd saved a lot of wrong things and thrown away some of the best, no doubt, and we needed to think about that, too.

There was a kind of unspoken rule that if you found something of particular interest to you—an old postcard, a letter, a recipe card, you could take your time and savor. What had begun as a wearying chore had begun to take on the flavor of a family reunion. "Remember when Eddie caught us stuffing our bras with Kleenex?" I said to Shilda. "Remember when he let us camp out all night in the mattress truck?" "Has anybody come across his recipe for tomato sauce? He hasn't made it for years on account of the white flies. Eddie could march right up to a copperhead snake and laugh right in its face, but the sight of a single white fly on a tomato leaf made him break out in a cold sweat. One fly meant the eventual destruction of the whole garden." "Remember Eddie's eyeball trick—how he could move one eyeball all around while the other stayed perfectly still?" "Gross!"

"I've decided *this* much," Mavis said one day. It seemed we'd come to a stopping place. "Eddie's big failing was that he never learned to let things go." She was, as his mother, perhaps the only one who could have said that. We'd all thought it, I'm sure. The attic seemed to explain Eddie's death in a way the professor's story hadn't. We watched Joe maneuver the last big box down the attic stairs. It brimmed with useless singular things: mateless socks, one tennis shoe, one flip-flop, a jar of unmatched earrings, single gloves. There were several books—mysteries—their bindings so rotten that they'd lost half their pages. Why hadn't he been able to toss them out? Yet I thought there was something so optimistic about saving bits and pieces of things. It's as if Eddie had believed that loss, no matter what kind, was never permanent. In one way Eddie seemed clingy; but in another way he'd been steadfast.

Mr. Clarence Monday, a go-getter realtor from Kernersville, drove over to check out the house with a couple of bank-officers. And Mavis hired a local lawyer to help untangle the knots of her guardianship, of both Shilda and the property. The day before she and Shilda left to go on vacation at Nag's Head, a FOR SALE sign appeared in the yard.

They had made reservations at the Carolinian, the best hotel on the beach, and they begged me to come along. But I said no. It just ached me to be with them, knowing our days together were so sparingly numbered. Shilda had decided not to live with us and finish high school at Orfax High; she was going to live with Mavis in Newark.

"I wish you'd come with us," Shilda said as Mavis revved up their rented car. It was a hot, bright morning. Instead of dark glasses they both wore old 3-D glasses they'd dredged out of the attic. The glasses had crumpled-up stems. They both wore short shorts and halter tops and flip-flops; they looked more like sisters than grandmother and granddaughter. Mavis adjusted her canvas beach hat that had MADE IN THE SHADE written across its bill. "We'd have such a great time," Shilda said. "Tell her a sample joke, Mavis."

"A sample joke," Mavis repeated, pretending to haul one up from an extensive repertoire. "Hmmmmm—oh, yes! What did the elephant say when he was pulled out of the ditch by the balls?"

"I give up."

Mavis grinned her boyish grin. "Thank you, Mr. and Mrs. Ball."

Shilda whacked both her thighs and laughed. "Think

of it. All the way to the beach, six hours of nonstop jokes and talk.''

"I'd be a third wheel, and y'all know it," I said.

"Poo!" said Mavis.

Shilda gave me a look of disgust.

"I'll miss you," I said.

"It's just a week," said Shilda. She pulled her flag of black ripply hair back from her face and lassoed it into a ponytail.

"Still," I said, "I'll miss you."

She patted my hand. "Take care of the house for us. Don't let Mr. Monday sell it to some creep."

Mavis began backing the car down the driveway, and I followed, holding the door handle. I wished I had the nerve just to jump right in and go, buy a bathing suit and a toothbrush when I got there. I felt as old as somebody's mother, waving good-bye to them. For a long time after the car had disappeared, I stood watching. I felt ready to be separated from Shilda, but I stood watching as if I couldn't believe they'd really left me. I expected any second the car would roll backwards up the street for a joke, and they'd leap out and pull me inside. But I knew that the loneliness I felt was the practice sort, because Shilda hadn't really left for good.

They'd given me the keys to the house on Proximity Street with instructions to make it available to anyone Mr. Monday chose to bring over. Also they wanted the mail checked. I walked up on the front porch and sat down in the glider and waited for Jim Dooley, the postman, who was chatting next door with a lady who still wore her bathrobe and curlers. Her little boy rode his tricycle up and down the sidewalk, trying to smash ants and whooping whenever he got one.

She looked like she'd be an attractive lady if she'd take out her curlers and put on some lipstick. She seemed to enjoy Jim Dooley's company immensely, tossing her head back and laughing flirtatiously in spite of her curlers—and that took confidence. Every now and then the breeze would blow back her housecoat and open her up to his view. Who could really tell what was happening there? But give me a guess and I'd say something was. Just the way she laughed. Unnecessarily. Just the way she bit the corner of an envelope he handed her. There she was, living in a nice brick house, a sporty Pontiac convertible in the driveway, a curly-headed little boy riding up and down the sidewalk walloping ants, and she wanted more than that already. You could tell. I gazed up at the porch eaves of Eddie's house so that I wouldn't see too much. A wasp glided stealthily in and out of its parched nest. I looked back at the woman talking with Jim Dooley, but they'd both gone inside and shut the screen door. I wondered if she knew the story of Eddie and Gloria Hawk, if the town's gossip had reached her and she knew not just the immediate facts of his death and her disappearance, but the histories behind them. But if she was of a mind to have a go at Jim Dooley, nothing would stop her, would it?

In a minute or so, Jim Dooley came out of the house, wiping his mouth on the sleeve of his postal uniform. Now, it could have been water—a drink she'd offered him—that he was wiping from his lips, or it could have been lipstick. Even though she wasn't wearing any lipstick, guilt might have caused him to wipe his mouth.

"Hello, Pally," he said to me, trotting up the porch steps. "How come you're sitting here?"

"Waiting on you," I said.

He looked flushed, but *maybe* it was the heat. He handed me a phone bill, a *Life,* and a letter in a gray envelope. "How's Shilda getting along?" he asked, shifting the weight of his mailbag to the other shoulder.

"She and Mavis have gone to the beach," I said.

"It'll do her good to get away."

"Fun stuff always does Shilda good," I said. "She's one of these people who's easily distracted."

"Good for her," he said. "I sure wish somebody could distract me from this heat. Whew!" He wiped his forehead with one palm. Then he asked for a glass of water.

☆ ♡ ☆

I opened some windows to air the rooms and laid the mail on top of the mantel. The letter was from Augustus Fuchs. He always wrote in black ink on pearl gray stationery. I held the letter up to the light, but I couldn't read through.

Inside the house there was hardly any furniture left. Beside the fireplace in the living room sat a beige sofa with cigarette burns on one arm, a telephone table, a big old Motorola television set about as heavy as a tank, and a pot of dusty philodendron that somebody had sent for Eddie's funeral. All the rest of the furniture had been shipped to Newark or put in storage. The empty house had an airy, blond quality to it. I liked walking through the large sunny rooms and touching the cool plaster walls. The windows, stripped of blinds and curtains, let in big yellow banners of light that fluttered over the bare, heart pine floors. In spite of everything, it was a cheerful house.

The phone rang, a sparkler of sound, and it was Mama asking if I wanted to go with her and Joe to Greensboro. They were going to pick up their wedding invitations. I felt excited for them, but I said no.

For a long time I just sat on the sofa with the cigarette burns, thinking. I thought of the solidness of the house, but how solidness had failed. I thought about how even with the walls painted yellow and rose and baby blue, the air had hung between people as gray and dim as bad weather. I thought how nobody, looking at that house alongside Mr. Monday, who would be pointing out the recently installed oil furnace, the narrow little butler's pantry off the kitchen, the sleeping porch upstairs off the bedroom where Gloria and Eddie had once slept, nobody looking would know the misery that had dwelled there as real and hulking as any person. There could have been a murder in the bedroom or a baby born there, and nobody could have told the difference.

I ambled out to the kitchen and cut the faucet off, hard. Every time it dripped it sounded like a bell. Eddie's recipe file was beside the sink, and I flipped through until I came to some blank recipe cards at the back of the index. All the cards had little black old-timey stoves printed at their tops and a headline that said: FROM THE KITCHEN OF EDDIE HAWK. I took one of the blank cards and rummaged in a drawer until I found the stub of a pencil. Then I sat down in the middle of the kitchen floor and wrote a good luck letter to that house. I wished it well; I wished its new owners happiness and everlasting love. I thanked the house for sheltering much of my girlhood. Then I folded the recipe card and I kissed it for a seal. I put it in a mason jar and screwed the lid on tight, and in the farthest corner of the attic, I dug a hole in the insulation and buried the jar. You'd never have guessed the letter was there; the attic was bare, a clean slate of an attic. All that marked the spot where the note lay hidden was a golden swarm of dust motes, spiraling in a shaft of sunlight. Like bees they seemed, anticipating blooms.

☆ ♡ ☆

It was later in the summer, while Mama and Joe Parker were on their honeymoon, that Eddie Hawk's house sold. Shilda was long gone to Newark with Mavis, and the summer was at the blowzy, overspent point when you are looking forward to school starting again. I could hardly get excited about the sale; the weather was so hot and breathless that it smacked excitement flat as if it were a pesky fly. I still had the keys that Shilda had left me. I'd been collecting any late mail and keeping the grass mowed. Usually Mr. Monday didn't bother to tell me when he was bringing somebody to have a look. But the last day in August—I was watering the petunias Mama had planted in a barrel—I recognized Mr. Monday's big white Buick pulling up beside our trailer. He waved at me and braked the car, gravel shooting out from under his tires. He jumped right out, as if his news was urgent, and he ran up to the trailer waving his hat. It was a white Panama hat with a madras hatband and he had on these prissy narrow black-and-white straw shoes. "Whahoo!" he cried gleefully, fanning his face with a one-hundred-dollar bill. "Looky, looky!"

"I see. What is it? Where'd you get it?"

"It's *earnest* money," Mr. Monday said happily. "I'm hoping we've sold the Hawk house. Mind if I sit down? I might faint I'm so excited and the weather's so hot." He sat right down on the trailer stoop and loosened his tie. He had a thrust-out, leathery-looking face, but the mustache on his upper lip was so delicate that it looked like tooling.

"Just let me catch my breath," he said, "and I'll take you right over to meet them."

"Meet them? What do I want to meet them for?"

"I thought you might like to case them out so that you could write Mrs. Davis and Shilda what you thought."

"All right," I said. But I wasn't sure of anybody's interest at this late date. In almost two months, Shilda had only managed to scribble me a postcard. Mostly it was a list of the names of boys she'd met and their vital statistics.

"Well, come on then," said Mr. Monday. "Let's hightail it before the doctor changes his mind."

"A doctor?"

"He's paying the full $18,000. Didn't even bat an eye. Didn't ask about the roof. Didn't inquire if the basement leaked. Didn't care if the fireplaces burned coal or wood. Knew exactly what a butler's pantry was. Didn't raise an eyebrow over the leaky faucets."

"Rich doctor," I said.

"I don't think it's that," Mr. Monday said.

"What did his wife say?"

"He's a widower," Mr. Monday said, and dropped his eyes appropriately. "He's got two little boys though, popping all around him like firecrackers."

"Children?" I said. "Well, let me go check them out."

☆ ♡ ☆

The doctor was sitting on the porch glider with his two little boys when we drove up. They were twin boys with taffy-colored hair as curly as wood shavings. Before Mr. Monday had cut the Buick's engine I could hear the children crying. Mr. Monday turned to me with a wise look. "See what I mean?" he said.

"Hello!" he called to the doctor, who stood up immediately and waved as if he'd lived there all his life. But up close you saw no such confidence in the man's face. His features seemed to rearrange themselves constantly in attitudes of worry or hesitation as his children clung to him or begged for release. He had a nice face, a square and manly face with a cleft chin. But there was a lonely, almost bookish quality to his face. His nose was fine-boned and beaky, as if it had been shaped by him falling asleep face-first on his books. He had blue, serious eyes, foggy with intelligence or grief or maybe just the distraction of his two boys. When he looked at me it was as if he couldn't quite concentrate. He was the youngest doctor I'd ever met, and introduced himself right away as William.

"Thank you for keeping the lawn mowed," he said. It was such a stiff and funny thing to say that I burst out laughing. "Somebody planted flowers, too," he said, uncertain.

"Oh, they're just crummy old petunias," I said. "And marigolds. They're just about the only flowers that can survive the summers around here. Nothing special."

"They set the house off nicely though," said Mr. Monday.

"Where are you from?" I asked William.

He stooped quickly to brush a bee out of one boy's hair. The other kid was busy tearing petunias up by their roots, and William hurried down the steps to snatch him up. "No, Francis!" he said. Then he turned to me, dazed-looking and apologetic. "What did you just ask me?" Francis went galloping after the bee that had been released from his brother's hair.

"I asked where you were from," I said. "You don't have a Southern accent."

"I'm from Colorado," he said.

"Colorado," I said. The word itself sounded cool and high. "The Rockies," I said. "Are they really that beautiful and jagged and snowy?"

"They are," he said, smiling. "They're something. Hey, are you trying to make me homesick?"

"Why on earth would you want to move to *Orfax*?" I just couldn't help myself. I pointed my lips at the ground and spat the word Orfax like a mouthful of poison. Maybe I was only showing off. Maybe I thought it would make me seem more worldly-wise if I pretended to hate the place. I was only flexing my straitjacket. Anyway, I wrenched my face into a pose of disgust and Mr. Monday blanched.

"What sort of nonsense is that?" Mr. Monday chided. "Orfax is a great town, Doctor. Pally's just fooling around."

I blushed. I wished Mr. Monday hadn't used the expression "fooling around." He was just so *out* of it. I wished I'd changed my clothes before we'd driven over, too. I

had on these godawful purple short shorts and this old
holey T-shirt of Joe Parker's that you could probably
see my bra through. I had on Joe Parker's FCX FEEDS
hat, but I wouldn't have taken it off for anything because there was a wad of lank brown sweaty hair underneath that should have been washed two days ago. In a
few weeks I would be seventeen, but, damn it, I looked
twelve.

"No, boys! Don't go into the street. Jesse! Francis!
No! Excuse me," he said to Mr. Monday and me before
he ran flying across the lawn to them. Of course they
weren't listening at all. They squatted by the street
popping tar bubbles with long sticks. "No, Francis," I
heard William say. "Don't put tar in your mouth. Yes,
Jesse, I know that it *looks* like licorice . . ."

Mr. Monday shook his head and fiddled with his delicate mustache. "Why on earth do people *do* it?" he
mumbled.

"*Do it*?"

"Get married, have kids. It's all a joke, isn't it?"

His bachelor's smugness irritated me. His aftershave
smelled like hyacinths. He blotted his forehead with an
ironed hankie that gave off a loveless, professionally
bleached smell. "It just seems like such a *battle,* having
a family," said Mr. Monday. "I mean in spite of the
sharing and the camaraderie, it's all so *complicated*. Just
look."

Now Francis was sobbing because he wanted the other
twin's stick. When William tossed the other boy's stick
into the drainage ditch, too, he also set up a howl.

"Sooner or later, people are going to wise up to all
this American family nonsense. 'First comes love, then
marriage, then comes wifey with a baby carriage.' You
can't treat life like the production line. But we're such
saps. We've all let Norman Rockwell take us for a
ride."

I wanted to challenge Mr. Monday. I wanted to challenge him for Betty and Joe Parker's sake if nobody else's. But I didn't. In fact, I sort of nodded. In my head I started making a list of worthwhile loves versus good-for-nothings. Betty and Speedy, Betty and Joe Parker. That's as far as I got. But it was the hottest day of the summer, and heat like that sort of flattens your hope. I watched poor William stumble toward us, Francis in one arm, red-faced and sorrowful, Jesse kicking and crying in his other arm. "If it's okay, Mr. Monday," the doctor said marching past us onto the porch, "we'll just spend the night here. We've got sleeping bags in the car."

"Fine, fine," said Mr. Monday, beaming. "I'll call the power company and see about having your lights cut on."

"We have flashlights," Francis said, wiping his tears.

"Well, I'll bring the contract out tomorrow then, since you seem to have your hands . . ."

But the miserable little family hurried inside the house before he could finish and the front door slammed shut.

XVII

☆♡☆　　☆♡☆　　☆♡☆

It seemed Indian summer was with us until Christmas that year. The trees never changed colors; the leaves simply burned brown and dropped off. By the time you'd walk to school and heard the eight o'clock bell, your clothes were soaked through with sweat. The sky was so blazing shiny blue that you couldn't look at it for very long. Football practice had to be held at six in the morning, which made the whole team pretty vicious, but that was *good*, Coach Weaver said. They didn't want any seventeen-year-old linebacker dropping dead of heat-stroke during some workout in full sun. This had happened to a college boy over at State College. Even the cheerleaders were told to cut back on the number of cartwheels and handsprings they normally performed. Without Mopsy Brownlee urging them on, they were an athletically limp bunch anyway. All their energy went into giggling with just enough left over for ironing their knife-pleated skirts.

The heat cast a dreaminess over everything. You kind of hauled yourself from place to place through air that felt like glue. It was too hot to eat. Butter kept in the refrigerator stayed soft, and Jell-O wouldn't set at all. Nobody could stand to cook, it was so hot, and I guess that Betty and Joe and I lived mostly on watermelon and peach ice cream and canned salmon until Halloween. On the verge of heatstroke myself and in a fit of practicality, I got my hair cut short in a Dutch-boy style. Mrs. Futrell passed me in the hall and complimented it: she referred to the cut as a "classic bob."

I baby-sat a lot for William Pickup, who wasn't a people doctor at all but a vet. Doodle Washington's wife, Lady, quit her job at the high school cafeteria and became William's housekeeper. He paid her better and took care of all Doodle's dogs for free. But in the evenings, when he made most of his large animal calls, I stayed with the boys. I'd feed them supper, and I'd give them their baths and read Dr. Seuss books until they were sleepy. They were sweet boys, really, but they liked to test you. They were only three years old, motherless, and living in a strange little town they'd never visited before in a house that smelled empty. William Pickup just didn't have time to fix the house up; he was busy day and night with his new vet practice. Those little fellas slept on the floor in sleeping bags until Christmas that year, when Santa Claus finally broke down and bought them bunk beds.

Often, after we'd read books for a while, I'd sing to them: a hymn, an Elvis Presley song, a nursery rhyme remembered from my childhood. Sometimes they sang with me, and their flat little voices echoed among the empty rooms and must have carried sweetly into the night. I'd watch them falling asleep, all the devilment going out of their faces, like some miracle healing right before your eyes. It made my heart swell with love for them, for their innocence and the hope that nestled within that innocence like a small, frail bird in straw.

Sometimes when William Pickup got home, if it wasn't too late, we'd sit on the glider and talk and drink tall sweaty glasses of iced tea with mint. He was usually so tired from his work that I did most of the talking. He liked that. He liked leaning his head back against the cool metal of the glider and listening. He loved Orfax the way outsiders always do. He doted the way converts always dote upon the religion that, at long last, they've finally embraced.

But I spared him nothing. I was eager to have him relax his enthusiasm just a bit. I wanted him to feel informed about the town, not merely entertained. It was the only way he'd ever blend in. In a very real way he'd entered a foreign country. It wasn't enough that he spoke the language or got used to the manners; he had to fill himself up with the lore. And when I told him, say, a story about Mrs. Oxendine, I was grateful for his laughter.

He didn't talk much about himself. About all anybody knew was that he'd lived in Denver all his life and won a scholarship to vet school down at State College in Raleigh. He'd married while he was in college and had two babies right away. There was a picture of his wife in a little gold heart-shaped frame which sat on the floor beside his sleeping bag along with his alarm clock. Maybe it was because I knew she'd died young, but she had a doomed look on her face. It was a thin, sober face with a little pinch of a mouth. Her hair, clipped and curly as a poodle's, looked artificially happy. Her eyes were small and sad, as if she knew something burdensome and was on the verge of flinging herself tearfully into somebody's arms. Nobody knew what she'd died from—although sooner or later somebody would find out and spread the word.

Sometimes when I'd pause, and there'd be a few moments of silence between us, I'd wish for him to fill it with something about himself. But he seemed to want to saturate himself thoroughly in everything I said, however slight and meaningless. "Tell me about your high school," he'd say. "What's it like now?" So I'd plunge right in and not spare him a single boring detail. I described Mrs. Futrell's pert outfits. I talked about Shilda's bathroom fight with Fayette Weems. I told him about Mopsy's Midsummer Night's Dream prom theme. I even told him about the time I got kidnapped by the LaMarrs. It was long enough ago so that I could laugh, too. There was something about William Pickup's audience that made me feel detached from my stories. I almost felt I'd never been part of them, and I told them like anecdotes. How could I now be so flip about something as harrowing as that joyride in the LaMarrs' Sardine? How in the world could I split my sides laughing about Bynum Jenkins's lint brush Christmas gift? But I could.

I supposed that William sat as rapt as he did because I was a new person in a new town. I didn't have one thing to do with the bleakness that had urged him to seek out a place like Orfax. I was pure-t trivial.

As the weeks passed, I noticed color creeping into his face. I saw the tenseness that squared his jaw loosen so that his face seemed rounder and more boyish. Around eight o'clock, after I'd gotten Francis and Jesse into their sleeping bags, I found myself watching the road for William Pickup's wood-sided station wagon. And if he was later than nine o'clock, I began to worry. Not so much that something had happened to him, although anything might have and I was no stranger to such possibilities, but that there wouldn't be enough time to linger on the glider with him before I rode my bicycle home. My curfew was still eleven o'clock on school nights.

Then, one day at the end of September, I went to school and found the whole place jiving and buzzing.

My first thought was that Mr. Curry had dropped dead of a heart attack or that there'd been some terrible fight in the parking lot with broken Coke bottles or some dreadful instruments that farm boys liked to carry: baling hooks or scythes.

Right away I saw Phoebe Jenkins making a huge scene. She was crumpled against her locker, sobbing, encircled by a clump of jabbering girls. "What's going on?" I whispered to somebody. Phoebe overheard. She dropped her hands from her eyes and glared at me. "He's *gone*, that's what," she said angrily. "*Now* are you satisfied?"

Of course I thought she was talking about Bynum. "But he'd *planned* to go, Phoebe," I said. "He'd signed up back in the spring for that extension course." It was an animal husbandry course at State College, and Bynum would be staying with his grandmother, who lived near the school, while the course lasted. It was no big secret that he'd planned to do this; just like it was no big secret that he and I had broken up for good.

"That's right," Phoebe said, "go ahead and pretend you don't know what I'm talking about."

The group of girls, pastel-colored as bonbons, tended to melt away from us.

"Will somebody please tell me what she's talking about?" I said to one of the girls.

"It's Bobby Rex," the girl said. "He's left town."

"And don't pretend you're sorry that we've broken up," Phoebe sobbed. "Bynum told me every jealous word you ever said about me."

"I'm sorry, Phoebe," I said. "I thought y'all were practically engaged."

"Ha! You sorry?" She snorted. "Sorry-*looking* maybe."

I said to one of the girls then, "Where did Bobby Rex go?"

"None of your goddamn beeswax," the girl said.

☆ ♡ ☆

Of course, there was no problem finding out. Everybody was all keyed up, expecting a real showdown between Bo Moseley, Bobby Rex's daddy, and Hogan Royal. That's really what all the buzz was about. Nobody gave a hoot about Bobby Rex dumping Phoebe. That's what had really gotten to her, I think: the tragedy of lost love playing second fiddle to a fight.

All summer Bobby Rex had worked at Hogan's Esso, part-time, and stashed his money in the bank. Bo Moseley was sore with Bobby Rex for not helping him with the tobacco that year, but he wouldn't pay him what Hogan did, and Bobby Rex argued that he needed a pile of money quick. Nobody could get it out of Bobby Rex what he needed the money for, and it wasn't until he'd left on the bus for Tennessee that people found out. He'd gone to Nashville to enter a talent show. He'd caught the bus in front of the Esso just a little past five that morning. He hadn't told Phoebe a thing. Only Hogan Royal had known and been there to see him off and wish him well and slip him a little cash bonus.

When I heard the news, the sharpest sense of loneliness crept over me. I had goose bumps despite the roaring heat, and I asked my English teacher if I might be excused. Slowly I walked to the bathroom, fingering the cool plaster wall as I walked. There were pockmarks all over it where people had taken hard money, quarters and fifty-cent pieces, and twiddled them back and forth against the wall, sneakily, until deep craters were formed. It took years to gouge out a wall like that, but it was some people's ambition. If anybody caught you rotating a coin against a spot on the wall, you could be expelled for vandalizing school property. But people risked doing it anyway like it was some great calling.

I felt like I was in mourning. I sat on the stone-cold radiator in the bathroom and cried my eyes out. Now I knew he was impossible. Now the phone would never ring. Bobby Rex Moseley was one chance gone from my life, and it seemed that as you got older what you lost, one by one, were chances. People talked about losing your youth, your health, your friends, love. But it all boiled down to losing the chances for those things.

I think what I cried over most was the knowledge that I wouldn't have known what to do with Bobby Rex Moseley if I'd had him. And if by some warped stroke of luck I *had* known, it wouldn't have made a bit of difference to him.

After school I didn't even try to hitch a ride home. I walked the long way, straight down Narrow Gauge to the trailer park. We'd soon be moving, farther out from town on Joe's farm, and then I wouldn't have the choice of walking. The hot dry fall was a blessing in one respect: Joe Parker had just about finished building the house of Mama's dreams. It was a split-level house with a sunken living room. Mama had already ordered miles of carpet to lay all over it, colors of carpet with names like "Persian Lamb" and "Chesapeake Bay Blue." The house was about five miles from the center of Orfax, less than a mile from Kernersville's biggest new shopping center. In a sense I'd begun to feel that I, too, was leaving Orfax.

I took a shower as soon as I got home and put a can of salmon in the refrigerator to chill for our supper. I put on all white clothes—I remember Mrs. Futrell once mentioning that white clothing reflects heat, while dark retains it—and stepped into some sandals. I lay down for a while with slices of cold cucumbers over my eyes to take away the puffiness of tears and heat. I even put my underwear in the freezer for a while like *Glamour* magazine said to do if you really wanted to feel refreshed on a hot summer's day. Then, after going to all that trouble, I did the dumbest thing: I started baking a pie.

You realize, of course, that you have to preheat your oven to 450 degrees in order to bake a pie crust. It takes about twenty minutes for a stove to get that hot. Then another fifteen minutes for the crust to bake flaky. In no time at all the little kitchen felt woolly with heat. I kept opening the refrigerator to gulp cool swallows of air. I fanned myself with the refrigerator door, otherwise I might have fainted. But I didn't rush making the pie. You can ruin a pie crust if you rush.

Pie crusts are tricky, and no two will ever turn out just alike. You're bound to ruin one, too, if you make it straight from a recipe book without ever having watched somebody first. If you glob in too much Crisco, then the crust turns out too short. If you skimp on the Crisco, then the dough won't roll out well. It will crumble and crack and burn without cooking all the way through. And the weather, like with everything, can make a real big difference. I didn't know how to allow for the weather. The heat wave was out of control, that's for sure. I just made certain I put in plenty of chilled water. Then I stirred the dough rapidly until it formed a ball. I rolled it out on waxed paper, thin but not too thin. There's a trick to rolling it out, too. You have to do some things by *feel*, that's all I'm saying. To be honest, you have to believe a little bit in magic for a pie crust to turn out well. It seems to me that I hold my breath for good luck the whole time I'm working.

I made a cherry filling this time. And with the leftover dough I rolled strips of lattice and braided the top of the pie. It was the prettiest pie I ever made, the fluting of crust as lacy looking as a doily around a valentine.

While the pie was cooling, I washed my face in the kitchen sink. I pinned my Dutch-boy hair back from my face with two silver barrettes. I put on fresh lipstick and sprayed myself with cologne. I changed blouses—from the white one to a boat-necked fuchsia one that made me feel like I was blushing from my collarbones up. Then I put the pie in a basket and hung it on the handlebars of my bike and pedaled over to William Pickup's house, quick, before any more of anything else could melt.

Part III: 1964

☆♡☆ ☆♡☆ ☆♡☆

MEET THE
BEATLES

☆♡☆   ☆♡☆   ☆♡☆

I'm awake early this January morning. All night we
have slept with the windows open because of the unexpected thaw. The room feels balmy, and, outside the
windows, cardinals and catbirds, chickadees, the brave
little winter wrens chitter excitedly in a tall gathering of
cedars. The breeze from the fields gives off the dewy,
wistful smell of false spring. There's the fragrance of
coffee brewing downstairs, the crackle of a newspaper.
Yet I find myself missing the cold weather, the brusque
feel of cold air on your skin like necessary hardship.
How else do you appreciate shelter? I hear sounds of
wakefulness downstairs, but I miss that prodigal feeling
of lying in bed and listening to another's earnest asser-
tions against the cold. This morning I'm eager to get up,
sweating as I throw the covers back. It's as if the peculiar weather has lit a fire under me.

I collect some urine for Billy to take into town. Downstairs, when I hand it to him, he doesn't say anything.
He just kisses me and says, "I think we ought to plant
our own corn this year. Just a little. Maybe five acres."

"Joe gives us all the corn we can use," I say. "You

don't have time to plant corn. You don't want to be a farmer."

"I guess not, I'm just talking."

"Look," I say, taking his hand. "I either am or I'm not. And let's make a pact. When the doctor's office calls, whether it's negative or positive, let's don't say which until after Mama's party. Let's be private about the whole thing, okay, Billy?"

"Okay."

"Let's don't even think about it today. There just isn't time, right?"

"Right."

"It's Mama's fortieth birthday, and the party's here, *tonight*, and I've got to make all the food plus a birthday cake, and I've got to keep the baby while Mama gets her hair done. Plus the twins aren't in school because it's Saturday, and you've got to work, as usual, and, my God, I'm even out of butter!" I snap the fridge shut.

"Where you going?" Billy calls, pouring coffee, but I'm already out the door, climbing into the old station wagon.

"Convenience Mart," I call. "Back in a sec."

"You've still got on your bedroom shoes, Pally!"

Riding along I could be anywhere. I could be *going* anywhere. If things got bad, which they won't, but *if* they did, I could just veer on off, right there, at good old Highway 21 and keep on riding. I have twenty dollars in my purse. I could ride up 21 into Greensboro and leave the station wagon at the bus depot and buy a twenty-dollar bus ticket someplace secret. One way. I'll bet you can go pretty far on twenty dollars. Why do people who are perfectly happy and have everything think this way? Because they just do, no matter what. Because maybe life has more choices than is good for anybody to know about.

I have to wait twenty minutes for somebody to come and open up. The Convenience Mart is owned by Hogan

Royal and sits right beside the Esso station. Today it's Leon Moseley opening up. He jumps out of a beat-up red truck, yawning. His shirttail is half out, and when he bends over to scoop up the dropped key, I see the band of his underpants, his brown sunken navel. Why am I watching for these things? Why do I feel a catch in my throat when I think that Leon Moseley is fifteen, maybe sixteen years old, almost a man? I look down at my bedroom slippers. My jeans are pinned together. I may be pregnant.

"I forgot my wallet," I call to Leon, and turn around for home.

☆ ♡ ☆

I am telling Mama the memory I have about her always bribing me with raisins when I was little and she wanted to leave me behind. I liked raisins well enough, but when they were all gone, she was still gone, too. It's like her absence was *emphasized* rather than diminished, and to this day the taste of raisins makes me sad. I'm telling her this story because she's brought little Joey over this morning for me to keep, and he's screaming his head off, and she's asking if I have any raisins to offer him.

"Whew!" she says finally, easing into a chair with Joey barnacled to her hip. "I'm too old for this. Say something funny, punkin. Cheer me up."

"He'll be okay once you leave," I say.

"Are you sure you don't have any raisins?"

"I've got some raisin bran," I say. "I guess we could pick a few out. But, really, anything will do, I think."

"Anything will do," she says, "but raisins *work*." She fetches the box of raisin bran from the kitchen and starts feeding him.

"How do you think I should have my hair done?" she

asks, ruffling the back of her head. "Pally, I'm about to cry. I can't stand turning forty."

"Look, it's only the next birthday after thirty-nine. You've *loved* being thirty-nine," I say.

"Only because of Jack Benny. It's such a famous age."

"Well, I'd tell you to stick with thirty-nine only I've already written 'Happy Forty' on your birthday cake, and once something's in print . . ."

She laughs. "You should hear my knees pop when I go down the stairs," she says. "They sound like castanets. It's having a two-year-old that makes me feel so creaky."

"Babies are supposed to make you feel young."

"Ha!" she says.

"Ha!" says Joey Parker, grinning. He has cinnamon-colored ringlets that you can't help touching in order to believe.

"Well, honey," Mama says to me, "how are *you* feeling? Have you found out anything?"

"Billy took a urine specimen by the doctor's this morning on his way to work. I *feel* pregnant. But it's probably a false alarm." My heart flutters; I tell her this, guarded. The possibility hints at a breakable sort of joy that I don't feel like bringing out and putting on display. "Better not count our chickens before they're hatched this time, Grandma," I say lightly.

"The word 'grandma' is not allowed on my fortieth birthday," she says, tossing her head indignantly. Then she smiles at me and kisses Joey, who's crooning to his raisins. "Do you think Ruby's capable of giving me one of those new Sassoon cuts? I've got a magazine picture to take with me so that she'll know. I'd like to get it frosted or dyed, too," Mama says. "Something different. It might perk me up."

"I like your hair," I say. "It's a nice color; it's always made me think of pennies."

"It's blah," she says. "Anyway, Ruby will probably

want to try to put it in a beehive. She'll tease it up so high that I won't be able to get back into the car. Do you think Joe would faint if I frosted it?"

"Probably. Remember when we did our eyes?" I say.

"Lord, yes."

"Joe's funny."

"That was back then," she says.

"But Joe's still funny," I say, and she laughs, nodding.

"Still," she says, hugging Joey, "I need a change. What is it about hair that makes you feel that if you arrange it in a new style, you'll be in a new style, too. It won't just be your hair that gets the permanent wave or the henna or whatever, but also your soul. Women are crazy," she says.

"You've never thought like this before," I say. "You've always been my inspiration because you never cared."

"Give me a break, Pally," she says, "It's my fortieth."

"You don't sound like you," I say. "Is everything okay?"

"No, it's not okay," she says and sighs. "I thought you'd never ask, Pal." She taps out a cigarette and lights it and blows the smoke through her nose thoughtfully. "Joe's thinking about selling the farm again," she says.

"But he's *always* thinking about selling the farm," I say, offering her an ashtray.

"This time somebody made an offer," she says finally, importantly. "It's a whole lot of money, Pally. So much money that we'd be rich. And I mean *rich* rich."

"How rich?"

"Joe made me promise I wouldn't tell you any of this, and just look at me sitting here, blathering."

"Why shouldn't you tell me?"

"Blather, blather," she says. "What's wrong with me?"

"It's your birthday," I say. "You can tell me any damn thing you like. How rich?"

"A million dollars."

"*What*? Are you kidding? A million dollars?"

"Aw shush, Pally. Francis and Jesse are going to hear everything."

"A million dollars, a million dollars," Joey chants loudly. He has such a precise way of speaking that we burst out laughing.

"*Who* wants to buy it? When? Would they run it as a dairy?"

"I guess. I don't know. That Mr. Monday from Kernersville is the one who called Joe up. It's a serious offer though. They offered $10,000 earnest money on the spot. Lord, it feels good to tell you this, Pally. My mind's been boiling over with it for a week."

"So did Joe take the money?"

"Of course not. You know how Joe is, Pally. The man can chew the same piece of straw all day."

"But if he sold the farm, what would y'all *do*?"

"We'd be free," Mama says. "I expect we'd do everything there is to do."

"Where would you live?"

"I don't know," Mama says. "That's part of the problem. Joe *says* he's always fancied the beach. Well, I have to tell you, Pally, it's news to me. He says he's always had it in his heart to run a bait and tackle shop someplace like Wilmington. He wants us to start over fresh—a whole new business—if you can believe it! I say, 'Hey, we could *retire*.' And he says, 'Retire and do what? I'm not even forty-five, Betty. You act all ready to choke me full of mountain oysters just to keep the gleam in my eye.' That's what he said. Man's been around farm animals too long, and it's a fact. He's one big mess and I expect I love him anyway."

"Wilmington, North Carolina?" I say, breathless with shock.

"It's probably just another of Joe's pipe dreams, nothing more," she says almost cheerfully. "Gee, now that

I've told you, I feel like I've gotten rid of the problem.
It's yours now. Kind of like passing a hot potato or the
flu on to somebody else. I feel so much better, I just
can't tell you."

"Wilmington's down on the *coast*," I say.

"I expect the best place to run a bait and tackle shop
is some place on the coast," she says. She pats my
hand. "Look, it hasn't happened yet. It's just an offer."

"What an offer though! It's a whopper."

"Joe says it might be double what the property's
worth. Whoever it is wants it real bad. Maybe for development, who knows yet?"

"You should find out," I say. "Maybe there's oil."

Mama laughed.

"But what about your dream house, Mama?"

"I know," she says wistfully. "But a *million* dollars,
Pally!"

"Now you sound like you're all for it," I say. "I can't
tell what you want. You're acting crazy, Mama."

"I'm just excited about everything," she says, her
eyes sparkling. "It's exciting not to know how everything will turn out. It's exciting to have your whole life
up in the air. It feels young."

"But how could you leave Orfax? After all these
years?"

"I don't know," she says, stroking Joey's hair, "but I
suppose it can be done. Pally, the dairy's about to kill
Joe. All the help wants to work a year or two then leave
for greener pastures: the cigarette plants, the textile
mills. There's a brewery opening in Winston-Salem soon
that's hiring people from around here at top dollar plus.
Joe can't compete with that and make a living. It's sell
now or sell later as far as he's concerned. If Joey were
older there'd be somebody to pass the farm on to, but
maybe he wouldn't even want it. You can't plan that far
ahead, Pally. Gosh," she says, taking a deep breath.
"You think you're finally all set, but I guess you never

are. You think that finally this is it, but I guess it never is.''

She gathers her purse and car keys, then buttons her coat back up. ''We'll be over at six for the birthday party. If you let on to Joe that I've told you all this . . .''

She transfers Joey from her hip to mine and he only smiles. He seems a little drunk on the raisins.

''You know,'' Mama says, pausing at the front door, ''it's silly to show Ruby that picture of the Sassoon. It's silly ever to take a picture to the beauty parlor. Don't you know the beauty operator is just splitting her sides, watching you flip open some picture like it's a treasure map. It's never just the hairdo you're asking for; you want the whole show: the face, no wrinkles, the body in the bikini. There isn't much a beauty shop can do for you except give you the *feeling* they're doing something for you.''

''Now you're sounding more like your old self,'' I say.

''Oh dear, then,'' she says. ''That's too bad.''

I watch as she slides into her car and turns on the radio. She rips through a bunch of channels, and I hear raspy snatches of ''My Guy'' and the Beach Boys and Chuck Berry's ''Nadine.'' She fiddles around until she finds this drippy version of ''Bye Bye, Love'' by the Swingle Singers, and she turns it up loud and drives off.

☆ ♡ ☆

Joey wants to watch Saturday cartoons with the twins, so I plop him down between them and bring everybody cups of apple juice. They want to bake Rice Krispie squares and drink hot chocolate because they've just seen an ad, but I say no, I've got to finish decorating Mama's cake. I've gotten so good at cooking it almost scares me. I baste the turkey, snap some pole beans, make some Jell-O with fresh oranges sliced up in it for the kids. I roll biscuits and finish icing Mama's cake.

I don't feel so hot. When I was pregnant with the child we lost, I hardly noticed. It was last summer, and I went swimming every day at Joe's lake. I pitched horseshoes. I helped Billy deliver a bunch of calves and foals, and that takes pulling. I rode my bike until I was too unwieldy to mount it. I never felt weak or sickly for a moment. For the whole six months I felt as natural and sturdy as an egg basket, and nobody had an inkling why things went wrong. But there's an old wives' tale that says if you feel *too* good then something's wrong.

Suddenly, as I'm squeezing out icing, my knees wobble, and I have to sit down to catch my breath. I flip on the radio and WCOG is playing "Tom Dooley" by the Kingston Trio. Hearing it is like opening a diary to a very particular page. I think of October 1957, when Bynum took me on our first real date to the high school midwinter dance, and we had our first true argument. We argued about whether "Tom Dooley" was something you jitterbugged to or slow danced. Bynum kept trying to pull me close for a bumbling waltz while I kept flinging us apart to snap up the pace. Most people dancing were confused, but they weren't *fighting* over what to do. You could either waltz or fast dance; big deal, what did it matter? But that sort of thing mattered right from the beginning with Bynum and me.

If I fiddle with the dial long enough, I'm sure to hear one of Bobby Rex's tunes, most likely "Pally Thompson." Everybody knows he got a gold record for that one; I don't know about the others.

I switch back to WCOG and they're playing one of my all-time favorites, so ringing sweet with memory that I scoot the bowl of icing out of the way so that I can lay my head down on the table and cry if I want to. "Go back with me to 1961," Johnny Dee the deejay says. "Kennedy has just been elected president, Brigitte Bardot is teaching us how to wear bikinis, and the Shirelles are asking 'Will you still love me tomorrow?' " Why am I crying? What was so good about any of it? What lasted?

"What's the matter, Pally?"

Jesse touches my elbow as tenderly as his father might.

"It's okay, Jess. It's nothing."

"But you're *crying*."

"Oh, you know me," I say. "They just mentioned President Kennedy on the radio, and it just wrecks me when I think what happened to him."

"He's the man they let school out for," Jesse says.

"That's right. Here, give me a hug and make me feel better." He even hugs like his father, as fiercely as if he's surrounded by water and can't swim and you're a life preserver.

"When are we going to eat lunch?" he says. "Little Joey's starving."

Pat Boone is wallowing in "April Love," and I snap off the radio and take out a jar of peanut butter.

☆ ♡ ☆

After lunch, when Joey goes down for a nap, the twins and I stroll up to the barn to see the two Shetland ponies. We've moved to the country because so many people want to pay Billy in animals and feed, it seems. Joe Parker sold us twenty acres with a nice tenant house, two stories with a chimney of fieldstones. There's a small tobacco barn where the ponies stay. We have a few goats and ducks and a rabbit hutch, and there are so many dogs and cats, I can't keep up. Many of the animals go unnamed. But the ponies are our first, and Jesse and Francis are excited about them. They carry handfuls of carrot stumps and apples gone soft.

It's downright hot. We've put on light jackets and sweaters, no hats, and by the time we've climbed the hill to the barn, the boys are taking off their jackets and knotting them by the sleeves around their waists. Sunlight falls generously through the spindly tree branches, enough sunlight to make you squint.

Both Shetlands are a drab black color and shaggy in their winter coats. Their hooves have grown out and are beginning to curl like elf slippers. Their necks feel almost steamy under their ragged, long manes. They butt their faces against the fence posts, sniffing the offered carrots and apples. Their muzzles are small enough to fit into my palm and feel round and velvety as furred fruit. The warm, sleepy smell of oats and barn straw rises from their coats.

"What are we going to name them?" I ask, fingering a strand of mane that feels as airy as cobweb.

"Blackie," says Francis in his serious way.

"*Duh*, they're *both* black, Francis," Jesse says, poking him in the ribs.

"Blackie and *Extra* Blackie then," says Francis.

"*Extra* Blackie?" Jesse laughs hard.

"Well, we don't have to decide right now," I say.

"I think the names should be stuff that goes with stuff," says Francis. "Like Sugar and Cream or Sun and Moon."

"I like Sun and Moon," I say.

"Well, I don't," says Francis. "I just said that."

"How about Salt and Pepper?" Jesse says excitedly.

"Cat and Mouse," I say, laughing.

But Francis says: "Cat and Mouse? Those are the dumbest names I ever heard. They're *horses*, Pally."

"I'm just being silly," I say.

"Well, stop," he says sullenly, kicking a rock. It skids under the fence and pops off the hoof of one pony.

"Hey, Fran," I say, "what's the matter?" I lay my hand on his shoulder, but he wrenches away from my touch and runs down the hill toward the house.

"What's bothering Francis?" I ask Jesse. "Did I say something wrong?"

Jesse shrugs manfully. He knows something, but he's honor-bound not to tell.

"I'll speak to Francis then," I say.

"He won't tell you," Jesse says. "He swore to die if he ever told you."

"Hey, thanks for telling me that much." He nods and bunches his shoulders under the stroke of my hand against his back. He's always been the loving one, the one who crawled up in your lap for no reason at all and planted a kiss on your cheek. Now, at eight, he's struggling to be aloof, secretive, and it takes all the bravery he can muster.

He has this new little boy smell that children begin to have when they spend less time in the arms and laps of loved ones. As I brush my lips across the top of his darkening blond hair, I smell him. It's not an unwashed smell at all. It's a smell of the many places he goes where I don't follow. Places where secret pacts are made, blood brotherhoods sealed. I smell a mixture of the dust beneath beds in the houses of friends, the unfamiliar mustiness of other toolsheds, the dust that floats as pungent as spice in the cavey spaces of barns and cellars. I smell the dry, souvenir smell of stones and insect hulls, the daredevil smell of climbing trees, creek mud and waterfall, the metallic smell, sunk almost visibly as tattoos into his hands, of toy guns and bicycle handlebars.

"Guess what Francis and I did yesterday." Jesse's tone is lightheartedly confessional now that he's changed the subject. He'll tell all of something he *wants* to tell. He won't even wait to be asked.

"We ate the ponies' sweet feed."

"*Ate* it?" I want to laugh. He's so earnest about divulging this secret because it means nothing to him. It's my consolation prize.

"We didn't actually swallow it. We took handfuls and chewed it just to taste the molasses. We spit the feed part out."

"Well, I hope you left the ponies a share," I say.

He laughs at me and squeezes my waist—another consolation prize—then turns and starts down the hill ahead of me, skipping. All of a sudden he wheels around. "Don't let on that we've been talking, okay? Don't act like I told you anything, Pally."

"You didn't really."

"I don't mean about Francis, I mean about eating the horse feed."

"You weren't supposed to tell me *that*?"

"I don't think I'm supposed to talk with you, period," he says.

"Well, we're getting to the bottom of this," I say firmly, striding past him, faster on the descent. "It's your grandmother's fortieth birthday and we're having a party tonight and I'm not going to have a bunch of sourpusses around, okay? Enough's enough."

I glance over my shoulder to see him lagging behind, his face suddenly long and sad.

"Jesse, I *count* on you."

"Francis says we aren't coming to the birthday party," Jesse says. Tears fill his eyes. "We aren't coming because she's not our real grandmother." Then, before I can reach him to pull him into my arms where he means to be because he's so befuddled, Billy pulls into the yard, honking like a maniac and waving one long-stemmed red rose.

☆ ♡ ☆

It's ridiculous. Everybody's crying. We just got the news that I'm pregnant again and everybody's a mental case. Joey wakes up from his nap howling so pitifully that I finally phone the salon. But Ruby tells me that Mama's under the dryer. I tell her it's no emergency, but I don't know if it's a nightmare or an earache. *What should I do?* It's no emergency, though, I repeat, don't frighten Mama. But now I think it's beginning to be. Then, as soon as Billy handed me the rose, I started crying. And I keep crying off and on because I'm so frightened of losing this one, too, and going through all that sorrow again. And there's a part of me that's afraid I'll lose Billy, too, if I'm sad too much. So then I start crying on top of my crying because I don't know how *not* to be sad when I truly *am*. I can't seem to hide things from Billy. And if I can't learn to, what will happen? But if I *do* learn, then I'll be a phony and we'll have a phony marriage. I'm already lying a little bit when I tell him that the real reason I'm crying is that I'm so happy. Happiness doesn't have a thing to do with it.

Billy nuzzles me and says, "It's hormones, Pal."

Jesse has gone to his room, crying, and nobody can guess what that's about except me, maybe. Only Francis, cool, thin-lipped, walks around the kitchen, pouring himself a glass of milk, opening a package of Oreos while I jostle little Joey and Billy rubs my shoulders. I've put the rose in a jelly glass and set it in the center of the kitchen table.

"I thought y'all *wanted* to have a baby," Francis says.

Billy kisses the top of my head. "Sometimes when you find out that you're going to get something you've badly wanted, you cry a little, Francis," Billy says. "It doesn't mean that you're unhappy. It's just that now you know that having a baby isn't really everything you wanted after all. Now you want to have a *healthy* baby, and you want everything to be fine. You want the mother to have a good pregnancy. One thing leads to another."

"I didn't cry when we got the ponies," Francis says. "I'd wanted a pony for a long time, too."

"It's a little different, Francis," Billy says softly.

"Not a whole lot different, Dad," says Francis. "We've had the ponies for weeks now and we still don't have any saddles or bridles. We still can't *ride* the ponies, but I'm not crying about it."

When the phone rings sharply, Francis answers. "Yeah, she called you," he says. "Joey kind of went nuts or something. Here." He hands me the phone.

I tell her Joey's better, so it must have been a nightmare. Or too many raisins. I throw that in for a laugh, but she doesn't seem to hear. "I'm pregnant," I tell her then, and she gasps and congratulates me, but there's something leaden about her voice. "I'm so happy," she says, but the word "happy" squeaks in her throat as if rusty.

"How did your hair turn out?" I ask lightly, and now Mama bursts into full-fledged tears.

In a little while Joe Parker comes to pick up Joey and I hear Jesse and Francis ask Billy if they can ride bikes over to a friend's house. I'm lying down, reading some movie magazine that Billy picked up in town. Wilbur Rice practically threw it at him. And for only one reason: inside is a picture of Bobby Rex Moseley escorting Leslie Gore to the opening night of *Cleopatra*. Beneath the picture, the caption reads: "Move over, Liz and Richard. Recently voted Hollywood's cutest couple, rock 'n' roll stars Gore and Moseley make the scene together at *Cleopatra*'s gala premiere. Hey, good-lookin's, whatcha got cookin'?"

You couldn't say it was a *good* picture, really, just a candid shot. Rushed-looking profiles. You can see only one of Bobby Rex's dimples, but his ducktail shows up perfectly and the way his naturally wavy hair struts itself back from his forehead. About the only change I can see in his looks is all the glitter. He's got more sequins on his shirt than Leslie has on her dress. He's got a bunch of chains around his neck, and one's probably for the little gold record charm they gave him for recording "Pally Thompson." You can't see it in the picture, but that would be my guess. I wish the picture didn't cut him off at the knees. I'd like to see his boots. Anytime you read anything about him now, they comment on his boots. He wears a new pair every concert. They're his trademark: new flashy boots. One time I read where he wore a pair of glass boots. Another time I read where his boots were made of candy. He tossed them into the audience after the show was over, and everybody ate them. Of course all that was back in 1961, at his peak, and he hasn't made a record since the "Pally Thompson" album. The army had him two years, and he's only just now getting back into circulation. But when Elvis was in the army, he went right on making music or there wouldn't be "G.I. Blues." Don't think people aren't making the comparison either.

"The article mentions he's signed a movie contract," Billy says, sitting on the bed beside me. "They're calling him the new Tab Hunter. The movie's called *Beach Party Werewolf*. It's bound to come to Orfax. I can't wait." He grins.

"I don't like scary movies," I say.

"I know, you only like a scary life," Billy says and bites me playfully.

"You're so handsome it's scary," I tell him, because he is, leaning over me: his blond hair crisp-looking with curl and light, his eyebrows as pale as gauze, tender-looking eyebrows, soft like the pony muzzles. I can't think of anything softer, really. I love the way he holds himself above me, watching my face as if he expects something wonderful to happen: I would only have to smile.

He kisses my mouth gently, slowly. "We have the house to ourselves," he whispers. "They've gone over to play with Woody Rice." He strips off his shirt. His

skin is golden, the hair on his chest and arms is golden,
too. Winter and summer his skin stays tanned, as if the
sun can find him no matter what. Sitting beside me on
the bed, stroking me, he looks as contented as a boy on
a river raft—Jesse, maybe, only larger and more confident.

I raise myself on my elbows, thinking of discontented
Jesse.

"Sorry," he says, "I guess I smell like flea powder."

"I don't smell a thing," I say, "except trouble."

"Hey," he says, pushing me back against the pillows.
"I didn't mean to get you sidetracked."

"Something's going on with the twins," I tell him.
"We had a big scene after lunch. It's something to do
with my not being their real mother. God, Billy, I thought
we'd thrown out all that garbage years ago."

"Hey." He lays a finger across my lips.

"Okay. I'm just distracted."

"You need to *concentrate*?"

"I can't help thinking about the boys. Something's
awfully wrong."

"Okay, then." He sits up and puts on his shirt. "Rain-
check. But I have to tell you," he says, zipping up his
pants in that deft, manly way that makes me want to
scramble right up and undress him again, "I think I liked
things better when you were my loose little baby-sitter."
He plants a kiss on my mouth before I can protest.

"I was never loose!"

"Ha!" he says.

"Not till we were engaged."

"You were still my baby-sitter then," he says, and he
winks.

We stroll out to his station wagon, our arms loosely
held around each other's waist. I think we share a feeling of lost riches, but the riches weren't the sort we're
used to: having the house to ourselves in the middle of
the day. Maybe we wouldn't know how to make love

unless we were dog-tired, at the end of the day with the
children sleeping nearby. Sometimes I think that tiredness is an aphrodisiac, the way it blots out everything
but feeling.

We agree that I must break the ice with Francis; but
it's Billy who suggests a way.

I watch him drive down the lane that's overhung with
mulberry limbs. It's such a warm day for January that I
can imagine the trees leafed out and fruity. Billy is on
his way to Bynum Jenkins's farm to inoculate some new
hogs.

For a moment I imagine myself married now to Bynum
and awaiting the vet's arrival. If I had married Bynum
and stood watching out a different kitchen window for
Billy Pickup to arrive, would my heart lurch when I saw
him alight from the station wagon? Was I in any way
destined for Billy? Love makes you feel that you're
destined. But would circumstances or cowardice or both
have prevented me from moving toward Billy? Would I
have felt nailed to the spot I'd chosen, however poorly?
If that were so, then luck is more important than love,
more true, more constant. I'd been simply lucky that
Billy happened. But in a moment of wearing-down pity,
especially after Eddie Hawk's accident, I might have
chosen Bynum. Not because I loved him, but because he
was here and I was here and neither of us associated
leaving Orfax with a greater gain of happiness. If the
truth were known about Bynum and me, we were natu-
rals. Not as lovers, but as survivors of this place. Still, I
think about watching for Billy out the kitchen window of
Mrs. Bynum Jenkins, and what my heart of hearts tells
me is this: I would have lurched toward him; I would
have pined. I would have lost sleep and agonized. But
just like with Bobby Rex Moseley at Sawyer's Creek, I
would never have acted.

Not so much that I care what the gossips of Orfax

think, maybe *some* of that. Mostly I wouldn't have left Bynum for Billy Pickup for the same reason that Mama didn't leave Orfax after Speedy died or that Shilda kept visiting the LaMarr boys after their accident or that Gloria picked up and went with whoever seemed to want her the most at the time: that quicksand sense of belonging. For better or worse, we all eased into it: the desire to feel not just needed but claimed, a zone of devouring safety.

I walk down the lane to Narrow Gauge Road and our mailbox. Inside there's a Sears circular advertising fences: chicken mesh, stockade, picket, split-rail. There's a post-card from Mavis Davis and a phone bill. I'm angry with myself for wishing the postcard was from Shilda, but she never was one for keeping up.

She's an airline stewardess now, Shilda is, and in love with a pilot named Ray. I swear I'll never fly in a plane, knowing how they met and what goes on in the cockpit after all the passengers have been fed and the food trays collected.

I take my time walking back to the house, thinking about the baby again, relishing the full feeling that I have. It has focus now, that feeling, definition. It's no longer simply a hunch. The mulberries will be ripe in mid-June, and I imagine myself seven months pregnant, eating a bowl of them with cream.

Behind me I hear the whir of bicycle tires, and before I can turn, the twins race past, their legs pumping hard. They split off from each other on different sides of the lane, as if avoiding a dangerous obstacle: me. When I reach the house, I find their bicycles lying in the grass, wheels still spinning.

When I was sixteen I remember living for goals: from Saturday to Saturday, as if the time in between didn't count. And if something sad happened, I'd wish it to be a week later, I'd wish away healing hunks of time in order to dull the impact of a disagreeable moment. Watching the spinning bicycle tires, I want to blink my eyes and make it months from now. By then the tension between the boys and me will be eased and forgotten. I want Mama happy again, not up in the air about uprooting herself. Why is it that so often I want to speed up my life to find out sooner how it all turns out? As if, looking back, you ever feel any better. As if, looking back, you are empowered to change anything.

Inside the house Francis is watching television and Jesse has gone to his room. Perhaps Jesse, too, is wishing it were months from now. He would like to climb the mulberry trees to pick the berries for me.

"Francis?" I say.

"Just a minute, please," he says. Mike Nelson has just had his air hose sliced in half.

"I thought you might like to ride into town with me to pick up saddles for the ponies."

He turns to look at me, wide-eyed, dumbfounded. I've taken him by surprise. But then his eyes narrow as if he thinks perhaps I'm lying.

"It's really Billy's surprise," I say. "But he won't have time to pick the saddles up today. He had to go inoculate some hogs. If we don't pick them up today, we'll have to wait until Monday."

He glares at me.

"I thought as long as we were going into town, I'd stop by the Variety and get some party hats and balloons for Betty's birthday. What's a birthday party without favors?"

But he turns back to the television. "You'd better go by yourself," he says sullenly. Mike Nelson wrestles furiously with his underwater adversary.

"Makes you wonder how he can hold his breath for so long," I say lightly. "It makes me feel *I* can't breathe just to watch him. He looks like he's about to pop."

"Shhhh," says Francis, although all you can hear are

the bubbles of a ripped open air hose. Suddenly Mike gets a grip on his opponent's headgear and mouthpiece and jerks them loose. Long, pale-colored hair spills from the rubber cap.

"A girl," says Francis disdainfully. But I'm surprised. Somehow you don't expect a pretty young woman to be trying to kill Mike Nelson. Then Francis says, "Get her, Mike."

"Why is she trying to kill him?" I ask Francis.

He shrugs. "Just watch."

Of course in the end Mike subdues her. She simply can't hold her breath as long as he can and goes limp in his big strong arms. He gulps a deep breath of air from her mouthpiece, then holds it to her lips, pinching her nose closed. Gently he carries her, buddy breathing, and travels upwards through the water, his flippers churning them to the surface as easily as if he were running up a glass staircase.

On the water's surface, a boat is waiting to pick Mike up. The crew helps swing the girl on deck; Mike hauls himself over the railing, snaps off his mask, and immediately starts giving the girl mouth-to-mouth. You can tell he's crazy about her; it's the closest he'll come to a kiss, though.

"She's coming around," I say like one of the watchful crew.

Her eyes flutter open. At first there's a tenseness about her face. But when she sees Mike she smiles. She has the budding look Mopsy Brownlee always had, the chirpy dimpled look of a winner. "You mad at me, Mike?" she says.

"You panicked, that's all," Mike says.

"Thanks, Mike," she says. "You're swell." And she closes her eyes and sleeps.

"Dames," says one of the crew in a striped shirt.

"She had her heart set on finding those jewels," Mike Nelson says. "You sure can't blame a girl for trying."

"Well," I say to Francis as the "Sea Hunt" theme music plays, "I think we missed a lot of that one. They seemed to be good friends, Mike and the girl."

"Yeah, I guess." He sounds disappointed.

"So would you come with me to pick up the saddles? Remember? That's what we were talking about."

He switches off the TV and stands, facing me, his arms folded across his chest. "Okay," he says sternly. "But don't think I'm some dumb kid." Then he says: "I want Jesse to come along, too, so I'll have somebody to talk to."

I feel suddenly under water, lowered and sinking, anger rippling the space between us. If we were under water I would cut his air hose in a jerk. Then I'd save him, of course. That would be easier than this.

"I need Jesse to walk over to Mrs. Mullin's house and pick up my dessert plates that she borrowed. I'm sending him on an errand while we run ours."

"I want Jesse to go."

"This is between you and me," I say. But I'm out of breath before I can finish the sentence. "This is between you and me, Francis," I repeat. Then, in desperation I say, "Nobody helped Mike Nelson out." It sounds so silly I almost laugh.

But it didn't sound silly to Francis. He seems to wince as if punched. He shrugs, pouting. "Okay, I'll go," he says, shuffling out the back door. "This one time."

On the way we listen to the radio. Johnny Dee is all excited about the Beatles' hit song, "I Wanna Hold Your Hand." He plays it three times in a row. Francis sits beside me in the front seat with his hands in his lap, one hand cupping the other. They are brown, husky-looking hands with dirt under the nails. But I've watched them while he sleeps, the way they curl and open on his pillow like young night flowers. They seem like such harmless little things; they've hardly been anywhere;

they've hardly done anything. Johnny Dee plays "She Was Just Seventeen" and I think that I was seventeen when I got to know Jesse and Francis. A loose little baby-sitter.

"Do you like the Beatles?" I ask.

He turns his face to the window, gazes at a forest of pine trees rushing past.

"Do you?"

"The Fifth," he says stonily. Then, relishing my blank look, he says, "The Fifth *Amendment*. It means I'm not talking."

"Well, I like the Beatles," I say. "I sort of like nongreasy music for a change. The Beatles sound fresh, don't you think?"

He shrugs and leans his head back and closes his eyes.

"They're coming on 'Ed Sullivan,' tomorrow night, Sunday," I say.

"Everybody in the world knows that," Francis says.

"Hey, look!" I swerve the car off the road and slam on the brakes. The stop is so sudden that Francis and I both shoot forward, and he bumps his head on the dash.

"Damn it, Pally, now look what you've done!"

"You don't talk like that!" I grab him by both arms; they are slim and rigid as oars rusted in their sockets.

"Turn and look at me!" I yell. "I Wanna Hold Your Hand" is playing again, but I feel too fierce to break momentum and switch off the radio. So that song vibrates goodnaturedly in the background of our quarrel.

He's got a slight cut on his forehead from hitting the dashboard. His lower lip is quivering; his face, pale as whitewash. "You almost wrecked the car!"

"I'm sorry," I say, trying to calm my voice. "I almost wrecked the car, but you're trying to wreck me. What's going on, Francis? Level."

He's puffing hard, fighting tears. He swats at his cheeks as if batting them away.

"Francis," I say, "*please* tell me."

"I can't," he says, his tone as desperate as my own.

"I'm *not* the wicked stepmother."

Then Johnny Dee says: "Back to the grooveyard, folks. We're exhuming a musty, dusty, and some local folks say lusty single from 1961. Here's Bobby Rex The Man Moseley from down Orfax way singing his big hit, 'Pally Thompson.' This song's enough to keep all us farmboys down on the farm, hey!"

"Please, Pally," Francis says, sobbing into his hands. His thin, narrow-chested body goes slack against the seat as if all the air has rushed out of him. "Cut it off."

"I always cut it off," I say, snapping the knob. "Now what, Sir Francis? As long as the car's stopped, should I lie down in front of it and let you drive over me a few times?"

He sighs a deep, ragged sigh.

"Well," I say, "if you won't talk, you won't talk. Let's go ahead and get the saddles and the party hats. I'm tired of all this." And I am. Suddenly the late afternoon sun is in my eyes, making me feel so tired I could lie down on the car seat and sleep on and on. I could miss setting the table, browning the rolls, blowing a party tickler in Mama's face as she and Joe arrive, miss the whole party and the Beatles, too, on Sunday night. I simply don't have any stamina for argument.

We don't talk during the rest of the drive to the Feed and Seed. We don't play the radio either. At the store Mr. Whitaker shows us two small western saddles that have been shipped all the way from Montana. The leather is squeaky, a bright, parched-looking orange.

"Billy said to put them on the account if you don't mind," I tell him. "They're beautiful."

"Need a good soaping and a dose of linseed oil once a week. Leather'll turn gleaming brown in no time," says Mr. Whitaker. "I thrown in two rope halters for free. There's two bridles in the box, too, come on special. I think the bits is wrong, though, unless them ponies have light mouths. Snaffle bits is only good on a light-mouthed pony, you know.''

Francis stands beside me, rubbing the diamond pattern embossed in the leather seats.

"Do you like them, Francis?"

"They're okay," he says. "I'd thought they'd be English.''

"*English*?" roars Mr. Whitaker.

"Cavalry saddles," Francis says, "like Robert E. Lee had for Traveler.''

"With all due respects to Mr. Lee," says Mr. Whitaker, "what's wrong with western, now? A lot of fellas would swear by them. Let's see, there's Buffalo Bill, Kit Carson, Jesse James.''

"Western saddles are okay," Francis says again.

"English saddles don't have nothing to grab hold to, boy," says Mr. Whitaker. "I only seen one new one in my life, and it come rolled up in a barrel tighter than a corkscrew. You remember how when you sleep on a hunk of hair wrong and it tries to run away from your comb the next morning? I never seen nothing so skunking ornery the way it won't lay down right as that English saddle come rolled up in the barrel. When they laid it on the horse, he looked like he was wearing a great big old cowlick. Hoho! It took a three-hundred-pound man riding that saddle twelve hours a day for too many days to lay that saddle flat. Then the horse plumb died, he was so wore out.''

Even though the saddles are packed in boxes stuffed with excelsior, the car begins to smell of them. It's a bittersweet smell like pipe smoke that you can taste in the back of your throat. "Well, now," I say idly, "that's that.''

We turn off Narrow Gauge and onto Main, driving past the old Texaco station. It still looks the same, little red and green pennants fluttering above the pumps. Inside the station house, the same growling old farmers are still sitting on their soft drink crates, still talking ugly about Hogan Royal's Esso. But everything else along Main seems to be changing. There are five stoplights now. The newest, on the east side of town, is at the intersection of a road they named Green Acre Drive. It heads toward a new development of modernistic houses that covers most of the territory between town and Mrs. Oxendine's property.

Dicks Hot Dogs sold out to McDonald's. The Tastee-Freeze turned into Ruby's Hairport. The Rexall Drugstore is still on the corner of Proximity and Main, but Mr. Caldwell, the owner, ripped out the soda fountain because he said he was operating it at a loss. The Piggly Wiggly and the Cash and Carry are still battling it out on opposite sides of the street, but both of them stopped free delivery at the same time, so it seems that they're friendlier than they ever let on. There's a spanking new Farmer's Hardware and the U.S. Post Office branch, side by side. And although the movie theater closed last year, a man and his wife from Chapel Hill moved in and turned the theater into a cozy little glass-fronted café called the Sunset. People are driving in from miles around to eat there, although I can't see it just for a club sandwich served on a checkered tablecloth, but people like anything new. Some beatnik types from the university over in Greensboro tried to take over the Sunset Café, I heard, but they got run off by some local thugs. About the only thing in town that hasn't changed one tiny dust particle of itself is Wilbur Rice's Variety. It's still as drafty and full of creaks as a beach pavilion. It's still got its oily, unwaxed wooden floor, its elderly parakeets; no surprise in broad daylight to see a mouse scurry down an aisle and leap into hiding among the paper products or candy section.

The only change that's come about is that, since 1961, the Variety has become a kind of Bobby Rex Moseley shrine. Above the music section of the store is a home-made sign, done with glitter, that reads: RICE'S FABULOUS VARIETY STORE: HOME OF BOBBY REX MOSELEY'S FIRST GUITAR. Of course, unless you know better, you don't realize he means one of those little plastic toy guitars that you crank rather than strum.

All over the store are planted life-size cardboard cutouts of Bobby Rex in all sorts of guitar-playing poses. These aren't for sale, of course. Most of the cutouts depict Bobby Rex during his Ordinary Look days, when he wore work shirts and Levi's and scuffed boots. Wilbur hasn't updated the cutouts, mainly because he doesn't sell anything made with sequins.

All around the record section of the store sit half-mannequins dressed in BOBBY REX, MOSTLY T-shirts —black shirts with silver lettering. There is something creepy about all those mannequins, staring dully into space, wearing those flashy T-shirts. But Wilbur Rice just loves them and refers to them as "the fan club."

It used to get to me, the Variety. But lately I can sail right in and pick up what I need without batting an eye. Half the time I don't even notice the fan club.

"You want to wait in the car?" I ask Francis. "I'll just be a sec."

"I'll wait."

It's a relief to remove myself from his thorny scrutiny. It seems that we've reached an impasse. Until I can think of some new tactic, I'm stuck in the middle of a brier patch.

Inside the Variety, there's the strong, fishlike smell of fabric sizing, the burned-toast smell of the lunch counter. Overhead the fluorescent lights hum and flicker; the wooden floor groans and dips underfoot. You can spend all day here, browsing for the little knickknacks of life: emery boards, leatherette change purses, key chains, charms for bracelets, giant all-day suckers on wooden sticks, Nickel-nips, barrettes, glasses chains, coloring books, paint-by-numbers sets, underpants labeled "Monday" through "Sunday."

In the Party Treats section of the store I find packets of balloons already labeled "Betty." I find feather ticklers that you blow and party hats and Chinese mystery balls that you unravel for Cracker Jack prizes. I've got my arms loaded when I see them. And there's no mistaking that it's them, heading down my aisle. Well, I'm trying to figure out what to *do*. Then it occurs to me that maybe they won't recognize me. So I sort of turn myself into the party supplies and hunker down as if I'm studying these singing yo-yos, two for a dollar, made in Taiwan, plays happy birthday when spun. I pick up a blue yo-yo and read the package. Then a red one. Then I look for a yellow one. I just can't seem to make up my mind, can I? They're moving so slowly because of the wheelchair, and I'm thinking, Why don't you just *beat it,* Pally, when Orst, the one who can walk now, touches me on the elbow with the knob of his cane. "Hey, gal, don't I know you?"

I'm thinking he only remembers me because I'm still the tallest girl in Orfax. But I jump even before the cane makes contact with my skin. I jump before the sound of his voice. I had never expected to meet the LaMarrs face to face again.

"I'm Valerie Pickup now," I say. "I was Pally Thompson back in high school. I'm Shilda Hawk's friend." It's all I can think to say. Good Lord, you'd think he held me at knifepoint the way I'm trembling.

"Shilda," he says flatly, as if he's mulling that one over. He nods to the woman who's pushing the wheelchair in which Hogarth is semireclined and covered to the chin. "Shilda," Orst says to me, "this is Junebug LaMarr, my wife."

"He's confusing me with somebody else," I tell her. "I'm Pally or Valerie Pickup. You can have your choice. Hello, Junebug." I offer to shake her hand.

"And it's *June*, not Junebug," she says, rolling her eyes at Orst. "*No* choice."

"June was my nurse," Orst says proudly. "I reckon I owe her my life, don't I, Junebug?"

June rolls her eyes again. "If you say so, Orst."

"When did you get married?" I ask, trying to be polite, I guess.

Orst scratches his head. He's balding now. The loss of hair makes his forehead seem less glowering. He has a constant look of confusion in his face that I find almost appealing. "When did we get married, Junebug?"

"Day after Christmas," June tells me. "*Private* ceremony. It's my third and I'm not tacky so no big to-do."

"Then you're still on your honeymoon. Congratulations!" I say just as heartily as I can.

June glances down at Hogarth. "It's been a real footloose and fancy-free honeymoon, let me tell you." She takes a Kleenex out of her pocket and blots the drool from his chin.

"We're shopping," Orst says, but the way his voice trails indicates he's forgotten what they've come for.

"New heating pads," June reminds him, "and diapers," she whispers to me. She speaks with the tone of a complaining mother but also a dutiful one. She likes her responsibilities clearcut, you can tell. She's lean and pale and muscular, with flat, blond hair barretted back from her face. She has a rough-looking complexion, and she doesn't wear lipstick.

"I *do* remember you," Orst says.

"I tell Orst that he's *lucky* not to remember everything," June says. "I wish *I* could get shut of some things I done. Especially some of the people I done them with. Lord!" She rolls her eyes heavenward. "I tell Orst every day that he should be grateful he's starting over fresh. It's a gift from God. A second life, like reincarnation."

"It's Shilda who knew you best," I tell Orst. "Shilda Hawk. I just went along."

"Then, of course, maybe *he's* the lucky one," June says, and she points to Hogarth sitting still as a stone, watchful, a slippery little smile on his lips. She wipes his chin with the tissue paper. "Maybe Hogarth has his mind in a place we'd all envy."

"He understands plenty," Orst says of his brother. "He can nod, and he can hold up his left hand. His brain's first-class. But he's mostly paralyzed from the neck down, even his vocal cords."

"I'm sorry," I say, "I didn't realize—"

"I know you!" Orst says suddenly, his eyes sparkling with excitement. "You were a cheerleader!"

"I *wanted* to be a cheerleader," I say. "I tried out, but I got cut. You and Hogarth and Shilda and I sat together in the bleachers and watched the tryouts one day. Can you remember that? It was back in 1958."

The look of revelation on his face is enough to break your heart. "Shilda came to see us in the hospital," he says.

"That's her!" I say. It's funny, but now I *feel* like a cheerleader.

"She used to tell us dirty jokes. Then, after they moved us to the County Home, she didn't come so much. I remember her," he says fondly. "She was the girl with the bright red hair, right?"

"Black hair," I say softly, embarrassed.

"You're confusing her with somebody else," he says. "It was red. Just hearing her name I see red hair. That Shilda," he says, grinning, looking past me into the dim distances of his youth. "She was a spitfire, I remember that much."

"You're right," I say. "That's Shilda."

"Brother's getting restless," June says, nudging Orst with her elbow. "Let's get what we came to get and go on home. I need to start you boys some supper."

I can tell Hogarth has been listening to every word. There's a fierce look in his eyes, and now he's bunching his lips and the one good hand, the left one, struggles loose from under the blanket and begins traveling up his chest, crablike, slow and shaky.

"Brother wants to say something," Orst says attentively. "Look, June! Look how excited he is."

"We should have had him back in bed hours ago, Orst," she says sternly.

"I think he remembers you, Shilda," Orst says. "See? He ain't no dummy, are you, Hog?" He brushes his brother's lank forelock back from his forehead, hair that's an ashy, innocent color like pussywillow. Hogarth is perspiring underneath. I watch Orst's gesture of gentleness and kindness and I feel a rush of downheartedness. It's the too-lateness of it all.

Then Hogarth LaMarr's eyes meet mine. They seem kindled by some kind of merriment, the memory of a joke. They don't crinkle up exactly; the pupils seem to dance with pleasure. Then we all watch as his upward-struggling hand finds his mouth and begins to tug at his puckered lips. Over and over he repeats the labored gesture, hand brushing lips, over and over. His eyes are locked on my own.

"Why, you dirty old boy, you," June tells him. "You blowing this girl here a kiss, I think."

"You old so-and-so. You ain't forgot nothing," Orst says, cackling.

"I believe you do remember me," I say to Hogarth, laughing, but I feel tears stinging my eyes. "I went riding with you once, didn't I, Hogarth?"

"What happened?" Orst says eagerly.

"You were there with Shilda."

"We went everywhere together, Hogarth and me," says Orst proudly.

I smile at Hogarth and I pat his hand. "You remember, don't you, Hogarth? Remember how everybody teased me for being such a prude?" I look up at Orst to find relief from Hogarth's devouring gaze. "I wouldn't kiss him. I was scared to death of him," I say. "So I acted like I was having a nervous breakdown. I started kissing the car instead."

"I remember something like that happening," Orst says, but I can tell that he doesn't quite.

I hold Hogarth's quivering claw of a hand between my own. Ever so slightly I feel him squeezing back. Maybe I do what I finally do so that I won't crazily burst into tears in front of them all. I lean forward and I kiss Hogarth LaMarr on the mouth. I kiss softly, quickly, the way you might kiss a charm for good luck. And when I do it, I feel as if I'm kissing all of us or who we tried to be good-bye. *Finally* good-bye: Shilda, Orst, Bobby Rex and Phoebe, Bynum, maybe even the dead girl. I am kissing that part of us good-bye that had no respect for time, that thought of time as needing to be wadded up, expendable as a paper ball, needing to have hell stomped out of it. And I am finally kissing that part of me that I was always afraid to brush up against before: the moment. And when I draw away, there is poor Hogarth LaMarr's face, expressionless as a stopped clock, stuck in his past forever. His mouth tastes like an old, delicate grandfather's.

"Well now, how about that, Hogarth?" Orst says, slapping his thigh, laughing. "That ought to fix you up for a few years, son."

I feel winded and speechless and useless after the kiss. I hardly know what to do with myself, which way to run. I gather up all the items I'd set down. "Well, I've got to go," I say. "Nice seeing everyone. I'll write Shilda and tell her how you are," I say. It sounds so casual, so normal. My heart is rapping like a door knocker inside my chest: let me out of here, let me *out*!

As soon as I turn I see Francis, standing at the front of the aisle, snaring me with his chaperone's gaze. His arms are folded across his scrawny chest. The look he gives me is not one of sullenness or anger, but one of power.

"You *said*—"

"I know what I said," I say, whooshing past him to the cashier. "I said I'd be back in a sec. Well, I was wrong."

Once we're beyond Main and zipping along Narrow Gauge, I turn the radio on. I choose a gospel station, anything different. Mahalia Jackson is singing "Ave Maria" so sweetly and begging that I can imagine she's on her knees. But Francis switches off the radio just as soon as my hand leaves the dial.

"Why did you kiss that crippled man, Pally?" he says bitterly. "I *saw* you."

"I'm not sure why," I say quietly. "I knew at the time, Francis. It was an impulse, that's all."

Maybe it's my honesty that catches him off guard. He looks at me, trying to understand what I've just said, trying to believe that a grown person can be confused, too, can act without thinking, the same as a child. There's a bond of confusion between us.

"Who was he?"

I don't hesitate. "He was the wildest boy I ever knew. I was scared to death of him and his brother, too; they were mean."

"They don't look mean to me," Francis says, "they look whupped."

"That's now," I say. "I'm talking about *then*. They had a car with the roof blowtorched off that they called the Sardine. It was a heap, and the one time I rode in it, I thought I was going to die."

"Why do you still like them?" he asked.

"It's easy to like people you don't really know anymore. You can even forgive them." Then I look at him meaningfully. "It's the people you know who are always the hardest to love. You expect so much from the people that you love that you are bound to be disappointed."

"You aren't supposed to kiss *strangers*," he says.

"It was strange," I say. "When I saw him, Francis, I felt such a rush of guilt. I remember the afternoon I went riding and how wild he acted and how scared I was, but what a fake, too. Instead of being forthright, instead of begging him to stop the car and let me out, I acted silly and stuck-up. I acted as if I were better than he was, acted like I didn't know how to be wild when, in truth, I knew as good as anybody. I was just picky. Not about the person, exactly, but about when I could best get away with being wild. I acted like my whole life was at stake instead of one little kiss."

"He wanted to kiss you?"

"I think that was the whole point of my riding with him. But when he made his move, I pretended to go crazy, and I started kissing the Sardine instead. I thought I was saving my reputation. Oh, I shouldn't be talking to you like this," I say. "It's all personal and private stuff that happened a long time ago. It doesn't count for much in the great scheme of things.

"And something else," I say. We've come to the crossroads at the top of the hill that fronts the Moseley farm. It's a four-way stop sign, and I stop. Although nothing is coming except an old yellow cat who skulks across the road and into the woods. She carries a limp mouse in her mouth. "It's hard to be a kid, I know that," I tell him. "But it's hard to grow up, too, because you're expected to *know* everything after a while. But what you know always has this *blinking* quality to it. Like there is no truth, just warnings, caution signs. And it's okay for truth to turn out to be a caution sign, it's not bad exactly, it just gets in the way of your feeling that you'll ever learn anything that can't be reversed, can't change on you. You keep waiting to get to a stopping place, a spot where you can sit down and see things more clearly. But when you finally do, you finally don't. The truth is always blinking. Oh, I'm just talking trash now, Francis. But it's important to talk, honey." There are no cars coming, but we are still stopped at the crossroads. "About this fight we seem to be having, Francis."

He looks up from his lap.

"I've been at some fights where I screamed and yelled and hit somebody. I've watched a few, too. But nothing makes you feel any sorrier than the fight without words. Nothing makes you feel more crippled up inside, more helpless."

The sun is setting; the horizon looks molten, not quite fixed. It's five o'clock at the least, I think, and here we sit at the crossroads of Highway 21 and Narrow Gauge. Beyond a break of broom-thick maple trees and cedars I see the Moseley farm: the white, two-story farmhouse with the green tin roof. The rust-red barn and outbuildings jammed with farm machinery. Somebody walks out on the porch and takes a seat in the swing. From this distance you can't tell if it's a man or a woman: a man waiting for his supper, or a woman resting after she's put it in the oven. A man daydreaming a man's daydreams about the fame and fortune of his son, or a woman daydreaming her dreams of a time when the whole family might sit down to dinner together. A man thinking forward, a woman thinking backward.

"I suppose we should get going," I say. "I just feel like sitting here and remembering everything that was ever good or possible. I'm a mess." I blot my eyes on the cuff of one sleeve.

"Daddy says it's your hormones," Francis says. Then he cuts his eyes at me, his face flaming: "Is that something whores can have?"

"Whores? Who told you about *whores*?"

He looks down at the floor mat; his eyes could drill holes in it. "Elmo and Woody Rice," he tells me quickly.

"They say you're a whore and everybody knows it because of Bobby Rex's song."

So this is it. The moment is full of shock and grace; it feels as if I'm leaping upwards to catch an egg.

"Thank you," I say, hugging him. "I was beginning to think I'd done something, Francis. I was beginning to think I was guilty of something truly terrible. Only I couldn't imagine what or when or how." I almost laugh until I see the look on his tearstreaked face. It's still real for him, Elmo's and Woody's accusation. It still stings. And all I can really do for him at this point is deny it: my word against theirs, my definition of whore against theirs. For the first time perhaps in my life I must take the town's gossip seriously. Not for my sake at all, but for his. Just as Mama and Joe must have, all those years they pretended to sleep apart. I'd often thought it was to set an example for me; but wasn't it to keep me immune to the town's gossip, to make me feel—if ever confronted by an accusation of their immorality—that I'd borne witness to the truth?

"Do you think your daddy, Billy, could still love me if I was a whore?" I say gravely. Of course I am inviting him to say no. I'm offering Billy's steadfastness as proof of my innocence.

Francis looks at me a long time, searching my face. His blue eyes seem to lighten with his own finer truth, not mine. "Yes," he says at last. "He'd still love you."

"I can explain everything," I tell him softly, realizing of course, that I can't. Realizing of course that he's already forgiven me whether I deserve it or not. And all the way down the twisting haunts of Narrow Gauge I'm thinking that sometimes we love best when we stop trying so hard to prove it.

☆ ♡ ☆

We're all waiting, Billy, the twins, and I, when Mama

arrives. It's not cold out, but she's wearing her mink hat—the one Joe gave her last year for Christmas. She's come to her party camouflaged.

"Okay, Mama, you're among friends," I tell her. "Take off the hat."

Joe says: "Y'all better sit down for this one."

She's over the shock of it, you can tell. The hat's merely to arouse curiosity. "Let's enjoy our supper first," Mama says, giggling. "I don't want to make anybody *sick*."

"What color is it?" Jesse says excitedly, grabbing her hand.

"King's Ransom Gold," Mama says proudly.

"It's the color of canned peaches," Joe says, and he's not smiling.

"Sort of an apricot," Mama says, lifting off the hat.

It's short and varnished-looking, it's so shiny. I would have called the color Gymnasium Floor, but of course I don't tell her. I like the cheerleader casualness of it, the raggedy kind of cut that already seems to need trimming. Mama tosses her head a few times, rushes her fingers through her bangs, and says: "The big advantage is that you don't ever have to comb it."

"I really like it," I say enthusiastically, and she beams. "Except you realize that you look fifteen." She really beams on that one.

"I like it, too," Billy says.

"Well, a little change never hurt anybody, now did it?" Mama says, seeming to consult Joe Parker's opinion by the direction of her glance. "Joe thinks it makes me look like a *boy*."

"I'm getting used to it," Joe grumbles and tousles it with one hand. "All she needs to do is get herself a guitar and join up with the Beatles."

We're halfway through dinner before I notice how quiet everybody is. I've been jumping up and down, waiting on all of them, and so I don't really notice the silence until I start my own meal. Now I'm aware of the tink of silverware against plates, somebody coughing politely into a napkin, the tuneless music of ice cubes stirred in tea. The mantel clock has a hastening-on sound.

"Hey," I say. "This is a party."

"Great supper," Joe Parker says, helping himself to some more of the stringiest pole beans on earth.

Even the twins aren't talking. Their whole faces seem occupied with eating. They seem to croon against their drumsticks as if holding microphones. Little Joey is busy fingerpainting with his mashed potatoes.

"Save room for the birthday cake," I say. "It's chocolate."

Now I'm even aware of the way people chew their food, the rhythm of their jaws, the tap and click of grinding teeth, the cushiony sound of a swallow. I hear the whispering sound of butter spread on a roll, the gleaming sound, like a dropped coin, of the butter knife being returned to its plate.

"I ran into the LaMarr boys at the Variety today," I say abruptly.

"I understand that they came into some money, selling their homeplace to some developer," Joe says. "Of course it's that nurse one of them married who manages everything for them."

Now it seems that all of them are busy swabbing up the last of their gravy with the last of their rolls. All of them look down at their plates as if into mirrors.

"Great supper," Joe says again, loosening his belt one notch.

Mama holds up a teaspoon and studies it. She turns it around and around in the candlelight. "What pattern is it?" she asks me, but she *knows* what pattern we have. Rambler Rose. It was Billy's first wife's pattern. Mama gazes into the spoon's back, studying herself. "Do I *really* look like a Beatle?" she asks.

"Okay," I say finally. "What's going on?"

"What do you mean what's going on?" Mama says, glancing at Joe.

"Nobody's said a word the whole meal," I say. "This isn't like us when we all get together. It's like a room filled with strangers, sitting around and trying to act mannerly, talking about noncontroversial stuff like hairdos, for Pete's sake!"

"I don't know," Joe says, "hairdos around here are always pretty controversial seems like."

"And silver patterns!" I say. "Really, Mama!"

Mama lights a cigarette off one of the candles.

"So what is it that everybody knows around here that I don't?"

"Pally," Francis says from across the table. His eyes have a mincing quality, cutting through Mama's cigarette smoke and searching out my own. "Bobby Rex Moseley wants to buy Joe Parker's farm."

When he says this, he pronounces the name Bobby Rex in an exaggerated way as if the two of us share a secret ourselves. Which we do, in a way, having warred so long and hard with each other all afternoon only to wind up with identical spoils. For better or worse we are attached to one another. There is our revived sense that who and what we belong to—our family—hangs over us, not so much for protection but strategy. It's the canopy under which we gather—an official shelter—where we not only identify loyalties but endure them. Perhaps part of Francis's anger this afternoon had been due to his not being able to tell me everything. He'd sworn some kind of oath to the rest of the family from which I'd been pushed outside. His had been the shaky offensive of an unloaded weapon. Elmo Rice hadn't removed the ammunition; his own family had. I saw his dilemma clearly. He'd overheard Joe Parker telling Billy about Bobby Rex's offer and that I shouldn't be told. He hadn't understood *why* I shouldn't be told any better than I did. Too many details got hush-hushed or avoided. Then,

Elmo and Woody Rice dumped their slander on top of the whitewash.

I gaze around the table. All the faces of the people I love look pale and scolded. Even Joe's, which is always so red and full of bluff.

"I need to say some things," I say. I swallow hard. I don't know if I'm mad most or hurt most. "It's been three years or more since that song came out, and nobody can seem to forget it. We *say* we've forgotten it. We switch off the radio whenever somebody digs it up from the grooveyard. The fact is, I'm the only person here who will ever be sure about what happened, and sometimes it seems unclear to me. I'm the only person who was there or wasn't there with Bobby Rex Moseley in whatever compromising situation occurred or didn't, take your pick. You have to base what you thought I did or didn't do on the me you know *now*. This very moment right here. The best I can hope for, maybe, is that by 1970—the way the world seems to be going—it won't matter to anybody whether I did or I didn't.''

"You're getting yourself all worked up for nothing," Joe Parker says. "I've already decided not to sell."

"Whether you sell the farm to Bobby Rex or not has nothing to do with what I'm trying to say, Joe."

"Let her talk, Joe," Mama says. "Go on, punkin."

"I don't really care about the 'Pally Thompson Special' on the Variety's counter menu. I didn't even flinch that time at Gizmo's, the first time Billy and I went, when Fayette Weems asked him to dance and punched 'Pally Thompson' on the jukebox. What gets to me is that for the last three years, Mother Pickup has been sending me all these Christmas and birthday presents that are such big *hints*. Potholders cross-stitched with religious messages, things like that. The first year we were married she sent me Pat Boone's *Twixt Twelve and Twenty*, for God's sakes!''

"Well, you were only nineteen," Billy says, but I

don't laugh. "Come on, Pal," he says then. "We thought it was funny."

"Back then we could laugh. It seemed silly and new. But now it's old as the hills and getting worse. Whenever she writes letters, they're always addressed to Billy, and only the P.S. includes me. 'P.S.,' she'll write. 'Enclosed is a Dear Abby piece I thought Valerie might find useful.' *Useful*? And it's usually about infidelity or premarital sex."

"Just be glad she lives all the way out in Colorado," Billy says.

"It's not just her," I say. "It's everybody who's supposed to be closest to me, who's supposed to know me best. It's Joe not telling me about the farm offer, or Francis afraid to tell me about some gossip he's heard. It's you, Billy."

"Me?" He looks stricken.

"Remember when I wouldn't do the interview with *Rockola Magazine*? Remember when we had that fight? You said it made no sense for me not to give an interview if nothing had ever happened. Well, the fight blew over, and we got married, but what about your doubts, Billy?"

"What are you saying, Pally?"

"Look at you, Billy, still bringing me home updates on Bobby Rex's latest doings. It's like you're waiting for a reaction that will *finally* give me away."

"You know what I think?" Billy says softly, but his eyes bore into my own. "Sometimes I think it's Pally Thompson who doesn't believe in her own innocence. Not that the song is true."

"What then? Say it, Billy."

"I don't know," he says, "it's just a feeling. And now it's gone."

"I know what he's trying to say," Mama tells me. "It's like *you're* the one who's always made the mountain out of the molehill."

"I didn't tell you about the farm," Joe Parker says, "because it was my decision and I didn't want anybody else to feel the burden of making it. I'm a plain and simple man, Pally. Don't make me out to be any more than that."

"I hate Bobby Rex Moseley," Francis says. "I hate his stupid guts."

"I feel like he's crashed my birthday party," Mama says.

"He's a stupid jerk," says Francis.

"A turd ball," Jesse says.

"A greaser."

"A big fat weenie head."

I feel them drawing their wagons in a circle around me, and I realize, selfishly, that I've been testing them all. I say selfishly because a large and genuine part of me wishes that song was true. Wishes I had once done something as reckless and impossible as being loved by someone as loveless as Bobby Rex. Such a memory it would have made! My one small and harmless way to leave Orfax while standing at the kitchen sink. It would be a way of not giving them everything, which I guess is allowed.

Why is what might have been always so crucial to what is? And why do we always tell ourselves that what might have been was expendable? A papery wad of an option. We act as if we can always claim control. I might have loved Bobby Rex, and maybe I came close—if that counts for anything. And I believe it does. All I know after twenty-one years of life is this: I am here, safe and loved with my family. I am always here. This is how people stay places. Always and forever. But I suspect that every now and then, an instant will flash like a shooting star when I'll wish otherwise. In the midst of argument, disappointment, loss, sorrow cinching my throat like a noose, I'll wish myself gone from here and into that moment that never was: that wispy girl of your song, Bobby Rex, lying down forever, young forever, pitiless and wasteful among all the other flowers.

Joe Parker is telling us now about his pipe dream of selling the farm. How it never was more than a pipe dream and we should have known all along, knowing him as we do. We should have known *ourselves*, each of us having climbed the very tallest of the black cherry trees that Joe Parker's father watched his father plant right after the Civil War. These are old, crotchety-looking cherry trees that border a branch of Sawyer's Creek that feeds Joe's lake before it runs on down to the Yadkin River. We've climbed them. You have to climb them if you want the best view of Joe's farm, which you do, the bonus being that it's a lush view of the county, too, because the cherry trees are clustered at the crest of the biggest hill for miles around.

What you take down with you from the trees is a sight that makes you feel deprived when you're back on the ground. From the tallest tree you see land dipping and rolling, gathered into pleats of cultivation. There's such an order and a calmness you might be dreaming. You don't see anything *particular*. There's no billboard, no car close enough to determine its make or the numbers of its license, no poster pinned up on some gas station door letting you know about some information you could or couldn't live without. You see a barn and a house and part of a fence. You see a little dot person on a little dot tractor, quietly twirling around a field. You see a dog running across the road, or maybe it's a small pony broken loose. Looking down on Orfax, it comes to you that it's the details in life that exhaust you: reading the small print, squinting your eyes so that you'll be certain to recognize the person coming toward you and speak to them or they'll hold a grudge. Not to mention that sitting in the cherry trees you not only feel like flying, you know for a fact that you can. And I suppose the only reason that you don't is that somebody might see and recognize you, bearing down on the details, and a great big deal would get made of something that's really so natural. But something you also know, sitting there in the elderly cherry tree, is that if you could fly, and you can, you'd also be grateful for a favorable wind that would return you, but not until you were good and dizzy from the world. I'm thinking that return to that rise would seem just as precious, just as necessary as departure, and maybe more urgent. A matter not simply of judging distances but of understanding them. I say, "Bobby Rex Moseley . . ."

"He's a has-been," Jesse claims excitedly.

"He's *nothing* compared to the Beatles," Francis says to me.

"He sounds like a popped-out string on Paul McCartney's guitar!" laughs Jesse.

"Hey, Pally," Francis says, slipping his arms around me, "*smile*."

About the Author
☆♡☆   ☆♡☆   ☆♡☆

MARIANNE GINGHER was born on Guam in the Marianas Islands, raised in Greensboro, North Carolina, and attended Salem College in Winston-Salem, North Carolina, and the University of North Carolina at Greensboro, where she received an M.F.A. in creative writing. Her stories have appeared in *North American Review*, *Redbook*, *Seventeen*, and *McCall's*, and her work has been cited for excellence in *Best American Short Stories*. In 1985 Ms. Gingher was awarded a North Carolina Arts Council Grant in Literature. She is married and the mother of two young sons.